For my family

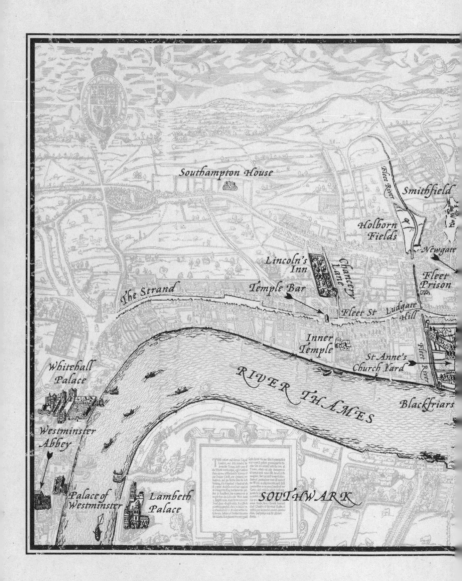

Southampton House

Smithfield

Fleet River

Holborn
Fields

Newgate

Lincoln's
Inn

Chancery
Lane

Fleet
Prison

The Strand

Temple Bar

Fleet St

Ludgate
Hill

Inner
Temple

Fleet River

St Anne's
Church Yard

Whitehall
Palace

RIVER THAMES

Blackfriars

Westminster
Abbey

Palace of
Westminster

Lambeth
Palace

SOUTHWARK

Sixteenth Century

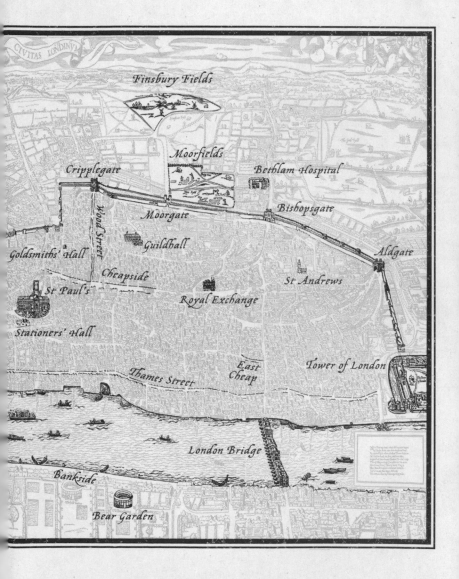

CIVITAS LONDINVM

Finsbury Fields

Moorfields

Cripplegate

Bethlam Hospital

Bishopsgate

Wood Street

Moorgate

Goldsmiths' Hall

Guildhall

Aldgate

Cheapside

St Andrews

St Paul's

Royal Exchange

Stationers' Hall

East Cheap

Tower of London

Thames Street

London Bridge

Bankside

Bear Garden

CHRONOLOGY

1530 Ambrose Dudley born
   Gabriel Browne born
1532 Robert Dudley born
1534 Caroline Lovelace born
1540 Christopher Radcliff born
1542 Henry VIII's 'Great Debasement' of the currency
1547 Henry dies
   Edward VI becomes king
   Protectorate established
1549 Popular uprisings
1551 'Dudley testons' first appear
   Simon Lovelace born
1553 Edward dies
   Mary I becomes queen
   Earl of Warwick and Guilford Dudley executed
   Ambrose and Robert Dudley held in the Tower of London
1556 Christopher Radcliff matriculates at Pembroke Hall
1558 Mary dies
   Elizabeth I becomes queen
1559 Christopher Radcliff graduates and becomes a tutor

CHAPTER I

London, February 1574

On the first day of February Christopher and Katherine had been on their way to Ludgate Hill from the house of her aunt, Isabel Tranter, in Wood Street and only by chance had found themselves at Smithfield as the clock of the church of St Martin struck twelve. Caught up in the crowd — at least one hundred strong, fuelled by ale and beer and seemingly impervious to the cold — they had been unable to drag themselves away and for reasons that neither of them could have explained, stood arm in arm, silent and expectant.

In their pens, pigs waiting to be butchered sensed the excitement, grunting and squealing and snapping at each other. Their steaming breath rose in the freezing air to mingle with that of the onlookers. It was as if the animals knew that the place which had witnessed so many executions was about to witness another.

Pie-sellers and fishwives with trays of oysters taken that morning from the beds downriver from the bridge touted their wares at double the prices they would normally ask and the tradesmen and -women who had gathered for the spectacle paid a penny for a small beaker of ale supplied by the girls sent out from the Crossed Keys or twopence for a tankard of kiss-the-donkey — a foul concoction, but popular on hanging and burning days.

Christopher felt a tug at his gown and looked down to see a filthy, barefoot child with palm open in the hope of a coin. He shook his head and shooed the child away. Give one a farthing in a crowd like this and, like ants, another ten would appear. Instinctively he checked that his purse was safe under his shirt and put a hand on the hilt of the slim blade tucked into his belt. Pickpockets and cutpurses would be moving through the crowd on the hunt for easy pickings. He had heard that an hour at a burning or a hanging could be worth a week's hard toil at Cheapside market or Billingsgate.

A cheer went up and a flat cart drawn by a half-starved pony trundled into the square from the direction of Newgate. An old woman only partially covered by the shreds of a filthy shift sat huddled on it, bound and tied and unable to protect herself from hands reaching out to scratch at her eyes or tug at her hair. Neither the magistrate, a fat, ruddy-faced man, nor the two blue-coated constables guarding her made much effort to stop them. An exposed breast hung loose and spent like the udder of a cow too old to give milk. A trickle of blood ran down a mud-caked cheek. Shaking with cold and fear, the woman raised her eyes to her tormentors and sent forth a stream of yellow spittle.

Beside Christopher a tall man in a leather jerkin hoisted his blubbering daughter on to his shoulders. 'There, child,' he growled, 'you'll see her burn from there. Now shut your mouth or you'll join the witch.' The child sniffed and did as she was told.

The magistrate and his constables used their staffs to clear a path through the crush, cracking knees and ankles as they went and ignoring the howls of protest. When they reached the middle of the square the constables dragged the woman off the cart and tied her to a post surrounded by a pyre of dry faggots laid ready for her. Her eyes rolled in their sockets and her mouth opened and closed as if she was trying to speak but could not. From the window of a house overlooking the square the contents of a shit bucket were thrown down and splattered over her. The crowd bellowed their approval. 'Burn the witch.' 'Send her to hell.' Each voice louder and more insistent than the last.

A butcher in a blood-soaked leather apron, brandishing a heavy-looking meat cleaver, stepped forward and faced the crowd, which had formed itself into a semicircle perhaps ten paces back from the unlit fire. 'Let me have the bitch,' he yelled. 'I'll cut her up for the swine.' Unwilling to be deprived of their entertainment, harsh voices soon shouted him down and he sloped off muttering obscenities.

A young mother with a child at her breast threw a stone with her free hand at the woman. Her aim was true and blood ran in a bright red stream from the woman's head. Again the crowd cheered. But when another old woman — this one covered only by a ragged kirtle — jumped out of the crowd and, holding her arms aloft, proclaimed tearfully that her sister was no witch and guilty of no crime, she was jeered until a constable shoved her roughly to the ground and ordered her to hold her tongue. The woman scrambled back into the crowd on her hands and knees and disappeared from sight.

A constable rang a bell and the magistrate held up his arms for silence. When he could be heard he spoke in a voice powerful enough to carry around the square. 'I am Gilbert Knoyll, magistrate of this ward. This woman . . .' he paused briefly to consult a constable, '. . . Jane Riley has been tried and found guilty of the crime of murder by witchcraft and has been sentenced to death by burning. Let all here take note that the same fate awaits any who offend God and the

Crown in this way.' He took a moment to cast his eyes over the grinning faces, saw that they would tolerate no more delay and signalled to the constables to put their torches to the pyre. They did so and watched while the kindling caught. The crowd strained to see the flames.

At first, there were but thin wisps of smoke. The woman had regained her voice. She struggled feebly against her binding and in a pitiful croak called down God's wrath on her killers. When the faggots caught and flames began to lick about her feet, she shrieked and shrieked and went on shrieking until one of the constables threw half a pail of water over her to slow the fire's progress and prolong her suffering. Soon the flames took hold again. Very quickly, they raced up her legs, her eyes opened wide in silent agony and she slumped forward, held in place only by the rope. Her head fell to her chest, her hair crackled and finally, in the torment of fire, she died. Intent upon the spectacle, the crowd, at first raucous, had gone eerily silent.

The stench of burning flesh — a sweet, sickly, gut-churning stench — filled the square. The pigs caught it and shrieked their terror, threatening to trample their post-and-rail pen to the ground and run amok around the square.

Their entertainment over, the crowd began to disperse — men into the Crossed Keys, women to their homes or to work. Christopher covered his nose and tried to cough the smell from his mouth and throat. Katherine turned her head to him and hid her face against his shoulder. He could hear her whispering the Lord's Prayer and put his arm around her. It did not stop her shaking.

They did not wait for what remained of the woman to be swept up and removed for disposal in the river or at some unmarked spot in Moorfields or Holborn, but hurried on to Ludgate Hill. They spoke no more that day of what they had seen.

CHAPTER 2

The clock of the church of St Martin struck seven. It had been as harsh a winter as any could remember and as yet no sign of spring. More snow had fallen in the night and icicles hung outside the window of the bed chamber. Christopher put a hand on the swell of a hip and squeezed gently. Katherine rolled over to face him and propped herself up on an elbow. Despite their excesses, her skin glowed and her green eyes shone. She brushed aside a strand of her auburn hair and traced a line down his cheek with a finger. 'How you have changed, Christopher,' she said quietly. 'There was never such ferocity in you as I felt last night. It was as if some ungodly hand had drawn it from you.'

He ran a dry tongue over his lips and tried to work some saliva into his mouth. 'It is injustice that draws it from me. Injustice and unnecessary suffering. The slaughter of innocent Huguenot women and children; a gobber-toothed old crone dying in agony on the fire.' The woman they had seen perish in the flames had been found guilty not only of practising witchcraft but also of causing her one-eyed husband to be seized by convulsions so severe that he had swallowed his tongue and choked to death. One neighbour had testified that he had seen her flying through the night sky, another that she had found a headless cat on her doorstep. Among the woman's possessions had been discovered a pestle and mortar suitable for crushing the poisonous berries of the laurel or the yew, and a child's rag doll with a single eye. Evidence enough for her to be tried at the assizes and sentenced to die in the flames.

'Did you not think her a witch?' asked Katherine.

'I did not.'

'The marks were on her. The jury was in no doubt.'

Christopher pushed himself up. 'I cannot buy a penny news sheet without its being full of reports of witch trials, yet how many of those who are tried can so much as lift a hand to defend themselves? As for the marks, you have three moles on your back, yet I do not think you a witch. The woman was old and ignorant — nothing more. Some may believe in the devil's handmaidens. I do not. Wise women with a knowledge of plants and herbs and their healing properties, even an ability to see into the future, I can believe in, but a pact with Satan? Nonsense. Superstition born of ignorance. Burning her was an act of barbarity. It recalled the streets of Paris and horrors I wish never to witness again.'

Katherine climbed over him to reach the smock lying on the floor. She pulled it into the bed and held it to her breasts to warm it before putting it on. 'Enough. I too regret the manner of the witch's death but I believe her execution was necessary. You will not persuade me otherwise and eighteen months have passed since the bloodshed in Paris. I understand that it still causes you anguish but let us not begin the day by speaking of it.'

'The slaughter in France has made irrational fools out of sensible folk. Fear of papists has become fear of the ungodly and fear of the ungodly has become fear of papists. Suddenly there are witches and conjurors and evil all about us. Suddenly that which was once thought absurd is commonplace — witches who fly at night, conjurors who commune with the devil. Fantasy is taken as fact and innocent men and women suffer. The gods of anarchy and chaos must be rubbing their hands with glee at what is to come.'

'Christopher, that is blasphemous. And you exaggerate.'

'Do I? You did not see what I saw on the streets of Paris and Amiens.' Not only did Katherine not see the unspeakable horrors of the slaughter in Paris, as a Catholic she was inclined to disbelieve half the stories she heard about that terrible time.

'I did not, and thank God for it. I pray the images that plague your nights and your mind will soon leave you.' She reached out to touch his cheek. 'Now, dress yourself and come down to the kitchen or you'll die of cold in this chamber. That window shutter must be repaired. It is no protection in the winter. The wind blew through it all night. Did you not hear it rattling?' She slipped into the smock and covered it with a simple gown.

'I was too busy with my dreams.' As if to banish them, he shook his head like a terrier with a rat. 'Be off, wench, light the fire and prepare breakfast. My stomach is empty and my mouth full of dust. I need food and drink.'

Katherine threw a shoe at him. 'I am neither wench nor cook, Dr Radcliff, and you will guard your tongue or sleep alone and go hungry.' When she slammed the door, the shutter rattled alarmingly.

Christopher knew that no amount of food or drink would rid his mind of what he had seen on St Bartholomew's Day in Paris two summers before. It never did. And the dreams, although less frequent, were no less intense. He lay back and closed his eyes.

As so often after love-making his thoughts turned to the strange journey that had brought him to this place at this time. From commoner pupil to Doctor of Law at Pembroke Hall, from convicted killer — albeit by accident in a drunken tavern brawl on the day of his mother's funeral — to service as intelligencer for the Earl of Leicester. Once the verbal swordplay of disputation in the comfort of a Cambridge college, now an endless search for England's enemies among the alleys and hovels and the halls and mansions of London. Unlike Katherine, he did not see the hand of God in this, or in any earthly affairs, such as his own misfortune. He had lashed out; the man had fallen, cracked his head and died. He had been tried and convicted, only saved from hanging by the testimony of John Young, Master of Pembroke Hall, and would have languished in Norwich gaol until he died had the earl not used his influence to have him released. Christopher had been a good recruiter of clever young men to Leicester's service and the earl had offered him a position as an intelligencer in London. The hand at work had been an earthly one. God had not been present.

He had grown close to Katherine after the death of her husband, Edward Allington, and she had travelled with him to the city, in part to care for her ageing Aunt Isabel, in part to be near him. She a devout Catholic, he a doubting Protestant, they argued often, on occasions bitterly, and, recently, even more often. He had wondered if they were nearing a fork in the road, at which they would either travel on in the same direction or go their separate ways.

Of course, there was no purpose in peering into a future he could not predict or in dwelling on what fate had brought him, yet sometimes he could not help himself. Even a lawyer's rigorous mind did not always behave rationally.

*

Katherine called from the kitchen: 'Make haste, Christopher. The fire is lit and your breakfast is on the table.' He stretched his long legs, forced himself out of the bed and struggled into the woollen shirt and trousers he had discarded the night before. He held up the little hand mirror that had once belonged to his mother, grimaced at what he saw and ran a hand through his thick yellow hair and over the stubble on his chin and cheeks. It was past time that he visited the jolly little barber in Fleet Street who would shave him, anoint him with lavender oil or rose water — 'purchased at great cost from an avaricious apothecary, sir' — pass on whatever gossip he had picked up as he trimmed beards and pared nails, and offer to let his blood — 'nothing finer for improving the balance of the humours, sir' — and all for three pence. The barber — barber-surgeon, he tried to insist upon — was one of a dozen or so tradesmen who had no inkling that their customer was the Earl of Leicester's chief intelligencer in London and cheerfully chattered away like songbirds: blatherers to a man. Much of what they said was empty twaddle but now and again a shiny nugget emerged from the heap of dross. It was worth encouraging them and paying attention just in case. He took a deep breath and, a little unsteadily, went down to the kitchen.

Katherine had prodded the fire into life and laid out manchet bread, beef and a jug of small beer. 'Why will you not permit me to find you a new housekeeper, Christopher?' she demanded. 'There is little enough food in the house without some of it humming with maggots.' When his elderly housekeeper had died the previous year Christopher had not troubled to replace her but chose to manage alone or to be ministered to by Katherine. He had hoped that the lack of a housekeeper might induce her to spend more nights here than at her aunt's house, but the hope had been misplaced. She had made it clear that, much as she loved him, she lived in Wood Street, not on Ludgate Hill. A widow, she insisted, must maintain at least an appearance of respectability. Privately, Christopher thought this absurd but he knew better than to try to persuade her otherwise. Katherine was not a lady who readily changed her mind.

'I would not be happy with anyone else after Rose,' he replied, pouring himself a beaker of ale. 'She knew my ways as another would not.' He rinsed the ale around his mouth before swallowing.

Katherine grunted and pushed a plate towards him. 'Then at least let me tutor you in the ways of the market. You pay sixpence for meat worth two pence and are content with bread a week old. The Earl of Leicester's chief intelligencer you may be, but at looking after yourself you are no better than a child.'

It was true. He had never been much concerned with money or the practicalities of daily life and, left to himself, was unusually inept at both. At Pembroke, a rattling shutter would have been swiftly repaired by a college servant or by a poor sizar in need of a few pennies. In London, it might never be done.

'This morning we will walk to Cheapside where we will buy fresh meat and winter vegetables at prices I agree with the traders. Then you will know how much to pay in future.'

Christopher speared a slice of beef with his knife and took a bite. Sure enough, it was tough and stringy and he knew that he had probably paid too much for it. Good meat and vegetables had become harder to find this last twelvemonth. But he would not surrender without some semblance of resistance. 'I have much to do and it will be bitter cold out there.'

'Your work can wait. Wear your thick coat. Think of yourself as a pupil newly arrived at Pembroke Hall. Cold or not, there will be traders about and you shall have your first tutorial in the art of purchasing. I should have given it months ago.'

Christopher grunted. 'I do not wish to break a leg. The streets will be icy.'

'Then we will take care. Argue no more. This morning we shall go to the market and count ourselves fortunate that we have money to buy food. Many do not.'

That too was true. Three poor harvests in a row and few country folk could now eke a living from the land. The religious houses that might once have sheltered them were long gone and every week more vagrants poured through the city gates seeking work and shelter, found neither and ended their days in Newgate or as dinner for the rats in a filthy alley. Some wards were swift becoming no more than noxious cauldrons overflowing with poverty, crime and disease. Talk in the inns and taverns was of little else.

And as if that was not enough, fearful Londoners awoke each morning half expecting to see Spanish ships on the river. The more scurrilous news books delighted in depicting the unsmiling King Philip of Spain lurking in his Escorial Palace and plotting an invasion of the island for which he reserved most of his papist venom. To Catholic Queen Mary Philip had been married; to her Protestant sister Elizabeth he wished only the fires of hell. With Spanish troops just over the narrow sea in the Low Countries it was not difficult to imagine their arrival at London Bridge one dark night. The trained bands were drilling for just that and if it happened, God alone knew what might befall England.

'If I must, Katherine, although I would rather be practising my lute. I have been idle of late.'

'How is it that today you are so keen to return to your lute? Nothing to do with visiting the market, I suppose.'

'Nothing. I merely thought that playing might lift my spirits after the horror of yesterday. I know I am a poor hand at the instrument but playing requires concentration and does not permit the mind to wander.'

'Christopher, you are not as poor a hand as you pretend and you can play later, after we have been to the market. I shall go to the chamber to dress. Be ready when I am.'

He waited until he could hear her in the bed chamber before going to the study, where he kept his lute in its fine, tooled leather case hidden under a heap of old clothes. In the eighteen months since it had been presented to him by the Earl of Leicester he had never allowed anyone, not even Katherine or Rose, to touch it. A housebreaker would surely ignore a pile of old shirts and look elsewhere.

He took the instrument from its case and sat as if to play. It was an ivory lute, made in Venice to the earl's order and had been a prized item in his private collection. He closed his eyes and ran his fingers over the body and down the fine lines of ebony that bordered it, savouring the smoothness and the gentle curves of the ivory.

The sound board had been fashioned from alpine spruce and the delicate trellis of the rose was gilded. The back of the neck was decorated with tiny ivory roses and on the peg box had been fixed an ivory plate showing the bear and ragged staff emblem of the Dudley family. It would have cost ten times the price of a common lute and there would be very few like it in England.

The day after the execution of the traitor John Berwick, who had conspired to blow up Whitehall Palace, assassinate the queen and replace her with the Catholic Queen of Scots, Leicester had summoned Christopher to Whitehall and asked to see his right hand — the hand on which the ring and little fingers were bent inwards. When Christopher held it up for inspection, Leicester had looked doubtful. 'Your first two fingers and thumb are unaffected by your condition, but your third and fourth fingers are a concern. It would be a pity if you could not use them. Using a goose-feather quill to play, as our grandfathers did, so limits one's range.'

Christopher had been astonished. He had no inkling that Leicester had so much as noticed his hand.

'There is nothing to be done but try.' From behind his enormous writing table Leicester had produced the lute. 'I hope that you will accept this in appreciation of your service in uncovering the *Incendium* plot and in capturing the traitor Berwick.' He dropped his voice in mock confidence. 'Any of the royal lutes would gladly sit in the stocks for a week for this. I thought Anthony Conti was going to faint when I showed it to him.' Conti's name was well known for his skill on the lute not only in Whitehall but throughout London. 'Have you ever played, doctor?'

Christopher had confessed that, as a boy, he had been taught. 'My mother had a fine singing voice, my lord, and insisted on my taking lessons in order to accompany her. When I left home and went up to Cambridge, however, I played no more. It is a source of regret.'

'Well, here is an opportunity for you to start again.' The earl handed the instrument to Christopher. 'Sit and try it out. Let us see what you can do.'

To refuse would have been unforgivably discourteous. Christopher took a seat, placed the body of the lute on his lap and the fingers of his left hand on the neck. When he rested the little finger of his right hand on the sound board and played a few chords, he found, to his surprise, that he could use his third finger without undue difficulty. The little finger would be more of a problem but one that with a little dexterity he could overcome.

Immediately he regretted having admitted to playing as a boy. 'I fear that I shall not do such a fine instrument justice, my lord,' he said. 'It is years since I played.'

'Nonsense, doctor. I can tell by your posture that you have been well taught. You read tablature of course.'

'I do, my lord, and music.'

Leicester nodded. 'The lute has been correctly tuned. Why not try something simple from memory?'

After more than twelve years, no tune would be simple. Christopher racked his brains. 'I recall learning one of Thomas Wyatt's poems set to music, my lord — "Wilt thou go walk through woods so wild". I could try that.'

'Perfect. Not a difficult piece. You will manage it with ease.'

Christopher breathed deeply, as his teacher had long ago instructed him, adjusted the angle of the lute slightly, and began, slowly at first, and then picking up speed as the movement of his right arm became familiar. His teacher's voice came back to him. 'Pluck the strings with the arm, Christopher, not the hand.'

When he reached the end, he put down the lute, knowing that although he had not made a fool of himself, he had coped poorly with one difficult change of stops and that his playing had been less than fluent.

Leicester clapped his hands. 'Bravo, doctor. Your thumb misbehaved a little and with practice you will play faster and with more divisions, but I believe you could be a fine musician.'

'Thank you, my lord, although I fear that you flatter me.'

'I do not. And I hope that playing will prove as beneficial to you as it does to me. A well-played tune is a sovereign cure for every malady from melancholy to gout. Harmony and balance in music as in life. Take the lute, doctor, and learn to play it well.' A sly grin crept over the narrow face. 'In fact, if you practise hard enough I might be able to offer you a position as a musician with my players. How would you like that?' Of the troupe of players he sponsored, the earl was inordinately proud.

'It would of course be a great honour, my lord, although for the present . . .'

Leicester had laughed. As his mood invariably mirrored that of the queen, Her Majesty must have been in fine spirits that day. 'Quite, quite. Just a jest. But do practise, doctor, and one day you may play at court.'

It had been typical of the earl — a thoughtful, valuable gift, polite encouragement, a touch of humour and care for his intelligencer's well-being. And a complete surprise. Christopher had left the palace clutching the lute and wondering at a man who could be so generous in word and deed, yet, when his humour was ill, also unreasonable and impatient. Rather than risk the carts and horses and mud and muck of Fleet Street, he had wrapped the case in his gown and taken a wherry to Blackfriars steps.

Since that day he had taken great care of the gift, cleaning it often and replacing broken strings and worn-down frets. He had bought music from the booksellers' market in St Paul's yard and from Mr Brewster's shop in Fetter Lane, practised regularly, and had, he thought, become tolerably competent again. He had also come to realize that his playing and his choice of music reflected his mood — light and fluent when happy, slow and dull when not. Sombre pavans, jolly galliards, and dompes for quiet contemplation. His favourite piece of all was entitled 'My Lady Cary's Dompe'. It lifted his spirits when they were low and he played it often.

Working for the earl was seldom easy and sometimes downright impossible, but he took quiet pride in the gift and wished that

Leicester would ask about his progress. He never had. That too was somehow typical of the man.

He was wondering whether to risk a chord or two when there was a knock on the door. He cursed, replaced the lute in its case and went to open it. An icy blast swept into the house. Despite being wrapped up in a thick, fur-trimmed coat and hat, the young man standing outside was shivering. Narrow in the shoulder and several inches shorter than Christopher, he looked as if a strong gust might send him hurtling down the hill. 'Roland,' said Christopher, surprised. 'Come in at once before you perish.'

Roland Wetherby stepped inside and stamped a sprinkling of snow from his shoes. Christopher closed the door quickly. 'God's wounds, Christopher,' Roland said, shaking his head, 'but it is cold out there, cold enough to freeze a man's balls. There is ice on the streets and they are treacherous. Take care when you go out.'

'I would much prefer not to go out, Roland. In fact I had a mind to devote the morning to my lute, but Katherine wishes me to accompany her to Cheapside.'

Wetherby pulled off his gloves and rubbed his hands together. 'There will be precious few traders about today and, in any case, my friend, the noble earl has other plans for you. He summons you to Goldsmiths' Hall immediately. The lute later, perhaps.'

'What in the devil's name does the earl want of me at this hour and why Goldsmiths' Hall?' It was unlike the earl to summon him when it was barely light although at least the Hall was nearby in Foster Lane. He would not have far to walk.

Wetherby grinned. He rarely knew something about Leicester that Christopher did not. 'I have an inkling, but better that you should ask the earl.' He glanced up. Katherine, now properly dressed and her hair brushed and arranged to frame her face, was coming down the stair. He bowed low. 'Mistress Allington, good day. I had not thought to see you this morning. Do you fare well?'

Katherine turned her smile on him. A ladies' man Roland Wetherby was most emphatically not, yet he was as susceptible to her charm, when she chose to use it, as any. 'Mr Wetherby, a pleasure to see you. I fare well, thank you. But I trust you have not come to take Christopher away. Today he is to be my pupil, although between you and me, I do not expect much.'

'Alas, I fear that the lesson must wait, madam. The earl has other plans for him.'

Katherine made a moue. 'How disappointing. I was looking forward to teaching a doctor of law how not to spend a shilling when sixpence will do. I am vexed but still I wish the earl good fortune. Christopher's head will be throbbing and his mind befuddled. Like so many of your sex, he is prone to excess.'

'We saw a woman convicted of murdering her husband by an act of witchcraft burned at Smithfield yesterday,' explained Christopher. 'I sought solace in a bottle.'

'Several bottles.'

'Very well, Katherine, several bottles, not that they brought much comfort. We should not have been there and I know not why we stayed. The woman suffered greatly.' He closed his eyes as if trying to banish from his mind the image of her fleshless face and blackened bones. 'Now, sit, Roland, and take a beaker of beer. Ignore Katherine. Her temper is never sweet before midday. The earl must wait until I have finished my breakfast. I will join him presently. How is his mood today?'

Wetherby remained standing. 'Sour. He frets about the queen's progress to Kenilworth although it is still eighteen months away and every day finds something new and unpleasant to say about

Christopher Hatton. Yesterday he was "a mincing prancer". Today, who knows? "Captain of the Gentlemen Prancers", perhaps.'

Christopher laughed. At only thirty-three, the handsome Hatton, the finest dancer at court, or so they said, had, to Leicester's annoyance, been appointed Captain of the Gentlemen Pensioners, a high office for one so young.

'And his mood will not be improved if you keep him waiting. You know how he dislikes it.'

'No more than I dislike being taken from my breakfast. I will say that the streets were dangerous and forced me to take unusual care. Or that I was detained by an old woman who had fallen and needed my help.'

'He will not believe you.'

Christopher shrugged, poured beer from the jug into a beaker and handed it to Wetherby. 'Sit down and tell me what I might expect at Goldsmiths' Hall. I am not at my strongest and do not wish to be ambushed by the earl.'

'I shall return to the bed chamber,' said Katherine, 'so that you may speak freely.'

'And quietly. You will of course be listening.'

Katherine poked out her tongue and flounced off. Wetherby pulled up a chair. 'Oh, very well, Christopher, if you insist. I will tell you what little I know but you must pretend to know nothing. You may happily incur his displeasure but I do not wish to.'

'Nor will you. Now what is it that I do not know?'

Half an hour later, when Wetherby had returned to Whitehall, Katherine handed Christopher his thick coat. 'Return directly,' she said, 'I shall be here and impatient to know exactly what the earl has in mind for you.'

CHAPTER 3

The Goldsmiths' Company was one of the city's oldest livery companies and its Hall — as grand as any in London — had stood in Foster Lane for more than two hundred years. Christopher had passed by it countless times but had never before had occasion to enter.

At the entrance he was met by a red-and-gold-liveried company officer, who wore a sword at his waist. He asked Christopher's name, welcomed him to the Hall and led him through the Goldsmiths' Great Chamber, past a chapel and an armoury and down a short passage lit by rows of long wax candles in silver sconces attached at head height to the walls. In the air hung the sweet smells of lavender and rose water.

It was still too early for the Hall to be busy. Their shoes clattered on the boards of the floor and echoed down the empty passage until they came to a tall oak door, guarded by another armed officer. The escort knocked with his fist, pushed the door open and announced the visitor's arrival. Christopher stepped inside, leaving the escort outside. The door closed behind him.

The panelled walls of the room he entered were adorned with portraits of Masters of the Goldsmiths' Company. Above them, narrow windows were set high as if to prevent unwelcome eyes from peering in. The room was bare but for a blazing log fire and a long oak table set in the middle, on which stood a dozen more candles in silver candlesticks and four neatly aligned wooden boxes about the length of a man's forearm and the depth and width of his hand, their lids open. Beside them were a pair of brass weighing scales such as might be used by a merchant or an apothecary. As he approached the table, Christopher saw that the boxes were highly polished, edged in gold and with the Goldsmiths' blazon — a pair of unicorns either side of a quartered shield above which stood a figure holding scales and a touchstone — inlaid on the lid. By their size and shape he guessed that the boxes were designed to hold coins.

He doffed his cap and bowed to the two men standing behind the table. One was the Earl of Leicester, black-eyed, black-bearded, and clad in a crimson doublet, high-collared and embroidered in silver and gold, and hose that matched his doublet. Christopher had never been able to reconcile his master's flamboyant dress with his puritanical leanings. His own leanings were far from puritanical but he dressed habitually in academic gown and cap. A bird might be known by its feathers but a man could not be, sumptuary laws or no.

The man beside the earl, shorter and heavier and red of face, wore a plain dark blue doublet and hose, as if he did not want to be accused of trying to compete with the earl. His narrow eyes were blue and his short beard streaked with grey. His hands were clasped behind his back.

Leicester spoke first. 'Here you are at last, Dr Radcliff,' he said, tossing a coin he was inspecting on to the table. 'We await you.' In both words and tone his impatience was plain. The man beside him picked up the coin and put it carefully in the box to his right.

'My humble apologies, my lord. I came at once but the streets are icy and delayed me a little.'

Leicester's black eyes bored into his. 'Yet they did not delay me. I have much to occupy me today and no time to waste. Did Wetherby not impress upon you the urgency of the matter?'

'He did indeed, my lord, and I came with all speed.'

Leicester sighed. 'I do not altogether believe you but you are here now. Mr Martin, this is Dr Radcliff, of whom I spoke. Dr Radcliff, Richard Martin is a senior member of the Goldsmiths' Company and Warden of the Royal Mint.'

Again Christopher bowed. 'Mr Martin. Your name is known to me.'

Martin smiled. 'As yours is to me, Dr Radcliff.'

'Let us proceed without further delay,' said the earl. 'Her Majesty wishes to discuss arrangements for next year's progress to Kenilworth and I must return directly to Whitehall.' As Master of the Queen's Horse, Leicester was responsible for every detail of the royal progresses from agreeing the prices of bread and meat to the exact route they would take and the standard of the entertainment. Her Majesty was fond of bear-baiting but woe betide the wretch who produced mastiffs of insufficient ferocity. Progresses were thought essential to the good governance of the country and could involve over a thousand people. The task occupied much of Leicester's time and could render him very short-tempered. Christopher had learned to tread carefully when the earl was fretting about stabling for the horses or clean bed linen for the queen's ladies.

Martin waved a hand over the table. 'Here are four boxes, each containing silver testons. Those in two of the boxes were

minted in one of our eight mints, those in the other two were not.'
He took a coin from the first box and examined it by the light of a
candle. 'This one was not.' He handed the coin to Christopher,
took another from a second box and put it in one of the shallow
cups suspended on the balance. The balance arm dropped with its
weight. 'If you put your coin in the other cup, Dr Radcliff, you will
see the difference.' Christopher did so. The balance arm fell but
remained well above its counterpart. 'There, you see: two testons,
one almost pure silver, the other counterfeit and much contaminated by copper.' He removed both coins and handed the lighter
one to Christopher. 'Hold it to the light and you will discern a red-
dening on the face.'

Christopher did so. 'I recall the slogan that appeared on walls
and in news sheets when I was a pupil,' he replied. *'Beware the coin of
reddish face, not silver pure but metal base,* was it not?'

Martin's eyebrows rose. 'It was indeed, doctor. Your memory
serves you well. On account of your legal training, no doubt.'

'Thank you, Mr Martin.' Thanks to Wetherby he was prepared
for something like this.

'So there we have two coins, one genuine, the other counterfeit.'
Martin took a coin from the third box. 'And, of course, thanks to Her
gracious Majesty's efforts to stabilize our coinage, we also have
another perfectly legal teston but one with little more than half the
value of the first.' He asked Christopher to put his coin back on
the balance and then did the same with the one in his hand. Again
the balance dropped but not as much as it had the first time. 'A better
teston and a worse one.'

Christopher could not see where this was going. Since the revalu-
ation of the coinage twelve years earlier, the value of purer testons
had been established at 4¼ pence and that of the more contaminated

at 2¼ pence, about the difference in the prices of a loaf of bread and a goose. Every trader in the country knew this.

The distinction had not come without its problems — particularly in the markets where buyers and sellers had at first disagreed on the value of a coin or the accuracy of a trader's scales, but the queen had brought over skilled German minters to improve and standardize the quality of the currency from gold sovereigns and angels down to silver crowns and testons, and, now, the better teston was marked with a portcullis, the worse with a greyhound.

'But they have been with us since the proclamation of 1562, Mr Martin. Are they now a matter of concern? Has there been a new outbreak of coining?' he asked, trying to keep the impatience out of his voice.

'I fear that there has,' replied Leicester, before Martin could speak, 'but coining of a new and yet more insidious kind.'

'How so, my lord?'

Leicester signalled to Martin, who took a coin from the fourth box and handed it to Christopher. 'This coin and others like it were passed to us by traders who had carelessly accepted them as payment in the markets. So far there have not been many but even a handful are worrying.'

Christopher turned the coin over in his hand. One face was stamped not with a greyhound or a portcullis but with a bear on one side and a ragged staff on the other. This Wetherby had not mentioned. He looked up sharply. 'But the bear and staff is your family emblem, my lord.' An emblem that adorned every room and almost every item of furniture in Kenilworth Castle, as well as Christopher's lute. Martin's demonstration had been no more than a preamble to this. No wonder the earl's mood was less than sweet.

'Indeed it is. The coiner has seen fit to replace the queen's likeness and the proper mark with my family crest. And the coiner is a man of some skill. See how well made the coin is and how clear the stamps. Her Majesty has been shown one of these and, not unnaturally, is shocked and angry. I have given her my word that I will discover the source of this treason without delay and put an end to it. And so I shall. It is not so much a counterfeit as an act of desecration.'

The words were out of Christopher's mouth before he could stop them. 'May I take it, my lord, that you mean it is I who will discover the source?'

Leicester stared at him, his dark eyes narrowed. 'Take care, doctor. This is no time for levity.'

Christopher swallowed and bowed his head. 'My apologies, my lord. I am not myself after witnessing an old woman burned at the stake for causing death by witchcraft yesterday. The spectacle has unsettled me.'

'Be that as it may, the matter of this false coinage is one of the utmost gravity, a deliberate insult to Her Majesty, to my family, to the country, and to me. Coining is an attempt to debase not only our currency but our monarchy. Not thirty years ago the country came close to anarchy caused in large part by our debased coinage and the role it played in fomenting unrest. Markets closed, coiners abounded, poor men starved and many died. I was with my father and brother at Norwich when the rebels led by the traitor Robert Kett were defeated. It was a cruel time.' He shook his head as if to banish an image from his mind. 'The bloodshed — of good men and bad — was almost beyond belief. I trust never to see the like again.' He took another teston from the box and held it up. 'This must be dealt with forthwith before dangerous discourse of our coinage and of these abominations surfaces once more.' He paused briefly. 'And in any event witchcraft in all its forms must be stamped out. If burning is the way to do so, so be it. I have no time for squeamishness in such matters and neither should you. Put it from your mind.'

From Leicester's tone Christopher knew that he had gone too far. 'Again, my lord, I crave your pardon. In what way may I be of service in the discovery of these coiners?'

'You can start by visiting the Royal Mint at the Tower. Mr Martin will explain more to you about the process of minting there.' Leicester glanced at Martin, who nodded his agreement. 'From there various avenues of inquiry will doubtless present themselves. I recall that among your agents there is a Jew operating from Fleet Street. A goldsmith. Perhaps he can shed light on the matter. But remember, discretion is vital. Here we have a blatant attempt to blacken the Dudley name. The felons must be caught and punished before word spreads.'

Although the earl spoke, as was his custom, quietly, the force of his words was unmistakable. It would be difficult to think of anything less likely to endear him to the queen than the substitution of his emblem for her own on coin of the realm. Nor would her displeasure be the worst of it. For Leicester's enemies awaiting their chance to strike, the coining would be a godsend. Christopher Hatton would dance himself silly.

'If you present yourself at the Royal Mint tomorrow at midday, Dr Radcliff,' said Martin, 'I shall be happy to show you its workings and to discuss the matter further with you.'

'Tomorrow, sir. You may expect me.'

'That is settled,' said Leicester. 'Now I shall return to Whitehall Palace. Dr Radcliff, report to me the minute you have news.' He took a false teston from the table and tossed it to Christopher. 'Take that. You might find it useful. But do not attempt to spend it.'

Christopher caught the coin. His ill humour had caused him to overstep the mark of civility — a mark the earl held dear — and he was glad to be dismissed. Katherine had told him to return straight to Ludgate Hill, but she would have to wait. And so would the lute.

Usually a heaving throng of beasts and beggars and men and women about their daily business, Fleet Street that morning was quiet. Even the shivering wretch with his ears nailed to the stocks on the corner of Whitefriars was spared the usual barrage of rotting food and muck. Christopher had to brush off but a few ragged urchins and avoid the pure collectors with their evil-smelling carts. The cold had kept traders in their beds and horses in their stables. He walked as briskly as the icy street would allow, past the shop of the garrulous barber and as far as an unmarked door beside a printing house about halfway along the street. While others had stayed at home, Isaac Cardoza, goldsmith, would surely be at work.

Isaac, a Marrano Jew, loved above all else to talk and had told Christopher much about his family and their desperate escape fifty years earlier from the Portuguese inquisition. While many Marranos had settled in Paris or Copenhagen, Isaac's family had reached London and had settled into the small Jewish community centred on Leadenhall market. Now his business thrived among the goldsmiths of Fleet Street.

They had spoken often of the same intolerance that had forced the Jews from their homes in Portugal and Spain and was driving Catholics out of England and Protestants out of France. Isaac liked to ask why. 'While you Christians fight amongst yourselves, we Jews are happy to share a country with anyone and we never seek to proselytize, yet we are looked down upon wherever we go. Why is that, my friend?' he would ask. Christopher had no answer.

Unlike some Marranos, who had converted to Christianity to avoid persecution, the Cardozas continued to practise their faith in private. If the Church or the law suspected this, they turned a blind eye to it. The Marranos were valued for their business sense and for the useful intelligence they brought back from their travels to France and the Low Countries. Witches might burn, Catholic priests might hang, but the Marranos were tolerated. Without their help, the traitor John Berwick might never have been caught and hanged and Christopher would not now be the Earl of Leicester's chief intelligencer in London.

Isaac was sitting at his weighing table, a pair of thick spectacles perched on his nose, examining a silver spoon by the light of six wax candles. The goldsmith prided himself on never spending an unnecessary coin but did eschew cheaper tallow candles, which gave off such a noxious odour. He reckoned that he recovered the extra cost in the higher prices he could extract from customers whose noses were not assailed by the smell of burning animal fat. When he looked up and saw who his visitor was, a crooked smile lit up his wrinkled face. 'Christopher, my friend, I wish you joy. It has been too long. Forgive my not rising — my back aches from this infernal cold. See how my hand shakes.'

Christopher took the outstretched hand in his and held it firmly enough to stop the shaking. 'At least it is not as bent as a meat hook, Isaac, and when the spring comes, your hand will be warm but mine will still be like this.' He held it up for Isaac to see. The fingers were bent inwards and almost touching his palm.

'It has worsened since last I saw you. Has no apothecary been able to help?'

'No, nor doctor nor surgeon nor mixer of magic potions. I have tired of handing over money to quacks and charlatans and have determined to let nature take her course. No more expensive, useless remedies for me.'

'Wise, no doubt. We Jews hate handing over hard-earned coins without good reason. But you have not come to talk of medical matters, Christopher, nor, I think, of money. What can I do for you?'

Christopher pulled up a plain pine stool and sat opposite the goldsmith. 'As chance would have it, Isaac, it is indeed about money that I have come. That and the pleasure of seeing you. How do your family fare?'

'Well, thank you. I thank God for the children. They make our days worthwhile. And Mistress Allington — not yet persuaded to marriage?'

Christopher laughed. 'Not yet, nor ever, I fancy, hard though I have tried. She still harbours notions of my returning to Cambridge as a Fellow of Pembroke Hall, despite the foolishness of it. Marriage of course would make that impossible.' He took the counterfeit teston from his purse and placed it on the table between them. 'It is about this that I have come.'

Isaac picked the coin up and peered at one face. Then, as Christopher had, he turned it over and looked up in surprise. 'Christopher, my friend, do you know what this is?'

'It is the emblem of the Dudley family. The bear and ragged staff.'

'Indeed, but the story behind it, do you know that?'

'I did not know there was a story.'

'It is newly minted and well made. Did the earl give it to you?'

'He did, and instructed me to find its source.'

'He told you no more?'

'No.'

'So you need my help.'

Christopher nodded. 'I do. I must discover how and why and by whom this coin was made and do so without asking questions that might give rise to alarm. Can you offer any advice on how I am to do this, my friend?'

Isaac scratched at his red beard. 'I do not like this coin and for any but you I would refuse. Merely holding it in my hand makes me uneasy. I imagine that Warden Martin knows about this?'

'He does, and I shall visit the mint tomorrow.'

'Then I suggest you ask Martin to share with you what he knows about it and its marks. It is new but its story is old.'

'Will you not tell me the story, Isaac?'

Isaac shook his head. 'No, my friend, better that it should come from the warden. If you wish, however, I will speak quietly to one or two trusted friends. Something might emerge.'

'Very well, Isaac. One or two, but no more, please. The earl was most insistent on the importance of secrecy.'

'That is no surprise. This coin must be a great embarrassment to the Dudley family and it might just as well have the word "treason" stamped upon it. You are too young but I remember the time when it first appeared. It was a bad time, one that men of peace do not want to see repeated.'

'Yet you will not speak to me about it.'

'I will not. We Jews are a superstitious race but rest assured that I shall be careful, and so must you. Call again in a few days.' Isaac put the coin in his purse. '*Shalom*, Christopher. Take care.'

'*Shalom*, Isaac. Go well and send blessings to your family.'

What was the story behind the coin and why would Isaac not say more? And why, for that matter, had Leicester not said more?

Finding the coiner would not be made easier by the earl not sharing intelligence.

Katherine was sitting in the little parlour he used as a study. He threw his coat over a chair and warmed his hands at the fire. 'It is bitter cold and snow is falling,' he said. 'A day for wise virgins to stay at home.' When Katherine did not respond, he straightened up and turned to her. 'But since you are neither wise nor a virgin, I expect you will be wanting to return to Wood Street.'

She ignored the jibe. 'You have been gone a long time, Christopher. Did the earl detain you or did you see fit to visit your whore? Is she to assist you in your work, while I may not?' In her voice there was no trace of humour.

Caught unawares, Christopher snapped, 'God's mercy, woman, what has brought this on? My day has been difficult enough without this carping. Can you not accept that Ell Cole is a valuable intelligencer and that she is not my whore?'

'So you have visited her.'

'I have not. I have been to Goldsmiths' Hall where I found the Earl of Leicester in impatient mood, and thence to Fleet Street to speak to Isaac Cardoza. He wishes you well. Now, for the love of God, may we talk of something else?'

For a minute Katherine was silent. Then she rose from her chair and embraced him. 'I am sorry, Christopher. It is sitting idly by while you are about the earl's work. I hate it. Can I not assist in some way?'

'In what way?'

'You could begin by telling me what you learned at Goldsmiths' Hall.'

Christopher pushed her gently away. 'I am sworn to silence and, even if I were not, have you forgotten how close to death you were at the hands of John Berwick when you last assisted me? He would have sliced open your throat without a moment's pause.'

Katherine frowned. 'Berwick is dead. I saw that evil traitor at the end of a rope with my own eyes. And have you forgotten who it was that persuaded Ursula Walsingham to speak to the earl for you when you were under suspicion and held prisoner in this very house?'

Christopher had not forgotten, nor ever would. 'I think of it often. All the more reason why I am unwilling to put you in the way of danger again.'

Katherine nodded. 'Very well. A compromise. Let us sit and you tell me what you can. At least then I may be your sounding board. For now I ask no more.'

It was a slippery slope but Katherine Allington was not an easy woman to refuse. Choosing his words with care, Christopher told her what little he knew, playing down Isaac's reaction to the counterfeit coin. There was nothing to be gained by alarming her unduly.

It did not take long and when Katherine returned to Wood Street she had promised to speak to no one, not even her aunt, about the matter. Christopher watched her go and wondered if he had been too easily persuaded. Again.

CHAPTER 4

Since taking up his position in the earl's service in London, Christopher had worked to extend his network of agents. Now he had Isaac Cardoza and intelligencers in the Guildhall, in the livery companies, among the traders in the markets and the boatmen on the river.

In Roland Wetherby, now in the service of the earl who had lured him away from Thomas Heneage, he had a brave and perceptive ally, and, to Katherine's oft-voiced displeasure, he had Ell Cole, upon whom he had come to rely more and more not only for the intelligence she extracted from her 'gentlemen' but also for acting as a conduit to other agents in the roughest wards of the city, just as Isaac did among the business community. If he wanted them all to know or do something he had only to tell Ell and Isaac. It saved him much time and trouble and Ell revelled in the role. 'Not just a whore, now, am I, Dr Rad?' she had boasted. 'Proper intelligencer, aren't I? Don't know what you'd do without me.'

'I do,' he had replied. 'I'd have an easier time with Mistress Allington. She won't believe I'm not swiving you.'

Ell's laugh was a chuckle that began somewhere deep in her throat and exploded with enough force to make her shoulders shake.

'Can't believe it myself, doctor. Here am I offering it to you for nothing and here's you saying even that's too much. Have I to give you a pound for it, is that it?'

'Now there's a thought. But my price would be a little higher. Say twenty pounds?'

'Fuck off, Dr Rad. If I had twenty pounds I wouldn't waste them on you. I'd buy a fine house in Southwark and never speak to another man. I might even become a witch and fill the house with cats. That'd keep the buggers away.' Very few things frightened Ell Cole, even being thought a witch. Christopher remembered that exchange and that he had left her with a grin on his face.

Ell's stew was in a narrow, unnamed alley off Cheapside, usually the busiest street in London but on such a bitter day almost deserted. Huddled into his heavy coat, his cap low on his head, Christopher hurried past the few traders who had braved the morning cold, and turned into the alley. When he came to this place he tried not to be noticed although, at over six feet tall and with hair the colour of hay, that was not easy. The alley was home to families of fat rats who fed off scraps from the market and the heaps of human waste lining it and to beggars and vagrants sheltering in dark doorways. He ignored their outstretched hands and plaintive pleas and fingered the hilt of the poniard that had saved his purse, and his life, more than once. Measured by the number of a man's strides the alley was no distance from the Goldsmiths' Hall; in every other way it might as well have been a thousand miles away.

The bloated stew owner opened the door, a long clay pipe in her hand. 'It's you, doctor,' she croaked. 'Ell's free. Go up.' As he had never asked for any other of her charges, she knew well enough whom he wanted although she would have been astonished if she had been told why. She simply assumed that Dr Rad was one of Ell's devoted customers and had been spoilt for any other girl. In this he would not have been alone.

He climbed the rickety stairs and knocked on Ell's door. 'Bugger off, Grace,' a voice called out. 'I've had a hard night and I'm sore. That last one was a foul brute. Don't want to see him again.'

Christopher ignored her and opened the door. A fire was burning in the grate. Ell's customers would not suffer the cold in her chamber. She was sitting up in bed, naked from the waist up, brushing her auburn hair. How a hard-working whore could look so lovely, even after a busy night's work — oval face, brown eyes, a touch of red to her cheeks — he could not imagine. Only the faintest creases around the eyes betrayed her age, not that either of them had much idea what that was. Why she was not the pampered mistress of some pampered courtier he had never understood.

'Oh, it's you, Dr Rad.' She grinned at him. 'Any other time and it'd be a pleasure but I wouldn't be myself this morning. One after another it was from dusk till dawn. I need my sleep.' He laughed. She knew that it would be business not pleasure that had brought him there. She put down the hairbrush and pulled on a shift. 'Don't know why I'm hiding them from you.'

'No need, Ell, if you don't want to. Quite happy to look at them. And you shall have your sleep. Any gossip worth reporting to the earl?'

She shook her head. 'Just the usual. A Spanish spy around every corner, a priest in every cellar, the queen on her death bed, the earl himself found swiving a sheep.'

'What?'

This time, Ell's laugh was like a child's gurgle. 'Just my little joke, doctor. Though since the queen pushed him out of her bed, they say he'll swive almost anything.'

'Nothing new, then?'

'Not that's reached my ears.' She tilted her head to look at him. 'You are unsettled, Dr Rad. Your face is drawn. Still the dreams?'

'Still the dreams. And I saw a witch burned at Smithfield two days since.'

Ell snorted. 'She wasn't no witch. I knew her. Just an old widow with marks on her skin. She wouldn't have hurt anyone. It was her man deserved to burn. Evil bugger he was. She was just a miserable old crone, stuck with a one-eyed scroyle for a husband.'

'Hmm. These days it seems that every miserable old crone has made a pact with the devil. Or so we are to believe. Are you sure you've heard nothing?'

'Not a rat's fart.'

'Well, keep your ears open, Ell, and look out for strange testons. Let me know if you see any or hear anything.'

'What sort of strange? More red than silver? We're used to those.'

'No. Testons marked with a bear and a staff. But keep it to yourself.'

'A bear and a staff. That's different. Reckon I'd notice one of those. Very well, doctor. And you know me. Open door, open ears, open legs, mouth closed. I'll slip a note under your door if I hear anything, then you'll know to visit again.' She smiled. 'Take care, Dr Rad, and remember I'm here if you need me.'

'I'll remember. And you take care, too, Ell. There's likely more to this than just a false coin.'

For all its stinking filth, Christopher had come to love the Thames. As different to the Cam that flowed quietly through Cambridge as a nettle to a rose, it was a busy, bustling highway, on which men and women lived and travelled and went about their business. On still days, their voices carried clearly across the water, many in languages he could not guess at. Here a man might see on the same day a black

African face, a narrow-eyed oriental one, a face burned by the Mediterranean sun and the pale skin of the Baltic. He often wished that he could converse with each in his own tongue, ask them where they had travelled from, how they lived and what they thought. The Thames carried not only goods to be traded but knowledge and ideas to be exchanged.

From Cheapside he walked down to Blackfriars steps where he found two moored boats and three wherrymen braving the cold and awaiting a fare. Most wherrymen were affable souls, given to chatter and gossip and not short of an opinion. These three were huddled over a game of dice.

Both banks of the river as far as he could see towards London Bridge were lined with tilt-boats, barges and cargo vessels at anchor or at work. Between them the current bore its detritus out to sea. He sometimes wondered where it all went. Ell thought it washed up in France where the barbarous French ate what they could and fed the rest to their beasts. Rather unkindly he had not tried to dissuade her from this opinion.

One of the men looked up. 'Across to Bankside, sir?' he called out as Christopher approached.

'Not today. Tower steps.'

The wherryman looked at him sharply. 'Are you sure, sir?' he asked. 'River's high and there's a powerful current running under the bridge. Might be dangerous. Could put you off at Swan Lane. Only a short walk from there to the Tower.'

'Have you been through the bridge today?' asked Christopher.

'I have not, sir, and have no wish to do so.'

'What about you two?' he asked the others.

'We've been through, sir, and are still here, rough though it was.'

'Then you'll have no difficulty in doing so again. Tower steps it is.'

'As you wish, sir. Sixpence that will be.' Fares across the river were regulated by law. Up and down they varied with the distance, the tide and the weather.

Christopher took a coin from his purse and handed it to the elder of the two. Wherrymen liked to be paid in advance rather than risk having to watch helplessly as their passenger leapt out at their destination and ran off.

The elder man took up his position on the planked seat in the middle of the boat. The younger held it steady against the pier as Christopher stepped on board, then jumped in after him. Christopher took a seat at the stern, facing the rowers. If it really was rough under the bridge, a larger boat would be safer.

At first the river was calm enough with but a gentle swell and the breeze was light. Children were scavenging on the mudbanks while fishers tried their luck with long lines. The wind was no more than a stiff breeze and the bridge should present no problem.

When the bridge came into sight, however, he began to have doubts. Where the channel narrowed under its arches, the water was heaving and rolling in fountains of white spray. He opened his mouth to shout at the wherryman to make for Swan Lane but too late. The wherry shot forward on the current and was swept towards the bridge. Christopher steeled himself for the impact and for a drenching. The wherrymen, their backs to the bridge, shipped their oars and waited for calmer waters or the crash of timber against stone.

Whether by good fortune or their skill in positioning the boat, they raced under the central arch and emerged damp but intact on the other side. Christopher tried to look unconcerned but knew that running the bridge had been foolish. He shook water from his hair and wiped his face with a corner of his gown. The elder man grinned toothlessly and said nothing.

At Tower steps Christopher alighted carefully and walked up the hill to the Postern Gate, still trying to dry himself off. Why had he done it? He could have walked from Cheapside to the Tower easily enough or he could have heeded the wherryman's advice and alighted at Swan Lane. For the devilment perhaps. Since Paris, devilment of one sort or another came readily to him. From the gate he was escorted between the curtain walls to the Salt Tower, from which ran a line of low buildings westwards towards Broad Arrow Tower. These were the mint workshops.

He waited in a small hallway while Richard Martin was summoned. From the workshops came the ring of hammer on metal and the crackle of flames in a furnace. Martin entered through a door off the hallway and grinned. 'Dr Radcliff, I see you have travelled by wherry. Was that wise?'

Christopher shook more river water from his coat. 'It would appear not.'

'Can I be of assistance?'

'Thank you, no, Mr Martin. I shall dry off soon enough.'

'Then welcome to the Royal Mint. I take it you have not visited us before.' Today the warden, in a red gown trimmed with white rabbit fur, was more colourful. Yesterday, careful not to exceed his station, today an effort to impress.

'I have not, sir,' replied Christopher, 'although the Tower itself is regrettably familiar to me.' The gruesome sight of a sheep, face down on the rack and stretched until its limbs were ripped from its body like corks popping from bottles, while the traitor Patrick Wolf was made to watch, came back to him. Wolf himself had avoided the same fate by being murdered in his cell that night. For Christopher, who would have been expected to witness the racking, his death had been half drawback, half relief. 'I should be happy not to enter it again.'

Martin laughed. 'Fear not, doctor, the mint is managed quite separately from the Tower and we seldom have need to venture within the inner wall. Now let me show you our workings.' Beckoning his visitor to follow, he led the way out of the Salt Tower to the first workshop.

The moment they stepped into the place, Christopher put his hands to his ears. On one side of the room, a row of beaters hammered at ingots of silver. On the other, the flattened ingots were laid on a long-handled tray not unlike that which a baker might use, and placed in a furnace to be softened. As he watched, trays of ingots were taken from the furnace to the beaters to be shaped and then back again to the furnace, back and forth, until they were ready for rolling and cutting. In each corner of the room stood an overseer. Beaters and overseers alike wore woollen caps with long flaps that covered their ears and were tied under the chin. Scant protection from the noise but probably better than nothing. It was as if twenty blacksmiths were hammering out horseshoes in a single forge. Conversation was impossible. They did not stay for long.

'Alas,' said Martin when they were outside again, 'many of our beaters are deaf. It is a price they, and we, have to pay for the work. They jest that their deafness brings them money for ale and spares them the carping tongues of their wives when they return from the taproom. Man is ever adept at finding humour in misfortune, don't you agree, Dr Radcliff?'

Martin did not wait for a reply but opened another door and ushered him into a second workshop. Here teams of men working in pairs were stamping the silver discs with trussels and dies. Compared to the first workshop, it was blessedly quiet. The men worked steadily, soon filling a wicker basket with minted coins. 'You are familiar with the Trial of the Pyx, doctor, I expect?' asked Martin.

Up to that point Richard Martin had seemed an agreeable enough fellow but the question irked Christopher. Martin knew perfectly well that Christopher was as likely to be familiar with the Pyx as he himself was with Justinian's Codex. He disliked self-regarding men who treated conversation like a player at *jeu-de-paume*, always looking to score points from his opponent. There had been scholars at Pembroke Hall who seemed to live for little else. 'Naturally I am aware of the ceremony of the Pyx, Mr Martin, but my knowledge is limited to the origin of the word. Do, please, enlighten me.'

Martin caught his tone and glanced sideways. 'Then I will be brief, doctor. *Pyxis*, as you know, is the Latin word for a small box, and refers to the chests in which randomly selected samples from each minting are taken to the Star Chamber to be tested by a jury of goldsmiths before the Privy Council and the lords of the treasury. The assessed samples are kept as standards in the treasury and any of inferior standard are sent back to us to be melted down and reminted.'

'Thereby avoiding the worst of the debasements common thirty or forty years ago and making the identification of counterfeit coins easier.'

Martin's eyebrows rose. 'Exactly, doctor. You are well informed. Not a perfect process but better than it once was and overseen at all times.'

The pairs of minters were also watched over by overseers and at the door, unguarded on the outside, were stationed two armed yeomen. Martin went on: 'We do what we can to prevent theft but in truth it is all too easy for our processes to be copied by coiners, not uncommonly men who have worked here before using what they have learned to their own criminal advantage. And it is hard to track them down. Illegal mints producing small quantities of false coins are hidden away in cellars and lofts and the coins are swiftly distributed through the markets.'

'The silver for their coins coming from clipping and culling good money.'

'That is correct, doctor, and also from collecting silver dust by shaking coins vigorously in a bag, but that produces only small amounts. It is known as sweating the coins.'

Christopher nodded. He had heard of this. It sounded inefficient — as if it was the coiner who sweated for scant reward.

'And then there are the Flemish. If they do not come here to practise their nefarious trade, they find ever more ingenious ways of smuggling their coins in. At the ports we must look out for wine barrels full of them. We recently found a large bag of crowns hidden in a consignment of Flemish lace.' Martin laughed. 'I wonder they bother. The lace is costly enough.'

'Surely you cannot check every barrel and crate coming across the narrow sea?'

'Indeed we cannot. Our informers are our best protection although they too are not always above suspicion. One coiner or shipper of false coins may inform on another to rid himself of a competitor.'

'But these new testons are different, are they not?'

'They are. Counterfeiting our coinage is treason enough, but replacing the head of the queen and the royal emblem is a yet more heinous crime.' Martin hesitated. 'Are you aware of the stories of such coins at the time the Earl of Warwick, Leicester's father, appointed himself Duke of Northumberland?'

'I am not.'

'Then I shall tell you. It will help you understand the earl's anxiety. Let us find a quiet corner where we can refresh ourselves.'

In Martin's office they sat with glasses of hippocras served by a mint official. Martin took a sip and smacked his lips in appreciation. 'Excellent. I insist on plenty of cinnamon in the making. How do you find it, doctor?'

'Very agreeable, Mr Martin,' replied Christopher, thinking that there was far too much spice in it. 'The very thing for a cold morning.'

'Now, the testons. In 1551, only two years after the uprisings that brought such bloodshed to the country, a coin now known as the "Dudley" or "bear and staff" teston began to appear in the markets. Remember that the Earl of Leicester and his brother Ambrose had been at Norwich with their father the Earl of Warwick, sent there by Protector Somerset to quash the Norfolk rebels, and the terrors of that battle would have been only too fresh in their minds. The earl spoke only yesterday of the horrors he witnessed.' Martin paused to take another sip of hippocras. 'Do you recall that time, doctor, or were you too young?'

'I was only nine years old at the time of the uprisings but I remember the fear and confusion they brought. One day news would come that the rebels in Dorset had won a great victory, the next that every camp in the west had been destroyed by the Protector's troops. It was hard to know what to believe. There was a camp outside Cambridge and another at Wisbech to which men from the villages flocked. As a schoolteacher, my father was neither landowner nor serf and so avoided being the object of either side's rage, but his sympathies were with the rebels. I remember him talking about their plight and about their leaders in Norwich, the Kett brothers, but I do not remember the Dudley testons.'

'Nor did I, until I joined the Goldsmiths' Company and heard them spoken of. It was by all accounts a strange episode

— short-lived and never explained. The testons bearing the bear and ragged staff emblem appeared and disappeared within a few months. Their source was never found.'

'What could have been their purpose? They must have been easy enough to identify.'

Martin shrugged. 'Who knows? Warwick, remember, had used his defeat of the rebels at Norwich to muster sufficient support to gain the Protectorship from Somerset, although he was not a popular man and had enemies.'

'Who does not?'

Martin laughed. 'Indeed. But here was a man who had made himself unpopular with his peers and hated by his inferiors.' He paused. 'I should not be speaking of the earl's father in such manner, but better, I think, that you know the whole story. I may, I am sure, rely upon your discretion.'

'You may, sir, and I daresay the earl would not disapprove if your candour leads us to discover these new coiners. In any case, his father is long dead, his title taken by the earl's brother.'

'Quite so. The "Good" Earl of Warwick. But back to 1551. More than one man was arrested and imprisoned on charges of seditiously bruiting abroad rumours about the strange coins but, nevertheless, they persisted. People were ready to believe almost anything they heard in the markets and on street corners that discredited the powerful landowners they despised.'

'Little has changed in twenty years. Spend a morning at Cheapside market and you will hear the same sentiments. Prices, naughty money, secret mints — public discourse might be illegal but that does not prevent it happening.'

'Indeed not.' Martin scratched his beard. 'And I recall now that there was some argument about whether the coins actually depicted a bear or a lion, so poorly were they made. Unlike the one you saw yesterday.'

'Did you ever see one, Mr Martin?'

'I did not. The rumours quickly died down but the Dudley name had been dragged through the mud and when the Protector was arrested for his support for Lady Jane Grey, fuelled by those anxious to be rid of him, they resurfaced.'

'And what is your opinion?'

Martin shrugged. 'I doubt the Earl of Warwick was a coiner, but there will be those who still think he was. Not that that accounts for these new coins. I am at a loss to explain those unless they are further intended to blacken the Dudley name.'

'A man with a grudge against the Dudleys might find a better way to take his revenge, do you not think? And he is taking a great risk in producing these coins. If found, he will die a traitor's death.'

'As did the earl himself, and at the time of his execution a prophecy surfaced that the treachery which had brought him to his death would do the same to any man who held a bear and staff teston in his hand. The council had to act with uncommon speed to suppress it.'

'As I held one only yesterday, I must hope that the prophecy is false. Is there more you can tell me, Mr Martin? A name or a place? Anything, however trivial, might help me in my search for the coiners.'

Martin shook his head. 'I can think of nothing more, but feel free to call on me at any time. Now, doctor, I advise against returning the way you came. The bridge might not be so kind a second time. I could find you an adequate mount in the Tower stables, if you wish.'

'Thank you, no, Mr Martin. I must stretch my legs and clear my head. I will walk.' A drenching and an uncomfortable ride in one day would be too much.

'Then good day, sir, and good fortune in your search.'

He was better informed about the minting process and the history of the strange coins but how was he to discover the coiners? The bear and staff testons were another matter entirely from the usual counterfeits and their true purpose was not obvious.

It was no wonder that Isaac had been alarmed and that Leicester wanted the coiners found and safely in Newgate without delay. For him, for any member of the Dudley family, the coins must be at the least a grave embarrassment, speaking of pride and ambition, and at the most an act of treason, punishable by drawing and quartering.

The earl had spoken of his father's error of judgement in promoting the claim to the throne of Lady Jane Grey at the time of the young King Edward's death, of the fearful time he and his brothers had spent in the Tower after their father's arrest and of the misery of his father's execution no more than a stone's throw from their prison. They did not see the Duke of Northumberland, father of five living sons and two daughters, Earl of Warwick and once Lord President of the Council, die on the scaffold but they heard it well enough. Public executions were seldom quiet affairs. Leicester had spoken of all this but he had never spoken of the strange coins that had appeared at the time of his father's regency.

In Eastcheap a small crowd, well wrapped up in coats and caps against the east wind, had gathered outside an inn on the corner of Pudding Lane. Christopher peered over their heads and was able to make out words painted on the inn wall. The red paint had run and the letters were poorly formed, as if written in haste, but they were legible enough.

When Hempe is spun, England's done had once been a familiar couplet. It had been seen in the reigns of Mary and Edward and in the early years of the present queen's reign and had been much discussed by bibulous tavern-goers. Most agreed that *Hempe* signified King Henry VIII, his three children, Edward, Mary and Elizabeth, and Mary's husband, the scheming Philip of Spain. Whether doomed owing to a Spanish invasion, by Elizabeth dying childless and the Privy Council being forced to seek a successor elsewhere, or from a papist plot, was not made clear. It was a prophecy, like so many, that was vague enough not to be easily gainsaid, yet specific enough to cause alarm. Strangely, this one was marked with a cross — not in the form of a crucifix but in that of the letter *X*.

The crowd chattered among themselves but it was an old slogan and it probably signified nothing. Such things appeared from time to time without apparent reason. He continued along Eastcheap, passed a chestnut-seller forlornly huddled over his brazier, threw a farthing to a persistent urchin and bought half a dozen marchpane biscuits from a street vendor, not bothering to haggle over the price. Katherine had the sweetest of teeth. She would berate him for the cost but still eat the biscuits.

The cold had cleared the street of beggars and pickpockets, although unless an unusually charitable priest had given them shelter in his church, he could only guess at where they had gone. Not for the first time he pictured them scurrying like rats to their underground nests, there to wait for spring and easier pickings from the market stalls. It was an uncharitable thought and he forced it from his mind.

Briefly he considered continuing down Cheapside just for the pleasure of seeing Ell again, but guessed she would be sleeping. He had never inquired too deeply about her sources, taking them to be women like herself and their customers, and content that she had proved as reliable as any in carrying out his requests and in passing on whatever she happened to learn that might interest him. A word here, a whisper there, and before long what might be thought of as scribbles on a page could take on a shape that he understood and could act upon.

The booksellers and stationers had also stayed at home and the churchyard of St Paul's was deserted. Not a single stall had been put out. He strode across the cobbled yard and hurried on to Ludgate Hill.

He let himself into the house, locked the door behind him, took off his coat and threw a log on the fire in his study. The room had been built as a parlour but served well enough for his work. Satisfied that the log would catch, he put the marchpane biscuits in the kitchen and returned with bread and ale to sit by the fire. He took a bite and a sip and grimaced. The ale was thin and the bread hard. Perhaps Katherine was right and he should find himself a replacement for Rose. There was joy to be had from solitude but none from poor victuals.

He dipped the bread in the ale to soften it and bit off a lump. Was there not a certain irony in the noble earl giving him, of all people, the task of investigating a matter of coining? A man who knew the price of nothing and cared less. A man who before yesterday could barely have told a false teston from a farthing.

In the years following the split from Rome, slogans and prophecies like the *Hempe* daubed on walls, commonly the walls of churches, had proliferated. Some had been enough to send a man to the assizes and possibly the gallows. But, strangely, the perpetrators were seldom caught *in flagrante* or informed upon and that in itself had fanned the flames of fear and superstition. Satan's handmaidens, it was pointed out, could disguise themselves as cats, kill with spells and fly at night. Christopher remembered no crosses, but the one he had seen was unlikely to signify more than did the name of the artist on a painting.

Nor had it been only men in their cups who had concerned themselves with the prophecies. Among the most credulous had been some of his colleagues in Cambridge, where words had appeared on college walls and churches. In public affecting to dismiss them as empty scaremongering, privately they had discussed and argued and searched for meaning. The theologians had pointed to the Book of Revelation and the prophets of the Old Testament, the philosophers to Chaucer and King Arthur and the mystical Merlin. Christopher had kept his own counsel, believing them to be no more than the work of the idle nobles who came up to Cambridge to study, did little or no work, seldom took a degree and spent their time in dice houses and at cock fights.

It was mid-afternoon when Katherine arrived. 'I have decided,' she began, biting into a biscuit, 'and there will be no more discussion. Tomorrow I shall start looking for your new housekeeper.'

Christopher shook his head in mock surprise. 'Have I no say in this?'

'None. A replacement for Rose or I shall not be inclined to visit. I am neither cook nor laundress, yet I perform both tasks for you. There will be no more of it.' She took another bite. 'A fine sweet biscuit. How much did you pay for them?'

'I forget.' It was an argument he did not want and another about a new housekeeper would be futile. 'As you wish, Katherine, but I must approve your choice.'

'That you may, although be assured that she is unlikely to be comely. She will be chosen for her skills, not her looks.'

'Might she not possess both?'

'No.'

Christopher grunted and stretched the bent fingers of his right hand. Playing the lute had made them no worse but neither had it improved them. 'I saw the old *Hempe* prophecy today in Eastcheap.'

'I remember the *Hempe*. Why would it appear now?'

'I could not say.' Christopher stood up. 'Let us hope that Isaac Cardoza discovers something about the testons. I will call on him again in a few days. What I can say is that I am hungry. Did you bring food?'

'I did. Did you learn anything at the mint?'

Christopher recounted his conversation with Richard Martin. 'I have heard it said that the Dudley family are doomed to suffer,' said Katherine. 'But someone somewhere knows who the false coiners are. We must find that person.'

'And so we shall. Did you buy mutton or beef?'

'Neither. Codfish.'

Christopher swore. As a child he had almost choked on a herring bone. He hated fish and never ate it, even on Wednesdays and Fridays or during Lent, if he could avoid it. 'Your efforts to improve my humour are unlikely to prove successful. I trust my new house-keeper will be less contrary.'

CHAPTER 5

From his dress and manner a man might be forgiven for taking Roland Wetherby for a cosseted courtier with tastes more suited to ease and luxury than the hard edges of political life. Christopher knew otherwise.

Wetherby had shown his courage in helping to capture the traitor Berwick and his loyalty to the Crown by putting aside his own wrongful arrest and imprisonment. Urged by Christopher, the earl had persuaded him to leave Thomas Heneage's employment and to join his own. The Treasurer of the Queen's Chamber had given way to her Master of the Horse. Christopher had no qualms about confiding in his friend and when Wetherby called the next morning he related his meetings with Leicester and Martin. 'Were you aware of the story of the strange testons?' he asked.

'I was,' replied Wetherby. 'Heneage wasted no time in making me aware of it when I first came to London. Although he professes in public to be Leicester's friend, in private anything discrediting the Dudley family puts a smile on his face. Although it happened five years later, he claimed that the proclamation ordering all naughty money to be cut up as if it were being drawn and quartered was a direct result of the Dudley testons.'

'I recall that proclamation. A warning both symbolic and gruesome but not wholly effective.'

'As we have seen.'

'I have asked for Isaac Cardoza's help. If anyone can find the source of these testons, he can. Not that many coins have appeared yet.'

'Many or few, the testons are dangerous — to the earl, to the country. And until the coiners are found, their true purpose will remain obscure. If you wish it, I too will make inquiries.'

It was tempting. Away from Whitehall, the circles in which Wetherby moved were inaccessible to Christopher or even to Ell and there was always the chance of his hearing a lover's whisper. But he was a friend, not an intelligencer, and he was Leicester's man, not Christopher's. 'No, Roland, the risk is too great. For now let us hope that Isaac learns something. Keep me informed of Leicester's mood and pass on any rumours you hear. That will be help enough.'

Wetherby chuckled. 'You make me out to be no more than a tittle-tattle.'

'Never. An excellent informant and a wise counsellor.' He paused. 'Roland, I saw the old *Hempe* prophecy yesterday. It was marked with a cross in the manner of a writer's signature. Can you think of any significance in a cross?'

Wetherby shook his head. 'Beyond marking his work as a dog fox marks its territory, I cannot. What other purpose could it have?'

'No doubt you are right. Now, I shall walk around Holborn Fields. Would you care to accompany me?'

A faint blush coloured Wetherby's cheeks. 'I would, of course, but I am on my way to Eastcheap. An appointment with a friend.'

There were houses in Eastcheap that catered for men of Roland's tastes. Christopher inquired no further.

'Then never mind. Call again soon and bring me news from the whispering passages of Whitehall.'

'That I shall.'

Christopher disliked horses as much as he disliked fish and rode only when he had to; he was pleased to find that even the parsimonious members of the Inns of Court had not left their horses tethered or hobbled in Holborn Fields in such weather and had been forced to pay for their stabling. It was too cold even for the trained bands to be drilling. Frost lay on tufts of winter grass and his breath steamed in the icy air. It was a lawyer's job to find answers to questions and solutions to problems and for Christopher solutions were often most easily found while walking by the river or in the Fields.

If the 'Dudley' testons revealed their purpose, he would find their source. If not, it would be difficult. Illegal mints producing false coins there may have been but this was different and about more than illegal gain. The earl had been rightly insistent. The coiners must be discovered without delay.

By the time he returned to Ludgate Hill, his face was numb and his shoulders were hunched against the cold. He let himself in, cursing as he stamped his feet and pulled off his gloves. 'By the devil's ball sack, it's cold out there.' From the kitchen came a warning cough. He turned in surprise. Katherine stood at the kitchen door, beside her a young woman he did not recognize.

Katherine grinned at him. 'Good morning, Christopher. You are dishevelled. Do you wish to rearrange yourself before I present your new housekeeper?' She did not wait for a reply but continued, 'Joan, this is Dr Radcliff. Christopher, Joan Willys is a cousin of Aunt

Isabel's housekeeper and comes highly recommended for her skills in cooking and cleaning and as a laundress. I have engaged her on your behalf.'

Christopher tried not to stare at the girl. Joan Willys was a short, plump woman of about twenty, with a sallow complexion, lank hair that hung in loose strands outside her coif and an unsightly cast in her right eye. In choosing her, Katherine had been as good as her word. She curtsied to Christopher. 'Joan Willys, doctor. Mistress Allington has told me of your requirements.' The unfortunate woman spoke as if she carried a pebble in her mouth.

He shot a glance at Katherine. 'My requirements are few, as I trust Mistress Allington has explained.'

'Do not be churlish, Christopher. Joan will make your life a great deal easier by cooking and cleaning for you and by saving you money at the market.'

Perhaps the market traders would take pity on the girl and lower their prices. In any event, he could hardly turn her away. 'Very well, Joan. Let us see how we fare. When at home I am usually to be found in my study. Please do not disturb me there or move anything in my absence. The shirts, in particular, are not to be touched. Is that understood?'

'It is, sir,' she mumbled.

'Excellent,' said Katherine. 'Now I suggest that you take the air while I instruct Joan on her duties and show her the rooms.'

'I have just taken the air. It was cold.'

'So I gathered. Take some more. You will only be in the way.'

He had not even taken off his coat. 'Twenty minutes, no more. I have work to do.' With rather more force than was necessary, he shut the door behind him and set off towards Fetter Lane where the affable Mr Brewster might have some new fancies to offer him. He liked fancies — light at heart and easy to play. If he turned towards St Paul's and walked round the church to Fetter Lane, there and back should take about the required time.

But he did not get far. In St Paul's churchyard, still devoid of stationers' stalls, twenty or more clamouring men and women were crowded around the church door. He worked his way through them until he could see the door clearly. On it, daubed in red, was another slogan, like the *Hempe* prophecy poorly executed in red paint but legible. *Conceived in lust in Mouldwarp's bed, the witch will die unloved, unwed.* It too was marked with an *X*.

Some believed that *Mouldwarp* had first appeared in a prophecy by the wizard Merlin. During the reign of the queen's father it had been used to insult him. The king himself had found the word amusing or intolerable, as the mood took him. Now, in a new form and long after his death, here it was again.

One man read the words aloud for those who could not do so. 'What does it mean?' asked a boy at the front. 'And what is *Mouldwarp?*'

'Hush, child,' replied one who might have been his father. '*Mouldwarp* is an ancient word for a mole. You need know no more.'

Without warning, the church door was thrown open and an elderly priest emerged, tears running down his veiny cheeks. 'Acts of sacrilege!' he shouted. 'The door of our church defaced and our *Book of Martyrs* also.' The crowd stared at him. 'A foul papist has entered our church and left his mark on the book.'

Christopher pushed his way forward and spoke quietly to the distraught man. 'I am Dr Christopher Radcliff, in the service of the Earl of Leicester. Permit me to examine the book.' At first the priest did not appear to understand but stood facing the crowd, wild-eyed and disbelieving. Christopher touched his shoulder and repeated what he had said. This time the priest nodded and stepped aside to allow him to enter the church.

On the death of her sister Mary, Cambridge had waited for religious guidance from the new queen. Would she espouse Mary's Catholicism or would she lead the country back to Protestantism, the faith in which she herself had been brought up? Within days of her making it clear that it would be the latter, every vestige of the old ways had been stripped from the Pembroke chapel. Gone were the Latin prayer books, vestments and images, gone were the elaborate furnishings, altar cloths and censers. In their place a copy of Foxe's *Book of Martyrs*, depicting the Protestant martyrs who had died at the stake during Mary's rule, soon lay, open and much read, on a lectern to the left of the altar. And now, sixteen years later, the queen was governor of the Church of England and a hated enemy of Rome. *Cuius regio, eius religio.*

The book was open at an illustration of three women burning at the stake. Christopher remembered it. It was a depiction of a mother and her two daughters on the island of Guernsey being burned at the stake for their Protestant beliefs. A large cross had been cut diagonally across the page, slicing through the flames and the face of the mother. 'When was this found?' he asked.

The priest's voice shook with anger. 'I have only now seen it. The book was unmarked yesterday.'

Christopher turned the page. The incision had cut into the next illustration. 'Are you sure?'

'As sure as I am of Almighty God. The act was committed during the night. The church is never locked and it would not have been difficult for a foul papist to enter unseen. He must be caught and hanged.'

'Inform the magistrate. He will investigate the crime. And have the words on the door removed at once or they will fan the flames of unrest.'

'Yes, doctor.'

'And you would be wise to lock the church doors at night.'

Hempe and *Mouldwarp* and the *Book of Martyrs* — all marked with a cross. Yet another papist plot to foment insurrection?

Mr Brewster would have to wait for another day. He carried on to Leadenhall before turning back, and on an impulse turned down Dog's Head Lane, the shortest route home. The lane was narrow and dark, barely wide enough for two men to pass each other and deprived of light by the upper storeys of the dwellings on either side which overhung so far that they almost touched each other. Some of the dwellings were boarded up and marked with a red cross to signify plague. The occupants would have been shut in and left to die. He would not normally have ventured down the lane but he was anxious to be home.

With a hand on the poniard, he walked quickly, seeing no one. But nearing the end of the lane, where a little more light penetrated, a noise behind him made him turn. There was nothing. A dog perhaps, or a rat scrabbling for food. He cursed himself for his foolishness and hurried on.

He had seen nothing and heard little, yet at Ludgate Hill he fumbled with the lock. Either his mind was playing tricks or he had been watched.

Joan and Katherine had gone. He reached under the pile of clothes and brought out the lute. It needed a little tuning — with six courses of strings, five double strings and a single treble, each of which had to be tuned, not a straightforward task — but he did not hurry. 'The musician, like the artist, never hurries,' his teacher had once told him after he had impatiently over-tightened a treble string and broken it. Outside London good strings were expensive and hard to find. There was nothing worse than running out of strings and having to wait for the next market day in the hope that a vendor would have some. Never hurry. A simply stated lesson which, like all good lessons, he had never forgotten.

At first he had taken himself back to the beginner's exercises he remembered having to repeat over and over again until he could do them without thought, even to the extent of reciting the courses as he played them. Treble, small meanes, great meanes, contratenor, tenor, bass, and back again in the reverse order. He had found unexpected pleasure in performing such a childish exercise and still performed it from time to time. It reminded him of his parents, both taken by the plague while he was teaching at Pembroke Hall.

He chose an almain, a slow, steady piece that would not test him unduly. He had always been more comfortable with English and French dance music than with Italian madrigal intabulations. He found in them more melody and harmony.

The thoughtful pace of the dance suited his mood. He played it from the tablature, striving especially for contrast between the louder notes played by the thumb and the softer ones played by the fingers.

But concentration was difficult and after playing the piece three times, he set the lute aside, knowing that he had not played well. He never did when he was uneasy.

CHAPTER 6

That night the dreams returned. A year and a half since the slaughter in Paris yet they had lost none of their intensity.

This time he had seen priests drinking the blood of a face sliced by knives and axes, a lipless mouth gaping in a silent scream and a young woman clutching her headless child as she fell to her knees. She had been a Huguenot — that he knew — and she had died in Cambridge outside Pembroke Hall. He had watched himself walk unharmed through the slashing blades and in vain stretch out his arms to the woman as she and her child dissolved into a pool of blood.

The dreams varied yet were always the same. Blood, agony, death. He had tried abstinence, excess and moderation. He had tried fasting, prayer and potions. None had worked. The terrors came and went as they wished. He longed for a physic to cleanse his memory and render him free of their grip. But if one existed he had not yet found it.

He tugged the covers around his shoulders, tried to clear his mind of the tormenting images and waited for sleep to return. It did not. His mind would not allow it.

Ancient slogans marked with crosses and the desecration of the *Book of Martyrs* at St Paul's, also cut in the shape of a cross, and false testons that had not been seen for a generation. A coincidence — or was there a connection and, if so, what? And without knowing their purpose how was he to find the coiners, save for an informer appearing from nowhere like a *deus ex machina* or Isaac catching a word on the breeze? Small numbers of false coins could be easily produced with the right tools and with little risk of detection. A cellar, a stable, a derelict building — all could hide a small-scale coiner and his work, as Martin had made clear.

In Dog's Head Lane he had been watched. He was sure of it. But in such a place there would be eyes in dark doorways and shadowy corners looking out for easy pickings. Of course he had been watched. He had been foolish to walk down that lane alone and was lucky to have done so unmolested.

He was in the study when Katherine arrived bearing food and accompanied by Joan Willys. 'Joan will set the fires while I prepare breakfast,' she announced. 'Go and dress.'

He glanced at the girl, who looked as if she were about to burst into tears, opened his mouth to remind her not to disturb his papers or touch the pile of shirts, thought better of it and went up to the bed chamber. Surely Katherine could have found someone a little more favoured in looks and manner?

He came down again to find the grate cleared out, a new fire set and a good blaze warming the study while the women busied themselves in the kitchen. Katherine indicated a chair. 'Sit down, Christopher. Joan will clean your bed chamber while you eat.'

Christopher managed a thin smile. 'It is cold up there, Joan. Better wear your coat.'

'I have arranged for Joan's cousin to mend the window,' said Katherine. 'He will come later today.' Joan nodded and went up to the chamber.

He took a spoonful of oatmeal porridge and opened his eyes in surprise. 'Excellent. Does the girl cook as well as you do?'

'Better. This recipe is hers. We bought the oatmeal together and her uncle keeps bees. It is the honey that gives the porridge its sweetness. The skill is in knowing how much to add and when to do so. The porridge must be neither too hot nor too cool.'

He lowered his voice. 'She seems timid. I do hope she will not take fright easily.'

'She will need time to become accustomed to you, Christopher, but she is hard-working and capable and she cannot help how she looks. At least afford her a chance.'

'I will, of course, although it would be easier if you taught her to speak clearly.'

Katherine pointed her finger at him and spoke sharply. 'You will soon become accustomed to her manner of speaking and that is an end to it.'

Christopher shrugged and scraped the last of the porridge from his bowl. 'Is there more?'

'Not today. I will ask Joan to make more next time.' Katherine cleared away the bowl and sat at the table. 'She is knowledgeable about plants. You might ask her to suggest a salve for your hand.'

Christopher stretched his fingers and grunted. 'They are past curing.'

The kitchen door opened and Joan came in. She carried a bundle of clothes wrapped up in a bed sheet under her arm. 'The chamber is cleaned, sir,' she said. 'I will take these to be washed. Should I return them tomorrow?'

'Yes, yes, Joan. Tomorrow.'

'Are you sure you would not like me to take the shirts in your study, sir? It would be no trouble.'

'No. Leave the shirts.' The words came out more sharply than he had intended.

Katherine stood up. 'Thank you, Joan, you have done well and the porridge was excellent. As you see, Dr Radcliff has eaten it all. Come at eight every morning but Sundays, if you please. The doctor will not expect you on Sundays. He will pay you two shillings at the end of each week and will advance you the money for food. Just tell him how much.'

Joan bobbed a clumsy curtsy. 'Thank you, madam. A shilling for food should suffice.'

'A shilling it is. You shall have it tomorrow.' Katherine waited until they heard the front door close before speaking again. 'You were short, Christopher. Be civil to the girl and be grateful that she is willing to put up with you.'

Christopher grunted. 'I will try. Is two shillings a week enough? Did I not pay Rose two shillings and sixpence?'

'It is enough.' She sat down again. 'Have you thought more about the testons?'

'I have. As yet we have not seen many of them and they are as easy to spot as a fox in a hen house. The coiners are not about their work for profit.'

'Then what?'

'An insult to the Dudley family. To embarrass the earl. To cause trouble. Your guess is as good as mine.'

'Why and by whom? A rival? Thomas Heneage, Christopher Hatton? Surely not.'

'It seems preposterous, but who else might wish him ill with such venom that they are willing to risk being hanged and quartered just to make him blush before the queen?'

Katherine laughed. 'A pretty picture you paint, Christopher. No, if the coiners of the testons are not seeking profit, they are surely seeking more than a mere lordly blush.'

'I hope for help from Richard Martin. Or perhaps Isaac will learn something.' He paused. 'I saw a *Mouldwarp* prophecy at St Paul's yesterday.'

'*Mouldwarp*? But we haven't seen that for years. What did it say?'

'*Conceived in lust in Mouldwarp's bed, the witch will die, unloved, unwed.*'

'*Hempe* and *Mouldwarp* and an attack on the queen.' She frowned. 'Could the slogans and the testons be treasonous bed-fellows, do you suppose?'

'I have thought about that. I do not see how but if they are not, it is a strange coincidence that they should all appear now.'

'What might we see next, I wonder?'

Next, it was not false coins or ruined books or graffiti scrawled on a wall, but sheets of paper scattered outside the Guildhall. Christopher had left Joan to her cooking and cleaning and picked one up as he passed. The paper was made from poor rags and was rough to the touch. Printed on one side was a third couplet. *If Amy's death had natural been, Would Dudley then have wed our queen?* It too was marked with an *X*.

A group of merchants in thick coats, some trimmed with rabbit or fox, stood at the entrance to the Hall, their breath clouding in the cold. Each held a paper in a gloved hand. Christopher asked them what they made of it.

'It is treasonous, to be sure,' said one, 'and an insult to the Earl of Leicester. The magistrate must be told.'

'I had thought this matter long closed,' said another. 'It is fourteen years since Amy Robsart died, is it not? Why would it come to the fore now?'

'Who knows what trouble is brewing at court?' replied the first man. 'The earl is not without enemies and they say that in Whitehall Palace even the walls have ears.'

A third man joined in. 'There have been slogans elsewhere. I saw one at St Paul's. It too was marked with a cross. And their *Book of Martyrs* has been cut and defaced. What mischief is afoot?'

'I am at a loss as to how the perpetrators of these crimes have gone undetected.' It was the first man again. 'What about the watch and ward? Where are the constables we pay for?'

'There are plague crosses appearing on houses where there has never been sickness,' added another voice, shrill with indignation. 'Who is doing this?'

'And what is their purpose?' asked the first man. 'Why mark healthy houses?'

Christopher left them to their chatter and carried on to Cheapside. God alone knew how and why the slogans had suddenly appeared and this leaflet had certainly come from an illegal press. No licensed printer would have risked producing it. But there were illegal presses tucked away in cellars all over the city. Any one of them could have printed it.

As he walked down Cheapside, it happened again. A certainty that he was being watched crept up his spine to his neck. He turned sharply. In a crowded street full of market stalls it would have been easy for a watcher to go unnoticed and he saw nothing odd — only traders and their customers about their business. Yet the uncomfortable feeling remained.

He laid the leaflet on his writing table and smoothed it out. *If Amy's death had natural been, Would Dudley then have wed our queen?* It was roughly printed in black ink and the paper was ragged around the edges. He turned it over and looked closely but there was no clue as to its source.

He had been twenty, a pupil at Pembroke Hall, at the time of Amy Robsart's death. The news books had reported on almost nothing else for weeks and the jokers and jesters among the undergraduates had run amok on the streets and in the taverns and inns. Contests had been held for the wittiest verses daubed on church walls. It had been the same, they said, in every town in England. Even the inquest jury's verdict of misfortune had not stopped tongues wagging. Some had pointed to Amy's frail health and spells of melancholy and had wondered if the wife of Robert Dudley had taken her own life. On the day she died at their home near Oxford, she had sent all her servants away to a local fair — evidence, they claimed, that she had planned to kill herself.

Others agreed with the jury that it had been an accident. She had fallen down a short flight of stairs and broken her neck. She was known to be unwell and might have fainted or been taken by a seizure. Yet others — the quietest but most insidious — had claimed that Dudley had arranged his wife's murder, leaving him free to marry the queen. After all, they pointed out, he spent much more time with Her Majesty than ever he had with Amy and he did not even trouble to attend her funeral. They dismissed the jury's verdict as 'convenient' and 'arranged'.

To a lawyer's mind any suggestion of murder was absurd because the suspicious death of his wife was hardly likely to endear Dudley to the queen and because he would have been taking a wholly unnecessary risk in acting so brazenly. There were more subtle ways of disposing of an unwanted spouse. And the Dudley Christopher had come to know was not a man capable of such a crime.

When, six years later, he had been invited to enter Leicester's employment as a recruiter of young intelligencers, he had not hesitated. He had never thought the earl guilty of anything more than zealous devotion to the queen. In other minds, however, he knew that doubts had lingered and festered and never quite been banished.

He poked the fire, threw a log on to it, and sat back with his eyes closed. He thought more clearly without the distraction of vision. As a pupil he had spent entire tutorials with his eyes closed. Now, if he could have closed his ears as well, he would have done so.

But there was work to be done. He must call again on Isaac.

CHAPTER 7

Invariably lit by candles arranged to give the goldsmith sufficient light to examine the coins and objects he was brought, Isaac Cardoza's shop, strangely, was in darkness. It was a Saturday, but Isaac would surely be there. 'How am I to feed my family if I am not here to serve my customers?' he used to say. 'You should see the boys eat.'

Christopher called out but there was no reply. Surely Isaac would never be so careless as to leave the door unlocked and the shop unattended, even for a few minutes. He called again but there still was no reply.

His eyes were becoming accustomed to the darkness. He found a candle and a flint and managed to light it. The back of the shop remained in shadow but the front appeared as it always did — two simple stools, and a table upon which stood weighing scales, a row of weights and a strongbox — but of Isaac there was no sign. Then the faintest of sounds drew his eyes to the shadows in a corner behind the table. Holding up the candle, he peered into the gloom. A body lay face down on the wooden floor. He stepped around the table and stooped to look more closely. His gorge rose and he had to steady himself with a hand on the table. Isaac's red hair was a mess of congealed blood. Beside him, in a pool of gore, lay a heavy brass weight. The goldsmith had been struck from behind with great force.

Gently, Christopher turned him on to his side and put a hand to his neck. There was a flicker of life. 'Isaac, it is Christopher,' he whispered. 'Can you hear me?' Isaac's eyes were closed and he did not respond. He tried again but still there was no response.

He hurried outside and looked up and down the street. Beside a printer's shop a few doors away a group of urchins were squabbling over something. He shouted out, 'There is sixpence for the one who finds a carriage and brings it here. Six pennies. Make haste. An injured man needs help.'

The boys looked up and stared at him. None moved. Then one, the tallest, shouted back, 'How much?'

'Sixpence. A carriage. Be quick.'

Pursued by the others, the boy ran off down Fleet Street towards the Strand to find a carriage or cart for hire. Christopher went back into the shop and closed the door. Isaac had not moved but he was still breathing. Christopher took off his coat and placed it very carefully under the stricken man's head, taking care not to touch the wound for fear of causing more blood to flow. Satisfied that he had done what he could, he picked up the candle and looked around the shop.

There was no sign of a struggle or of theft. The lock on Isaac's strongbox, a heavy iron casket, had not been touched. His scales and weights — all but the one used to attack him — were on his table. Even his pens and papers were in order. His purse was still attached by a short chain to his belt. Christopher slipped the chain off the belt and opened the purse. Among the coins was a key. He took it out.

Christopher swore. This was no robbery. Isaac had been attacked for what he knew, not for what he owned. And it had been Christopher who had brought this upon his friend. He was as much to blame as if he had struck Isaac himself. He sat on Isaac's chair and tried to breathe slowly. It was difficult. He had killed one man. Was Isaac to be the second?

The tall urchin crashed into the shop. 'A cart is outside,' he panted. 'I brought it.' He held out his hand. 'Sixpence, you said.'

Christopher ignored the hand. 'Help me with this man and you shall have it.'

The boy wiped his nose with a sleeve and grunted, 'You said nothing about help.'

'Just do it, boy, or you'll get nothing.'

The boy shrugged and stepped forward. At the sight of Isaac, he started. 'Been attacked, has he? Does he live?'

'He is alive. Take his legs, gently now, and I'll take his shoulders. Be careful.' They manoeuvred him out of the shop and into the street where the cart was waiting.

The driver took one look at Isaac and spat into the dirt. 'A Jew. Why take the trouble?'

Christopher snarled, 'If you want the fare, hold your tongue. This man is my friend and he needs help quickly.'

'I want no Hebrew blood in my cart.'

'Then drive with care. I will travel with him.'

They laid Isaac on the seat with the coat under his head. Christopher returned to the shop to lock the door with the key he had taken from Isaac's purse, took a shilling from his own purse and gave it to the boy. 'You did well.' The boy grinned and ran off, waving the coin above his head and shouting to the other urchins. Christopher climbed on to the cart. He laid Isaac's head on his lap and held it steady. 'Leadenhall, driver. Make haste but with care.'

The Cardozas lived near the meat market at Leadenhall. It was a year and a half since Christopher had been led to their house by Isaac's sons, Daniel and David, but he remembered where it stood well enough. The lanes were too narrow for a cart so he alighted at the market, paid the muttering driver and managed to carry Isaac down one lane and then another and from that into a small yard, one side of which was formed by three narrow dwellings. At the door of the middle house he called out. Nothing happened.

Reluctant to put Isaac down, he tried again, more loudly. This time he heard footsteps and the door was opened by a red-haired boy of about sixteen. Christopher knew him. Daniel was the elder of Isaac's two sons. 'Daniel, your father has been attacked.'

The boy stepped forward to help Christopher bring his father inside. They carried him up to a bed chamber and laid him on the bed. 'I will tell my mother,' he said, a tremor in his voice.

Christopher had met Sarah Cardoza only once and that briefly. He remembered her as a slight figure with an aquiline profile, bright eyes and a clear gaze — a strong, handsome woman, who smiled often. She bent over Isaac, kissed his forehead and whispered to him in Hebrew. 'Fetch Saul Mendes,' she ordered Daniel. 'Tell him it is urgent.' When Daniel had left she took Christopher's hands. 'I thank you for bringing him. What happened?'

'I know only that he was attacked in the shop, where I found him.'

'A robbery? It is what I have always feared.'

'I think not. There was no sign of one and the door was unlocked.'

Sarah took a handkerchief from her sleeve and dabbed at her eyes. 'Not a robbery.' She took a deep breath and spoke slowly. 'Of course I know a little of the work Isaac does for you, doctor, work he is proud to do for the country that shelters us. Is this connected in some way to it?'

It was not the time to speak of the counterfeit testons. 'That I cannot say, Sarah, but you have my promise that whatever the reason for this, I shall find it. Has Isaac mentioned anything unusual or acted strangely in the last few days?'

Sarah shook her head. 'No. The children and I would have noticed anything out of the ordinary. His humour has been as it always is.'

Christopher handed her the purse. 'I have kept the key so that I might go there again.' Sarah nodded. 'Do you know where the key to his strongbox is?'

A tiny smile played fleetingly around Sarah's mouth. 'He did not like to have it with him in case he lost it. It is under a floorboard at the back of the shop.'

'When did he leave this morning?'

'Around seven, immediately after our morning prayers, as was his habit.' Sarah began to sob. 'No more than a few hours ago and now . . .'

Christopher took her hand again. 'I will return to the shop. Send word to Ludgate Hill when he wakes.'

'Be sure that I shall, doctor. Our community will pray for him and Saul Mendes is a skilled physician. He helped deliver all three of our children. He will save Isaac.'

Christopher retrieved his coat and let himself out. Already the sun was low and such warmth as there had been was fast disappearing. A few flakes of snow were falling. He shivered and pulled the coat tighter around his shoulders.

It would have been the same route that Isaac took from Leadenhall to Fleet Street that morning and every morning. Christopher walked as quickly as the streets would allow, trying to keep his mind clear and his thoughts on the crime, rather than the victim or his family. He hurried on, barely noticing the children tugging at his cloak and begging for coins, the forlorn cries of traders trying to sell off the last of their stock before packing up their stalls for the day and the painted fruit-sellers lurking in dark doorways.

Inside the shop, he lit half a dozen wax candles and spread them about. Isaac's strongbox was constructed of thick oak with iron fixings and nails and a heavy, hinged lock. The box and lock were intact. Isaac's attacker had made no attempt to rob him. He found the key under the loose board and opened it. Inside were a number of silver objects — a pair of spoons, buttons, plate, a pair of small boxes — but nothing of very great value. He took them out and put them on the table.

He found no coins but Isaac was a clever man. He felt around the edges, found a flaw in the wood and pulled gently. A panel slid open. In it was a small leather pouch, much the same colour as the wood of the box. In it was the Dudley teston that he had left with Isaac.

He put the other items back in the strongbox, locked it and replaced the key under the board, stuffed the pouch into his purse, pinched the candles and locked the door behind him.

He hurried home to Ludgate Hill and let himself in. Without bothering to remove his coat, he went to the kitchen and found a bottle. He filled a beaker and emptied it quickly. It did not help. He could not put his mind to the crime, only to Isaac. The blow had been cruel enough to fracture his skull. If it had, he would be lucky to live. Even if not, it was a deep wound from which much blood had flowed.

When had he last shed a tear? Even on the day his mother died, even in Paris where he had seen babies skewered like piglets and old women roasted on fires he had not cried. Not once. Later he had felt guilty, wondering if the lack of tears betrayed a lack of true feeling. But it was not that. It was the need to survive, to act, to return to London with intelligence of the *Incendium* plot, that had enabled him to push those terrible sights to the back of his mind and to concentrate on his task. The suffering had come later when the plot had been foiled and the danger was past. Still there had been no tears but a mind battered by what his eyes had seen and his ears had heard. And his nose had smelled. The woman burned at Smithfield had recalled the sickly stench of seared flesh, but there had been no tears.

Now, the tears did come and he howled. Was his distress for Isaac, a good man who had served the country in which he lived but of which he was not a citizen, was it for his wife and children, or was it for himself and the dreadful certainty that it was he who had caused Isaac to be attacked? It was for all of these. He let the tears run their course and made another feeble effort at prayer. He hated himself for praying. His faith in God was flimsy at best but at times of pain or grief he still found himself doing it. What else was there?

One bottle became two and, eventually, slumped in his chair, his eyes closed. Sometime later he awoke and knew that he should have gone straight to Whitehall.

A guard stationed at the palace's Holbein Gate escorted him to the earl's apartments and asked him to wait while word was sent to the earl. Even an agreeable scent of lavender could not endear the earl's antechamber to him. It was furnished to impress, even intimidate, and dominated by a large portrait of Her Majesty, but he had been obliged to sit there often enough and no longer found it as unsettling as once he had.

When the earl swept in, immaculate in gold-trimmed doublet and grey silken hose despite the early hour, Christopher rose from his chair and remembered to bow low. After their last meeting, the earl would be watching him closely. Christopher followed him into his private apartment. It, too, was furnished and decorated every bit as richly as might be expected of a man of such high office, with a huge walnut writing table and a smaller companion on which had been set a chess board with ivory pieces and a cylindrical brass clock, which had been a gift to the queen from a Bavarian admirer and had never worked. She had passed it on to Leicester.

Even before Christopher could open his mouth to speak, the earl thrust the leaflet into his hand. 'There, Dr Radcliff, read that. What devilment is behind it? It is as if some evil force, too cowardly to show itself, is set upon dragging up ancient falsehoods and blackening my name. Well, what do you make of it?'

Christopher glanced at it. 'It is lamentable, my lord. I saw one such at the Guildhall. I have come to report—'

Leicester's black eyes bulged. 'God in his heaven. Even while I was grieving for my wife, gossipers and rumour-mongers were spreading falsehoods about her death. No matter that the coroner's jury rightly found it to have been an accident, the muck-rakers would not be silenced. And here is the damnable thing again. *If Amy's death had natural been, Would Dudley then have wed our queen?* Marked with a cross. A double insult and not only to me and my family but to Her gracious Majesty. It is treason.'

'There has been an outbreak of such slogans, my lord. This is but the latest example.'

'I am aware of that. Most are not worthy of attention, but this is different. What must we expect from the next example, do you suppose? An attack on my sanity? A threat to the queen's life?'

'I trust not, my lord.'

'Why have the criminals not been apprehended? They must have been observed or are they sorcerers, able to render themselves invisible while they carry out their evil work?'

'*Mene, mene, tekel, upharsin,*' whispered Christopher, before he could stop himself.

Leicester glared at him. 'What do you say, doctor?'

'The Book of Daniel, my lord. The writing on the wall at Belshazzar's feast, prophesying his death and the end of his kingdom.'

'Yes, yes, I remember, of course.' Leicester frowned. 'Why do you mention it?'

'Here is another invisible hand at work, my lord. A hand that signs its name with a cross. I have seen three slogans, each marked in the same way. And my agent Isaac Cardoza has been attacked in his shop and is close to death. He has not spoken.'

'The Jewish goldsmith. Was it a robbery?'

'It was not, my lord. Nothing was taken. But I fear the attack was connected to the false coins. I had asked him to look out for them.'

'You instructed him to be discreet, I trust?'

'I did, my lord. He would have been most cautious. And mindful of your wish for discretion, I have spoken to no others.' An untruth which once he would not have countenanced, but what was to be gained from mentioning Ell or Katherine?

'Although not, it seems, sufficiently cautious for his own protection.' Leicester walked to the window and looked out on to the queen's garden below. It was his habit when pondering a problem. 'We shall have to search out the coiners and the authors of these malignant slogans by other means.'

Leicester turned to take a coin from his desk and tossed it in his hand. 'These are a monstrous affront to my family. No doubt you know about the false accusations of counterfeiting made against my father.'

So Leicester was willing to speak of the matter. Christopher had thought he was not. 'I do, my lord. Mr Martin has informed me of the history of these coins. He thought I should know.'

It was as if the earl had not heard him. 'My own father, Earl of Warwick, Duke of Northumberland, a privy councillor and loyal servant of the Crown, a counterfeiter? Ridiculous, yet there were some who believed it. And the mere belief damaged not only him but the country. Currency that cannot be trusted is more dangerous than an enemy in plain sight. It does not oil the wheels of trade but brings poverty and conflict. That and the treason they represent are why these felons must be found and punished without delay. As must the slogan-writers. We shall have to risk tongues wagging. Find them.'

'I shall endeavour also, my lord, to find Isaac Cardoza's attacker.'

Leicester nodded. 'Of course, of course.'

Christopher felt his temper rising. The counterfeit testons and the slogans had unsettled the earl in a way that news of Isaac's condition had not. 'The *Book of Martyrs* in St Paul's church has been defaced and plague crosses are appearing on houses that have never been afflicted by plague.'

Leicester slumped on to his chair. 'Plague crosses? Good God. It has the appearance of a conspiracy to cause not only harm to my family but also confusion and unrest when our eyes should be on our enemies across the narrow sea. Who in the name of all that is holy is behind this? Spanish spies? French Jesuits?'

'Someone who wishes England to suffer. Someone who wishes you to suffer. Someone clever enough to carry out these crimes without being caught.'

For a while Leicester sat with his head in his hands and his eyes closed. When he spoke his voice was firm. 'Put aside all your other work, doctor. Use whatever resources you can muster. Our enemies must be found and destroyed.'

'Without Isaac Cardoza, my resources are diminished but naturally I will do as you say, my lord.'

'I depend upon you to repay my faith in you, Dr Radcliff. You will have my support in any action you take.'

As he hurried back to Ludgate Hill, Christopher replayed the words in his head. 'Support in any action you take.' That was something he had not heard before from the earl, a man not given to relying on others or to encouraging independence of thought or deed. A man, rather, who hated being less than fully informed or in less than absolute control. And there had been an unusual brittleness to his tone. If the reappearance of the stories about his father and his wife were intended to unsettle him, they were succeeding.

CHAPTER 8

By the time Joan arrived on Monday morning, he was in his study. She disappeared into the kitchen, prepared a large bowl of honey-sweetened oatmeal porridge and went up to clean the bed chamber while he ate it. He washed the porridge down with a beaker of ale and felt the better for it. Too much wine and too little food did not make for a good humour or a settled stomach.

Breakfast made and house cleaned, Joan left for the market. She did not ask what he liked to eat. Katherine would have told her. Perhaps he would become accustomed to her more easily than he had feared. An ill-favoured young woman but a capable one.

He heard the scrap of paper being pushed under the door and knew at once what would be written on it. The hand was childish but the letters were clear enough. *ELL*.

He took his time in locking the door. If eyes were on him he wanted to be sure that they had seen him leave. He walked slowly, not breaking his stride or looking back, lest he appear wary or uncertain.

The bitter cold of the past few days had eased, traders were back on the streets and, with them, even more beggars and urchins to fight over their scraps, taking what they could before the rats scuttled out from their nests and the kites swooped from the rooftops. In London there were hungry mouths wherever one looked.

Twice he had been sure that he was being shadowed. He had seen nothing on either occasion but the sensation had been uncomfortable. And difficult to describe. Somewhere between anticipation and dread was the best he could do. Next time he would be more alert and move faster.

On Ludgate Hill he sensed nothing and turned towards Newgate, hoping that its dark corners and hidden alleys might serve his purpose. Outside the prison — a hateful, doom-laden place made worse by the agonized cries of the wretches inside it — he ran the gauntlet of beggars and whores, ignoring their pleas and promises and brushing away grasping hands. Many of them would have travelled no further than the few yards from the prison gates to where they stood. What would a newly released prisoner gain by going further? He loathed prisons and the knowledge of what lay within Newgate's walls tempted him to quicken his pace. With an effort he did not.

Nearing the end of the street, he stopped and turned quickly, hoping to catch a glimpse of a coat or a hat disappearing into the shadows. He saw nothing. Apart from beggars and whores he was the only person on the street. He carried on.

The lanes here were old and narrow, twisting this way and that without apparent reason. Like Dog's Head, had he not had good reason he would have hesitated to venture into them alone. Poniard to hand or not, there were too many dark corners for a man to feel safe. Just the place for a malevolent shadow to strike. And thereby show himself.

None did. Half relieved, half disappointed, he emerged on to Cheapside to join the throng of buyers and sellers. At one stall he paused to examine a cheese, at another he asked the price of a mutton pie, stealing a look around the market each time. Still he saw nothing untoward. There were too many people and a shadow, if there was a shadow, would look no different to the next man. He had not intended to buy anything — Joan would see to his needs — but a tray of cakes on a vendor's stall caught his eye. If Katherine were with him, he would have been given no choice. For her, gingerbread and marchpane were irresistible. He reached for his purse.

The boy who ran past him from behind jolted his arm with enough force to make him look up sharply. Thieving children frequently hunted in packs and he clutched the purse tightly as he watched the boy disappearing into the crowd. It was at that moment that he glimpsed a shadowy figure and knew. At once and without doubt, he knew. Whether it was the wide felt hat low on the head or the breadth of the shoulders or the scarf wound around the lower half of the face, he did not know. But he was certain. An unremarkable figure whom he might never have noticed but for the boy who had made him look up suddenly from his purse.

The shadow's eyes, for an instant, met his. Then he turned and was gone. Still clutching his purse, Christopher ran after him, yelling at the man to stop and forcing a way through the crush of bodies. Just as he thought he had lost his quarry, he saw the felt hat dart between two low houses, followed it and found himself in an alley so narrow that two men could not have walked along it side by side. Just a thin thread of sunlight penetrated its gloom. He strained his eyes but could see no hat. The shadow had melted into the darkness.

There was no point in continuing the chase. The wretch could have vanished into any number of secret places. The chance had gone. But he had been there and Christopher had seen him. He had been right. There was a shadow.

Ell herself answered the door. 'Dr Rad!' She laughed. 'Thought you'd come quick. Can't stay away from me, can you? Grace is out. Come into the parlour so we can sit by the fire.'

When they were settled, Christopher asked, 'What have you for me, Ell?'

'Not sure. Might be nothing, might be something.'

'I have heard you say that before. What is this something or nothing?'

'There's mischief about.'

'What sort of mischief?'

'I could not say exactly. It's like a smell. You know it's there but finding words to describe it is not so easy.'

Christopher smiled. 'Could you try, Ell? I need something more.'

Ell frowned. 'It's a mood, Dr Rad, a humour such as you might have when you wake up in the night after one of your dreams. You know it was only a dream but still it's in your mind as if it was real.'

'A humour familiar to me, but how does it come about?'

'Different ways. A cat hanging from a tree in Aldgate, a dead child pulled out of the river. Folk are frightened.'

'Folk are always frightened of what they do not understand and cannot explain. Anything else?'

'Naughty money as you told me to watch out for. Silver testons with false marks. Like this one.' She handed a coin to Christopher.

He turned it over. A bear and a staff. 'Where did you get it, Ell?'

Ell grinned. 'A nice gentleman. Spoke to me like a lady. Hadn't had the pleasure before. I wouldn't have taken it but for you asking me to keep an eye open, so I pretended not to notice. Is it what you wanted?'

'It is. What was his appearance?'

'Tall. Not as tall as you, doctor, but taller than most. Black hair and a black beard. Brown eyes. Well dressed. White shirt and blue doublet. Spoke like you. Not as handsome as you, though.' She pursed her lips and looked him up and down. 'Not many are, though.'

'Did he have a name?'

'Not that he told me. They seldom do.'

'Anything else?'

'Said he'd call again.'

'Good. If he does, find out what you can. You're right: it might be nothing but a gentleman knows when he is passing a false coin. Make him happy and get a name. And a place, if you can; he must live somewhere.'

Ell chortled. 'Don't I always make my gentlemen happy, doctor? If he comes again, I'll let you know.'

'Thank you, Ell.' He rose to leave. 'Take care. Do you still have your blade?'

'Under the mattress, doctor, same as always.'

'Good.' Christopher pulled his cap over his brow and tugged his coat around his shoulders. 'And remember, if your gentleman comes again, find out what you can about him and send word.'

'I shall, doctor. Especially if I'm feeling lonely.'

He ignored the lewd grin. 'And carry the blade when you go out. There are strange things going on, Ell, things I don't yet understand.'

'God's teeth, Dr Rad, if you don't understand them, what hope is there for a poor whore?'

'I mean it, Ell. Be doubly watchful.'

*

They sat in the study, where Christopher's table was still an untidy mess of paper and pens, inkpots and sand shakers but the window was newly cleaned and the chairs dusted. 'I have learned very little for certain other than that I am being watched,' he said.

'Watched, Christopher? Why did you not say so before?' When Katherine was angry or alarmed a blush spread up her neck.

'I am only now sure.' He told her about the man in Cheapside. 'If I am being watched, it is possible that you are too. Be alert and take care.'

'A watcher and Isaac Cardoza. Should you not visit Isaac's wife again, Christopher?'

Christopher shook his head. 'I cannot help but feel that Sarah holds me responsible for what has happened to Isaac and I am reluctant to distress her further by calling unbidden. She promised to tell me if there is any change in his condition and when she is ready to speak to me. Until then . . .'

'Until then, Christopher, we know nothing.' Katherine's voice was shrill. 'Explain the seriousness of the situation — exaggerate if you must — and she will help. If Isaac spoke to anyone else about the testons she may know who. We cannot sit on our hands waiting at her pleasure.'

Christopher stared at the fire. 'The earl would not be pleased if he knew we were doing so. Not that I shall be the one to tell him. But he has eyes and ears everywhere, as you well know, and he did tell me I had his full support. Doubtless you are right. But the guilt hangs heavy upon me. I will think on it.'

Katherine stood up. 'Do not think for too long. If you really cannot bring yourself to do your duty in this way, I shall do it for you.'

Christopher bit his tongue. Katherine could be shrewish but an argument now would do no one any good, least of all Isaac. But she was right and he would do it. Of course he would do it. He would put his guilt to one side and call on Sarah Cardoza. 'Very well, but I shall visit the mint again first.'

Warden Martin had been affable enough, yet Christopher could not help feeling that he had been holding something back. He arrived only a little damp from the wherry ride and found Martin in his office in the Salt Tower. Martin greeted him politely, dismissed the official to whom he was talking and waved Christopher to a chair. He did not offer refreshment. 'Dr Radcliff,' he began, 'I wish you joy. Have you made progress?'

'As yet, I have not, and, worse, an agent of mine has been attacked. Isaac Cardoza, a goldsmith in Fleet Street. Do you know him?'

'Cardoza.' Martin shook his head. 'No, doctor, I do not. A Jew would not be welcome at the Hall or here at the mint.'

'I am aware of that but thought that you might at least have heard of him.'

'I have not.'

'Has nothing else occurred to you? The minter of the false coins is no beginner and must have learned his skill somewhere.'

Martin's eyebrows rose. The Warden of the Royal Mint was unaccustomed to being addressed so bluntly. 'There are eight royal mints in the country, doctor. The coiner you seek might have worked in any of them.'

'Or none of them, Mr Martin. I am aware of that. But he must be found. Have you searched your records?'

'I am a busy man, Dr Radcliff. There has not been the time. I will send word to you when I have had the chance to conduct a thorough search. Not that I expect to find anything.'

Why was Martin being unhelpful? 'Why is that, sir, if I may ask?'

'Because, first, as the noble earl himself has pointed out, it is clear that these testons are not so much a matter of counterfeiting as an attack on his family. Why then suppose that a man who has worked here or is at least known to us is involved? Is it not more probable that one of his lordship's rivals is behind the coins? And, second, because, with the right tools, these coins could have been made in small quantities anywhere and by any skilled minter or goldsmith. You have seen the process for yourself.'

'Mr Martin, you are not only Warden of the Royal Mint but a senior member of the Goldsmiths' Company. If there exists a rogue member of the company, surely you would have a suspicion.'

Martin leaned forward. 'Dr Radcliff, not all goldsmiths are members of our company. The Jew of whom you spoke, for instance.' So that was it. Blame the Jews.

Christopher swallowed an oath. 'Isaac Cardoza has in the past performed brave and loyal service for our country. He is above suspicion of any kind.'

'Perhaps, but can you say the same of all the Jews working in London? Might there not be one with the necessary skills who wishes the earl ill?'

'Isaac has been attacked in his own shop.'

'So you said. Do you know by whom?'

'I do not.'

'Then I suggest that you find out. If you enlisted the help of the Jew, might he not have discovered the coiner or at least approached too close for his own safety?'

Of course it was possible. But was Martin a little too ready to shift attention away from the mint and the Goldsmiths? 'Have the false testons been tested?' he asked.

Martin hesitated as if taken by surprise at the change of direction. 'They have. Their purity is about three parts in four. That is to say that three honest coins could have been melted down and copper added to make four false ones.' He laughed. 'I have seen worse, much worse, but not, of course, marked with the Dudley emblem.'

Christopher chose his words with care. 'Mr Martin, I am charged by the Earl of Leicester to discover the source of these false coins and to do so without delay. If you, as Warden of the Royal Mint, are unable to help, where do you suggest that I turn?'

Martin barely reacted. 'As I have said, doctor, I suggest that you use your contacts among the Marrano community. There you are more likely to discover intelligence of value.'

Christopher shrugged. 'Then good day, sir. I will leave you to your work.'

Academics were just as bad. Agreeable when they felt at ease, but defensive when challenged and ever ready to cast blame elsewhere. In the presence of the earl and on Christopher's first visit to the mint, Martin had been obliging and informative. Not so this time. What had changed? Anxiety for his position, a grudge, guilt?

The door was opened by Daniel Cardoza. 'There has been no change in my father's condition,' he said quietly. 'What may we do for you, Dr Radcliff?'

Christopher knew immediately that he was not welcome. 'I would not intrude if the situation were not grave,' he replied. 'And I am most anxious not to distress your mother. If she is willing to speak to me, however, I believe it might be of great help in finding your father's attacker.'

Daniel stood in the doorway, showing no inclination to let him in. When he spoke his voice could have been that of a man twice his age. 'I am reluctant to ask her and I doubt she would agree. She does not like to leave my father's side.'

'Your father is fortunate to have such a family.'

'But less fortunate, it seems, in his friends,' replied Daniel sharply, before raising a hand in apology. 'I am sorry, doctor, that was inappropriate. We are under great strain.'

Christopher said nothing. Daniel sighed. 'Come in, doctor, and I will tell my mother that you are here. If she will not see you, you must leave. I can do no more.' He stepped aside. 'Wait in the parlour, please.'

Christopher heard the young man's steps on the stair and the faint sounds of voices. While he waited, he looked around the room. On a small table in one corner was an open Talmud. Heavy drapes covered the windows, the furnishings were sombre, as if waiting for a death, and the floor was bare. A simple room in which the family would come together to talk or pray.

He knew from the weight of the steps descending the stair that they did not belong to Daniel. He took a deep breath and prepared himself.

Sarah Cardoza had been weeping and her skin was so waxen that Christopher doubted she had left the house since Isaac's attack. She made no attempt to smile or to offer words of welcome. 'There has been no change,' she said simply. 'Isaac has not opened his eyes or spoken.'

'Has your physician offered an opinion?'

'Only that his life is in the hands of God. I said that I would send Daniel, Dr Radcliff. Why have you come?'

'I was reluctant to do so, Sarah, but strange things are happening in the city and we have very little idea why. Our best hope is that Isaac spoke to someone he trusted about the matter he was assisting me with and that that someone might be able to lead us to his attacker. I hoped you might be able to suggest a name.'

Sarah took a seat and gestured to Christopher to do the same. She sat quite still with her hands clasped and spoke without hesitation. 'It is often easier for a Jewish family to accept the death of a loved one than his prolonged suffering from sickness or injury. When a man dies he simply travels from one life to another. That is God's plan for us. We show our respect by mourning our loss but his death, by whatever means, is not a tragedy. When a man falls sick, however, or is mortally injured, what can one do but wait and pray? There is no period of *shiva* and thus no return to normality.' She took a handkerchief from her sleeve and dabbed at her eyes. 'It is hard to bear.'

'If I could undo what has been done, I would, Sarah,' replied Christopher, 'and I too pray for Isaac's recovery. But I have a duty to my master, the Earl of Leicester, and to the Crown. The very fact that Isaac was brutally attacked shows how serious may be the threat we face. There is treason simmering on the streets of London and its source must be found. Others will suffer if it is not.'

Sarah went on as if she had not heard. 'We are forbidden to do anything that might hasten a man's death, even if it would be merciful to do so. God alone must decide the time and manner of death. In the case of my husband, a good man who has striven always to do his best for his family, I can only imagine that God is thinking about it. He will have his reasons although I do not know what they are.'

'God's purpose is very often obscure to me, as it is to you, Sarah. I find it more profitable to concentrate on earthly matters than to ponder on that which I will never understand.'

Sarah nodded. 'I know that you are not a pious man, doctor. Isaac would wish me to help you but I am not sure that I can. I do not know to whom he speaks each day. He is a goldsmith, a trader who has contact with dozens, scores of others.' She paused. 'However, if there is one person to whom Isaac might have spoken it is my cousin Aaron. Aaron Lopes. He is a merchant dealing in precious stones. He and Isaac are like brothers.'

'Where will I find your cousin, Sarah?'

'He left for Antwerp the day before the attack. I do not know when he will return.'

'Has he a family?'

'Aaron is unmarried.'

If Aaron Lopes did not leave until the day before the attack, there would have been time for Isaac to have spoken to him. 'I must speak to him as soon as he returns.'

'So you shall, but remember, it is only a thought. Aaron may know nothing. Leave now, please, doctor. I must return to Isaac.'

With half his mind still on Isaac, he was playing idly on the lute when Katherine arrived again at Ludgate Hill and let herself in. He glanced up. 'I had not expected to see you again today. Is there news?'

'Not news of the kind we would wish for. Joan Willys is in Newgate.'

'What? Of what is she accused?'

'Of witchcraft.'

'God in heaven, what next? It will soon be dark. We will go first thing tomorrow morning.'

CHAPTER 9

Newgate. Home to pickpockets, cutpurses, thieves, murderers and felons of every hue awaiting death by gaol fever or their turn in court. There could not be a darker, more noxious, verminous place in London nor one so devoid of hope. The last time Christopher had been inside its walls he had sensed the cold stone closing in and felt his breath being squeezed from his lungs. For nearly four hundred years it had been a place of misery, pain and despair. Over the centuries it had been rebuilt and enlarged but it was as close to hell now as it had ever been.

They were admitted by the guards and escorted down to the cells. It was here in the depths of the common side that the poorest prisoners were kept, those who had not the means to buy their way to the master's side above ground. For all the good intentions and ordinances of the Court of Aldermen, London prison wardens seldom thought further than their own pockets. To recover the outlay necessary to secure the wardenship, they extracted from the prisoners and their families every penny they could for food, bedding and the most basic of comforts and spent not a farthing more than they had to. And Newgate wardens were the most notorious of all.

Katherine held tightly to his arm as they followed a gaoler down a flight of stone steps to a narrow passageway, dimly lit by rush lanterns fastened to the walls. Barred cells, each crammed with prisoners, lined the passage on either side. Christopher put a hand on a wall to steady himself and pulled it back at once. The stone ran with slime. The air was thick with the stench of excrement and disease.

Ignoring the pleas of the prisoners — some feeble, others loud and threatening — and being careful not to slip on the flagstones, they reached a small cell at the end of the passage. The gaoler chose a key from a number on a ring attached to his belt, and unlocked the door. 'There she is,' he growled. 'Alone for her own safety. Witches don't last long in here, except those that can fly. There's a guard at the steps so if she's not here when I return, we'll know for certain she's a witch without the trouble of trying her.' He clattered off, chuckling to himself.

Their eyes had adjusted sufficiently to the lack of light to make out a shape in one corner of the cell. 'Joan?' whispered Katherine. 'Is that you?'

The shape moved and Joan pushed herself up until she was sitting with her back to the wall. 'Mistress Allington,' she mumbled, 'I feared you would not come.'

Katherine carried a cloth bag from which she took a round loaf and a small block of cheese. She squatted down beside Joan and handed her the food. 'Here, Joan, eat this. It will help you keep up your strength.'

Joan took the bread and bit into it; then she took a mouthful of cheese. She swallowed them with difficulty. 'My mouth is dry, mistress. I need water.'

Christopher produced a bottle from under his gown. 'The water here will be foul, Joan. Do not drink it. I hope this will suffice instead.' He pulled the cork and gave her the bottle.

She tipped wine into her mouth, spluttered and managed a weak smile. 'It will, sir. Thank you.'

Katherine took her hand. 'Joan, can you tell us what happened? Your cousin told me that you had been arrested for witchcraft. Is it true?'

Joan rubbed her eyes with a sleeve and sniffed. 'I have done harm to no one.'

'I am sure of it,' replied Katherine gently. 'But who is saying that you have?'

'My neighbour, Alice Scrope. She told the magistrate that I had caused her to suffer pain in her stomach after the birth of her baby. Said you only had to look at me to know I was a witch.' Tears ran down her cheeks and dripped off her chin. Kathcrine handed her a napkin.

'Why would she do that?' asked Christopher.

'She's a thief. I know it and I've told her so but I've no proof, only what my own eyes have seen.'

'So she wants to be rid of you?'

'She does.'

It was not an uncommon story. One person suffers illness or misfortune and takes the opportunity to accuse another, against whom he or she holds a grudge, of causing it by supernatural means. When faced with such an accusation a magistrate would examine the accuser and the accused, take depositions from them and from witnesses and either dismiss the case or refer it to a grand jury who would declare a *billa vera* or *ignoramus*. If the former, the accused would appear at the next sessions. It was unusual, however, for the accused in such a case to be held in gaol before the examination.

Joan was shivering. Katherine took off her cloak and wrapped it around the girl's shoulders. 'You must prepare yourself to be examined by the magistrate, Joan. The law requires it. But Dr Radcliff will speak for you and the case will be dismissed. Take courage from prayer. We will soon have you home.'

Joan nodded. 'When will the examination be?' she asked.

'In a few days, I expect, when witnesses have been summoned,' replied Christopher. 'I will find out from the magistrate. And Mistress Allington is right. You won't be alone, I promise you. I will be there.'

She looked at Katherine. 'And you, mistress?'

'I too will be there. And we will arrange for you to be moved from this place immediately. Are you warm enough?'

'It will be cold tonight.'

'Then keep the cloak — that should help. Try not to be afraid. God will watch over you.'

Just as he watched over the woman at Smithfield, thought Christopher. I wish I believed it. 'From what you have said the accusation is malicious and it should not be difficult to persuade a judge to dismiss it.'

'I will come tomorrow, Joan,' said Katherine, patting her shoulder. 'Be sure to remember your prayers.'

The gaoler was waiting at the bottom of the steps. Christopher took a crown from his purse and held it up. 'Joan Willys is to be moved at once to a clean cell on the master's side and given food and drink. Not just bread but meat, and good ale to drink. No foul water. Is that clear?'

The gaoler grunted, took the crown and peered at it by the light of his torch. 'There's funny money about, they say, but this looks right. Meat and ale it shall be, sir.'

'And a cell on the master's side. We will return tomorrow.'

Joan lived with her crippled mother in a lane not far from Wood Street. There was no purpose in knocking as the old woman would not be able to reach the door unaided. The door, however, was unlocked and they let themselves in.

'Goodwife Willys,' called out Katherine, 'it is Katherine Allington and Dr Radcliff.' When there was no reply she called again. This time they heard a weak voice and pushed open a squeaky door. Inside, Joan's mother lay on a narrow cot against one wall, huddled under bed covers, with only her head visible. A black cat was curled up at the end of the cot. The fire had gone out and the room was icy. Katherine pushed the cat off. 'Have you fuel?' she asked.

There was a nod of the head. 'A little wood in the kitchen.'

'Are you hungry?'

Another nod. 'Where is Joan?'

'Joan is safe. I will fetch food while Dr Radcliff sets a new fire.'

At least there was good food in the house. They waited until the fire had warmed the room and she had taken a few mouthfuls of soup. 'Can you tell us what happened?' asked Katherine.

'The magistrate came with two constables. I did not hear what they said but they took Joan away. Where is she?' Her voice was a little firmer now.

Katherine nodded to Christopher. 'I am Christopher Radcliff,' he said. 'I am a lawyer in the service of the Earl of Leicester.'

'Joan has spoken of you.'

'Your neighbour, Alice Scrope, has made an accusation against Joan. Do you know anything of it?'

Suddenly the old woman's eyes blazed and her voice took on new strength. 'That doxy. A liar and a thief. Spread her legs for a dog, she would, if she was offered a shilling or two. And three babies dead — no wonder her man ran off. What lies has she told about Joan?'

'She has accused Joan of practising witchcraft.'

'Joan, a witch? A foul lie. No mother could have a better daughter. Where is she?'

Katherine and Christopher exchanged a look. 'Joan is in Newgate. We have seen her. She has food and is safe there for now.'

'Newgate.' It was a sob. 'In the name of God, my Joan in Newgate. I cannot believe it.'

Katherine took her hand. 'Do not alarm yourself. I will see that she is well cared for and Dr Radcliff will speak for her. Joan will be released and will be home soon.'

The old eyes turned to Christopher. 'Will she, doctor?'

'I will do everything in my power to ensure that it is so.'

Tears ran down the wrinkled cheeks. 'Joan a witch. A foul lie. It is that whore who's a witch. Did the magistrate's bidding, I expect, and turned him against Joan.'

'If that is so,' replied Katherine gently, 'we will soon discover it. Now, I shall ask your niece Margaret who serves my aunt to stay with you until Joan returns. She will come within the hour.'

'Thank you, mistress.'

'I will lock the door and give Margaret the key. You will be safe.'

'Which is the house of Alice Scrope?' asked Christopher.

'Three houses down towards Wood Street, but take care, sir, she is a rough woman.'

Christopher smiled. 'Don't worry, I shall be careful.'

Once outside, Katherine's anger boiled over. 'An accusation as plainly false as any could be, yet the magistrate leaves a crippled old woman alone and unprotected. It is he who should be in Newgate.'

'It is. I will hear what the man has to say when I have spoken to Alice Scrope. Go now and find Margaret.'

'I will find Margaret and when I have done so I will pray for the magistrate to reap just reward for what he has done.'

*

Alice Scrope might once have been pretty. Her narrow face might once have lit up in a smile, her grey eyes might have been clear and her mean lips might not have turned down so markedly that they dragged the skin of her sallow cheeks with them. As it was, however, she was an ugly creature, battered by a miserable life and old beyond her years. When she answered his knock, Christopher was tempted to walk away. But he could not. Joan Willys was his housekeeper and he carried a responsibility for her, just as he did to see that justice was served, which it would not be if she were sent to the assizes on the word of this slattern.

'Goodwife Scrope,' he began, speaking slowly, 'I am Dr Christopher Radcliff, in the service of Her gracious Majesty's adviser, the noble Earl of Leicester.' When the unlovely face did not move, Christopher tried again. 'The earl is anxious that all the facts pertaining to accusations of witchcraft are investigated and brought to the attention of the authorities.' Not true, but entirely plausible. The red eyes narrowed a little. 'I understand that you have made such an accusation against Joan Willys. Is this correct?'

'The woman's a witch, as anyone can see. She caused me much pain after my child was born. I only did what's right for the sake of others.' She spoke in a voice shrill with indignation.

'Then you would be wise to answer my questions. What evidence have you of witchcraft?'

'Hemlock and belladonna and henbane. The magistrate found them all in the devil woman's house. She mixes them at night.' Katherine had mentioned that Joan had a knowledge of plants and their properties. 'And her face. It is the face of a witch.'

'Allow me to enter, goodwife, so that we may speak in private.'

'There is no fire.'

'That is no matter.' Christopher took half a step forward, forcing the woman to step back. He slipped past her into the hovel. 'Thank you.'

Inside it was as foul as its occupant — cold, dirty, unloved, empty but for a few sticks of furniture. Without asking, Christopher found a small room and stood with his back to the unlit fire in the vain hope that there might be a little heat left in the ashes.

'Where do you work, goodwife?' he asked.

'The Fox in Bishopsgate. I serve the customers.'

'And your child?'

'She comes with me.'

'Have you other children?'

She looked up sharply. 'They were taken from me. Three of them. I will answer no more of your questions.'

'Then you will be made to answer them in court before the magistrate. It will go easier for you if you do so now. How did your children die?'

She shrugged. 'Same way most children die. They were sick.'

'Your pain. Is it still strong?'

'It comes and goes, according to the witch's thoughts.'

'Has she ever accused you of thieving?'

'Can't remember.'

'What about thieving from the market?'

'Ha. I paid no mind to that. There are thieves in any market, cutpurses and rogues and queer-birds too. She mistook me for one of them. Or lied, more likely, just to cause me trouble. And she knows things.' From another room came the cry of a child. Alice Scrope ignored it.

Christopher kept his face impassive. 'What manner of things does she know?'

'She knows how to cure ailments.'

'You will have to swear to all of this to the magistrate. Will you be willing to do so?'

'The magistrate will believe me. He knows me to be an honest woman.'

'Think hard, goodwife. The penalties for making a false accusation can be severe. Tell an untruth in court and you may find yourself in Newgate.'

Alice Scrope screeched, 'Then fuck off. Leave my house or I'll call for a constable. Try to stop me and I'll cry rape. Go and comfort the witch. Tell her to ask for the devil's help. It's all she'll get.'

'Joan Willys will suffer no punishment. If you are lying, you will be the one to suffer.' Christopher slammed the door behind him, half hoping that the hovel would collapse on top of the worthless whore.

If found guilty, Joan would spend twelve months in prison and four days in the stocks. He doubted she would survive that.

The magistrate's house stood in Gresham Street, on the corner of Gutter Lane. Christopher had last seen the man at the witch-burning at Smithfield. It was he who had read out the proclamation condemning the poor woman to die in the fire. He knew the man well enough and that he was ready and willing to profit from others' misfortunes and as industrious as a fat sow reluctant to heave herself off her bed of straw. Most magistrates were honest, hard-working men, trying to do their best for their community. Not this one.

Gilbert Knoyll did not rise when Christopher entered but put aside his plate and nodded a greeting. 'Dr Radcliff, you find me at leisure. Can the matter not wait until tomorrow?'

'It cannot, sir.'

Knoyll poured wine into his glass. 'Then will you take a glass of wine?'

Christopher waved a hand in refusal. 'I have come about the false accusation made against my housekeeper, Joan Willys.'

'False, doctor? Is it false?' He pursed his lips in distaste. 'Why do you think so?'

'Of course it is false,' snapped Christopher. 'Joan Willys's accuser is no more than a slovenly whore intent upon revenge for being called a thief, which she undoubtedly is. Her claim to have suffered pain is a fabrication and her accusation should be dismissed at once.'

Knoyll steepled his hands in front of his bloated face and peered over the spectacles perched on his snub nose. 'That is not for you to say, doctor. An accusation has been made and there must be due process of law. I will summon witnesses and will hear depositions and examine the accused. Then, and only then, shall I decide if the case should be referred to a grand jury. That is the law, as you well know.'

'And I know that it is within your power to dismiss the case now and prosecute the woman Scrope for a monstrously false accusation.'

Knoyll shook his head. 'That is not something I am prepared to do without a proper examination. I believe that the accusation has been made in good faith. If the accused's innocence is plain, she will be released. If not, the case will be presented to a grand jury. If the jury finds the case to be true, they will send it to the next session. You are a Doctor of Law, sir. You are aware of the procedure. Now, good day.' He adjusted his spectacles and returned to his food.

'When will you carry out the examination?'

'On Friday next at midday.'

Friday — two more days and nights for Joan to suffer Newgate. 'Where?'

'In the sessions house.' The sessions house stood next to Newgate prison — convenient for delivery of accused awaiting trial at the next assizes.

'I wish to be present.'

Knoyll's eyes narrowed. 'I cannot prevent you doing so.'

'Then I shall be there, Mr Knoyll.'

The magistrate shrugged. 'If you insist.'

'On Friday at midday. In the sessions house. Good day, Mr Knoyll.'

Outside the house on Ludgate Hill, Daniel Cardoza was waiting for him. 'Dr Radcliff, my mother asks that you come with me to Leadenhall.'

Christopher took a deep breath. 'Your father?'

Daniel shook his head. 'My father's condition is unchanged but Aaron Lopes has returned from Antwerp. He is at our house now. Please come.'

By the time they arrived at the house, Christopher was panting with the effort of keeping up with the young man. He took a few deep breaths before following Daniel inside.

Sarah Cardoza's cousin rose from his seat when Christopher entered the room. He was narrow-faced, with dark eyes and a black beard so long that it might at another time have been comical. As Isaac habitually was, he was dressed in the black of a respectable merchant. And he was about the height of a ten-year-old boy. He held out a hand and spoke in a voice not much above a whisper.

'Dr Radcliff. I am Aaron Lopes. Sarah is with Isaac. She has told me what has happened.'

'May I sit, sir?' asked Christopher, not wishing to tower over him.

'Of course. Sit and tell me how I may be of service in finding Isaac's attacker. He is not only my cousin's husband but a dear friend and a good man. I pray that he recovers soon.'

'As do I. Did Isaac mention to you the appearance of strange counterfeit testons?'

Aaron shook his head. 'He did not. In what way are they strange?'

Christopher took the pouch from his purse and handed the teston to Lopes, who held it up to the light. 'Isaac is the goldsmith,' he said. 'I deal in precious stones — diamonds and rubies for the most part — but I have heard tell of these coins and their connection to the Dudley family. They caused much trouble when first seen, did they not?'

'They did, and are doing so again. The Earl of Leicester is understandably exercised about them and has instructed me to find their source. So far, I have made little progress.'

'The Goldsmiths, the Royal Mint?'

'Nothing.'

For a while they sat in silence. Eventually, Aaron spoke again. 'I will make inquiries among our community.'

'Thank you, Mr Lopes. But be discreet. The earl has insisted that the fewer who know about the coins the better. You should know also that there have recently appeared several slogans, some of which refer to the earl. The testons might be connected to them.'

Aaron's shrewd eyes narrowed. 'And have added to the noble earl's discomfort, I daresay.'

'They have. The perpetrator of the one might lead us to the perpetrator of the other.'

'And thus to Isaac's assailant.'

'Let us hope so.'

The door opened and Sarah Cardoza entered. To Christopher's eye she was diminished even since his last visit. Her face was drawn and her cheeks hollow. 'Dr Radcliff,' she said in a voice almost as quiet as Aaron's, 'have you news?'

'None as yet, I fear, Sarah, but with Mr Lopes's help, perhaps we shall make progress.'

'And with God's help.'

'Indeed. Mr Lopes, Daniel knows where to find me.'

'*Shalom*, Dr Radcliff.'

Mr Brewster's shop in Fetter Lane was tucked between a seller of legal books and a supplier of court dress to judges, lawyers and clerks. Lincoln's Inn and Gray's Inn were both close by. Christopher called on Brewster not only to buy new compositions but also for the pleasure of his company. Brewster could get his hands on rare printed books from abroad, and, when he could not, engaged professional copyists to produce elegantly penned music manuscripts.

Brewster, like Isaac Cardoza and the barber in Fleet Street, loved to talk. A grey-haired, smiling man of about forty, he had no family but he did have an opinion on anything he read in a news book or overheard in an inn. He knew Christopher only as a customer and would have been astonished to learn that the tall, fair-haired Dr Radcliff was the Earl of Leicester's chief London intelligencer. If he had been less talkative, it would not have suited Christopher's purpose. He encouraged Brewster to share his gossip and occasionally learned something useful. So he claimed that his ivory Venetian lute had come to him from his late father.

At first, they had discussed suitable pieces and Brewster had gone to the trouble of looking out some that required the use of only the thumb and two fingers. Later Christopher had bought a copy of Le Roy's Lute Book and a number of pieces by Richard Edwards and the Italian Francesco da Milano. Both were dead but Brewster thought their music would suit Christopher. He had been right. The serenity of da Milano and the melodies of Edwards, Master of the Children of the Royal Chapel in the reign of the queen's father, perfectly suited Christopher's taste.

Brewster had also offered advice on where to find good strings and how to avoid the poor ones shipped from France and Germany. The quality of strings varied with the seasons and even the merchants in Thomas Gresham's new Royal Exchange could be tricked into buying parcels of old strings that would soon perish.

Today, however, Christopher was not in the mood for talk. He had come to buy some new music, in the hope it would take his mind from Newgate. He explained that he had little time to spare and asked for Brewster's suggestions. 'Do you know any of Master Johnson's tunes, sir?' asked the shopkeeper. The name was not familiar. 'Well, then, I suggest that you try this.' Brewster held out several sheets of music, rolled and secured with a blue ribbon. 'It is his latest composition and has already become very popular. I believe Mr Johnson has a bright future ahead of him, perhaps even a place at court.'

Christopher took the roll and read the title written on it. It was 'The Delight Pavan'. He thanked Brewster and fumbled in his purse for coins.

'No funny money, if you please, sir,' said Brewster with a grin. 'I hear there's much of it about. Strange testons, they say, although I have seen none.'

Christopher handed over a silver sixpence. 'Thank you, Mr Brewster. I shall take care to avoid anything with a red hue.'

'And the slogans, sir. Have you seen them?'

'I have, but paid them little attention. I doubt if they are of any consequence. Good day, Mr Brewster.'

'Good day, sir. Call again soon when you have more time.'

CHAPTER 10

The man beside the earl was heavier set and without the earl's aquiline good looks. Only the Dudley eyes gave him away. He did not rise when Christopher entered the room.

Leicester's tone was brisk. 'Dr Radcliff, my brother Ambrose, Earl of Warwick.'

Christopher doffed his cap and bowed as low as he could. 'My lord, it is an honour.' Ambrose Dudley did not reply or even smile. Christopher recalled hearing that Ambrose Dudley, the 'good' Earl of Warwick, seldom smiled. There was certainly none of his brother's charm about him. An austere Puritan, by all accounts, who had distinguished himself both in war and in the administration of the realm. He too had been sentenced to death and imprisoned in the Tower at the time of their father's execution, had been reprieved and had gradually worked his way back into royal favour. It seemed to be the story of the Dudley family.

'You sent for me, my lord. How may I be of service?' The elder Dudley's eyes did not leave Christopher's face but still he did not speak.

'My brother is aware of the recent slogans and of the testons that falsely and treacherously carry our family emblem and of the attack on your agent in Fleet Street. Naturally, he is as concerned as I am. What news is there?'

'Isaac Cardoza lives, my lord, and we are making inquiries that I hope will lead to the source of the false coins.'

'Hope, doctor? We had expected rather more by this time, and so had Her Majesty.'

'It is not easy to locate the source of small numbers of false coins, my lord. The mint could be anywhere and the warden has been unable to offer any suggestions as to the identity of the coiners.'

Leicester held up a hand. 'I am aware of the difficulties but our family name is being impugned and that we will not tolerate.' He glanced at his brother, who nodded. 'And what of the scurrilous scribblings concerning my late wife? Has their author been arrested?'

'I fear not, although I am confident that he soon will be.' The words were out of Christopher's mouth before he could swallow them. He had no idea if the slogan-writer would ever be caught. His attention had been elsewhere.

'Confidence as well as hope. We are fortunate indeed, Ambrose, to have the services of Dr Radcliff, are we not?' When Leicester was in this mood, it was best to say as little as possible. Christopher stifled a protest and remained silent. Leicester sighed. 'Well, we must hope that your confidence soon proves justified, must we not, Ambrose?'

For the first time, Ambrose Dudley spoke. 'Indeed we must.'

'Now, Dr Radcliff, I summoned you here to tell you that tomorrow I must travel to Kenilworth and do not wish to leave these matters unattended to. While I am away, you will report to the Earl of Warwick and carry out his instructions. Is that clear?'

'It is, my lord.' Christopher turned to Warwick. 'How will I communicate with you, my lord Warwick?'

'Deliver messages to Wetherby. He will ensure that they reach me without delay. If I wish to see you, I too will send word by his hand.'

'As you wish, my lord.'

'The earl will contact me if necessary,' said Leicester. The black eyes narrowed. 'I trust it will not be necessary. Have you any more questions, doctor?'

'None, my lord.'

'Then I shall expect the coiners and those behind the slogans to be in Newgate by the time I return. Good day, Dr Radcliff.'

'Good day, my lords.' Another low bow and he took his leave. He hurried along the gallery and down the steps to the Holbein Gate. Outside the gate, he squared his shoulders and breathed deeply. Whitehall Palace was a place he had once found oppressively intimidating and which even now after nearly four years in Leicester's service made him uneasy.

The Brown Bear tavern was wedged into a narrow space between a baker's shop and a cobbler on the Strand. From time to time Christopher went there after visiting Whitehall. It was a quiet place where he was unlikely to be bothered by acquaintances or troublemakers and the ale was less watery than in most London taverns.

He sat in a corner with a beaker and tried to remember what more he knew about Ambrose Dudley, Earl of Warwick and elder brother of the Earl of Leicester. At first he had been taken aback by the earl's lack of courtesy in not rising when Christopher was introduced to him, particularly as his brother insisted on good manners at all times, but now he recalled that the queen had sent Ambrose Dudley to France at the head of an army in support of the Huguenots. In the defence of Le Havre he had been badly wounded in the leg and now walked only with difficulty. Standing must also be painful for him.

What else? A strict Puritan, owner of Warwick Castle not far from Kenilworth, twice — or was it thrice? — married, childless and close to his brother. He too had served in his father's army at Norwich. Lacking Robert's looks perhaps, but not his loyalty or his ambition. And to hold the position of Master of the Ordnance, as Warwick did, showed favour with the queen. Christopher swallowed the last of his ale and left. He had hoped to have heard from Aaron Lopes by now and perhaps from Richard Martin, although their last meeting had been less than fruitful. A word with Warwick about him might not go amiss. Or it might. Wiser perhaps to bide his time until he could better judge the earl's reaction.

In Fleet Street a dozen or so men had gathered outside an apothecary's shop. He could guess why. Sure enough, the letters were poorly formed and it was marked with the letter *X*. *Beware the coin with Staff and Bear, Not minted royal but in Dudley's lair.* Another direct attack on Leicester, on the Dudley family. Another act of sedition without apparent purpose other than to discredit them.

This time he could not pass by. He stood in front of the apothecary's wall and faced the onlookers. 'Did any man see who did this?' he called out. There was no response. 'The writer of this is guilty of treason and so is any man who knows him but does not speak.' A shuffling of feet and eyes downcast but still no response.

Then a woman at the back spoke up. 'The words appear as if by magic. The writers are never seen. It is witchcraft.' The crowd murmured its agreement.

Christopher raised his voice. 'It is not magic; it is not witchcraft. The slogans are the work of a man of flesh and blood, no different to you or me.' He stepped to one side and pointed to the slogan. 'See how the letters are poorly made. A sign that this felony was carried out at night when the felon could not see well what he was writing.'

The woman spoke again. 'What of the crosses? Have these writings not all been marked with crosses?'

'They have, goodwife, but they mean little. They are not Christian crosses, merely the mark of the writer as a painter would mark his work with his name. There is nothing to be afraid of here. A wretch who has not the courage to say what he means clearly and by the light of day is not to be feared by honest folk.' Another thought occurred. 'If these words had been written by the hand of a witch, would they not be impossible to remove? Surely they would. Yet all the slogans we have seen have been scrubbed off with nothing more than water from the river. See here.' With the corner of his gown he rubbed hard at the letter *D*. It immediately faded a little and some fell away on chips from the wall. 'There. A witch's work made worthless by a humble gown and a little effort. Fetch water and be rid of this treason. Do not be cowed by it.' Among the onlookers he sensed a change of mood.

'I will bring a pail,' volunteered one man.

'Make haste,' said Christopher, relieved that the crowd had been persuaded. He was about to walk away when out of the corner of his eye he glimpsed a face he knew, or thought he knew, detach itself from the crowd and walk briskly off towards the Strand. Was it his imagination or had he seen that face before? If he had, it might have been anywhere — an inn, a shop, on the street. But something about the face unsettled him. Perhaps it would come to him.

The small figure standing outside his door was also familiar. He saw Christopher coming and raised a hand in greeting. 'Dr Radcliff, Daniel Cardoza led me here.'

'Mr Lopes. I hope you bring good news. How is Isaac?'

'Isaac is unchanged. As far as Sarah can tell, he is neither better nor worse. She manages to drip a little ale and broth into his mouth. Without that, I believe he would not have survived.'

'He has said nothing?'

'Nothing.'

Christopher unlocked the door. 'Come in, Mr Lopes, and tell me your news. It is a day for new developments.'

They sat in the study, Christopher behind his writing table, Aaron perched on a chair opposite, his feet barely touching the floor. 'It is not much,' he began, 'but I thought to tell you at once. There are two men — father and son — John and Hugh Pryse, skilled men who worked at the mint until three years ago when they were dismissed.'

Christopher kept his face impassive. Martin had said nothing of this. 'Why were they dismissed?'

'An argument with a supervisor. Tempers frayed and blows were struck.' Aaron smiled. 'Over a woman, it seems. Is it not always a woman?'

Christopher rolled his eyes. 'Not always but often enough. What of these men?'

'Both were highly regarded minters and the warden was sorry to lose them. The father left swearing revenge.' Aaron took a false teston from his purse and held it up. 'I have shown this to three goldsmiths. Two of them suggested the Pryses on account of the quality of the work but none could guess at where they might now be. After their dismissal, they disappeared.'

'Surely there are others who could have done work as good?'

'There are, but without the motive of revenge. It is a powerful weapon, Dr Radcliff.'

Christopher thought of John Berwick, a traitor motivated by revenge for the killing of his father, who had been driven to attempt to assassinate the queen and set fire to Whitehall Palace. 'As I am aware, Mr Lopes. The whereabouts of these Pryses are not known?'

'They are not. In or out of London, in a cellar or an attic, they could be anywhere.'

'Richard Martin, the warden, made no mention of them. Why would that be, I wonder?'

'Martin might not have connected them to the false coins.'

Christopher found himself stretching his fingers. 'I shall call again on Mr Martin. It can do no harm.'

Aaron stood up. 'I wish you good fortune, doctor. Tell me if I can do more.'

'You have acted swiftly and you have done more than anyone else, Mr Lopes, and I thank you for it. If Martin can shed light on these Pryses, we might at last make progress. Please tell Sarah that I think of her and hope daily to hear news of Isaac's recovery.'

'I shall, although the longer he is as he is, the less likely a recovery. A painful thought but we Jews prefer to face the truth. Ignoring it does no good. *Shalom*, doctor.'

'*Shalom.*'

'What is unclear to me, warden, is why you have not mentioned the Pryses to me before. They must have occurred to you as possible suspects.'

Christopher had wasted no time. A wherry had taken him to Tower steps, from where he had marched unbidden to the mint and demanded to see the warden. Told that the warden was otherwise occupied, he had insisted on waiting. An hour later an ill-tempered Martin had appeared and now they sat in his office.

'They did not.'

Christopher squinted at him. 'That is strange indeed. Two men, expert minters, dismissed from their positions and leaving with threats of revenge. Surely they would have been watched?'

'It seems not. And remember, doctor, that they were not dismissed for a crime but for brawling with a supervisor. Why would anyone suspect that they would become illegal coiners? And if they did, why would they produce coins which would pass not the slightest scrutiny? It makes no sense.'

'Is it possible to trace their whereabouts? Might other workers in the mint know where to find them?'

'They were dismissed three years ago. It is unlikely.'

'May I have your permission to ask them? Any man here at that time, that is.'

'It would be an unwelcome intrusion into our work, doctor. We are already stretched.'

Christopher glared at him. 'Mr Martin, before he departed for Kenilworth my lord Leicester was adamant. The minters of these monstrous affronts to his family name must be found and arrested. Am I to report that the Warden of the Royal Mint was unhelpful in my commission of this task?'

'I cannot help what you choose to report but I must weigh your request against the work we do. Coins do not mint themselves.'

'I doubt you would say so in the presence of the earl, sir. If I must I will speak further to him. Good day.'

The man was a fool. Was he merely being difficult as officials often were when they felt their authority threatened or did he have something to hide? Either way, Christopher would have to ask Wetherby to speak to Warwick.

Outside the Postern Gate there was a small green where Christopher, at the behest of the earl, had witnessed the execution of

Thomas Howard, Duke of Norfolk, for his part in what had become known as the Ridolfi Plot, after the Italian who had been caught entering the country with letters proving that the Queen of Scots was plotting the death of her cousin Queen Elizabeth.

Today the green was deserted but for a single man lolling against the tree under which Christopher had stood to watch the execution. He was broad-shouldered and well wrapped against the cold. His hat was low over his eyes. Seeing Christopher, he tipped the hat, turned and disappeared down a lane.

He had given Christopher a glimpse of his face. It was the face of the man in the crowd outside the apothecary's shop. And now he remembered where he had seen it before — the man at the market who had run off. It was the face of his shadow and this time the shadow had wanted to be seen. What game was the man playing? Why was he following Christopher? Was he setting a trap? If he was, for what purpose? To find out, the shadow would have to be caught.

Chapter 11

Roland Wetherby enjoyed the use of a small apartment overlook-ing the bowls lawn in Whitehall Palace, blessedly far from the bear-baiting pit by the tiltyard. Christopher knew Roland disliked the baiting of bears and bulls with mastiffs as much as he did him-self, although, as the queen greatly enjoyed the sport, he kept his own counsel on the matter. Privately he thought it strange that a woman who abhorred the use of torture, even on traitors, could laugh and clap at the sight of dogs being torn to bloody shreds by a furious bear.

The apartment had been one of the earl's lures to tempt Wetherby away from Heneage. As ever, he was pleased to see Christopher. 'Christopher, my friend, I wish you joy of the day. And how fares Mistress Allington?'

'Unchanged. A lovely bloom but beware the man who risks the thorns to reach it. And you, Roland?' He looked about the room. 'You are much favoured. A comfortable nest, as I have remarked before.'

'I am well, thank you, although truth to tell a little bored and lacking in occupation. The earl's affairs are easily dealt with.'

'Then I am happy to be able to bring you matters with which to exercise your mind.'

'Not too much exercise, I trust.'

'Not too much. Matters three only.'

'Ah. Three. Should I sit?'

'It might be wise.' When they were settled, Christopher went on: 'First and most important, Richard Martin is being unhelpful and knows more than he is telling me. I do not know why.'

'And you need the noble Earl of Warwick's help to encourage him to speak?'

'I do. Secondly, I am being watched and intend to set a trap to catch the watcher. I cannot do so alone.'

'Could you do so with my help?'

'I believe so.'

Wetherby nodded. 'Not too onerous so far. And the third matter?'

Christopher hesitated. 'The third matter is more personal. Not an affair of state. My new housekeeper, Joan Willys, a willing girl although ill-favoured in looks and manner of speech, has been arrested on a charge of witchcraft. She languishes in Newgate, although she is plainly innocent of any crime and should be released. Unfortunately, however, a lying whore of a neighbour testified against her, claiming that Joan caused her pain after childbirth, and the magistrate decided that she must be examined.'

'Poor woman, to be subjected to such an ordeal. Why would her accuser make a false declaration?'

Christopher shrugged. 'That is what I must find out. If she were tried at the assizes Joan might suffer at the whim of a jury and her appearance would certainly tell against her. That of course would be a monstrous injustice. Could you speak to Warwick?'

Wetherby sighed. 'For anyone but you, I could not. But for you, Christopher, I will try. Hold out no hopes, however. I expect to be brushed aside like a fly.'

'I could try myself.'

'No. Let me try first.' He grinned. 'I would not like you to be skinned and roasted over the earl's fire.' Wetherby seldom failed to raise a smile.

'God's wounds, does the Earl of Warwick eat human flesh?'

'Only, I believe, on feast days. He is at present at Warwick Castle but is expected back in a day or two. I will speak to him about your housekeeper and about Richard Martin. Which leaves your watcher. Have you a plan for him?'

'Let us devise one together.'

Christopher left the palace an hour later. Marvelling as he always did at the opulence now on display on the Strand, where merchants were showing off their wealth by building their grand houses with views over the river and private landing steps, he arrived in Fleet Street. A pang of guilt gave him pause as he passed Isaac's door. Wetherby's way of finding humour in times of trouble had made him forget his friend. He checked that the door was locked and secure, and hurried along Ludgate Hill, half expecting Daniel Cardoza to be waiting for him with news of his father.

What awaited him, however, was not Daniel but a red cross painted on his door. The paint was still wet and had run as if it were blood dripping from a wound. A pair of ragged urchins, so alike they might have been brother and sister, were watching from the other side of the street. He called out to them: 'Did you see who did this?' Neither spoke. He tried again. 'Who made this mark? There is no plague here.'

The urchins exchanged a glance. 'He said there was,' said the boy.

'Who said this?'

'The man who gave us a halfpenny to keep watch,' replied the girl, holding up a coin.

Christopher took a pace towards them. 'I must know who the man was. What was his appearance?'

He was too slow. In a trice they had run down the hill and disappeared. Two urchins just like every other urchin in London but a halfpenny richer.

'I do not understand this, Christopher,' said Katherine. 'If you are being followed, why would a follower alert you by painting a plague cross on your door? What purpose can it serve?'

'I do not know, unless his purpose has changed from observing me to having me boarded up in my own house and left there to rot,' replied Christopher with a shrug. 'But I have asked for Warwick's help with Martin and Roland's with setting a trap for my shadow.'

Katherine reached up to kiss him lightly on the cheek. 'I am glad of it but do not ignore the danger. If the coiners are watching you, they know you are an enemy and will waste no time in getting rid of you.'

Christopher smiled. Katherine was not given to gestures of affection. 'You worry too much, Katherine. Am I not always careful?' Not waiting for an answer, he asked how Joan was managing.

'The poor child is losing hope by the hour. She thinks the world is against her and she is certain to die in Newgate. Surely there is more we can do for her?'

'I have asked Roland to speak to Warwick on her behalf, although he doubts it will do any good.'

'And if it does not?'

'Then we must extract the truth from the whore who accused her and have the magistrate's decision overturned. Have you learned anything about her?'

'I have been too occupied with Joan to speak to the doxy.' There was a gentle knock on the door. 'Tush. What now? I will send them away.'

Christopher heard the door open and close and Katherine returned holding out a scrap of paper as if it were poison. He did not need to ask and barely glanced at the paper. 'Your whore ran off. It seems she has need of you. Make haste or she might be smitten by another.'

'Ell is not my whore, Katherine, as I have told you a thousand times. She is an intelligencer, and a good one.'

'And a whore. No better than poor Joan's neighbour. A stinking whore from whom you are fortunate not to have caught the French gout.'

'An intelligencer, not my whore. I have never so much as touched her.' A flash of anger and his voice rose. 'But if you continue to think otherwise, I shall be happy to do so. It would be a pleasure to escape your sharp tongue in the arms of a whore.'

Katherine's look was icy. She did not speak but picked up a beaker and hurled it at him. He yelped when it struck him above the eye and would have lunged at her, but in a moment she was gone, leaving him fingering the bruise and staring after her. He was used to her throwing things — a slipper, a hat — but only in jest. The beaker had been in earnest.

For some time he sat in the study, trying to justify the outburst to himself. It was her fault. She had no real reason to disbelieve him yet she persisted in doing so, or pretending to do so. He was sick of it.

Never laid a hand on Ell, yet accused of swiving her every time her name came up. Never an apology, never a word of regret. Ell a whore, Christopher her eager customer, whatever he said. No wonder his temper had betrayed him.

But a whore she was, and a lovely one. A woman without learning who had survived by using what she had been given. Her beauty brought her money from her customers and her intelligence brought her more from Leicester's coffers. She harmed no one and served the Crown as best she could. Not a saint, but certainly not a sinner.

Often tempted he may have been but he had never succumbed, although perhaps he should not be surprised that Katherine thought otherwise. And there still remained the matter of the other whore, Alice Scrope, and her false accusation against Joan.

For once, Ell was dressed and waiting for him in the stew owner's tiny parlour. 'Thought you'd be coming, Dr Rad, so I wanted to be ready. I heard voices — who was with you?'

'Mistress Allington, I'm afraid, and she saw your note. She'll take a while to simmer down.'

'Is that where you got your bruise?'

He grinned. 'She has a strong arm.'

'Oh, mercy, doctor. If I'd had my wits about me . . .'

'It's done, Ell. No point in fretting over it. What is so urgent?'

'The gentleman who paid with a naughty coin like the one you showed me.'

'Has he been back?'

'He has, doctor, last night. Very talkative he was, full of questions. Wanted to know about my customers, had I any regulars and did they like special favours?'

'Did you get a name?'

'Afraid not, doctor. I tried but he wasn't saying.'

'Did he ask about me?'

'I thought he was going to. Asked if I had any favourites.'

'What did you tell him, Ell?'

'Not much and it doesn't matter now. He was found in the lane with his throat sliced open.' Ell had seen enough death not to be much moved by it.

'When?'

'This morning. The rats were helping themselves, so we called a constable to take him away. He'll be in the deadhouse now.'

'Think hard, Ell. Did he say anything about the coins or about himself? Where he lived, what his work was, anything at all that might help?'

Ell ran a hand through her hair. 'Afterwards, he did say that it was worth the price of a wherry to see me, so I suppose he'd come from over the river. Very polite, he was, same as last time, and well dressed. Blue doublet, white hose, buckled shoes. If he was not a real gentleman he'd have been on the stage. Could have made anyone believe him.'

'Nothing else?'

'Not that I can recall.' She pulled a coin from under her gown. 'Except that he paid me with one of these again.'

Christopher took the coin. It was a 'Dudley' teston — the bear on one side and the staff on the other. 'I'll keep this, Ell. Don't want you using it in the market — you might get into trouble.' He took a coin from his purse and gave it to her. 'Have this one instead.'

'Doesn't seem fair me taking a coin from you, Dr Rad. Wouldn't you like something for it?'

'Another day, Ell. I must go to the deadhouse now. And you've done enough.'

'No trouble, doctor. He wasn't rough like some. I'm sorry he's dead. Any idea who did it?'

'Not yet. Might just have been a thief after his purse. Take care, Ell. And a note under my door if you learn anything new.'

Ell chortled. 'Won't learn anything new at my age. Been at it long enough.'

'You know what I mean, Ell. I don't want to find you with your head stove in.'

'I'll be careful, doctor, same as always. And you too.'

The deadhouse was beside the coroner's house, not far from St Bartholomew's church. It was an old, single-storey building, seldom repaired and nondescript as if unwilling to draw attention to itself. The coroner, Clennet Pyke, was fond of saying that the occupants never complained so there was no purpose in spending good money on it.

Pyke was a flat-faced little man with an unusually small mouth, resembling nothing so much as a flounder on a Fish Street slab, reeking of drink at any time of the day or night and disobliging even when sober. He was well known, as many in his profession were, as a 'basket coroner', for the basket he carried in which to put the bribes that came his way and the fees he exacted for his services. And he was no more competent than he was honest.

Pyke answered the door himself. 'Dr Radcliff,' he spluttered, 'I trust you are not requiring my services. I am much occupied with important affairs.'

'I require you only to unlock the deadhouse so that I may inspect the body of the man murdered near Cheapside and brought in this morning.'

Pyke's suspicious eyes narrowed. 'And what is your business with this man?'

Christopher stood tall and stared at the mean, close-eyed face. 'I have no time to argue, Mr Pyke. Kindly unlock the door and allow me to examine the body.'

'Why should I do that, doctor?'

'I am about the Earl of Leicester's business and that of his brother the Earl of Warwick. Do as I ask and be quick about it, else their lordships will soon know.'

The callow Pyke did not take long to make up his mind. Safer to leave his ale than risk the anger of the Dudley brothers. 'I trust it will not take long.'

'It will take as long as is necessary, Mr Pyke, and then you will be free to return to your ale and your victuals.' Another tiresome official. Self-important and stupid in equal measure.

Pyke shrugged and disappeared into the house, returning with a large key. He pushed past Christopher, opened the door of the deadhouse and went in. Christopher followed him.

At first, it was so dark that he could see nothing but he knew the design of the place well enough and was able to follow Pyke into an inner room — the deadroom — where bodies were kept until they were claimed or buried. Despite the law, unexplained deaths were not always investigated and unwanted inquests could easily be avoided by describing them as 'accidents', even when evidence to the contrary was overwhelming. Summoning a jury and holding an inquest made for work, not something Pyke enjoyed, and when inquests might be embarrassing to the relatives of the dead man, his opinion could generally be bought for a pound or two.

Although he was expecting it, the lingering stench of death and decay made Christopher's gorge rise. The place was little better than Newgate. He swallowed the bile in his throat and breathed deeply.

Pyke watched him and smirked. 'Do you wish to return another day, doctor?' Christopher shook his head.

The coroner lit a tallow candle and with it three torches attached to the walls at about the height of his rheumy eyes. Four low tables had been set down the middle of the room, on only one of which lay a body. With a theatrical flourish, he pulled off the grubby sheet that covered it, placed the candle beside it and stepped back. 'There, doctor, the man you seek. I will wait outside.' The sheet was tossed on to another table.

Christopher approached the body. The dead man lay on his back, his eyes closed, naked and exposed. A gaping wound revealed that his windpipe had been severed. His assailant had been strong and his weapon heavy — a butcher's knife, perhaps. Despite spending the night in a filthy alley, however, his face and hands were clean save for the teeth marks of the rats which had dined on him.

He picked up a limp hand and examined it. The nails were clean and newly pared; the palm and fingers, apart from the rats' marks, devoid of cuts or calluses and free of ink stains. He stretched out his arms to assess the man's height. Ell was right — her customer had been tall. And, as far as Christopher could judge, well favoured. A narrow face, trimmed beard, black hair, brown eyes. A handsome man, showing no signs of a trade or profession, who paid twice for the services of a whore with false money. Judging by his hands, he had not been a coiner himself but that did not signify much. Men and women of all sorts might be employed to distribute the coins in markets and inns and brothels.

He slid his arms under the body and, with a grunt, carefully turned it over. Thankfully it was too soon for putrefaction to have set in. There was nothing, no marks and no clue as to who he was. Just a foolish man in a filthy alley at night or a coiner with a reason to be there? He had no purse, but that could have been taken by his killer, his finder, a constable or even Pyke. As could his clothes and shoes. Items of value found their way into baskets as readily as coins.

He turned the body back and looked again. The blood on his cheeks was odd. How did it get there? He picked up the discarded sheet and used a corner to wipe some of the dry blood away. Then he saw it. On the right cheek, a deep cross had been cut. There was another on the left. More crosses. Not a foolish man leaving a stew at night but one with a connection to slogan-writers and minters of false coins. And perhaps with the attack on Isaac Cardoza.

He took a last look, saw nothing more and left the deadroom to its lonely occupant. Pyke was waiting in the outer room. 'Did you find that which you sought, doctor?' he asked.

Christopher ignored the question. 'What was he wearing when he was found?'

'He was just as he is now. His clothes and shoes had been taken. That ward is a filthy nest of felons and whores. He would have been stripped and robbed within minutes of being found.' True or not, the man's belongings had indeed gone and, as like as not, would not reappear.

'Has a hue and cry been raised?'

'Of course, as the law demands, although I doubt it will do any good. It seldom does.' In London that, at least, was true.

'When will a day for the inquest be set?'

'When a jury has been appointed. Now, doctor, if that is all, I have work to do.'

'As have I, Mr Pyke. Did you notice the crosses in the form of the letter *X* cut into his cheeks?'

'Crosses? No.'

'They are there. I wiped off some of the blood to reveal them.'

Pyke looked startled. 'You should not have done that, doctor, as you well know. Interfering with a corpse awaiting an inquest is a serious matter. I should report you for doing so.'

'To whom, may I ask? And if you do chance upon someone interested in your complaint, I shall certainly draw their attention to your incompetence in failing to notice the cuts yourself.'

Pyke blinked. 'What do they signify?'

'I have no idea. I will attend the inquest. Good day, Mr Pyke.'

It was Pyke who deserved to be in Newgate. If he could, he would throw the ugly little toad in there with the thieves and murderers who infested the foulest cells. With luck they would steal his food and the toad would starve.

Back at Ludgate Hill, he poured himself a beaker of beer, swallowed it in one gulp and poured himself another. He glanced at the pile of shirts under which he kept his lute, realized that he was in no mood to play well and slumped down on his chair.

Daniel Cardoza arrived at dusk, just before the curfew bell sounded. Not that Christopher paid much heed to the curfew. If the watch stopped him he had only to mention the Earl of Leicester. Daniel was too polite to inquire about the plague cross on Christopher's door but wasted no words. 'My father is awake,' he said, 'and asks for you, Dr Radcliff.'

The news cut through the fog in Christopher's mind. Two beakers had become four and would likely have become six if Daniel had not knocked loudly and called out for him. If Isaac was awake there was hope – for Isaac himself and perhaps for catching his attacker.

Katherine would have to wait. He would take a peace offering in the morning. Now, suddenly clear-headed and trying not to pester Daniel with questions, he followed him swiftly to Leadenhall.

Sarah Cardoza greeted him. 'Our prayers have been answered, doctor,' she said, 'and I thank you for yours.' Christopher merely smiled. Praying did not sit comfortably with him but he would not say so. Her face was composed although she had been weeping and she dabbed at her eyes with a white napkin. 'It is God's will that he lives. Let us go up.'

Isaac lay in his bed, eyes closed, his face so peaceful that for an instant Christopher feared that he had woken briefly before dying. He knew this could happen. But Isaac had heard them and his eyes opened.

Christopher bent to take a hand. It was almost weightless and the skin was as dry and brittle as parchment. He held it as gently as he could without letting go and spoke very quietly. 'Isaac, my friend, it is a joy to see you awake. We have been anxious for you.'

The faintest of smiles touched Isaac's lips and he whispered something which Christopher could not make out. He bent lower. 'Water.'

'Sarah, he asks for water.' A pitcher and a beaker had been placed on a small table beside the bed. Sarah poured water into the beaker and held it to his lips while Christopher supported his head. After a few sips, Isaac lay back. 'Has he eaten?' Christopher asked.

'A spoonful only.' She touched his face. 'He will need fattening up. God has spared him and I will feed him.'

Isaac's voice was a little stronger. 'I am not a calf to be fattened for the feast.'

Sarah laughed. 'Nor you are, husband, but I shall go to the kitchen and bring a little more broth. Do not tire him, Dr Radcliff. A minute or two only.'

Christopher pulled up the chair Sarah had used during her long vigil and sat as close as he could. 'There are strange things happening, Isaac, bad things, but at least you will live to be a hundred. I rejoice for it.'

'A hundred? God have mercy.' He paused to gather himself. 'I remember nothing before the day I was attacked but the man's face is clear to me. A tall man, brown-eyed, bearded and dressed as a gentleman. He wanted to sell a gold ring. I asked him to show it to me and turned away to get another candle. After that, nothing.'

'He hit you from behind with a weight from your table. I found you on the floor. Can you describe him any further?'

'Dressed in doublet and hose. I cannot recall the colours.'

'I found the false teston I gave you in the secret compartment in your strongbox.'

'Did you? I do not remember putting it there. So you found the key.'

'With Sarah's help.'

Sarah came quietly into the room bearing a bowl of broth. 'That will have to do, doctor. Isaac must eat and rest. Call again tomorrow.'

'I will. Tomorrow, old friend. Do as Sarah bids you.'

'Always.'

A tall man, well dressed, bearded and brown-eyed, and who now lay in the deadhouse? The attacker himself attacked and killed? Why?

Infernal woman — sweet as one of her marchpane biscuits one moment, jealous witch the next. Every time Ell's name came up, she flew into a rage. He was sorely tired of it. Damn her — his conscience was clear. Ell could not be easily replaced and he would not abandon her. Katherine must fester in Wood Street until her humour was better. He fingered the bruise above his eye. It was still tender. Let her stew in her own bile.

How different life would have been if his friend Edward Allington had not been killed in a fall from his horse. His childless widow would not have become Christopher's lover and would not have followed him to London. And he would by now have married her, had she not stubbornly clung to the belief that one day he would return to Pembroke Hall as a fellow. Fellows of colleges could no longer take wives and convicted felons, as he was, could not become fellows. Stubborn, wilful, impossible woman.

Mark you, without Joan the cupboard was bare and without Katherine it would be barer still. It was a price he would have to pay. Isaac had been attacked and he needed Ell. This time he would not be swayed.

CHAPTER 12

He went early back to Leadenhall. Despite the hour, he found a tall, stick-thin, dark-skinned man with Sarah in her parlour. She introduced him. 'Dr Radcliff, this is Saul Mendes, the physician who has worked a miracle on Isaac. Saul has been at his side for most of the night.'

Mendes bowed to Christopher. 'Sarah has told me much about you, Dr Radcliff.' The voice was surprising, almost too deep for the body.

'We are all indebted to you, Dr Mendes. It is a miracle that he lives.'

'A miracle? No, no, those are the work of God. I am but a humble physician, plying his trade among his own kind.'

Christopher feared that he had given offence until the physician's eyes told him otherwise. 'Of course, doctor. How fares the patient today?'

'Improved. Sarah has nursed him night and day and I am tempted to say that it is her broth that has brought about his recovery. The wound was severe and he left us for a long time. I was very concerned.'

'You are too modest, Saul,' said Sarah. 'The salves you applied and the powder you mixed with his water were efficacious, even though you will not tell me what was in them.'

'Ah, we physicians have our secrets, too, just like Dr Radcliff.' He nodded to Christopher. 'Sarah has told me about the work Isaac did for you. Of course, there must be no more of it. Isaac will need rest and care for a long time yet and anything likely to fatigue him unduly is out of the question.'

Christopher was tempted to reply that Isaac would wish to decide that for himself but this was not the moment. 'May I speak to him?'

'You may, but not for long and not without Sarah present to make sure he is not over-taxed. I will return this evening.'

Sarah showed him out and led Christopher up to the bed chamber. Isaac's eyes were closed and he was breathing evenly. She touched his face and whispered his name. The eyes opened and he smiled. 'I was sleeping,' he said.

'You were not. When you sleep, you snore like a dog.'

'So Saul has cured my snoring. He is a magician.'

Christopher laughed. Here was the Isaac he knew — frail, yet alert and able to see humour in his own predicament. 'I would not tire you, my friend,' he said, 'but has your memory of what happened returned? Even the smallest thing might prove useful.'

'I remember nothing, but you mentioned a teston in my strong-box. Why was a teston there? I have more valuable items.'

Christopher explained. 'It is likely the attack was connected to the false coin.'

'At least whoever sought it did not find it.'

'Do you remember where it came from or speaking to anyone about it? A fellow goldsmith perhaps?'

Isaac shook his head. 'I fear not. Might I have done so?'

'You might. To my shame, I asked you to.'

'You will have had good reason, Christopher. Let there be no shame.'

'That is enough, doctor,' said Sarah firmly. 'If Isaac remembers anything more, Daniel will bring a message.' At the door, she added, 'Come again whenever you please, doctor. Seeing you will aid his recovery but do not tax him beyond his strength. His memory will return or it will not. Let us leave it in God's hands.'

'Why do I spend so much of my life waiting outside your house, Christopher?' asked Wetherby in mock irritation. 'It is no occupation for a gentleman and it is damnably cold.' He folded his arms over his chest to make the point.

'For the same reason that I spend much of mine running around London on the earl's business. We are mere servants and must obey our masters.'

'How fares Isaac?'

'Awake and lucid, but remembering nothing. I am happy and disappointed both.'

'I too am happy and perhaps his memory will return. For now, however, you must accompany me back to Whitehall. There the good Earl of Warwick awaits you.'

'You spoke to him?'

'I did. He asked to see you himself.'

Christopher sighed. 'Do you know why? I must be at the sessions house by midday.'

'I do not.' He pointed to the cross painted on the door. 'Whoever did that has a strange turn of humour. You could be boarded up inside and left to rot.'

'I know. I will have it removed.'

'Do not delay. Now let us be gone. The elder brother is no more patient than the younger.'

Warwick's apartment lacked the opulence of Leicester's and exactly reflected his character: plain, functional oak furniture, neither carpets nor drapes, a portrait of the queen and another, smaller one of a woman Christopher took to be the earl's wife. He still could not remember whether she was the second or the third but she had been very young when it was painted.

Warwick looked up from the paper he was reading. 'Dr Radcliff, forgive my not rising. This infernal leg tries my patience.'

'I grieve that it pains you so fiercely, my lord.'

'It does. The surgeons advise me to have it off but as that is likely to kill me, for now I shall bear it. Wetherby has told me of your difficulty with the warden. What exactly has he done?'

'Mr Martin has refused me permission to speak to workers in the mint. I know not why.'

'And you need to do so in the commission of your task for the Earl of Leicester?'

'I do, my lord. Until now there has been neither whisper nor hint of who is behind the false testons, but at last a line of inquiry has presented itself.'

Warwick stroked his beard. It was greyer and longer than his brother's. When he spoke he was precise. 'Richard Martin is a mercurial soul, whose mood ebbs and flows like the tide according to the state of his gout. With that I can find some sympathy. But he is also ambitious and obsequious in equal measure. Not that there is any excuse for being obstructive. I will write to him today, instructing him to afford you whatever access to his staff you might require.'

'Thank you, my lord. There is also a second matter.'

'Yes. Wetherby told me of it. In this case, however, I can be of no help to you. As I understand it, guilty or innocent, the woman will be examined by the magistrate and depositions will be taken. I cannot interfere with the proper process of the law.'

Unlike your less cautious brother who did just that in securing my release from Norwich gaol, thought Christopher. 'I understand, my lord, but in this case—'

Warwick held up a hand. 'My decision is made, doctor. Let the law take its course. Is there any other matter that requires my attention?'

'No, my lord.' It did not seem an appropriate time to mention his shadow or the plague cross on his house.

'Then I suggest you concentrate your efforts on finding the coiners. These testons continue to be, to say the least, a grave embarrassment.'

Christopher bowed and took his leave. He had held out no great hope of securing Warwick's support for Joan but still it was a disappointment. The poor girl would have to take her chances in front of the magistrate.

Warwick had been brief and businesslike and certainly not ill humoured, as his brother could be, yet Christopher had left with the feeling that there had been more to the encounter than he had expected. There had been no need for Warwick to summon him to Whitehall – Wetherby could easily have acted as messenger – yet the earl had done so. The brothers were known to be very close. Perhaps Leicester had asked for Warwick's opinion of his intelligencer.

CHAPTER 13

The sessions house in which the assizes for London and the county of Middlesex were held had been built on the street known as Old Bailey, close by Newgate gaol. The court was roofed but otherwise open to the weather and to the stench that rose from the foul underground cells of the gaol. Happily, Knoyll had decreed it too cold to conduct Joan Willys's examination outside. It would be held in a small room within the sessions house.

In front of the magistrate's table a low bench had been set. At one end of it sat Alice Scrope, at the other Joan Willys. Katherine stood behind her and when Christopher arrived a few minutes before midday she was leaning forward to whisper in Joan's ear. Joan saw him and managed a tiny smile. Her hands were clasped in her lap and she was shaking. He returned the smile and found a place at the back of the room. His instinct was always to stand at the back of a room or a crowd, whether because of his height or because he did not care to have people behind him, he had never been sure.

He was wondering why Joan had been brought into the court to hear the accusation against her, it being more common for the accused to be sent for after it had been made, when Gilbert Knoyll waddled in, red-faced and dishevelled, and followed by his clerk.

Knoyll lowered himself on to his chair and looked around the room, nodding briefly to Christopher and peering at Joan. He sniffed, cleared his throat and began by explaining the nature of the accusation and that the purpose of the hearing was to judge the substance of the allegation of witchcraft made against Joan Willys. He would make his judgment by hearing depositions and by questioning the accused.

The accuser, Alice Scrope, was first to speak. Her deposition did not take long. She claimed that Joan had caused her to suffer great pain after the birth of her child and that she suffered still. 'The woman's a witch,' she cried, pointing a filthy finger at her, 'as anyone can see. Who but the devil himself would give a woman such a face? And she is wise. She knows how to use plants to cure and to poison. And she keeps a cat. It is her familiar spirit.'

'It is true that poisons were found in the house of the accused,' said Knoyll, 'and there is a cat. Why, however, do you suppose that the animal is her familiar?'

Again Alice Scrope pointed at Joan. 'She speaks to it. I've heard her. And she feeds it milk mixed with her own blood. I've seen that too.'

Knoyll nodded and glanced at the clerk whose task it was to keep an accurate record of the proceedings. 'Did you write that, master clerk?' he asked.

'I did, sir.'

'Good. I would hear now from the midwife who searched the accused.'

Christopher frowned. He had not been told of a searching.

A large woman of perhaps thirty stood up. She wore a thick skirt and a shawl around her shoulders. 'I am the midwife, sir.'

'What is your name, midwife?'

'Abigail Cooper, sir. I examined the girl in Newgate with two others. We all agreed.'

'What did you agree?'

'She carries a devil's mark on her left thigh. It is unmistakable.'

'How is it unmistakable?'

'I have seen many such marks, sir, and they were all the same. This one is no different. It is in the form of a woman's teat.'

'How do you account for such a mark?'

'It is made by the teeth of a familiar sucking blood from the witch.'

Knoyll's eyes swept the room. 'I see. Have you any doubt about this, Mistress Cooper?'

'None, sir. I saw it myself. A familiar spirit's mark.'

'Thank you, mistress.' Abigail Cooper sat down. 'Are there others here who would speak in support of the accuser?'

There were two, both elderly women, who did so. One repeated everything Alice Scrope had said; the other claimed that Joan did not attend church on Sundays and had caused her house to be infested by mice. The clerk dutifully wrote it all down.

Throughout, Joan had sat silently with her head bowed, dabbing with a handkerchief at her eyes. When Knoyll addressed her, she glanced up but did not reply. He said, 'It is now the accused's turn to speak. Joan Willys, what do you say to the accusation made against you that you are a witch?' Joan looked down at the floor and said nothing. When Knoyll repeated the question she remained silent.

'If you do not answer my questions, Joan Willys,' he said, 'you will certainly be referred to a grand jury.' He looked around the room. 'A year in Newgate might loosen her tongue.' There was a ripple of laughter, but Joan did not even look up.

Knoyll tried a volley of questions. 'When did you become a witch? Where did your familiar come from? Do you know of other witches?' Still Joan said nothing, even when Katherine whispered to her.

The silence was broken by the magistrate. 'In the name of God, child, you are foolish. You give me no choice,' he thundered. 'An indictment will be sent to a grand jury and thence, I do not doubt, to the next sessions. You would do well to speak there lest you are made to suffer pressing.' But even the threat of being crushed to death did not bring a word from Joan.

Was the girl hiding something or was she simply terrified? Christopher pushed his way to the front. 'Mr Knoyll, the accused is my housekeeper and I would speak for her.'

'Dr Radcliff, I have made my decision. The accused has not co-operated in her examination and must be tried. And she is not entitled to witnesses to speak on her behalf.' His eyes swept the room and he laughed. 'Where would we be if a woman accused of being a witch could produce whomever she liked to a hearing? We would be here for weeks.'

'I do not seek to be a witness, sir, but rather to speak in her stead, as it is plain that she cannot do so herself. She is frightened and cannot at any time speak clearly. It is only just that someone speaks for her.'

The clerk shrugged his shoulders and addressed the magistrate. 'I am unsure, sir. It is irregular, but I know of no law against it.'

Knoyll threw up his hands. 'Oh, very well, Dr Radcliff, but be quick.'

'I shall endeavour to be quick, sir. In answer to your first ques-tion, Joan Willys denies that she is a witch or that she has ever practised witchcraft. She has no so-called familiar spirit and she knows of no other witches. How would she, having no knowledge of witches' work? Further, the cat in her house belongs to her infirm mother and is fed on scraps and an occasional spoonful of milk and she speaks to it only as any woman might speak to a pet animal. The poisons found she used for the treatment of ailments. In small amounts they can be beneficial. It is the dose that makes the poison. These being the facts, it is clear that her accuser, the woman Alice Scrope, has made a malicious accusation which should be dismissed.'

True or not, it was the best Christopher could do.

'Why would she do that?'

'Because Joan Willys knows her to be a thief and has said so.'

'Is there evidence of this?'

'I know of none but have no doubt of the truth of the accusation. The woman Scrope is a liar and a whore.'

Alice Scrope was on her feet at once. 'It is the witch who is the liar and the whore. I am her victim and seek justice,' she screeched.

'And you shall have it, goodwife,' replied Knoyll. 'What of the devil's mark on her, Dr Radcliff? How do you account for that?'

'I hope Joan Willys will forgive me if I say that she is not well favoured. There may be many marks upon her skin, but not one of them was made by the teeth of a familiar — cat, rat or spider. I can also say that while she has worked as my housekeeper, she has been reliable and efficient in her duties.'

Knoyll's eyes narrowed. 'For how long has she been your house-keeper, doctor?'

'Not long. A matter of days.'

'Hardly long enough for you to form a valid opinion.'

'There is no evidence against her, sir. The accusation is false and malevolent, made out of the spite and rage that we have just seen.'

'Have you anything more to say, doctor?'

'No, sir.'

'That is a comfort. As you are speaking for the accused, kindly ask her to stand.' Joan stood up but did not raise her head. 'The recent increase in cases of witchcraft has led the Privy Council to issue instructions to magistrates to observe a special presumption on account of the fact that a witch's work is by its very nature secret. The presumption is that if an accusation is lawfully and honestly made, the accused shall be referred to a grand jury. I will therefore be referring Joan Willys with the depositions taken today.' Still Joan did not raise her head but in the room there was a murmur of agreement. 'The constables will return you to Newgate to await the sessions at Easter.'

'One more question, sir,' shouted Christopher. 'Who has paid for this accusation and who will pay for the case to go to trial? Has the woman Scrope the money to do so?'

Knoyll ignored him and marched out of the room. The clerk gathered his papers and followed. Smirking foully, Alice Scrope, flanked by her two witnesses, flounced out behind him.

Joan was taken out by two constables. She was weeping. Christopher smiled at her but she did not see him. Katherine followed behind her. As she passed, Christopher said, 'I did not know about the searching.'

Katherine barely glanced at him. 'Would it have made a difference if you had? Were you not too busy about your master's business to spare a thought for a poor, innocent woman made to suffer searching?'

She was gone before he could reply but the arrow had hit its mark. He had let Joan down.

CHAPTER 14

Yet he could not dwell on it. Not on Katherine, not even on Joan, made to suffer by an unjust process that came close to presuming guilt on the feeblest of evidence. He would turn his mind to her when he could. For now, whatever Katherine might think, he had the earl's work to do. It was back to the mint.

It was as if Richard Martin, self-important, defensive, obstructive Richard Martin, Warden of the Royal Mint and senior member of the Goldsmiths' Company, had travelled the road to Damascus and seen the light as Saul had seen it. He welcomed Christopher into his office, offered him wine and inquired politely after his health. Only when his visitor was comfortable did he turn to business.

'Dr Radcliff, I regret that our last meeting was less than satisfactory. I have assured the Earl of Warwick that it was no more than a misunderstanding and that you will naturally have my assistance in apprehending these coiners in any way you request.'

Christopher swallowed hard. Whatever Warwick had written to Martin had brought about an instant and remarkable transformation. The Puritan earl could not have minced his words. 'Thank you, warden. I request that each member of the mint staff who was here at the time of the Pryses' dismissal be brought to me to be questioned. I will start immediately.'

Martin's smile revealed two rows of small, white teeth. They reminded Christopher of a rat's. 'I had anticipated that, doctor. There are three men to whom you should speak. Use this room and I will send them in one at a time.'

The first man could not have been less than fifty and could hear only if Christopher stood close and shouted at him. The deaf man remembered nothing of note about John or Hugh Pryse except that they were father and son and the son was fond of ale. Christopher got no more from the next one and was beginning to wonder if Martin was having sport with him. The third man, however, was more interesting.

Edward Gibson had been working at the mint for five years. He was a well-fed, jocular fellow who claimed to be twenty-eight years old and to have been on friendly terms with Hugh Pryse. 'We often drank together,' he said, 'and a few other things too.'

'What other things?' asked Christopher.

'Nothing against the law, sir. Just ale and women and a game of dice when we had the money.'

'Do you still enjoy these pastimes, Gibson?'

Gibson shuffled his feet. 'Not often, sir, but is it not Hugh you want to know about?'

'Hugh, yes, and his father, John. You must have known both of them.'

'I did, sir, although I tried to keep my distance from Hugh's father. He was a miserable old goat, as ill-tempered as his son was cheerful.'

'Good workers, I am told.'

'They were, sir. I am sorry they've gone, for all John's cussing and grumbling.'

'What did he cuss about?'

'The noise, the supervisors, the rest of us, not enough money. One day it was too hot, the next too cold. John Pryse would always find something to cuss about.'

'Why did they leave?'

'There was a fight. Hugh's woman lay with a supervisor, or so he thought. He knocked the fellow down, kicked him where it hurts most and would have kicked him again if John had not pulled him off.'

'Who was the supervisor?'

'Don't recall his name. Matters little — he's long dead from the pox.'

'Then what happened?'

'The supervisor complained and wanted Hugh in front of the magistrate. I think a deal was struck because John and Hugh were both soon gone and we heard no more about it.'

Christopher nodded. 'Anything else?'

'There is one other thing, sir. I believe the Pryses were inclined to the old ways.'

'How so?'

Gibson lowered his voice, as if afraid of being overheard. 'I am one who cares not a jot for how a man chooses to worship — Protestant, Puritan, Jew or Catholic — but others do. Hugh never spoke of it but I do know he carried a rosary in his purse. I happened once to see it.'

'Thank you, Gibson. Is there anything else?'

'No, sir, not that sits in my mind.'

'Where did the Pryses live?'

'Southwark, sir, not far from the bridge.'

'Could you point out their house to me?'

'I believe so, yes, sir.'

'Good. I will speak to the warden.'

Martin was back at his desk. Christopher stood in front of him. 'Why did you not speak of the Pryses, Mr Martin?' asked Christopher. 'You must remember them.'

'Indeed I do, but the matter was a source of some embarrassment and I had hoped not to reopen the wound. I was in error, of course. I realize now that they should be found and questioned.'

'And so they will be. Edward Gibson knows where they live. I shall also need your assistance.' Gout or no gout, Martin must suffer a little discomfort in the cause of justice.

'Mine? Of course, doctor. When do you plan to go?'

'Now, Mr Martin, now. There is sufficient light left and it is not far to Southwark.'

They threaded their way across London Bridge, between the new-built mansions of the rich and the cottages and hovels of the poor. The bridge heaved as ever with merchants, tradesfolk, carts and beasts. Unusually, at the great stone gateway where traitors' heads were commonly displayed, only one spike was occupied. A gaggle of noisy urchins threw stones at the blackened skull and shrieked with delight when one of them hit it.

Under the arch whose wooden galleries extended over the river on both sides, and they were in Southwark. If the contrast between Goldsmiths' Hall and the alleys off Cheapside was stark, it paled beside that in this borough. Christopher never felt at ease there.

Gibson led them to a narrow, cobbled lane, coated with layers of mud and muck and running westwards, roughly parallel to the river. This area, to the east of the bear-baiting and bull-baiting rings in Paris Garden, was infested with stews and dice houses. Outside the control of the city aldermen, it was a place of vice and violence, populated by whores and beggars, cutpurses and vagrants. Further away from the river stood the shops of the bakers and confectioners for which Southwark was famous and the workshops of the many joiners and carvers and furniture-makers who had arrived here from France and Holland. It was exactly where a man might go to hide.

Gibson and Christopher walked as quickly as the mud would allow, leaving Martin struggling to keep up, limping along with the aid of a stick and blowing hard. After a few minutes they came to a dark lane leading away from the river. 'It is down there,' Gibson said. 'Do you want to go down there?'

Christopher looked at Martin, who shook his head. 'Of course, Gibson,' he replied. 'We will not find the Pryses by standing here.'

About forty paces into the lane, Gibson pointed to a mean cottage in the middle of a row of three, all roughly built of stone and timbers so black and rotten that they might have been washed up on the riverbank. Their doors and windows were marked with red plague crosses. 'That is it,' he told them.

Christopher hammered on the door with the handle of his poniard and shouted for John Pryse. There was no reply and no movement inside. It was the same with the cottages on either side. He glanced up and down the lane, saw no one and put his shoulder to the door. It was locked but a few hefty blows and it would break.

'Hold, Dr Radcliff,' cried out Martin. 'If there has been plague here, we would be unwise to enter.' He had a point but Christopher was in no mood to leave none the wiser about the Pryses. Without them, or some information about them, he would be back at the start of the game with his chess men unmoved.

He tried again but the lock held. He was about to give it a kick when an old woman, her back bent from the load of washing she was carrying, a clay pipe clenched between her teeth, appeared from the direction of the bridge. Christopher called out to her. 'Goodwife, we seek John Pryse and his son Hugh. They lived here. Do you know them?'

The washerwoman eyed him suspiciously, took the pipe from her mouth and sent a stream of brown spittle to the ground. 'Long gone and left the plague behind them. Daresay it'll be back come the spring.'

'Do you know where they went?' Christopher took a coin from his purse and held it for her to see.

'No. Dead and buried for all I care.' She held out a bent hand. 'I'll take the coin though.'

Christopher flipped the coin to her. It bounced off her arm and into the dirt. 'Take care, goodwife,' he said. 'A penny won't keep the plague away.'

'Well now, doctor,' said Martin, as the old woman shambled off, muttering to herself, 'are we to knock on every door and question every man and woman? Or will you break this door down and search for the Good Lord knows what?'

Christopher ignored him and kicked hard at the door. A timber splintered and when he kicked again, the lock broke and the door swung open. 'I doubt there has been plague here,' he said. 'If there had been, the house would have been boarded up. More likely whoever lived here made a feeble attempt to keep curious eyes away with the crosses.' He stepped inside.

The washerwoman was right. Whoever had lived here was long gone. He coughed dust from his mouth and held a hand over his face against the musty stench of vermin. At first he could see little but when his eyes became accustomed to the gloom, he made out a low wooden bench and a plain chair. There was nothing else.

A single door led off the room. He pushed it open. The room beyond was small, barely larger than a cupboard, and windowless. A wooden box stood in one corner. In it were a hammer, a chisel and a pair of dies. He held the larger die to the light from the doorway but could not make out the stamp.

Martin and Gibson were waiting at the front door. He showed them the dies. 'Taken from the mint, almost certainly,' said Martin, 'although the stamps are too worn for me to tell what they are.' He held them out.

'Keep them, Mr Martin,' said Christopher. 'I have what I need and I thank you for your help. If you think of anything more, Gibson, kindly tell the warden, who will tell me.'

'I will, sir. Glad to have been of service.'

'Now, Mr Martin, I shall leave you and Gibson to return to the Mint. I must put my bloodhound to work.'

He crossed the river by wherry and hurried to Cheapside, where he found Ell sleeping. 'The devil's prick, Dr Rad,' she grumbled when he woke her, 'is an honest whore not to get any sleep?'

'Sorry, Ell. I need your help.'

'Funny money, doctor, or bodies that get up and walk?'

'What?'

'You haven't heard then. That gentleman of mine who was found in the lane with his throat cut and taken to the deadhouse. He's gone and nobody knows how.'

'Somebody must know, Ell. Bodies do not remove themselves. Another visit to the coroner for me but for you I have a different request.' He told her about the Pryses. 'They might be dead or they might be alive and up to coining those testons. Can you go to Southwark and ask about?'

'For a crown or two, Dr Rad, I will. Pay me now or later?'

Christopher gave her a crown. He always gave Ell a coin even when her intelligence was of no value. The earl's comptroller did not know what was useful and what was not and never grumbled about the money he spent. 'One now, another later. Must keep you wanting more.'

Ell gurgled. 'Don't you always? Mistress Allington back in Wood Street?'

'She is.'

'Thought she might be. Note under your door then, same as usual.'

He heard them before he saw them. A furious crowd, several dozen strong, had gathered in the street and was hurling whatever it could find at the deadhouse. Stones and refuse and muck splattered the walls while a man in a leather jerkin battered at the door with his fists and bellowed for it to be opened.

Christopher looked around for Clennet Pyke. There was no sign of him. No doubt the little toad was cowering in his parlour. 'What has happened here?' he asked a young woman holding a baby at the back of the crowd.

'Witches' work,' she muttered. 'A body has gone from the deadhouse, taken for the devil.'

'How do you know this, goodwife?'

The woman eyed Christopher suspiciously. 'Word spreads fast.'

He moved forward into the crowd. One man called for the deadhouse to be burned down, another for a priest to be fetched. 'There is sorcery here,' he shouted, waving his arms about. 'Find the witch who has taken the body and burn her.' There was a roar of approval and a surge towards the door.

A shot rang out. Heads turned and the surge was halted. To their left the magistrate, holding a pistol, and six blue-coated constables, armed with clubs, stood and watched. When he could be heard, the magistrate spoke. 'I am Gilbert Knoyll, magistrate of this ward. This assembly is unlawful and will disband at once. My constables have orders to arrest any who do not obey.'

'Find the witch, magistrate, and burn her,' yelled a woman's voice, 'that we might live in safety.'

'Aye,' said another, 'bodies do not disappear but when a witch has need of a corpse.'

Knoyll signalled to his constables who raised their clubs and took a step forward. The crowd formed itself into a ragged line to face them. The woman shouted again: 'Who has written words on walls if not a witch? Who has painted plague crosses on our doors if not a witch?'

A youth picked up a stone and hurled it at Knoyll. It missed and clattered against a wall. The crowd surged forward again. Another shot was fired. Knoyll had a second pistol. Christopher pushed his way through the line to the front and stood with arms raised. 'There has been no witchcraft here. Return to your homes.'

'Who are you to give us orders?' growled the man in the apron. 'Stand aside that we may burn this evil place to the ground.'

'The body will be found. There is nothing of which to be afraid. Go home.'

Knoyll had been watching. 'Do as he says or you will find yourselves spending the night in Newgate. Witchcraft or not, there will be no more law-breaking in my ward.'

A few sloped off. The rest stood and stared at the constables, apparently unmoved. 'Where is the coroner?' demanded a fishwife. 'Where is Pyke who has charge of the deadhouse? What has he to say?'

Other voices took up the cry. 'Where is the coroner? Drag him from his house and let him speak.'

Knoyll glanced at the coroner's house, as if considering what to do. He was spared having to do anything by the door being cautiously opened and Pyke's flat face emerging. The coroner had been listening. He took a quick look and darted back inside, but not before he had been seen. 'There's Pyke,' shouted a woman's voice, 'skulking in his house. Haul him out and let him answer for this.'

'A body missing is the coroner's business. Bring him out, magistrate, or we'll do it for you,' added another voice.

Christopher was wondering what he would do in Knoyll's place when the magistrate gave another signal and the constables, side by side, charged into the mob and set about limbs and bodies with their ballows. Blood spurted from heads and bones snapped. Unarmed and unable to defend themselves other than with their arms and hands, the mob panicked, turned and fled, leaving their wounded to the mercy of the constables. Very quickly the street was clear.

Christopher had not drawn his poniard for fear of causing more blood to flow and had been fortunate enough to avoid all but a few glancing blows. He held his ground and shouted to the magistrate, 'Call off your constables, Mr Knoyll. The deed is done.'

Knoyll heard him and ordered his men to let the stragglers and the injured go. 'Dr Radcliff, I had not thought to find you at such an unlawful gathering.'

Christopher approached him. 'I heard that the body of the murdered man had disappeared and came to speak to the coroner about it. It seems I was among the last to hear.'

'Why would you wish to speak to the coroner?'

Before he could reply, Pyke opened his door again and stepped into the street. 'How fortunate you were alerted, Mr Knoyll, else more blood might have been spilt. And I see that Dr Radcliff was among the troublemakers.'

'That is untrue, sir, and had I been, the blood spilt would most likely have been your own. For cravenly hiding in your house that would have been no more than you deserve.' Christopher glowered at Pyke and was pleased to see the ugly face redden, although whether with anger or embarrassment he could not tell. It was enough that the little man was silenced. To the magistrate he said, 'Mr Knoyll, I wished to speak to the coroner because the disappearance of his body strengthens my opinion that the dead man was connected to another serious matter that I am investigating for the earl.'

'How is that, doctor? Connected how?'

'That I cannot say. However, at present there is no body and without one there can be no inquest. Those wishing to keep the identity of the murdered man secret might have concluded that their best chance of remaining undetected was to remove it.'

'Was the lock on the deadhouse forced, Mr Pyke?'

'It was not, sir,' replied Pyke with a smirk at Christopher. 'And I can be sure that the door was locked because I locked it myself. What is more, it was locked when I tried it this morning. Without doubt we are dealing with another act of witchcraft.'

'Let us examine the door and the deadhouse,' replied Knoyll. 'Dr Radcliff, to satisfy your own curiosity, you might care to join us.'

Pyke unlocked the door and led them inside. He lit a torch and guided them into the deadroom. All four of the low tables were devoid of bodies. 'There, sir,' announced Pyke, 'as you may observe, no body, although it was here yesterday evening when I carried out my usual check. I am most particular in that.'

'No doubt, Mr Pyke. Were there other bodies here?'

'There were not, sir.'

'Is that unusual, Mr Pyke?'

Pyke scratched his chin and looked at his feet. 'Not very unusual, sir.'

No indeed, when the surgeons would pay well for a fresh cadaver. 'And there was no sign of a forced entry and nothing left behind by the intruder?'

'I believe there must have been more than one intruder, Mr Knoyll,' said Christopher. 'The dead man was not small.'

Knoyll scratched at his beard. 'Either that or we are indeed dealing with a case of witchcraft. The door was locked before and after entry, no sound disturbed the coroner's sleep and there is no trace of the intruder. I am in agreement with Mr Pyke. It seems to me most likely that the body was spirited away by supernatural means.'

'Or was removed by someone with access to the deadhouse and who knew of a buyer for the body. There are those who pay well for cadavers upon which to practise their surgical skills.' Christopher looked pointedly at the coroner.

Pyke exploded. 'That is a monstrous slander, Dr Radcliff. Only I hold a key to the house and I will not be accused of malpractice. Ask any surgeon in London and he will tell you that he has never had a body from Clennet Pyke. Mr Knoyll is undoubtedly correct. This was an act of sorcery. The sorcerer must be found and tried according to the law.'

Christopher ignored him. 'Mr Knoyll, this is no more a matter of witchcraft than is the pain claimed by the woman Scrope.'

Knoyll bridled. 'A jury will decide Joan Willys's fate and when the perpetrator of this outrage is found another will decide his or hers. I will order a hue and cry and instruct those with suspicions to come forward. Those with nothing to hide need have nothing to fear. The guilty person must be found before fear and unrest spread through the ward. We have seen enough of both already.'

They left the deadhouse. Pyke made a show of locking the door and turned to Christopher. 'Am I to understand that you are not a believer in supernatural acts or powers, Dr Radcliff?'

'There is much neither I nor any other man understands about the world, Mr Pyke, and only a fool would claim otherwise. That there exist witches and sorcerers at the command of the devil I believe unlikely, if only because I have never been shown proof of it.'

'Then beware lest the doubts you profess are taken as evidence of your own guilt, doctor. I have often seen it.'

'I shall take great care, Mr Pyke. And now I suggest that you and Mr Knoyll set about finding the true felon.'

Christopher strode off rubbing his bent hand and hoping that the odious Clennet Pyke would soon get his comeuppance. But if it was not a witch, who was it and why? And how had the news spread so fast?

John Johnson's 'Delight Pavan' had lain untried on his table since he had brought it home from Mr Brewster's. Perhaps it would calm him. He took the lute from its case, ran his hand over the cool of the ivory and tested the strings. The single treble string needed tightening. He turned the peg carefully and tried again. A little more was needed. He gave the peg another touch. And swore mightily. The wretched thing had broken. A pox on Pyke and a pox on Knoyll. A pair of poxed pricks.

Still cursing, he chose a replacement from a box purchased in the Exchange, tested the evenness of its arc by stretching it out and plucking it with his thumb, and fitted it to the lute. It was a task he disliked because his hand made tying the knots correctly difficult.

Once fitted, he tested the string again. It was not perfect but he was not in the mood to change it again, so he fiddled with the frets until he was satisfied.

He started to play. Mr Brewster was right. Master Johnson's pavan was a light, lilting piece, not greatly demanding for the lutenist but requiring some dexterity in the faster passages. It was not surprising that it was so popular. In the right hands it would be joyful.

But Christopher's were not the right hands, at least not that day. He played the pavan through but his rendition was flat and clumsy. He adjusted the frets once more, moved his right hand nearer the rose and tried again. Still he could not find the sweet sound the 'Delight' deserved. His playing was as ponderous as a plodding cart-horse. He gave up. The lute went back in its case under the shirts. 'The Delight Pavan' must wait for another day.

Daniel Cardoza arrived as the bright February day was fast becoming night. He wasted no words. 'Dr Radcliff, my father asks for you. Please come.'

'You should not have come alone at this time, Daniel. The streets are dangerous after dark.'

'My brother is helping our mother.'

'Were you not stopped by the watch?'

'I was not seen, doctor.'

Christopher put on his coat and slipped his poniard under his belt. Isaac would not have sent the boy out alone and during the hours of the curfew without good reason.

Isaac was sitting up in his bed, a pillow behind his head, holding a beaker of beer. He wiped his mouth with the back of his hand and sighed. 'Tastes all the better for the waiting. One can tire of pottage, even Sarah's.'

'You are improving, Isaac,' replied Christopher. 'That is good. You asked for me?'

'I did. I have been trying to picture the man. He had a gold ring to sell, I remember that, and I think he did speak about the testons.'

'What did he say?'

'He asked me if I had seen any and if I knew about them — in a casual way, as a man might ask another if he has heard that a friend is unwell. I said that I had heard tell of new counterfeits but had seen none.'

'What then?'

'I must have betrayed myself because when I turned away to find a candle, he hit me.'

'Either that or his purpose had always been to kill you.' Christopher paused. 'Describe him to me again.' Isaac did so. 'A man exactly fitting that description was found murdered in Cheapside. I saw his body in the deadhouse.'

Isaac's eyes sparkled. 'Take me there. I shall know him.'

'Alas, that will do no good. His body has disappeared.'

'Disappeared? How?'

Christopher shook his head. 'I do not know, except I doubt it was the work of a witch, as some are saying.'

'Are they? A corpse taken for some foul ritual? It is possible, I suppose, but men turn too readily to magic to explain what they do not understand. Have you considered that it was the dead man's murderer who took him from the deadhouse?'

'I have, but can find no reason for it, although his face was marked with two crosses in the shape of the letter X. The slogans that have appeared recently have been marked similarly and plague crosses have been painted on houses where there is no plague, my own among them.'

Isaac shook his head. 'Then you are in danger, Christopher.'

'If I cannot discover who is behind these things, we will all be in danger. In the meantime, old friend, I will continue to search them out while you recover your strength. You know where to find me if anything more occurs to you.'

'I will send one of the boys. Go down now and Sarah will give you some of her pottage.'

'That is kind, Isaac, but really . . .'

'She will be offended if you do not eat with us. As will I.'

Christopher hesitated for only a moment. 'Of course. And you have spoken highly of her pottage.'

Isaac grinned. 'It is excellent. And plentiful. Eat as much as you can.'

'I shall. And shall hope to see you further improved next time.'

The Cardozas ate in a small room attached to the kitchen at the back of their house. Around a circular table sat Sarah, her sons Daniel and David and her daughter Ruth. Their heads were covered and they all rose and bowed to Christopher when he entered.

There were two empty seats. Sarah indicated one of them. 'Sit there, doctor,' she said. 'The other chair is Isaac's.'

On the table stood a thick loaf of bread and huge bowl of pottage. The bowl was richly painted in red and blue with a gold border. In front of each of them was a smaller, matching bowl and a wooden spoon. All but Daniel took their seats. 'Daniel will bless our meal,' said Sarah with a smile. 'In deference to you, doctor, I have asked him to keep it short.'

When the prayer had been said, Sarah spooned soup into each bowl while Daniel cut a slice from the loaf and took a bite out of it, before cutting a slice for each of them. They spoke during the meal but took care not to interrupt one another or to speak with food in their mouths. Having eaten in this house once before, Christopher knew the most important Jewish customs and was careful not to transgress.

'It is a sadness to us that we must observe our customs in secret,' said Sarah, 'and it is rare indeed for us to have a Christian guest at our table. We thank you, doctor, for accepting our invitation and for saving the life of my children's father.'

'I am honoured,' replied Christopher, 'and I join you in thanking God for his recovery.'

'Dr Radcliff,' said Daniel, a note of surprise in his voice, 'our father once told me that you are not a believer in any God.'

Christopher grinned. 'I am far from being certain but there are times when I find that I can believe.'

'Then we must hope that your belief is not misplaced,' replied Sarah. 'Isaac's recovery will take time.'

Christopher managed three bowls of pottage and two slices of bread and could see that Sarah was pleased with his effort. Afterwards he stayed only as long as courtesy dictated then hurried home through the dark streets, keeping to the wider ones and clutching the poniard tightly. If he were attacked from behind, he would be ready. It was not a thing he commonly did but to his annoyance the mysterious shadow had unsettled him. Who was he and what was his business with Christopher? Somehow he must find out.

Chapter 15

They sat in Christopher's study before a feeble fire. He had not laid it well and it was giving off little heat. Joan would have done a good deal better, had he managed to secure her release. Poor woman. It was bad enough to be afflicted by her appearance. Being accused of witchcraft was a monstrous injustice.

He had returned late from Leadenhall and after a day spent hurrying from there to Whitehall, to the session house, to the mint, to Southwark, to the deadhouse and back to Leadenhall, he had slept until dawn, and might have slept longer had Wetherby not hammered on the door and shouted for him to open it.

'There is much left to chance in this plan,' said Wetherby. 'Your shadow has to appear, I have to see him while remaining hidden myself and we have somehow to apprehend him. It seemed sound enough when we first discussed it but now I am less sure.'

'Of course there is chance. But in the absence of better, this is what we are going to do. We cannot stand by and wait for Ell Cole to find the Pryses, if indeed they are the coiners. The body of Isaac Cardoza's attacker has disappeared, the false testons are still appearing and I must soon report on our progress to Warwick.' Christopher paused, took a sip of ale, and peered over the top of his beaker at Wetherby. 'Unless you would like to do so on my behalf?'

'I hardly think the noble earl would be pleased if I did. He would imagine you skulking in your bed chamber, quite unable to speak for yourself or do anything but fill your piss-pot.'

'And he would not be far wrong. That is much how I feel. However, let us give the plan a try. If it works I shall feel much better.'

'And if it does not?'

'You will find me in my bed chamber.'

They left the house together, hoping that the shadow was about his work. They did not see him but nor did they expect to. At the bottom of Ludgate Hill, they parted company. Christopher waved his hand in farewell and turned towards St Paul's churchyard. Wetherby disappeared into Creed Lane. It had been agreed that he would circle back from the south end of the lane to St Paul's, keeping to the shadows. As he had much further to walk, Christopher would dawdle, giving the other man time to catch up.

Taking care not to look back over his shoulder, Christopher walked slowly. He stopped to buy a small pie from a vendor and again for a cup of milk from a milkmaid. He did not look round but concentrated on sensing the shadow. He felt nothing. Disappointed, he moved on, arriving in the churchyard just as a trained band troop marched through it on their way to drill in Holborn Fields.

The market in St Paul's yard was the place for members of the Stationers' Company, whose Hall was nearby, to show off their wares. There a man could buy not only rare books but also fine writing materials — duck-feather pens, good oak-apple ink, well-made rag paper. Most of the books were beyond Christopher's purse, but he would not stint on pens and ink. Good penmanship had been instilled in him from an early age by his schoolmaster father.

On busy days the bustle of the market could even spread into the nave of the church. There news was exchanged and bargains struck. Today, however, once the trained band had gone, it was quiet, which suited their purpose well. It would be much easier to identify and apprehend a man who could not disappear into a throng of bodies. He wandered around the square, stopping to exchange a few words with the stationers he knew and to browse at their stalls, thus giving Wetherby plenty of time to take up his position in the unnamed lane to the side of the church, where he could hide in the shadows without much risk of being seen but from where he had a clear view of the churchyard.

When Wetherby identified the watcher — it should not be difficult as Christopher had given him a description of the man, whose eyes would be firmly on his quarry — he would run at him shouting for the thief to be arrested. Traders in any market hated the thieves who plagued them and invariably observed the unspoken rule that a thief to one was a thief to all. They would rush to Wetherby's aid and bring down the watcher. A constable would be called and the felon taken into custody, accompanied by Christopher and Wetherby. Not a perfect plan but not a hopeless one.

When the church bell struck ten Christopher realized with a shock that he had been in the yard for an hour. There was no point in continuing. If the watcher had been there, Wetherby would have seen him and raised the alarm. He made his way to the corner of the church where Wetherby would be, intending to call off the plan, perhaps to try again on the morrow.

But of Wetherby there was no sign. Christopher peered down the lane and called out for him. Surely he would not have deserted his post without warning, yet where was he? Christopher went further into the lane, straining his eyes against the gloom and keeping a tight hold on his purse.

The sound he heard might have been made by a cat or even a newborn left to die. It was a sorry cry, feeble and pitiful. But when he moved towards it he made out a human form lying across a doorway, its head resting on the cobbles, its feet in a pool of muck.

He knew at once that it was Wetherby and swore mightily. First Isaac, now Roland. He squatted down to lift the stricken man's head. His eyes were closed but he was breathing freely. Christopher spoke his name. At first there was no response. He spoke it again and Wetherby's eyelids flickered, and then opened. He turned his head to the side and vomited.

'Can you stand?' asked Christopher once the retching had stopped. Wetherby nodded and Christopher helped him to his feet. 'Lean on me until you are steady,' he said with an arm around Wetherby's shoulders.

They stood like that until Wetherby whispered, 'I saw nothing. A blow from behind.' He reached down to where his purse should be. 'A thief. My purse has been taken. May the fellow rot in hell.'

'Did you see the shadow?'

'I did not. I am sure he was not in the market.'

'You saw nothing, heard nothing, Roland? A skilled thief indeed.'

'Nothing. I was intent upon watching out for our man.'

'Could it have been our man who surprised you?'

'If so, he was more than skilled. The eyes of a hawk and invisible. And my purse has gone. Not that the devil will have found much in it. Come now, Christopher, an army of drummers are playing inside my head but with a little help I can walk back to Ludgate Hill. For the love of God let us be gone from this place.'

They had taken a single step when Christopher felt an arm encircle his neck from behind. Instinctively, he let go of Wetherby and reached up to grasp it. Wetherby slumped to the ground.

Christopher had heard nothing, not a sound, just as Roland had not, and the arm was thick and knotted like a ship's rope. He could not dislodge it and could barely take a breath. A muffled voice whispered in his ear: 'A foolish trick. Try again and your pretty friend will lose his looks and you will lose your eyes.'

Christopher let go of the arm with his right hand and reached round to find his blade. Immediately the arm strengthened its hold and forced his head backwards. 'Did you not hear me?' growled the voice.

Christopher tried again. He bent his knees and let his weight pull him downwards. With luck the assailant would not be able to hold him up and he might slip through his grasp. The grip loosened a little but not enough. The man held on until Christopher had to either stand up or fall back. He tried a sudden jerk upwards and felt the back of his head hit the man's chin. There was a yelp of surprise and the grip loosened enough for him to wriggle free. He turned sharply but his vision was blurred. He caught just a glimpse of a broad back hurrying off and disappearing around a corner in the alley, nothing more. Christopher rubbed his head. The man had been strong and skilled. And, Wetherby's purse or not, no common thief.

Wetherby was still on the ground, his face turned to the wall. Christopher knelt down to him and gently turned him on to his back. 'Roland, can you hear me?' he asked, and immediately wished that he had not. The words had come out in a fiery rasp. He put an ear to Wetherby's face and heard the sound of soft breathing. He was alive but Christopher dare not leave him to fetch help and calling out for help would have been pointless. Even if he were heard no sane man would be lured into that alley by what might be a trap. He sat down beside Wetherby and waited.

The attacker could have killed them both but had not. Neither of them had seen his face but was there any doubt that he was the shadow? If he was, what was his purpose? Had he been Isaac's attacker? Or had that been Ell's murdered customer who had disappeared from the deadhouse?

Wetherby stirred and opened his eyes. 'Has he fled, Christopher?' he croaked.

'He has. I had to let you fall. Can you stand?'

'I can try. Help me up.'

Christopher slipped an arm under his shoulders and heaved him up. 'How is that?' he asked.

'My legs feel like bowls of rice pudding. But hold on and we might just find our way home.'

They had to stop twice but eventually staggered back to the house. Christopher sat Roland in the study and gave him a beaker of beer. 'Best I can do, Roland. Good French brandy would be better for you but I have none,' he said.

'A pity.' Wetherby sighed, putting aside the beaker. 'This beer tastes foul. Was it a thief, do you think?'

'No. It was the shadow but what his purpose was or is I cannot say. We were unlucky.'

Wetherby spluttered and put a hand to his head. 'We? In what way, pray, were you unlucky, Christopher?'

'My head too is a little painful but I meant only that we did not catch him. How does yours feel? Would more beer help?'

Wetherby stood up and put a hand on Christopher's desk to steady himself. 'No, thank you. I shall return to Whitehall.'

'Are you sure? You are welcome to use my bed until you have recovered a little more.'

'Quite sure. At the palace I shall be safe from cudgel-brandishing vagabonds and I may expect rest, brandy and consolation.'

Christopher rubbed his head gingerly as he watched Roland make his way unsteadily down the hill. The plan had failed hopelessly but they were alive and would both recover.

There had been no word from Katherine since she had stormed out in a fury and for all he knew she had left London and returned to Cambridge. She had neither apologized nor recanted nor made any effort to speak to him. It went with her flame-red hair — stubbornness, pride, a refusal to admit error. Sometimes, not often, these qualities were appealing. Increasingly, they were wearisome beyond measure.

CHAPTER 16

The coroner's boy arrived that evening. A body had been fished from the river and lay in the deadhouse. Dr Radcliff might care to examine it.

He followed the boy to the deadhouse where the coroner was waiting for him. The little man smirked. 'Dr Radcliff, it seems that our man has come to pay us another visit.' Christopher ignored him.

The stench of decay lay even heavier than it had on his last visit. The corpse lay on one of the four tables, covered with a grey sheet which did not quite reach his ankles, leaving bite marks exposed on a pair of bloodless feet.

Pyke removed the sheet, unleashing a blast of corruption that made Christopher gag. 'There, Dr Radcliff, your man, I rather think.' Pyke was clearly enjoying Christopher's discomfort.

'My man, coroner? I do not understand your meaning.'

Pyke grinned. 'The man in whom you showed an interest when he last paid us a visit. It is he, is it not?'

There was no doubt. Even after some time in the river, even after the predations of the crabs which had feasted on the bloated carcass and the fish which had nibbled at its feet, even after the removal of an arm — by beast or human? — leaving a ghastly stump at the elbow, it was the body of the man murdered outside Ell's stew. The eyes had gone but the hair and beard had not. The shape of the head was right, as was the height of the man. His throat had been cut and the crosses cut on his cheeks were still visible.

'Where was he found?' asked Christopher.

'At Tower steps by a wherryman not two hours ago. Most of our river-bodies wash up there. It's on account of the current.'

'And what now is your opinion of how a dead man managed to escape this room and jump into the river?'

'He was taken from here and thrown in the river. I cannot say by whom but I believe it was an act of *maleficium* — a witch's doing. How else could it have happened — and why? No, when asked, I shall give my opinion that this man was the victim in life of an attack by an unknown assailant and in death by a trick of one of Satan's foul followers.'

Christopher shook his head. Clennet Pyke was an imbecile. 'Will there now be an inquest?' he asked, trying to keep his temper.

'I think not,' replied the flat-faced coroner. 'The body is already decayed and will decay still more before a jury can be summoned. It would not be right to expose them to such a sight.'

The deceased's body was displayed at an inquest so that members of the jury and the public could inspect it, unless the coroner thought it prudent for reasons of health or sensibility not to allow this. Coroners, of course, varied in their judgement and in how they then treated the death. The most idle, of whom Clennet Pyke was certainly one, would simply record the death and give as its cause 'killed by an unknown hand'. No jury, no inquest, no work, no cost.

'Unless you have good reason to delay, doctor, I shall order a burial for Tuesday next. The common graves at Moorfields will accommodate him.'

Christopher could think of no reason to delay burial. Before long the remaining flesh would fall away and the corpse would liquefy. That was when its evil humours would be at their worst, spreading disease and yet more death. Best to bury it under the soil.

That night he awoke with a start, not because of another dream or because of the attacks on Isaac and Roland but with a sharp stab of guilt. Joan Willys was in Newgate awaiting trial. He must visit her. Katherine would have made sure she had sufficient to eat and drink and clothes to keep her warm but he should go and he would do so in the morning.

At dawn, however, he was jolted awake by a persistent hammering on the door. Cursing the Earl of Warwick for sending a messenger at such an early hour, he struggled into the shirt and trousers discarded the night before and stumbled down the stair.

'What can the noble earl want at this hour?' he grumbled, opening the door. But the visitor was not whom he expected. 'Oh, it is you,' he said. 'If you are looking for Ell Cole, she is not here.'

Katherine pushed past him and into the house. 'Joan has been moved,' she told him. 'She is in a crowded cell with a dozen others accused of murder and other felonies. I doubt she will last a day.'

'Why was she moved?'

'I do not know. The warden would not speak to me.'

Christopher put on his coat. 'I will come at once.'

They walked in silence to Newgate. At the gate, Christopher gave his name and a coin to a guard. 'Show us where the prisoner Joan Willys is kept,' he ordered. 'We must see her at once.'

The coin did its job. With a torch to light the way, the guard escorted them inside the gaol and down the flight of steps to the lowest cells. At that time of the morning, there were usually bodies to be carried up and off to the burial ground at Moorfields or to await the arrival of a relative who might be prepared to spend money on a proper burial. On the steps they were forced to stand aside for a burly gaoler with the body of a woman over his shoulder. 'One belly less to fill,' he muttered. 'Only four today. Must be feeding them too well.'

The women's cells lined a narrow passage leading off the main one. Here the cries were yet more pitiful, more terrible than those from the men's cells. Each cell was crammed with prisoners, some lying, others sitting, a few standing at the bars, stretching out for succour as beggars might. 'Take care not to venture too close,' advised the gaoler. 'If one gets her claws into you, you'll be lucky to escape unharmed.'

Christopher edged Katherine into the middle of the passage, out of reach of grasping hands. He had once read a pamphlet in which these cells were described as 'body upon body, the air fetid and corrupt, each one awash with human waste, a hell from which it would be kinder to take the prisoners, guilty or not, and hang them at Tyburn'. It was a description that had stayed with him and it was no exaggeration.

When they came to the last cell, the gaoler stopped and pointed into it. They strained their eyes into the gloom. What looked like a bundle of rags had been heaped in a corner. 'Joan,' called out Katherine, 'are you there?'

The bundle moved and Joan's face peeked from under the rags. 'In the devil's name,' screeched a voice, 'keep your witch's face hidden or you'll be the death of us all. Show it again and you'll feed the rats.' Joan pulled the rags back over her face.

Katherine tried again. 'Joan, listen to me. You should not be here and we will soon have you moved. Dr Radcliff is here. You have nothing to fear. Say your prayers and God will watch over you.'

The screeching voice was even louder. 'God? What God? The God that has abandoned us to die here or on the scaffold? Or perhaps you mean the evil one, the devil.'

Another voice spoke. 'Aye. One man's God is another's Satan.'

'She's a witch, more than likely, with that face. Should have been smothered by the midwife.'

'Won't be pleading her belly. No judge would believe the bitch.'

'Enough,' shouted Christopher. 'Joan Willys is under my protection. If any harm comes to her, every one of you will regret it.' Beside him, the gaoler shuffled his feet. Christopher carried on before he could say anything. 'Joan will be moved without delay. Until then, keep in mind what I have told you. Do her harm at your own peril.' It was hard to tell how much effect his words had and in any event he doubted it would last long. They must get her out of this hellhole at once. He spoke to the gaoler. 'Come, man, we will have words.'

Outside, he turned on the man. 'What outrage is this? We paid for the prisoner to be held in a better cell on the master's side. Why has she been moved into that place?'

'Price goes up for witches with the mark of the devil,' growled the gaoler. 'Another two crowns if you want her out of there now.'

'That is monstrous,' said Katherine. 'We will see her moved at once. Now.'

The gaoler shook his head. 'Victuals to be paid for and clean straw once a week. It'll be two crowns to see her through to the sessions.'

Katherine stared at him. 'You will have a crown now and another in two weeks. And we will have full value for our coin.'

The gaoler scratched at a pustule on his face and held out his hand. 'Very well.'

Katherine nodded. 'A crown, Christopher, have you one?'

He took five testons from his purse and handed them to the gaoler, who peered at them. 'Funny money about,' he grunted.

'Go and fetch Joan Willys now and bring her up here. We will see her safely into a cell worth the money.'

They waited in silence while the gaoler fetched her. Although the sky was grey, she blinked in the light. Katherine took her arm and the three of them followed the gaoler across the yard, through a door and along another passage to where Joan had been held until she was moved. She was put in a cell with only two other women, both of whom must have had the money or a benefactor with the money to pay for their comfort. They were clean and well enough dressed in smocks and gowns.

This time it was Katherine who addressed the women. 'For what crimes are you being held?'

'They say I stole a purse, though I did not.'

'And I am no doxy.'

'Joan Willys is under my protection. See that she is well treated and you will be rewarded. If she is harmed, you too will be harmed. Is this clear?'

The women glanced at each other and nodded. 'Yes, mistress,' replied one.

'How large a reward, mistress?' asked the other.

'Large enough,' snapped Katherine. 'And mark my words carefully.' To Joan she said, 'You will be safe here and I will come every day to make sure you are.'

'And I will continue to work for your release, Joan,' added Christopher.

Joan's voice was barely above a whisper. 'I thank you, mistress, and you, doctor.'

Outside the prison gate, Katherine said, 'I will return now to Wood Street.' She took a sheet of paper from her sleeve. 'Here is a list of prices you should pay in the market. They are prices for good, fresh food. Do not buy cheaper meat or fish which will be inferior and perhaps rotten.'

Christopher took the list. 'Why have you given me this?'

'I have decided that I will take care of Joan and keep an eye on her mother but no longer will I cook for you or share your bed.'

'Katherine . . .'

'I have decided. Let that be an end to it.'

Christopher watched her go. She did not look back. No kiss, no touch, not even a smile. And not a hint of regret in her voice or her eyes. Was it really all because of Ell Cole, whom he had never touched? Or had they simply reached that fork in the road?

'Dr Rad, wasn't expecting you, but here you are. Always a pleasure, even on a Sunday. My busiest day, Sunday, after my gentlemen have done with their praying.' Ell, fully dressed for once, was sitting in the stew parlour, gnawing at a chicken leg. 'Stringy old bird. Less meat than a sparrow.' She tossed the bone into the fire. 'I've been to Southwark and asked around, if that's what you've come for.'

'Have you learned anything about the Pryses, Ell?'

'Not much. They packed up and left a year since, or maybe even two years. No one knows where they've gone, or if they do, they're not saying.'

'Nothing else?'

'Odd pair, they say. Father a miserable old goat, son fond of his drink and the ladies. One in particular but I didn't find out anything about her.'

'Is there a wife or mother?'

'Died giving birth to the boy.'

Nothing to go on there. 'Pity. But you did your best, Ell.'

Ell's eyebrows rose in surprise. 'Not giving up, are we, Dr Rad? Not like you.'

'Isn't it? No, I suppose not. Not myself today.'

'Mistress Allington?'

Ell always knew. Christopher nodded. 'Impossible woman.'

'Loves you, though, and lucky to have you. Be patient, doctor, she'll come round.'

'Perhaps.'

'And we're not giving up yet. How about if I ask about the boy's lady friend? Might lead somewhere. Worth a try.'

'Very well, Ell. But take no chances. I don't want to lose you too.'

Ell laughed. 'You won't lose me and you haven't lost Mistress Allington. Now be off with you. I'm expecting a visitor.'

'A note if you hear anything. I'll come to you, Ell.'

'Best you do. I don't want to interrupt you swiving her.'

Not much chance of that. 'Goodbye, Ell.'

CHAPTER 17

He had hoped that the effort would restore his spirits but it did not. With brush and water he had scrubbed the plague cross off his door but felt no better for it. Might as well have left it there and waited for the house to be boarded up with him inside it. At least then he would not have to go to Whitehall to inform Warwick that he knew very little more than he had a week ago. Even Ell had cheered him only briefly.

Katherine sulking in her tent like Achilles at the walls of Troy, Wetherby attacked by an invisible hand, Joan in Newgate, a body marked with a cross taken from the deadhouse and thrown in the river. And who was the dead man? A customer of Ell's, but what was his name and how was he connected to the false coins? And who was this man who'd threatened him — the shadow? God in his heaven, but a glimmer of light would be welcome.

At least there had been no more slogans or crosses, Isaac was recovering and if Ell had any luck in Southwark, there might yet be cause for hope.

Do not lose heart, Dr Radcliff, do not sit in your study and mope. Use your lawyer's brain. Think.

He chose 'The Duke of Somersett's Dompe'. If anything helped it would surely be a gentle melody. The best of them had been known to send listeners into a state of reverie perfect for quiet contemplation.

He took up the lute and began. His last effort at playing had been a failure but, to his surprise, today his hands moved lightly over the strings, the music flowed and he found himself playing while his mind was elsewhere. The questions had answers and he would find them. Katherine would emerge smiling from her tent. Joan would be released from Newgate and return home to her mother. He played the dompe twice and began to play it again.

The knock on the door was insistent. He put down the lute and went to answer it.

'Come at once, if you please, Dr Radcliff.' It was Daniel Cardoza. 'Dr Mendes is concerned.'

'And does your mother wish me to come, Daniel?'

'She does.'

'Then let us make haste.'

The lute went into its case and under the shirts and they were off within a minute.

They did not speak as they hurried through the lanes to Cornhill and thence to Leadenhall. Daniel unlocked the door of the house. Christopher ducked his head and followed him inside and up the narrow stair. Sarah and Saul Mendes stood by Isaac's bed. Dr Mendes looked up at Christopher and shook his head. 'I feared this could happen,' he said quietly. 'A false recovery is not uncommon in cases of head wounds.'

Isaac's eyes were closed and he was as pale as he had been on the day Christopher had found him in the shop. 'Can he hear me?' he asked.

'He is asleep, doctor,' replied Sarah. 'He cannot hear you, nor did God hear our thanks.'

'His breathing is shallow,' added Mendes. 'The loss of blood was too great for him. That and the shock.'

'Shock, doctor?'

Sarah held up a leather bag. 'These were left on the doorstep this morning. I showed them to Isaac, God forgive me.'

Christopher took the bag and rummaged inside. It was full of coins. He took out a handful. They were false testons, marked with the bear and ragged staff. 'Was he seen, the man who left these?'

'No, doctor,' replied Daniel. 'I found the bag when I left the house.'

'What is the meaning of it, Dr Radcliff?' asked Sarah, dabbing at her eyes with a napkin.

'Sarah, I do not know.'

'These coins will bring only death. They must be thrown in the river.'

'No, Sarah, I will take them to show to the Earl of Warwick. He should be told about them.'

'As you wish, doctor. Take them and do as you will but do not bring them back here. They are a curse on this family.'

'What I am wrestling with,' said Wetherby, 'is why, if it was your shadow, he struck with so little force. Why did he not break your neck and cave my head in like poor Isaac's?'

'I do not know. He took a risk in not disposing of us for good. After all, we might have caught a glimpse of him.'

From Leadenhall Christopher had made his way to Whitehall and now sat in Wetherby's apartment. Outside the bowling green was covered with a thin layer of white frost. The room was warmed by a fire and smelled of the beeswax that had been used on the furniture.

'Alas, we did not. We must try again.'

'I would not put you in harm's way again, Roland. And Isaac's condition has deteriorated. When I visited him he did not open his eyes or speak a word. Dr Mendes fears the worst.'

'I am cruelly sorry to hear it,' replied Wetherby, 'but it should not deter us from our task of finding our man. Surely he will lead us to the source of our troubles.'

Christopher handed him the bag of testons. 'These were left on Isaac's doorstep.'

Just as Christopher had, Wetherby put a hand into the bag and took out a few coins. 'Bears and staffs,' he said. 'What can be the meaning of this? A warning?'

'I think not. If it were, surely the bag would have been left outside my door, not Isaac's.'

'Warning or not, we must try again, Christopher. What else is there to do?'

'Ell Cole is trying to trace the Pryses. The son, it seems, was fond of women and not overly particular about their station. Ell is clever. I am hopeful.'

'Good. When shall we try again?'

'Roland, you have been badly injured. I am reluctant to put you in danger's way again.'

'Nonsense. Did I not spend a long night with you in St Ann's church in the vain hope of catching the traitor John Berwick and did I not fire the shot that disabled him and allowed you and Katherine to escape his clutches? Am I now to be denied the chance to catch the scroyle who did this to me?' He touched the back of his head and winced. 'Still painful.'

'When you are recovered we will speak of it again. Until then rest. Eat well and do not go to Eastcheap.'

Wetherby grinned. 'I? Never.'

'Hmm. Now I shall call on the noble Earl of Warwick. If he is like his brother he will expect to be told everything.'

Warwick was in his apartment, and, after a short wait, Christopher was ushered in to see him. 'Dr Radcliff,' said the earl, not rising from his chair, 'what have you there?'

'Testons, my lord.' Christopher handed him the bag.

Warwick took one out and held it close to his eye. He sucked in his teeth. 'God's wounds, the bear and staff again. They are all the same?'

'They are, my lord.'

Warwick shook his head and put the coin back in the bag. 'Where were they found?'

Christopher told him about the bag, about Wetherby, about Isaac and about the body taken from the deadhouse and recovered from the river. Warwick sat silently with his hands steepled under his chin until Christopher had finished. After a moment or two, he asked, 'What do you make of this, Dr Radcliff?'

There was no future in dissembling. Warwick would know at once if he strayed from the truth. 'Very little, my lord. I see only disconnected events without obvious purpose.'

'Surely these testons have a purpose, as have the slogans daubed on walls. Their purpose is to shame my family.'

'Yes, my lord, but what of the plague crosses and the attack on Isaac Cardoza?'

Warwick pushed himself painfully to his feet and limped to the window, where he stood facing into the room with his hands behind his back. He spoke quietly so that Christopher had to strain to hear him. 'When my brother and I were incarcerated with our father in the Tower, we spent many hours at the chess board. At first we were evenly matched but in due course, if I may be permitted to say so, I became the stronger player and won almost all our games. The reason for this was that although he was as skilled as I at making a plan, he did not pause to consider what my plan might be and then to take steps to counter it. He ignored the possibility that I might be setting a trap for him and played as if there was no connection between the positions my pieces occupied. His strategy was one of all-out attack while mine was more watchful and more adaptable.' He turned to look out of the window.

Not entirely sure where this was leading, Christopher remained silent until the earl turned back to face him. 'The point of my telling you this is twofold. First, we must assume our enemy has a purpose beyond these apparently random acts, even if we cannot yet see it, and second, I cannot help but feel that he is playing a game with us. A game full of bluff and deception. A game of confusion and disorder.'

'If he is, my lord, it is a violent game.'

'Which shows us only that he is determined to win it.'

'And what prize is he playing for?'

'That is what we must ascertain.' Warwick paused. 'The Earl of Leicester will return from Kenilworth soon. Until then, proceed with your inquiries and apply your mind to what our opponent might be planning next. Assume there is a connection between his actions and search for it. What connection could there be, for example, between a body taken from the deadhouse and slogans painted on walls or between these coins and plague crosses on plagueless houses?'

It was, like his chess strategy, a more considered approach than his brother's would have been. Not that Leicester was a fool — far from it, no man who had risen as high as he could be other than clever and perceptive — but he could be impetuous, even rash, as his various failed ventures had shown. But who am I to judge, thought Christopher, the man who spent eight weeks in Norwich gaol for striking and killing a man in a fit of temper?

'Yes, my lord. I shall think on it.'

Warwick picked up the bag of coins. 'And I shall keep these. We do not want them flooding the markets and stews of the city.'

CHAPTER 18

It was all very well Warwick telling him to think. He had been
trained to think. What he had not been trained to do was buy
food and cook it. But a man had to eat. Since Katherine had stormed
off, he had managed on what had been in the house but now the
cupboard was bare.

Armed with her list, he started at Smithfield, where they had
witnessed the woman found guilty of witchcraft dying in the flames.
For a small chicken he handed over one penny, as she had instructed.
But the trader, it seemed, had been instructed differently and
demanded another halfpenny. 'I have been advised to pay only a
penny,' replied Christopher.

The trader laughed. 'Then you won't be eating chicken for your
dinner, sir. A penny-halfpenny it is and you won't find cheaper.'

'Why has the price gone up, goodman?'

'It's the false coins, sir. Never know when you might take one by
mistake. Have to cover the risk.'

'I thought the counterfeits were only testons, and they with the
Dudley emblem. Easily detected.'

The trader dropped his voice. 'Can't be sure of it, sir, and no telling what the mint might mix with a little silver to make it go further. My father spoke of the trouble naughty money caused in the time of King Henry. False testons one day, crowns made of tin the next, I should not be surprised. A penny-halfpenny, if you please.' Christopher shrugged and gave him a halfpenny. 'Thank you, sir. I see you have a full purse. Take care. There are cutpurses about.'

Christopher moved on. At the next stall he asked the price of a pound of good mutton. 'A penny-halfpenny last week,' replied the trader, 'two pence this.'

'Is there bad money about?' he asked.

'No more than usual so far, sir, but there are rumours.' He took the two pennies Christopher gave him and handed over the mutton. It was a poor start. Only two purchases and a penny over Katherine's prices already.

It was no better in Cheapside. A penny-halfpenny for six eggs, two and a half pence for a small loaf of bread and two pence for six ounces of hard cheese. Everywhere the same story — traders in fear of counterfeit or devalued coins and raising their prices accordingly.

If the testons were intended to cause panic, they were succeeding. The price increases had been sudden and steep. If they continued, two pennies would become three, then four, then five until the poorest could no longer afford to eat. That would mean violence on the streets, more crime, more beggars, more homeless families, more dead children. The spreaders of rumours were as guilty as the coiners. Reality and perception confused and leading to disorder, even chaos. Leicester was right. What society could survive without faith in its currency? And that, of course, was why public conversation of it was against the law.

A pedlar had taken up position at the Eastcheap end of the market. An ancient pony stood beside him, two large sacks slung over its sway back. The pedlar held up a bottle. 'Less meat, good people, and more wine. Wine to sharpen the blade and bring a smile to her face.' He looked around the thin crowd that had gathered in the hope of a bargain. The wine would certainly have been stolen and probably watered. 'Excellent Spanish wine for but a few pennies. Take a bottle home and you won't be sorry.'

'No, but she might be,' shouted a voice from the back.

Christopher was about to part with a few pennies when suddenly the pedlar put his bottle back in one of the sacks and took up the pony's leading rein. 'Constables on the horizon,' he said, 'but the wine will be as good tomorrow.'

Christopher could see no constables. The pedlar would have a boy, his son perhaps, perched among the kites on a roof, whose job it was to signal if he spotted a constable approaching. A pity, a few bottles of cheap wine would have made up for the cost of the eggs and cheese.

Once again he was tempted to visit Ell. Truth to tell he was always tempted to visit Ell, although he preferred not to admit as much to himself. He had no real reason to do so — she was entirely reliable. If she said she would let him know if she had anything to tell him, she would do so. With the lovely Ell, whore and intelligencer, he had never had cross words and she had never let him down. Let her sleep or swive or do whatever she was doing without interference from him.

Christopher sensed the shadow before he saw him. The man was there somewhere, hidden among the traders and the bickering clusters of men and women complaining about the prices they were having to pay, or he was lurking in the shadows, his eyes fixed on his quarry.

He managed not to turn suddenly but took his time, pretending to think about another purchase, and giving the hunter no cause for alarm. He made his way slowly along the line of stalls until he reached the corner of Gutter Lane. There he turned into the lane and immediately quickened his pace, hoping the shadow would follow him. A narrow alley ran off the lane about halfway along it. He ducked into it, put down his bag and waited. When he heard footsteps approaching, he took the poniard from his belt and held it ready to strike.

The footsteps stopped. Christopher saw in his mind's eye the shadow hesitating before going further into the lane. He willed him to carry on. But the shadow had thought better of venturing further. The footsteps retreated.

Christopher stepped out from his hiding place in time to see a hat he recognized disappearing back down the lane. He shouted in vain for the man to stop and sprinted after him, hoping to catch him before he reached the safety of Cheapside.

It was a forlorn hope. Christopher was not the only one to sense the presence of another. In the lane, his shadow had sensed him. By the time Christopher reached the corner, the hat had gone.

Once again he had come close but the man who watched him had escaped. He went back to retrieve his bag.

The bread and the cheese had been not less than two days old and he had left the chicken to cook for too long. Even washed down with a decent claret it had been a poor affair. Damn the shadow and damn Katherine. Leaving him to fend for himself was like throwing a man who could swim only feebly into the sea, and she knew it.

He swallowed the last of the wine. Was she mocking him? Was she waiting to see how long he stayed afloat before rescuing him? Or would she let him drown? Should he fight against the waves or pretend to sink below them?

He sat up straight. Through the fog of drink, a thought was trying to find expression. Fool that he was for finishing the bottle. The thought was elusive. Something to do with order and disorder. He tried to concentrate but it was no good. Whatever it was would have to keep until his mind was working better.

He spoke aloud. 'Next time, sir, whoever you are, next time, you will come too close and I will snare you and find out who you are.'

That night it was not burning witches or screaming babies but the Petit Pont in Paris where he and Sir Francis Walsingham had found themselves trapped by mobs of blood-crazed Catholics in search of Protestant prey. Sir Francis had bravely faced down their leader and they had escaped. In the dream he was not with Sir Francis but Katherine and they did not face down the mob but threw themselves off the bridge and into the Seine. He woke, his forehead damp with sweat, struggling to take a breath of air. Before Paris he had never suffered from such night terrors. Now they plagued him whenever they pleased.

It was too early to rise. If Katherine were beside him, they would make love and go back to sleep. Without Katherine, sleep would not come and he could only wait for dawn. At least, since the window had been mended by Joan's cousin, the bed chamber was tolerably warm. The thought jogged his memory. Joan might indeed know of a remedy for his hand. He would ask her. No more duplicitous apothecaries would gain from his ailment but Joan would surely give him honest advice.

Order and disorder. Bluff and deception. Why had the words given him pause? He remembered the blind frustration of being unable to play a piece properly until he realized that the composer had written the music on five lines instead of six. The result had been chaos.

Chaos. The word came from the ancient Greek for what existed before the world began. Or was it an empty void between the world of the gods and the world of man? Or both? It was certainly Greek. He could visualize the letters. *Chi, alpha, omicron, sigma – XAOΣ.*

It jumped at him. The first letter, *chi*, was formed in the shape of an *X*. Was his memory playing tricks or had *chi* been used by the ancients to signify a state of chaos? Why did that suddenly matter? Because what he had thought was a cross might just as well have been the letter *chi*. The slogans were marked with it, as was the *Book of Martyrs* in St Paul's church. A cross signified plague yet had been daubed on healthy houses, and it had been carved into the dead man's face. False coins, plague crosses, the writer's mark – all intended to cause panic, fear and chaos?

He abandoned the warmth of his bed, pulled on breeches and shirt and went down to his study. There was a flicker of life still in the fire. He threw a handful of kindling on it and gave it a poke. The ashes sparked and the kindling caught. He lit a candle and sat and watched as the flames took hold.

Was he being absurdly fanciful and too clever for his own good? How many men in London would recognize a Greek letter? And what would it mean to those who did? Nothing.

Yet the idea nagged at him. He thought about Warwick's advice. If their enemy was playing a game, the letter could be the connection between his moves. But why *chi*, not *alpha* or *omega*? Because his purpose was chaos. And he was willing to use violence to achieve it. The attacks on Isaac and Wetherby could be explained, that on Ell's gentleman could only be guessed at. Perhaps he had been a piece that had to be sacrificed. Perhaps.

His mind was too active to return to the bed chamber. He was beyond sleep. He sat in the study, examining the facts, as a lawyer should, considering the evidence, and searching for flaws in his argument. He found none but that was not enough. He must test his ideas on another. Not Warwick, he was not ready for Warwick, and he doubted Katherine would speak to him. Roland Wetherby would be his sounding board.

Daniel Cardoza arrived at dawn. 'Dr Radcliff, my father died last night,' he said simply. 'My mother wished you to know at once.' The boy's face was drawn with exhaustion and he had been weeping.

They had eaten together and given thanks for Isaac's recovery but even so to a Jewish family sympathy would have been inappropriate. Christopher blinked away a tear and put a hand on Daniel's shoulder. 'Your father was a good man and my friend. I shall miss him and respect his memory.'

'Thank you, doctor. He will be buried today. Although we will receive visitors of our faith during our period of mourning, my mother asks that, as a Christian, you do not call until the seven days of *shiva* are over. It is her wish.'

'Of course, Daniel. Tell your mother, please, that I will call after you have observed *shiva* and that your family will be in my thoughts.'

'I will. Good day, Dr Radcliff.'

Two murders now, one of an unknown gentleman, the other of a dear friend. More pain, more death. More chaos?

CHAPTER 19

Dr Mendes had warned them but still it was a shock. When a man is alive, however sick or injured, there remains a spark of hope. When that spark disappears with the spark of life, the finality is brutal.

Christopher had never dealt well with death. He had watched both his parents die from plague and in Paris he had seen death in terrible forms. And in a fit of anger he had killed a man in a brawl. But without the comfort of prayer — a comfort he had forsaken — he found it difficult to accept loss. He had learned, however, that the best remedy for grief was action.

Unable to face Fleet Street, where he must pass Isaac's shop, he took a wherry from Blackfriars to Whitehall steps and walked from there up to the Holbein Gate. For once, he paid no heed to the river — his thoughts were on Isaac and Sarah and their family. Daniel Cardoza was not much younger than he had been when his father died. Unlike him, however, Daniel had a grieving mother and two younger siblings, for whom he would now be responsible. Not in law — he was too young for that — but in practice. For all the support of the Marrano community, it would be a heavy burden for him.

At that hour, Roland Wetherby was barely awake. 'By Jesus, Christopher,' he protested at the door to his apartment, 'may a man not wash and dress before receiving visitors?' Then, seeing Christopher's expression, he reached out to take his arm and his tone became serious. 'What is it?' he asked.

'Isaac has died.'

'Come in, my friend, and tell me.'

Christopher kept his account brief. When it was done Wetherby cursed. 'May the man who did this rot forever in the depths of hell. I did not know Isaac Cardoza well but I know he was your friend and our world will be a poorer place for his loss.'

'It will and I will find his killer. Also, there is a matter upon which I need your advice.'

'Anything if it helps us find Isaac's killer.'

Christopher told him about his encounter with the shadow and the thoughts that had come during the night. 'Am I being fanciful, Roland?' he asked. 'Or might there be some substance to the idea?'

Wetherby considered. 'Not fanciful and we have no better explanation for the marks. But even if it is so and our enemy is playing a game whose purpose is simply to confuse and frighten, we do not know *why*. Nor does the idea lead us in any direction other than the one we are set on. Have you heard any more from Ell Cole?'

'Not yet.'

'Then we must try again and this time we must succeed.'

Christopher shook his head. 'If you mean that we will set another trap, I forbid it, Roland. Our watcher knows you and will be on the lookout for you. I do not wish to lose another friend.'

'What else do you propose, Christopher?' Wetherby's voice was suddenly shrill. 'Or are we to do nothing?' Christopher stared at him. 'Forgive me — that was unfair.'

'So it was and I will not put you in danger again. Next time the blow may kill you.'

'Or you.'

'Or me or Ell or, for all we know, our gracious queen.'

Wetherby threw up his hands. 'God's wounds, but I pray not. The French and the Spanish would be in London within the week.' He paused. 'Could they be behind all this?'

'I have considered it, of course, and they may be. Chaos and insurrection in London would certainly suit their purpose. But for now put your mind to it from the safety of this palace.'

'Must I remind you once more of the bullet that struck down the traitor Berwick?'

'I am serious, Roland. You are more use to me safe and thinking than in danger on the streets. Think of Isaac Cardoza if you believe otherwise.'

At the door Wetherby asked, 'Did you know that Leicester returned last night?'

'I did not. Thank you for the warning.'

Katherine too must be told, much as he would prefer not to call at Wood Street and half hoped that she would not be at home. Then he would be able to leave a message with Isabel Tranter.

Katherine was at home. 'Christopher, have I not made my feelings clear?' she asked, barring the door.

'Abundantly. Isaac Cardoza is dead. I thought to tell you.'

'Well, now you have and I am sorry for it.'

'The prices in the markets are rising. I paid two and a half pennies for a small loaf.'

A glimmer of a smile crossed Katherine's face. 'I trust it was fresh.'

'It was not. How fares Joan Willys?'

'Better than her mother who does little but weep and curse the Scrope wench.'

'Should I visit her?'

'No. I will see that Joan and her mother are safe. You be about your business.' Katherine made to close the door.

'One thing more, Katherine. Unless Alice Scrope has a hoard of coins hidden in her house, someone gave her the money for the hearing and will have to give her more for a trial. If we can discover who that is, we may be able to help Joan.'

'I have thought of that. Is there anything more?'

It was not the time. 'No.'

'Then I shall bid you farewell. And buy fresh bread in future.'

Thinking he would do just that even if the price was another halfpenny, he made for Cheapside. Approaching the market, he knew there was trouble. The sounds were not those of bartering voices but of timber breaking and iron crashing against iron. He hurried towards them.

Cheapside was in disarray. Stalls were being overturned and smashed. Apprentices picked fruit and stones from the ground and pelted the stallholders, who were battering them with lengths of wood and iron bars.

A boy went down screaming and clutching his leg. Another bent over him to help, only to be laid out with a blow to the head. Two stallholders picked him up by the ankles, shook out his purse and dropped him on to the cobbles. Blood was streaming from his head. Christopher barged into the mêlée and dragged him out.

Crouched over the stricken boy, he looked back over his shoulder. The battle was raging. A tall youth thrust a buckler into a trader's face, which spurted a fountain of blood. A stallholder jabbed a stick into another apprentice's groin, watched him collapse and landed a heavy kick to his head. In no time, the street was strewn with wounded bodies and the remains of broken stalls. There was no sign of a constable.

The apprentices began to gather up their wounded and with-draw. The traders watched them go, brandishing their weapons in triumph and shouting abuse. Christopher approached one of them, a vendor of sweets and confections from whom he sometimes bought Katherine's biscuits.

'What has happened here, fellow?' he asked.

'It's the prices we are having to charge, sir,' replied the confec-tioner, struggling to regain his breath. 'Some can no longer afford to buy from us, although we try to explain why a halfpenny bag of almond sweets now costs more than twice as much as it did two weeks since. The young men will not accept the need for it.'

'That is no surprise but why so sharp an increase? Are almonds suddenly dearer now than they used to be?'

The confectioner wiped his brow with the back of his hand. 'No, sir. It is fear of the coins we take. A busy trader cannot examine every one and must protect himself against the bad ones by increasing his prices. What else is he to do?'

'Are there more bad coins about?'

'The word is that they are breeding like maggots.'

'Have you suffered many?'

'I, sir? No, I confess that I have not but others say they have and I am expecting the worst.'

Christopher picked an almond biscuit from the cobbles and wiped it on his gown. 'How much for this, goodman? I will not pay full price for a biscuit that has lain in the dirt.'

The confectioner looked at him and smiled. 'Seeing as it's you, sir, there will be no charge. Enjoy the biscuit, but next time you come I fear the price may have risen again. So don't leave it too long.'

'Thank you. I won't.'

Nibbling at the biscuit, which truth to tell was too sweet for his taste, he made his way through the debris scattered down the street and the vendors struggling to rebuild their stalls from the wreckage the apprentices had left behind.

Perception and reality. Fact and rumour. In the matter of currency, one could be as damaging as the other. Once the earl had spoken with his brother, Christopher would be summoned. Would that he had better news to report. Finding a quiet time simply to think or play was not so easy in the employ of the Earl of Leicester, whatever Warwick had urged him to do. There were ever matters to be dealt with, often urgent, sometimes important matters, and the mood on the streets of London was both.

Leicester had been to Kenilworth to oversee arrangements for the queen's progress, although it was still more than twelve months away. What was it about her progresses, that were considered so important to the good government of her realm and which occupied so much of his time? To be sure, they gave her people — not many, but some — the chance to see their queen in the flesh rather than in a painting or on the face of a coin, but upwards of a thousand men and women travelling from town to town had to be billeted and provisioned and equipped with mounts and carriages and all manner of household necessaries. The cost to the exchequer was prodigious and a considerable burden to the landowners with whom she and her courtiers stayed. Leicester, not to be outdone by anyone, was planning displays of jousting, bear-baiting, archery and fireworks, hunting trips in the Warwickshire countryside, and feasts with enough meat and drink to feed half of London for a day. He had spoken of his plans not boastfully but with pride at being able to serve the queen with such splendour. Yet could the cost really be justified? Or could it not?

Elizabeth, of course, was very far from the first monarch to set store by such displays of extravagance. A hundred years earlier, Philip the Good had turned the quietly prosperous town of Bruges into a haven for artists and writers as well as for wealthy merchants and bankers by going to extraordinary lengths to create an illusion of even greater opulence. A golden throne actually made of wood, for example, and unproven stories of a treasury bursting with gold and silver. And the queen's grandfather, King Henry VII, had been among those who had followed Philip's example and passed the tradition on to his son and thence to his granddaughter.

There had been a purpose to their illusions, of course, just as there was to Elizabeth's. They were designed to impress the impressionable and the bigger and bolder they were, the deeper the impression of a country secure and at peace. A progress of the queen, a dozen courtiers and a small troop of guards would hardly have the same effect.

Were the coiners of the false testons up to the same trick? Were they intent upon creating exactly the opposite illusion to that intended by Leicester — one of an unreliable currency, a state of unrest and an impotent government? The traders at Smithfield and Cheapside had spoken of their fears but none had claimed to have held a false coin in his hand. Their fear was that of the unknown, of what might happen, of consequences only guessed at. Spanish ships in the Thames could be seen and sunk by cannon. This was hidden, secret, insidious and just as dangerous. England's enemies across the narrow sea would be watching closely.

And the questions remained: who and why?

CHAPTER 20

The summons to Whitehall came by messenger the next day. Christopher ran a razor over his face, rubbed his teeth with a rag, combed the knots out of his hair and put on the cleanest shirt he could find. Damn that magistrate for his stupidity. Joan Willys should be at home with her mother and looking after him. As it was, he would have to find a laundress.

This time there was no waiting in the antechamber. He was shown straight in to Leicester's apartment, where both earls were waiting for him. 'Dr Radcliff,' said Leicester without preamble, 'I am grieved to learn from my brother that since my departure you have made little progress. Indeed, I hear stories of riots in the markets and an attack on Mr Wetherby. Are they true?'

'They are, my lord. The market traders are much alarmed by rumours of false coins and the losses they will have to bear.'

'Rumours, I suppose, caused by the treasonous testons bearing our family emblem, a bag of which now rests in a secure place in this palace.'

'I believe it likely, my lord, although I cannot yet say how this has happened.'

'I have told Dr Radcliff that I believe that the coiners, whoever they are, may be playing a game with us. That might also explain the recent slogans,' said Warwick.

'And the murder of my intelligencer, Isaac Cardoza, and the removal of a body from the deadhouse.'

'What are we doing about it?' snapped Leicester.

'Thanks to my lord Warwick, Mr Martin has proved helpful and has given us the names of two minters dismissed from their posts.'

'I am aware of this. What else?'

'We are searching for them. Meanwhile, there have been no more slogans or false plague crosses.'

'I suppose that is something for which to be thankful but really I am beginning to wonder if I should appoint another man to the task. What is your opinion, Ambrose?'

Ambrose Dudley hesitated before replying. 'I doubt another man would have achieved more than has Dr Radcliff. He seems to me to have acted with the energy and thought that you would have expected, brother.'

Christopher silently thanked him. An unsmiling man but a fair one. More predictable than Leicester. What had the other brothers been like? he wondered. John, Henry and the unfortunate Guilford, husband of Jane Grey and executed with his father for his part in the ill-fated attempt to make her queen. To take such a risk, Guilford must surely have been more Leicester than Warwick, but the others?

'Hmm. Perhaps it is my ill humour to blame. As always, my dear brother, I bow to your judgement.' Leicester fixed his dark eyes on Christopher. 'But be in no doubt, doctor, this affair must be brought to an end and soon or even my lord Warwick's patience will run out.'

Better not say that he was hopeful or confident — the words went down badly the last time he used them. 'Be assured of my determination to bring it to an end, my lord.'

'Good.' Leicester's tone softened. 'I am grieved that your Jewish goldsmith has died. Will you replace him?'

'In due course, my lord. For now I am fully occupied upon the task that you have given me.'

'Are you? No more appearances at the sessions house in front of the magistrate?'

Good God, was there nothing the man did not know? His spies must lurk behind every wall and in every corner. 'The circumstances were particular. I see no reason for them to be repeated.'

'Then be about your work, Dr Radcliff.'

Christopher bowed and took his leave. An uncomfortable meeting but no worse than he had expected. Thank God for Warwick.

He should call on Roland but he lacked the energy. The encounter had drained him.

Ell had spoken of a mood — intangible, invisible, yet unmistakable. And she was right. Walking down the Strand, he too could sense it. More beggars outside King Henry's Savoy Hospital, more whores in dark doorways, the stalls on the corner of Carting Lane deserted and a heaviness to the air, a blackness that in summer might presage a thunderstorm. In February it felt more like the end of days. He could not help but hold on to his poniard tightly, and looked constantly back over his shoulder. But if the shadow was there, he kept well hidden. There was no sign of him. Was this what the coiners and slogan-writers, the unseen creators of chaos, intended?

With a last look around, he unlocked his door and stepped inside the house. He made straight for the kitchen and poured himself a beaker of ale from the pot on the table. The beaker still held the dregs from his breakfast, but the ale tasted well enough.

He was carrying it to the study when he heard a gentle knock. He had seen no one but someone had seen him. Beaker in hand, he opened the door to find a slight figure standing there. 'Good day, Dr Rad,' she said with a wink and a nod at the beaker, 'you look busy. Can I come in?'

He stepped aside. 'Come in, Ell. I am all alone. I hope you weren't seen.'

'No need to worry, doctor, there's not much of me. I can hide behind a militiaman's pike staff if I have to.'

He gave her a mug of ale and sat her in the study. 'Sorry there's no fire, Ell. My housekeeper's in Newgate.'

'What's she done?'

'Nothing except be accused of being a witch, which she is not.'

Ell scoffed. 'Another one. There's too many telling lies about their neighbours. Hope she doesn't go to the sessions.'

'So do I. What brings you here, Ell? Why no note under the door?'

'I knew Mistress Allington was away so it would be safe to come and I've been asking around about those men you mentioned. The Pryses, father and son. Word is, they only lived in Southwark for a short time and then went to the town of Guildford to look for work. Where is Guildford, Dr Rad?'

'Not far. About thirty miles south of London on the Portsmouth road. I've not been there.'

'Nor me. Never been further south than Southwark, thank the Lord.'

'How did you find this out, Ell?'

'You told me that the son, Hugh, was fond of the ladies and fond of his ale. Liked plenty of both. I found a lady who knew him and remembered him saying he was going to a town named Guildford. Didn't mean much to her but the name stuck. Proper swordsman by all accounts and with drink inside him talked more than a priest on a Sunday. Had a temper, too.'

'Could she be mistaken?'

'Could be, of course, and there's no saying he's still there. It's a year or two ago. Still, I thought you should know so I risked coming.'

'You were right to do so. Guildford. It's a start. Well done, Ell.'

'Thank you, doctor. Well enough done for a crown?'

Christopher took a crown from his purse and handed it over. 'Certainly. Check it though, it might be false.'

Ell chortled. 'Don't think so, not with you chasing the coiners.' The brown eyes sparkled. 'Anything else I can do for you?'

Katherine had left him, his spirits were low and the thought of a woman's touch — especially this woman's — was almost irresistible. Almost. 'Can you cook, Ell?'

'Cook? I'm a whore, Dr Rad, in case you hadn't noticed. I earn my keep in my bed chamber, not in a fucking kitchen. I'd poison you, like as not.'

'Better leave me to manage, then.' Christopher stood up. 'I'll see you safely out.'

'Tush. One day you'll say yes, doctor. That's if I ever ask again.'

In spite of everything he couldn't help but smile. 'Keep asking, Ell. One day I'll say yes.'

He opened the door, made sure there was no one lurking on the street, and let her out. 'Go safely, Ell. If you don't hear from me I shall be in Guildford.'

'Hope there's not a single woman under a hundred in the place. That would teach you a lesson.'

A thought struck him. 'One more thing, Ell. My housekeeper, Joan Willys, lives with her crippled mother near Wood Street. Mistress Allington is looking after the old woman while Joan is in Newgate. It was a neighbour, Alice Scrope, who accused her of witchcraft. Can you find the house and keep an eye on her whenever you have the chance? Regular customers, brawling, drunkenness — anything that can be used against her.'

Again the eyes sparkled. 'A whore, is she, doctor? It's a respectable trade, you know, and we look out for each other. Yes, for you of course I will. And for Joan Willys, poor wretch. She won't be any more a witch than I am.'

'Thank you, Ell. Take care.'

'Goodbye, Dr Rad.' A flashing smile and she was gone.

He watched her go and wondered why he had not said yes at once. Next time, if Katherine was still sulking, perhaps he would.

'I had not expected to see you again quite so soon, Dr Radcliff,' said Leicester. 'Is once not enough in a single day?'

'My apologies, my lord. I would not have troubled you had the matter not been urgent. It seems that the Pryses, John and Hugh, the minters who were dismissed for brawling with a supervisor and who we believe might be involved in the counterfeiting of the testons, left London for Guildford. I request your permission to travel there at once.'

'Guildford. Not much of a place to hide in. I will issue a travel warrant and have it delivered to you. Are you intending to travel alone? What about Wetherby?'

'With your permission, my lord, and if he is well enough, I thought to take Roland Wetherby with me. Two heads, two pairs of eyes.'

'Quite. Take Wetherby. He has served us well in the past. I will furnish you with two good mounts.'

There was no avoiding it. He could hardly ask for a carriage and thirty miles was too far to walk. 'I am obliged, my lord.'

Wetherby was in his apartment, reading a book by the window. 'Rabelais,' he said, holding it up for inspection, '*Gargantua*. Shock, bluff and paradox – I thought to read it again.'

'You will have little time for reading, Roland. Tomorrow we leave for Guildford.'

'Do we?'

'If your health permits.'

Wetherby put down the book. 'Naturally it permits. Now tell me why we shall be travelling to Guildford. I know of no particular entertainments to be had in the town.'

CHAPTER 21

A pale sun in a clear sky hinted at the first signs of spring. Although Christopher never felt comfortable on a horse, claiming that his legs were too long for riding, there was some benefit to working for the queen's Master of Horse. Leicester had provided them with as fine a pair of black coursers from the Whitehall stables as a man would find anywhere in England, and saddlery made to his own orders by the royal saddler and polished until the leather had taken on a deep richness that did justice to the horses. A pair of decent palfreys would have done as well but the royal stables did not provide palfreys, decent or not.

They each carried a leather bag slung over the saddle for their travelling necessaries and full purses tucked under their shirts. Wetherby wore a hat and coat trimmed with rabbit fur, and a pair of leather gloves that reached almost to his elbows, Christopher his thick coat and academic cap. 'You will be cold, Christopher,' Wetherby had warned him.

'I hope so,' he had replied. 'It will numb the pain of sitting on this beast.'

If the state of the highway allowed, they would try to cover the thirty miles or so to Guildford in a single day. Barring accidents or the throwing of a shoe, it should be within the range of the horses and would spare them a night in a miserable coaching inn where the food would be slop and they would be more at risk of being robbed than they were on the road. For the unwary traveller, robbers and rogues posted accomplices in the inns to alert them to those who ordered the best wine and the most expensive rooms. For that reason they would not even stop at an inn to eat.

Once over the bridge and through Southwark they broke into a canter. Here, so close to London, the villagers along the way had made some effort to discharge their duty to keep the road in a reasonable state of repair and the pitfalls and potholes were few. Wetherby, naturally, rode well, his back straight and his balance steady. Christopher at least did not fall off.

At midday it was just about warm enough to break their journey. They hobbled the horses and let them find what grazing they could on the strips of fields that flanked the highway, while they refreshed themselves from Wetherby's supplies. The palace kitchen had provided good beer, manchet bread and a roasted capon, which he cut in half. Sitting under a leafless oak by the roadside, they saw no one and heard nothing but a little birdsong.

'Strange how a man's actions may be the same in one place as another but be seen as those of either a wise man or a lunatic,' said Wetherby through a mouthful of chicken.

The ride had done nothing for Christopher's spirits. 'If you must speak with a full mouth, Roland,' he grumbled, 'kindly do not speak in riddles. I am not in the mood for it.'

'Hardly a riddle, dear doctor. I merely meant that if we sat with our beer and bread on the side of the Strand, we would certainly encounter ridicule and abuse. Here, however, a passing traveller would barely give us a second glance.'

'If we took our dinner on the paving of the Strand we would most likely be removed by the constables directly to Bedlam and it would be no more than we deserve.'

Wetherby threw away his chicken bone and stood up. 'You are an ill-humoured companion, Christopher. I trust that your mood will improve once this journey is over.'

'As do I,' replied Christopher. 'My legs ache and my backside has not been as sore since my father took a birch stick to it for stealing apples from the parson's tree.'

Wetherby laughed. 'Now that is a sight I would wish to have seen.'

They remounted and set off again, riding side by side but saying little. The further from London, the worse the highway and the more care they had to take. It would be all too easy for one of the horses to break a leg in a pothole. Here and there they passed an isolated farm or a cluster of houses but very few travellers either on horseback or on foot, and hardly anything that might be called a village. As the population of London had grown, so that of the countryside around it had declined. Poor harvests, the closure of the religious houses, plague and pestilence had rendered life intolerably harsh for those who tried to eke a living from the land.

The distress could be seen not only in the poor state of the highway but in the deserted cottages and hovels and the lack of animals on the land. Where were the sheep and goats? Where were the pigs and cows? The answer was plain enough — when nothing else had remained, they had been slaughtered and eaten. And then their starving owners had walked to London where they found neither work, nor shelter, nor charity. If they got through the city gates at all, they were likely to be arrested for vagrancy and to end their days in prison or in the river. Jumping off London Bridge had become frighteningly popular in spite of the Church's warnings of eternal damnation for all who took their own lives.

Approaching Guildford, they clattered across a stone bridge over a narrow river, flowing fast after the winter rain and snow, past a silent mill and a deserted friary. 'Dominicans,' said Wetherby scornfully as they rode by.

'How do you know?'

'Looks gloomy enough. Miserable lot, the Black Friars. Or were. Who would not be, dressed from top to toe in black every day?'

The town itself, even at a time of such widespread hardship in the countryside, had a prosperous look to it. From a grammar school at the top of a hill to the River Wey at its foot, a broad street ran down between new-built brick dwellings on either side. Here and there a tailor or a cobbler had set up shop among them.

They walked their mounts carefully over the cobbles and down the hill. To their left, beyond the houses, stood the remains of a castle – Norman by the look of it – while from their right came the distant roar of furnaces. Christopher looked at Wetherby and raised his eyebrows.

'Glass-making, Christopher. The French are very skilled at it. I believe there are many of them employed here.'

'You are well informed, Roland.'

Wetherby coughed. 'Yesterday, after you had left, I sought out a friend, a French friend, who I knew had lived here and had been involved in the glass trade. He was able to provide me with much useful intelligence about the town.'

'I don't suppose he was able to tell you where we might find the Pryses.'

'I did not ask.'

'Or an inn of the quality we require.'

'About that, happily, I did inquire. It seems that the Prince Harry is the best Guildford has to offer for the weary traveller.'

Christopher looked to left and right and down the hill towards the river and fields beyond. Prosperous the town might be but it was neither Cambridge nor London: no pupils, no milling crowds, no hawkers or beggars — and no hint of an inn. 'And where is this splendid establishment?' he asked.

'My excellent friend informed me that it was at the bottom of the hill on the left side. We are to look for a sign above a wide arch.' They rode slowly on until Wetherby swept off his hat and held it out with his arm extended. 'And unless I am mistaken, here it is, awaiting our arrival.'

They dismounted and led the horses under the arch and into a broad cobbled yard. An ostler came running out to take their bags. He summoned a stable boy who led the horses off with instructions to brush them down and give them a good feed.

Inside the inn, a fire was blazing. The innkeeper appeared through a door at the back of the taproom. 'Good day, sirs,' he said. 'A room for the night, would it be?'

'Two rooms,' replied Wetherby. 'The best you have and not to be shared. We do not know for how long. And we will eat in an hour. What have you to offer?'

The innkeeper rubbed his hands together. For a room let to a single traveller who was not willing to share, he could charge five times his usual rate. 'Good pottage, sir, bread baked this morning, and the best ale in the county.'

'It will have to do. We will see the rooms now.'

The rooms were next door to each other. Christopher dumped his bag on the bed and asked for hot water to be brought. While the innkeeper scuttled off to fetch it, he unpacked the bag, put the contents in an oak coffer provided for the purpose, and tested the bed. His ankles hung over the end but otherwise it was passable. The mattress was filled with feathers and the sheets looked tolerably clean. Roland had done well to discover the Prince Harry. God willing, his efforts would be rewarded and the Pryses would be found.

The innkeeper himself served them. They brushed aside his questions about their purpose, saying only that they were on important business, and sent him off to fetch more ale. Roland put down his spoon, set aside his bowl and looked around the taproom to be sure he was not being overheard. 'By now,' he said, 'half of Guildford will know that two gentlemen on fine black coursers have arrived in the town and will be asking themselves what these gentlemen's business can be. It is a little early in the year for us to be buying wool, although I suppose we might be buyers of glass for a wealthy London merchant or for one of the guilds.'

'I had thought of that, of course,' replied Christopher a little testily. 'Our best strategy is to come as close to the truth as we can. We will say that we are officials of the Royal Mint, looking for John and Hugh Pryse who we believe moved to the town from London a year or two since, because a new mint is planned for Guildford and will be in need of experienced workers.'

'What about the circumstances of their departure from the mint? They may be known.'

'Our need is too great to let that stand in our way.'

'How many mints are there outside London?'

'Seven, I think.'

Wetherby rubbed his chin. 'I suppose it might work. Or the Pryses might take fright and disappear.'

Christopher had not yet recovered from the journey and his backside still ached. 'Unless you have a better idea, it will have to work. We will begin tomorrow by speaking to the justice and asking about in the market and the inns. If the word spreads that the Pryses are being sought, it will reach them.'

'In a town of no more than fifteen hundred souls, it should. If they are here.'

Christopher stood up. 'If not, we will return to London empty-handed. Now I am going to my bed in the hope that it will afford some comfort.'

'And I will finish my ale and follow shortly.'

Christopher locked the chamber door carefully, undressed and lay on the bed. They had spent the best part of a day in the saddle and had little reason to suppose that the journey would prove worthwhile — just a guess that the Pryses were involved in the false testons and the word of a Southwark doxy that Hugh Pryse had left London for Guildford more than a year since. Hardly proof incontrovertible.

The justice, Richard Lovell, was as different from Gilbert Knoyll as he could possibly have been. In appearance he might have been a prosperous farmer — ruddy-faced, well fed and dressed in a plain black coat and grey hose. In manner, he was cheerful and welcoming.

When a servant showed Christopher and Roland into his parlour, he rose to greet them. 'And what service may I perform for two gentlemen of the Royal Mint?' he asked after they had introduced themselves. He spoke well, in a deep baritone with a hint of Hampshire or Dorset.

They needed Lovell's help and it would be a mistake to deceive him. Christopher explained the true purpose of their visit and the deception they had agreed upon. 'I fear that the name means nothing to me, Dr Radcliff,' he said. 'Pryse is certainly not a name common in the county and I would have remembered it if the men you seek were here and their name had been mentioned. Could they have moved on?'

'They could, Mr Lovell,' said Wetherby, 'but if they have, we hoped that someone would know where they have gone.'

'Then let us make your search more widely known,' replied the justice with a wide grin. 'I will have a notice printed asking for information on their whereabouts on a matter to their great advantage.' He paused and chose a pen from the box on his desk. 'Would you care to offer a small reward to the provider of such information? I do find coin of the realm to be a powerful motivation.' Realizing what he had said, he laughed. 'I intended no jest, sirs. Coin of the realm, money, the mint. Merely a turn of phrase.'

'Have no care of it, Mr Lovell,' said Christopher. 'And, yes, I believe we can offer a small reward for information that leads us to the Pryses. I suggest two pounds.'

Lovell made a note on a sheet of paper. 'Splendid. Leave it to me, gentlemen. If the men you seek are in Guildford, I have no doubt that we shall find them. Did you know that there was a mint here in Norman times?'

'I had heard this,' replied Wetherby without hesitation. 'But did it not close long ago?'

'It did. I do not even know exactly where it was.'

They thanked Mr Lovell and took their leave. 'How did you know about the Norman mint?' asked Christopher as they walked back to the Prince Harry.

'I did not. I merely thought that as senior mint officials, we should have known.'

They checked on the horses, which appeared well cared for by the stable boy, and found a quiet corner in the taproom.

'At least we have an ally in Mr Lovell,' said Christopher. 'Another Gilbert Knoyll would have sorely tested my temper.'

'This afternoon, if I visit the inns and taverns of Guildford, will you go to the market?'

'Beer and wine for you, Roland, sheep and vegetables for me, is that your plan?'

'It is. Let us take dinner and then be about our work.'

Once fed and watered, they went their separate ways, Roland to the nearest tavern, Christopher to the market, where a weeping woman in the stocks was a sharp reminder that Joan Willys was still in Newgate and if sent by a grand jury to the assizes and found guilty of practising witchcraft, she would suffer the same fate. A monstrous injustice which he had so far been unable to prevent.

The market was small compared to Smithfield or Cheapside — merely a dozen or so stalls — but he checked that his purse was safely under his coat and the poniard in his belt. Even here, in a town that seemed peaceful and law-abiding enough, there would be foisters and nippers about, ready to take advantage of an unwary stranger. He started with an unsmiling baker, who shook his head at the mention of the name Pryse and returned his attention to his loaves. It was much the same at the next stall, a cheese-seller, who tried to persuade him to pay two pence for a round cheese with a touch of green to it and which he claimed came from the finest sheep in the county. He too knew nothing of the Pryses.

Conscious of curious eyes on him, he went up and down the lines of stalls, asked the same questions at each one and received the same answers. No one knew of the Pryses or could suggest anyone who might. No one, indeed, was much interested, as soon as they realized that the tall, yellow-haired stranger in a black coat and soft academic cap was not there to spend his money. After two fruitless hours, he returned disappointed to the Prince Harry.

Wetherby had fared no better. 'I have never before visited six taverns in one afternoon and taken not a single drink,' he complained. 'Nor did I learn a thing about the Pryses. The best I got was a silly jest about "Pryses rising". If they are here they must live the lives of hermits.'

Christopher sighed. 'A day spent learning nothing. Let us hope for better tomorrow.' Damnation. It began to look like Ell's intelligence had been wrong and that the Pryses had never been anywhere near Guildford. A journey wasted and, more importantly, they were no further forward in finding the coiners.

CHAPTER 22

'I have thought more about the good Earl of Warwick's suggestion,' said Wetherby the next morning, 'and I believe he is right. Someone is playing a game, or at least enjoying a jest at our expense.'

'Killing Isaac Cardoza was no jest, Roland. I think of him every day and every night.'

'Indeed not. But *Mouldwarp* and *Hempe*, the testons – a bag of which were left outside the house of the Cardozas – the crosses which may or may not signify chaos: all in all a strange confection with no obvious meaning. Shock, confusion and obscurity.'

Christopher waved a finger at Wetherby as a schoolmaster might to admonish a pupil. 'I do believe that you have been reading too much Rabelais. Damned Frenchman.'

'I have. I brought him with me and the more I read of his fantastical creations the more I see of our enemy in him. Stories about giants should be simple tales for children but they are not. The vulgarity, for example, and Rabelais's grievances against the Church are hardly fare for the young. Both *Pantagruel* and *Gargantua* are full of such outbursts. Odd, often incoherent, sometimes funny, sometimes instructional.'

'Are you suggesting that Rabelais is our enemy?'

Wetherby laughed. 'You know perfectly well that he has been dead for twenty years.'

'His son, then?'

'He was a monk. As far as I know he had no son.'

'Then let us please abandon Monsieur Rabelais and turn our minds to the task before us. One of the men I questioned at the mint claimed to have seen Hugh Pryse with a rosary. Let us begin by asking the excellent Mr Lovell if he can suggest where we might start in that direction.'

'How goes your search, gentlemen?' inquired Lovell. 'Have you heard any word of your quarry?'

'No, sir,' replied Christopher. 'Neither market nor taverns proved fruitful. However, we do have a further request to make of you.'

'Of course, doctor. And how may I be of service?'

'We believe that the Pryses are inclined to the old ways of worship.'

Lovell frowned and pursed his lips. 'Catholics?'

'Just so.'

'And you wish me to direct you to those of a similar persuasion?'

'We do.'

Lovell sat back in his chair. 'Of course, as a magistrate, I have taken the oath of allegiance to Her Majesty and am conscious of the grave threat posed by Jesuits arriving from France. I have no sympathy with the trappings of papism or outlandish popish pronouncements, never mind the monstrous papal bull calling on Catholics to rise up against our queen—'

'But?' interrupted Wetherby.

'But, Mr Wetherby, there are men and women of the Catholic faith who worship privately and serve our community well. They are good people who cause no trouble and I would not wish to cause them any.'

'Rest assured, Mr Lovell, that we are not here to seek out Catholics, still less to prosecute them for their beliefs.' Wetherby glanced at Christopher. 'Neither Dr Radcliff nor I hold strong religious views. The coiners we seek, however, are guilty of treason and they must be found and brought to justice before they can do further damage. For this we need your co-operation.'

Lovell nodded. 'Counterfeiting is indeed a serious crime, but still I am reluctant to put anyone in danger on account of their beliefs. Before her excommunication, did our gracious queen herself not say that we all worship the same God and that how we choose to do so is mere detail?'

'She did, Mr Lovell,' replied Christopher, 'and I am wholeheartedly in agreement with her. However, having found no trace of the Pryses by other means, we must try what we can.'

The magistrate's face betrayed nothing and he did not reply immediately. At last he said, 'Very well, gentlemen, with your promise that no harm will come to any man or woman simply on account of their faith, I will speak privately to a friend who may be able to help. Do I have that promise?'

'You do, sir,' said Christopher. 'And we thank you for your co-operation.'

Lovell stood up. 'Return this afternoon at about two. I will do what I can. But remember — I promise nothing and I want no bloodthirsty pursuivants in this town.'

'No more do we,' replied Wetherby. 'And we thank you for your help, sir.'

*

'A good man,' remarked Christopher as they left the magistrate's house. 'Would that all justices were cut from the same cloth. Now, how shall we occupy ourselves until two?'

'Unless you would like to discuss why it is that Rabelais tells us that Gargantua emerged into the world from Gargamelle's ear, in the same manner as Minerva from the head of Jupiter, I suggest we see that the horses are being well taken care of before dining on the best our landlord has to offer at the Prince Harry. A pity you did not bring your lute. You might have passed yourself off as a travelling minstrel and paid for our dinner with a song or two.'

'You try my patience, Roland. Horses first, then food.'

They were back in Richard Lovell's parlour on the stroke of two. He wasted no words. 'I have explained your purpose and given my personal guarantee that you are to be trusted. With that assurance, although today is Sunday, Lady Paulet has agreed to meet with you at her house.'

'Lady Paulet? The name is familiar,' said Wetherby.

'You are too young to have known her, Mr Wetherby, but she was at court during the reign of Queen Mary. A notable beauty by all accounts. Perhaps you have heard the name at Whitehall. Lady Paulet is now past her fiftieth year and feels the passing of time. Her body is frail but her mind is still sharp. She will know at once if you are in any way dissembling and will tell you nothing.'

'There will be no dissembling, Mr Lovell,' replied Christopher, 'and Lady Paulet will be treated with the respect her age and position merit.'

'Good. You will find her house half a mile south of the town on the Portsmouth Road. It stands alone and set back from the highway. It is an old house, built a hundred years ago, and reached by a narrow path between two rows of elms. She is expecting you this afternoon.'

'We are in your debt, sir,' said Wetherby. 'And have no fear that your confidence in us is misplaced.'

'I have no such fear, sir,' replied Lovell, 'but I cannot say that Lady Paulet will be able to assist you. In the meantime, do you wish me to proceed with the notices we discussed? It did occur to me that they might have the opposite effect to that desired and frighten your quarry away.'

Christopher nodded. 'Let us hold them back until we have spoken to Lady Paulet. A more discreet approach is probably better to start with.'

They took their leave. 'Ride or walk?' asked Wetherby outside.

'Walk. It is only half a mile.'

'I thought you would say that.'

They saw the grey-slated roof of the house through the bare branches of the elms as they turned a corner. It stood well back from the highway and without any other dwelling in sight. They turned up the path towards it.

It was two storeys high, the upper storey overhanging the lower, stone- and timber-built, with shuttered windows and an oak door that looked as if it would resist any amount of battering. In its day a grand house, but now old and strangely sad, as if it knew that the end of its life was near. Christopher used the handle of his poniard to rap on the door. Almost immediately they heard the clatter of shoes on a stone floor and the pulling back of bolts.

The door was opened by a white-haired servant, rheumy-eyed and slightly stooped. 'Dr Radcliff and Mr Wetherby?' he inquired and, without waiting for an answer, said: 'Lady Paulet is in her library. Follow me, if you please.'

The library was not a large room and was made smaller by the shelves of books that lined three of its walls. A round table stood in the middle, with four plain chairs around it. On one of them sat Lady Paulet.

Past her fiftieth year, Mr Lovell had said, yet she might easily have been past her sixtieth. A narrow face, deeply lined around the eyes and from nose to chin, grey hair drawn back from the forehead and partly hidden by a black coif, a grey gown, and tiny hands resting on the table. Like her house, the beauty of youth now gone. 'Be seated, gentlemen,' she said, 'I know who you are.' The voice, however, was clear and precise — the voice of a lady accustomed to giving orders.

When they sat facing her, Christopher noticed her eyes. They were the palest shade of blue, unblinking and unafraid. 'Lady Paulet,' he began, 'we are indebted to you for agreeing to see us, the more so on a Sunday. Be assured that we mean you no harm and are concerned only with finding the men we seek. Their name is Pryse, a father and his son.'

'Why do you seek these men, Dr Radcliff?'

'We believe that they are involved in treasonous coining.'

'And why do you think that I can help you?'

'We believe that they left London for Guildford between one and two years ago, and if they continue to worship in the old way Mr Lovell thought that you might be able to direct us to them.'

'So he told me. Richard Lovell is a dear friend and if these men are counterfeiters, they must be found. False coins benefit no one, whatever their faith. I am old enough to remember clearly the problems caused by King Henry's debasements. Silver coins were so contaminated that every man with a hammer and a fire seemed to be making them. I am not sure, however, that I can help you in your search.'

'Coining of any sort is an act of treason, madam,' said Wetherby, 'whether by Puritan, Protestant or Catholic.'

The blue eyes held him in their gaze. 'I am aware of that, sir, but I cannot direct you to two men of whom I have no knowledge. The name Pryse is unfamiliar to me.'

Christopher cursed silently. Why had she agreed to meet them if she could not help? Mr Lovell would certainly have mentioned the name. He stood up. 'Then, madam, we will trouble you no further.'

Lady Paulet waved him down. 'Be seated, doctor. I would not have entertained you without reason. Mass is said here for those who wish to take the sacrament in the true form of the body and blood of our saviour. Very few people are aware of this and Richard Lovell chooses not to interfere. It must remain so.' Again he felt the blue eyes looking deep into his soul.

From somewhere inside her gown, Lady Paulet produced a rosary, which she twisted around her fingers as she spoke. 'Almost two years ago, I was approached by a man who claimed to have recently settled in the area and wished to worship as I do. I do not know how he learned of me. His name was Jack and he claimed to have travelled here from London. He said little but I believed him if only because he did not have the wit to dissemble. He did tell me that he had no wife, but a son, Henry, who did not care to worship with us. Their name was not Pryse. It was Brooke.'

Christopher cursed himself for a fool. Of course a stranger might give any name and be believed. 'What more can you tell us about Jack Brooke, my lady?' he asked.

'Not a great deal. We do not encourage conversation here other than with God and I do not know where they lived.'

'Lived, madam?' asked Wetherby.

'I have not seen Jack Brooke these past six months. I assumed that they had moved away. I do remember, however, mention of a forge. One day Jack came with his hand bandaged. He had burned it in the forge.'

'Did he arrive on foot or on horseback?'

'On foot.'

How far might a man walk to attend Mass? A mile? Two? 'At what time are your Masses held?'

'In winter at six in the evening, in summer at ten.' So a mile or two in the dark. Probably no more than a mile.

'Is there anything more you can tell us about this man, madam?'

'His appearance was unremarkable and his clothes those of a working man. He spoke as a working man of London would — without artifice or pretence. That was partly why I trusted him. I remember nothing more about him.'

'Nothing?'

'As I have said.'

'Then we thank you, my lady. We will leave you now. Come, Roland, we have tired Lady Paulet enough.'

The pale eyes held his. 'Remember, Dr Radcliff, I have trusted you. Do not betray my trust. If the Brookes are innocent of any crime, do not pursue them.'

'If they are innocent,' said Wetherby, 'be assured, my lady, that they will not be pursued or harmed in any way.'

'Then God go with you.'

The ancient servant showed them out. They had barely walked down the path to the highway before Wetherby was complaining.

'Have a care, Christopher. My legs are not as long as yours and you are testing me beyond endurance. For the love of God, slow down. A few minutes more or less will make no difference.'

Christopher slowed his pace a little. 'We must speak to Mr Lovell. He will be waiting for us.'

Mr Lovell was indeed waiting for them. 'Was Lady Paulet able to help?' he asked.

Christopher nodded. 'She was, sir.'

Lovell grinned. 'That is a relief. It means she trusted you.'

'It seems that we are not looking for Pryses but Brookes,' said Wetherby.

'Brooke, eh? A Henry Brooke is known to me. A young man with a temper and a taste for ale and women. If he has a father, I do not know him. Could he be the man you seek?'

'That is what we must find out. Where does Brooke live?'

'There is a farmhouse a mile west of the town. I believe he lives there, although I have never had occasion to visit him.'

'We shall need the services of two constables, Mr Lovell,' said Christopher. 'Are you able to provide them?'

Wetherby's voice held a note of impatience. 'Christopher, it is almost dark. It would be foolish to go now. Why do we not wait until the morning?'

The magistrate agreed. 'Mr Wetherby is right, doctor. I could not send constables out at this time. Tomorrow at dawn would be more sensible.'

Christopher was outnumbered. 'Very well. We will be here tomorrow at dawn, Mr Lovell. Two stout constables, if you please.'

*

It was a long night with little sleep. Christopher thought of Isaac and Sarah, of Joan in her Newgate cell, of Ell and of Katherine. He thought of the horrors of Paris and the traitor John Berwick. And he wondered if Jack Brooke would prove to be John Pryse and the key to unlocking the riddle of the Dudley testons.

Before first light he was up and dressed and waiting impatiently in the taproom for Wetherby, who appeared just as a weak winter sun rose above the horizon. 'Make haste, Roland,' he urged. 'The sooner we are at the Brooke house the more likely that we shall find our man there.'

'We will arrive sooner if we take the horses.'

'It is only a mile. If we walk quickly we shall be there in no more than fifteen minutes. And we are more likely to be unobserved than if we ride.'

They collected the constables from the magistrate's house. Both were broad-shouldered, heavy-set men, with swords at their sides. They greeted the two intelligencers politely but otherwise said nothing. Mr Lovell had chosen well. While the town was still quiet they set off on the highway leading west. Used regularly by drovers bringing their sheep in from the downs, it was a broad, well-trodden road, bordered on both sides by ditches which carried away excess water and kept it from flooding. In the distance they heard the glass furnaces being fired up.

They encountered but a single milkmaid trudging into town and a vagrant who jumped over the ditch and ran into the woods when he saw them. The few hovels they passed were deserted.

After twenty minutes or so they saw smoke rising from a building ahead. Christopher whispered to them to make no noise as they approached. Soon they could see that it had once been a farmhouse — straw-thatched, stone- and timber-built, and with a substantial wooden barn with a pitched roof beside it. The house was all but derelict. The window shutters hung loose on their hinges and part of the roof had caved in. The only sign of life was the smoke which drifted up through the gap in the thatch.

Crouching behind the mound of a stinking midden, Christopher whispered to the constables: 'Remain hidden here while I approach from the front. Mr Wetherby will circle around to the back in case our friends try to make a run for it. Remember that we must be sure that they are the men we seek before we arrest them.'

'There may be others in the house,' said Wetherby.

'If there are, we will soon find out.' Christopher stood up and strode towards the door. Wetherby slipped cautiously around the house to the back.

Outside the door he called out. 'Good day, master farmer. I was passing and thought to buy a beaker of milk from you.'

There came the rasping of iron upon iron and a rough voice replied from within. 'Who are you?'

'A traveller on the road to Farnham. I have not breakfasted and will give two pence for a beaker of milk.'

'There is no milk. Be on your way, traveller.'

'May I not rest here awhile? I have a long journey ahead.'

Bolts were pulled back, the door was thrown open and a young man of perhaps twenty-five stood menacingly on the threshold, a pitchfork in his hand. He wore a ragged woollen shirt, leather trousers and a leather apron. He was a few inches shorter than Christopher but thick-necked and muscular. His hair and beard were red. Both were filthy. He stared at his visitor through slits of eyes. 'Did you not hear me, traveller? Be on your way.'

Christopher feigned disappointment. 'I had heard that the Brookes were hospitable folk. It seems I was misinformed.'

'How do you know my name?'

'The name of Brooke is well known in these parts. Jack Brooke and his son Henry — good men and good company, I heard.' He waited for a reaction, saw none and added, 'As is the name Pryse.'

In a trice, the pitchfork was pointed at his stomach. Pryse lunged but Christopher was ready for him. He stepped back and a little to his right and grabbed the shaft with his left hand. A sharp pull and Pryse shot forward. He stumbled and fell on his face in the dirt. 'Constables,' shouted Christopher, but the two men had been watching and were already beside him.

One held Pryse down while the other bound his hands behind his back and slipped a rope around his neck. 'There,' said a constable, 'now you can lead us home. But take care. One stumble and the pitchfork will be up your fat arse.'

Pryse managed a strangled croak: 'What is this?'

'We are officers of the law, here to arrest you.'

'What law have I broken?'

'Why did you try to skewer me with that pitchfork? What are you afraid of?'

'I took you for a thief. It seems you are worse.'

'Where is your father?'

'What business is that of yours?'

'He too is to be arrested.'

Another coarse laugh. 'That will be difficult. My father died six months since.'

The constables hoisted Pryse to his feet. 'What did he die of?' asked Christopher.

'Who knows? Pox, plague, old age? Who cares?'

Christopher snapped. With a sudden backhand stroke across Pryse's face, he brought blood streaming from the young man's nose. 'Where is he buried?'

Pryse put his hands to his bleeding nose and grunted. 'Buried?' he spluttered. 'Inside the pigs' bellies, that's where he's buried.' With his sleeve he wiped his nose and spat out a stream of red spittle.

'I see no pigs.'

'All gone to market. Fetched good prices.' Blood was still dripping from his nose but he managed a coarse laugh. 'Perhaps you ate a leg.'

Christopher shuddered. 'You fed your father to the pigs. A foul crime, Pryse, and an evil one that will surely see you burn in hell. Take this creature back, constables. I will speak to it more in the gaol. Where is Wetherby?'

'I am here, Christopher,' said Wetherby from behind him, 'and look what I have found.'

Christopher turned. Wetherby was standing in the doorway holding a skinny girl by the elbows. Her face was streaked with grime and under only a thin shift she was shivering. 'Do you live here?' he asked her. She did not reply. 'What is your name, wench?' She wriggled but could not get free.

'What is yours, you poxed prick?' Her voice matched her face — rough, mean and foul.

Christopher bent down until his nose was almost touching hers. 'It will go better for you if you tell us what we wish to know. If you do not, a plague-infested cell awaits you as it does Pryse. Who are you?'

She glared at him but there was a hint of fear in the voice. 'Who are you?'

Christopher sighed as if speaking to a troublesome child and held the point of the poniard to her eye. 'How many one-eyed whores do you know, Roland?'

'Very few. They do not last long on the streets. Food for the rats within a week.'

'Do you suppose our master would be pleased to receive a whore's eyeball as a gift?'

'I think he would be delighted.'

Christopher thought the woman was still going to resist, but when he touched her eyelid with the point, she screamed and struggled. 'Let me go and I will tell you what you wish to know.'

He withdrew the blade. 'You will tell us anyway. Take her inside, Roland, and hold her fast.'

Wetherby marched the woman into the farmhouse and sat her on the single stool that served as furniture. He stood behind her, holding her just above the elbows. A slight squeeze and she would squeal like a piglet. A pile of faggots lay beside the fire and a heap of rags in one corner. Otherwise the room was bare. Christopher had followed them in. 'Now, woman,' he growled, 'what is your name?'

'Agnes Fayle.'

'Do you live here, Agnes Fayle?'

'No. I come when he wants me. He is often in town. Tell your pretty friend to let me go.'

'For how long have you been doing this?'

'A few months. He told me his father had died and he was going to return to London.'

'What work did he do?'

'None, as far as I could see. Ouch. My arms hurt like buggery. Let me go.'

'So he had money. Did you see it?'

Agnes Fayle snorted. 'A miserly coin or two. I've had better payers.'

'No hoard of silver?'

'Would I have seen it if there was? Let me go, shit bucket.'

'Mr Wetherby will let you go when you have answered all my questions. What did he call himself?'

'Henry. Henry Brooke. Came from London.'

'Had he an occupation there?'

'Couldn't say. He never spoke about it. Just wanted to swive. Good at that, he is. Prick like a bull's.'

'He didn't speak about minting coins?'

'Coins? Ha. Had precious few if he did.'

Christopher looked at Wetherby, who shrugged. 'We'll let you go now, but if you make trouble, the blade will be back at your eye. Do you understand?' She nodded. 'Let her go, Roland. She's no more use to us.'

When Wetherby released his grip the slut stood up and rubbed her arms. 'Pair of evil buggers you are. Could have taken my eye and broken my bones. And for nothing. Whatever it is you're after, I haven't got it and I don't know where it is. Who are you?'

'Never mind who we are. Get dressed and go. You won't see him again.'

She found a smock among the heap of rags and slipped it over the shift. Her shoes were by the fire. She put them on, picked up a faggot, threw it at Christopher and ran. 'I know who you are,' she shouted from outside the house. 'Two of the queen's arse-lickers. Well, fuck off back to Her royal Majesty and earn your crust.'

Christopher put a hand on Wetherby's arm. 'Let her go. She knows nothing.'

'Nothing, I agree. Once again I am astonished at your ability to turn from gentle Doctor of Law to monstrous inquisitor in the blink of an eye. You should have been a player.'

No, thought Christopher, not a player but a contented Doctor of Law who valued justice above all else and abhorred violence. But fate had chosen a different path for him. 'Needs must and she was unharmed. Isaac Cardoza, remember, is dead.' He looked around the squalid room. 'Before we return to speak yet more harshly to Master Brooke or Pryse or whoever he claims to be, we must have a good look around this hovel. If there was coining here, there will surely be some sign of it.'

They threw aside the pile of rags and the heap of faggots and found nothing. Nor was there anything in the adjoining room that, judging by the blankets and straw strewn about the floor, served as a bed chamber. When the father was alive, one of them must have slept by the fire.

There was neither parlour nor kitchen. 'Neither food nor drink,' observed Wetherby, 'nor beasts nor tools. Our man was not planning to be here for many more days.'

'No. I fancy we were barely in time.' He paused. 'And we might have saved the whore's life. A man who can feed his dead father to the swine would have no scruples about burying his whore under the midden. Let us try the barn.'

The south side of the barn was partly open to allow access to carts and beasts. Muck-splattered straw littered the floor, a stone drinking trough stood against one wooden wall and a pile of rusting scythes, shovels and pitchforks against another. The back wall was covered by heaps of empty sacks.

'There is something amiss here,' said Wetherby almost at once, before leaving the barn and walking down one side of it. He ran his palms along the timbers that formed the wall and every few steps rapped his knuckles on them. At the far end he turned and said, 'I thought as much. This barn is a trick. The inside is too small for the outside. The back wall is false.' He chortled. 'Might have been designed by Rabelais.'

'God's teeth, Roland, I thought we agreed no more Rabelais. But you are right. Help me move some of those sacks.'

Starting in the middle, they heaved aside armfuls of sacks until the wall was exposed. They found nothing and carried on until they came to a corner. Christopher tugged at a sack on the top of the heap and jumped back in surprise. It tumbled down bringing all those underneath with it. The sacks in the corner had been cunningly sewn together so that they could be easily moved and replaced. Behind them was a low door. Christopher crouched down and entered. Wetherby followed.

The hidden room was in darkness and at first they could see nothing. Gradually, however, their eyes became accustomed to their surroundings and they could begin to make out what they had found.

In the middle of the hidden room, as far from the wooden walls as possible, stood a brick-built kiln which would have been used for melting down the silver and copper. Above it, a hole, invisible from outside, had been cut in the roof to allow smoke to escape. On each side were thick oak work benches, on which lay an assortment of tools – flat shovels, hammers, shears and dozens of iron dies. An old barrel was brimming with evil-smelling water. In such a place the risk of fire would have been great – a spark from the kiln or even from a hammer striking metal and the timber walls would soon feed the flames.

'The ashes are cold,' said Christopher, withdrawing his hand from the kiln. Wetherby held up a chipped minter's iron trussel and pile. 'Bring them outside and let us see what we've found, although I think we can guess.'

They ducked back through the hidden door and into the open part of the barn. Wetherby handed the dies to Christopher, who held them up so that he could see the designs clearly. He laughed. 'A bear on the trussel and a ragged staff on the pile, both stamped into the iron, and as far as I can tell, well made. Certainly the work of a skilled man.'

'John Pryse, no doubt. His son does not strike one as a man of skill.'

'No doubt he would have kept the fire going and done the hammering and annealing while his father made the dies and trimmed the finished coins ready for use. The two of them would have been able to turn out as many counterfeits as their supply of silver and copper allowed. Someone brought them old coins and silver to be melted down. For other coiners this would not be profitable but it served the purpose of whoever was paying the Pryses.'

'Their purpose not being profit but something more subtle,' said Wetherby.

'And more sinister. My guess is that Pryse ceased work soon after his father died and would have set fire to the farm and the barn before leaving.'

'We have only Pryse's word that his father is dead. The story of the pigs might be to explain the lack of a grave.'

Christopher scratched his chin. 'It might. The father might simply have left.'

'Or his son might have killed him. Either way, Pryse must have accumulated enough money or at least thought that he had. They would have been well paid and I'll wager not all the silver ended up as bear and staff testons. Perhaps there's a hoard buried nearby.'

'If there is, we'll leave Mr Lovell and his constables to find it. We have not the time although I doubt Pryse will tell us where it is. Give me one of the dies to carry and we'll go and make sure he's settled comfortably into the gaol.'

Guildford gaol had at one time been the dungeons of the now ruined castle. While the turrets and towers had long since collapsed and the ancient walls were crumbling, the dungeons, largely safe from wind and rain below ground, were still intact and usable.

At the top of the stone steps leading down to the cells, Richard Lovell was waiting for them. 'Your man is ready for you, gentlemen,' said the magistrate with a big grin. 'I must say that he has not worn well since last I saw him. Drink and debauchery, I daresay. Odd that the father never came into town or, if he did, I did not come across him. Where is he now?'

'Dead, according to his son. Of old age or pox or a pitchfork in the guts, we may never know. Nor will a trace of him be found.'

Lovell caught his tone and raised his eyebrows. 'I see. What are your intentions now?'

'I will speak to Pryse but I doubt he will tell us much here,' replied Christopher. 'If you are able to provide us with a cart and a constable to drive it, we will take him to London. A few nights in Newgate and the prospect of a traitor's death should loosen his tongue.'

'Dr Radcliff, are you quite sure that he is the man you seek?'

'Quite sure, Mr Lovell. Go to the farm yourself and you will find a secret mint in the barn. That is where Pryse and his father produced the counterfeit coins, stamped with these dies.'

Lovell looked at the dies and nodded. 'A bear and a ragged staff, just as you said. That is evidence enough. I will make the arrangements for tomorrow.'

Dark and dank and foul, yet the dungeons of Guildford Castle were less awful than the hellish cells of Newgate. There was a little more light and air and the stench was less gut-churning. And there were but a few prisoners crying out for pity. King John's enemies, it seemed, had fared rather better nearly four hundred years earlier than did the gracious Queen Elizabeth's.

A gaoler led them down to Pryse's cell, where he sat in a corner on the stone floor. He looked up when they entered but did not move or speak. 'Let us begin with your name,' said Christopher. 'Are you Hugh Pryse?'

'I am Henry Brooke. I know no Pryse.'

'Do not waste our time, Pryse. We know who you are.' Christopher held up the two dies. 'And we found these in your barn. How do you account for them?'

'What are they?'

'For the love of God, man, do not make matters worse for yourself,' snapped Christopher. 'I have no time for this. Try our patience more and you will certainly suffer a traitor's death. Have you ever seen a man hanged, cut down while still breathing, his guts drawn from him and his body cut into quarters? Have you? Because that is what awaits you if you lie and dissemble. Tell the truth and you might yet be spared such an end. You know what these are and we know what they were used for. Where did you get them?'

Pryse shrugged and said nothing. 'For whom were you working?' Nothing. 'For whom were you working?' Louder this time. Still nothing. Christopher sighed. 'As you wish. Tomorrow you will be taken to Newgate for questioning. Think on what awaits you there and, if you still refuse to speak, what awaits you in the Tower. Inside the curtain wall, not outside it in the mint.' A flicker of fear crossed

Pryse's face. 'And I suggest you start by telling Mr Lovell where your silver is hidden. It will save his constables much time in searching and might spare you a beating.'

They waited for a response but there was none. 'Very well. Mr Lovell, he is well enough fed. I suggest neither food nor water. We will leave at dawn tomorrow.' They heard the key turning in the lock behind them as they climbed the steps.

At the top Christopher asked if he might accompany the magistrate briefly to his house. 'I have a task to perform and a small favour to ask of you,' he said.

Seated at the magistrate's desk and using one of his pens and his inkpot, he wrote a letter. It did not take long. He sanded it, folded it and handed it to the magistrate. 'You would be doing me a great service if you would have this delivered to Lady Paulet,' he said. 'And my thanks also to you, Mr Lovell. The Earl of Leicester will be told of your part in capturing Hugh Pryse. Be sure of it.'

Lovell inclined his head in thanks. 'Tomorrow at dawn, doctor. All will be ready.'

Outside, Christopher clapped Wetherby on the back. 'Progress at last, Roland, and now it is time we paid a visit to the glass-blowers.'

'With what purpose?'

'I have been wondering why the coiners chose Guildford for their mint and how the coins were smuggled into London. Could it be that Guildford was chosen so that the testons could be hidden in a shipment from the glassworks? It would not have been difficult to ferry a crate or two of glass across the river and bring them in through Lud Gate or New Gate without arousing suspicion.'

'It would not. Nor would we have ever known had Pryse not spoken of the town before they left London.'

Approaching the glassworks, the roar of furnaces reminded Christopher of the mint. And as they reached the cluster of low buildings in which the glass was blown and shaped and annealed, the heat from the furnaces greeted them like a burning blast of wind. Instinctively, they put their hands to their faces and turned away until the shock subsided.

To one side of the buildings stood a small dwelling — stone-built and tiled. Christopher hammered on the door, hoping that it was where they would find a supervisor or someone else in authority. It was opened by a tall man with a neat beard and dressed more appropriately for Whitehall than for a glassworks. His doublet was red and his hose white. 'Good day, sirs,' he said in a strong French accent. 'Have you come to inquire about our glass?'

'In a way, we have, sir,' replied Christopher. 'I am Dr Christopher Radcliff and my companion is Mr Roland Wetherby. We are in Guildford on my lord the Earl of Leicester's business.'

'I am Jacques l'Église, a sharer in this enterprise. Do you wish to order glass for his lordship? If so, it would of course be an honour to serve him. Be aware, however, that demand for our glass is high and we are very busy.'

'The quality of your glass is well known in London, sir,' said Wetherby with a slight bow, 'and on another occasion it would be a pleasure to examine your wares. Today, however, we would like to inquire about a man we are seeking.'

'What man would that be, sir?'

'His name is unknown to us, but he would have made regular visits here and would have purchased glassware for his customers in London. Small amounts, probably.'

The Frenchman's eyes narrowed. 'Why do you seek such a man?'

'That we cannot say,' replied Christopher, 'but the earl is most insistent that we trace him and will certainly look favourably on all who assist us in our task.'

'If you were to furnish us with a sample of your glass — say a small flask — we would be pleased to present it to his lordship with a view to his placing an order for Kenilworth Castle,' added Wetherby. 'Next summer, the queen herself will be visiting Kenilworth on her progress.'

'The queen's progress? That is most gracious of you. I will certainly find a suitable item for the earl. A flask, yes. We are noted for our flasks. But as to the man you seek, we have many customers and I . . .'

'He would have paid in silver coin.'

'As do many of our customers.' L'Église stroked his beard. 'Although there was one man — we have not seen him for some weeks — who ordered glassware on each visit, paid in silver, and placed another order for the next time. Never a large order but he came every month. We understood him to be buying on behalf of London gentlemen.'

'What was this man's name, sir?'

'He went by the name of Fossett. Gerard Fossett.'

'Can you describe him?'

'A tall man, black hair and beard, finely dressed. Always courteous. One would not have guessed that he had travelled from London. He came by a coach which he drove himself. Unusual, but he was a regular buyer, so I said nothing about it.'

'For how long was Mr Fossett a customer?'

'About a year and a half, I think. I could check my records, if you wish.'

'Thank you, Monsieur l'Église,' said Wetherby, 'that would be helpful.'

They followed him into the house where a thick ledger lay open on a table. L'Église turned back the pages until he found what he was looking for. 'There,' he said, tapping a page with his finger, 'Mr Fossett placed his first order on the tenth day of August 1572. It was for two dozen hock glasses at a price of ten pounds. He collected them on the twelfth day of September and paid in silver. On that day he also placed another order for hock glasses.'

'His masters must have had a taste for German wine,' said Wetherby. 'Personally, I find it somewhat insipid.'

L'Église turned over the pages. 'Mr Fossett returned every month until November of last year. I do not know why he no longer came after that.'

'Thank you, Monsieur l'Église,' said Christopher. 'That is most helpful.'

'A pleasure to serve the Earl of Leicester. Come now and I will find a flask for him.'

Christopher followed the Frenchman. Gerard Fossett, l'Église had said. Tall, well dressed, drove his own carriage, black-haired and courteous. And found with his throat slashed in a mean alley off Cheapside before his corpse was removed from the deadhouse and dumped in the river? Ell's handsome customer? He smiled. First Pryse, then Fossett. A little more progress and each step taking them closer to their prey.

By the time they trundled over London Bridge, the church clocks were chiming five in the afternoon. The journey from Guildford with the prisoner bound on a flat cart pulled by a sturdy pony had taken almost twice the time of that from London.

Pryse had not revealed the whereabouts of his money and on the journey had said almost nothing. To the name Gerard Fossett he had shown no reaction. Not a glimmer. Even at a crossroads near the village of Esher, where the constable had pointed to a thief swinging on a gibbet, his eyes taken by crows and his hair by wig-makers, and had amused himself with remarks about the dead man at least having died in one piece, Pryse had not spoken.

On the way up from the bridge to Newgate, they encountered few stares. Felons on carts being taken to gaol were a common enough sight on the streets of the city.

They left him at Newgate with instructions to the warden to put him with the penniless wretches in the lowest cells on the common side, paid off the constable with more than enough for his work and for a bed for the night, and returned the earl's coursers to their stable in Whitehall. Newgate had reminded Christopher again that poor Joan Willys was still held there. Somehow he must find time to visit her.

'A carriage next time,' he said, stretching his back. 'The older I get the more I dislike riding. And now it's time to face the earl.'

The earl, they were told, was with Her Majesty but a message would be given to him that they awaited him in the anteroom to his apartment.

The earl's audience with the queen must have gone well. They had been waiting no more than twenty minutes when he strode into the antechamber and summoned them straight into his apartment. 'You have returned sooner than I expected,' he said. 'I trust this signals good news?'

'Mr Wetherby and I believe it does, my lord.'

CHAPTER 23

Had the shadow disappeared? Had he lost interest or completed his shadowy task, whatever that was? There was no sign of him on the way to Newgate and Christopher sensed no presence. Joan first or Pryse? Let Pryse fester a little longer. Hopefully, Joan would be pleased to see him.

She was. When he entered the cell the unsightly face lit up in a lopsided smile and she rose from the cot on which she sat to bob a clumsy curtsy. 'Dr Radcliff, I had not thought to see you. Mistress Allington said you were much occupied with your work.' The pebble was still in her mouth, poor child, and she was not easy to understand.

'I have been, Joan, or I would have come sooner. How do you fare?'

'As you see, doctor, I am well and Mistress Allington brings me food each day. And she is taking care of my mother, may God bless her.'

'That is good. Are the gaolers treating you properly?'

'They poke fun at me, doctor, for my appearance, but I pay no heed to that. I am quite used to it. How much longer shall I be here?'

Christopher touched her arm. 'The next assizes are at Easter, but I am hopeful that we will find a way to have you released before then. The evidence against you is weak and Alice Scrope is a whore and a liar. We have only to prove it.'

Joan looked doubtful. 'If you are occupied with your work, doctor, how will you find the time to prove it? I would not wish to cause you more trouble.'

'There is no trouble, Joan, I will find the time and there are others working on your behalf. We will keep you from the court.' To describe Ell Cole as 'others' was stretching the truth only a little and he felt no pang of guilt. 'If you think of anything more that might help us, be sure to tell Mistress Allington. She will tell me.'

'I will, doctor, although I know no more than that Alice Scrope is a spiteful whore. May God give her what she deserves.'

'No doubt he will, Joan. Be brave and we will somehow get this foul charge dropped. You may be sure of it.'

'I will try, doctor.'

Hugh Pryse was brought up from the cells to a small room by the gate, in which prisoners were questioned or, occasionally, allowed to speak briefly to a relative. His hands and ankles were chained, one eye was half closed and a thin line of congealed blood ran down a cheek. Newgate was a dangerous place.

'Have you thought more, Pryse, or are you still determined to say nothing?'

The voice was a dry croak. 'I need food and water.'

'You will have neither until you have told me your name and those of the men you serve.'

'I am Hugh Pryse.'

'Not Henry Brooke. That is a start.'

'Water, for pity's sake.' In Newgate, water was as likely to kill a man as the lack of it and they needed him alive.

'Pity? What pity would you have shown your whore when you were done with her? Would she have gone to feed the pigs too? Give him a mug of small beer, gaoler.' From a pitcher on a table in the corner, the gaoler filled a mug and gave it to Pryse, who tipped it down his throat. 'The others, Pryse, who are they?'

'What others?'

'You try my patience again. You and your father were not working alone. Someone employed you to produce false testons stamped with the Dudley crest. Who were they?'

'My father was a farmer. I helped him.'

'Your father was a coiner, as you are. I have seen your mint. Where did the silver come from? Who supplied it and who collected the false testons from you?'

'I do not know.'

'You do know. Or did they come only when you were out drinking and whoring in the town? Was his name Gerard Fossett?'

'I know of no such man.'

'That is unfortunate, Pryse. Let us see how many days pass before you are begging to speak. Back to the cell with him, gaoler. Enough food and drink to keep him alive, not a scrap more.'

'As you say, sir.' The gaoler led the prisoner out of the room and back down the stone steps leading to the subterranean hell below. If Pryse lasted two days it would be a surprise.

He saw her before she saw him. As he left the gaol through the great oak doors, she was approaching with a wicker basket on her arm. Her face was half hidden by a coif but he knew her gait and the set of her shoulders at once. He stood still and waited for her to reach him.

'Good day, Katherine, have you come to visit Joan?'

She did not stop but brushed past him towards the prison. Not a look, not a word. He called after her. 'I have seen Joan. She is well. And I have found the coiners.' Still no word. She disappeared through the gates without so much as a glance.

He hesitated. Should he follow her and risk another rebuff or leave her to bring succour to Joan? He let her go. There would be a better time. And he wanted to see Ell.

Grace opened the door with her clay pipe clamped between her teeth. She wished Christopher good day but did not bother to ask him why he was there. He climbed the stairs and knocked on Ell's door.

'Come in, Dr Rad,' she called out, 'I am decent enough.'

Christopher opened her door. 'How did you know it was me?'

Ell was lying on her bed, covered by a thin shift. She gave one of her throaty chuckles. 'Should know your knock by now, shouldn't I? A very polite knock, it is. Not like some. How are you, Dr Rad? Been to that place — something "ford", wasn't it?'

'Guildford. Yes, I've been and come back with a coiner.'

'The strange testons?'

'Yes, the testons.'

'That's good. Everything back to normal now, is it? No more funny money?'

'Not quite, Ell. There's much I still don't know. Did you find Alice Scrope's house?'

'I did, doctor. The woman's a whore, to be sure, and not too particular about her customers. A rough lot most of them, all except one.'

'How so?'

Ell grinned as if she had a secret to tell. 'The coroner. Saw him twice, dressed up like a gentleman in his doublet, but just the same as all the others underneath. Except you, that is.'

'The coroner? Clennet Pyke? Looks like a haddock?'

'That's him. Ugly bugger. Perhaps that's why he swives a hag like Alice Scrope.'

'Well, well. Good work, Ell. Clennet Pyke of all people. Foul little toad.' He laughed. 'Perfect.'

'No trouble, Dr Rad.' She held out her hand. Christopher took a crown from his purse and gave it to her. It was one crown he should not reclaim from the earl's comptroller, but a crown well spent nonetheless. 'Anything else I can do?' she asked.

'Keep watching that house, please. Whenever you're not busy, that is.'

'Busy as I want to be these days, but for you I'll make time. How are the dreams?'

'Not so bad. Having a difficult job to do helps. Takes the mind to other places.'

'I'm glad of it. Go well, doctor.'

'Thank you, Ell. You've brightened the day.'

Clennet Pyke reeked of drink and looked as if he had only just risen from his bed. He was bleary-eyed and dishevelled. And far from pleased to see Christopher. 'Dr Radcliff,' he grumbled, 'have you come to cause more trouble? Kindly be brief. I have much work to attend to.'

In Pyke's study there was little sign of any work being attended to, but Christopher let it pass. 'I have come about one Alice Scrope who lives near Wood Street. Do you know her?'

Pyke's eyes betrayed nothing. 'I know of no such person, but if I did, what business would it be of yours?'

'Alice Scrope, a whore who has falsely accused my housekeeper, Joan Willys, of witchcraft.'

'If your housekeeper is a witch, Dr Radcliff, take care that you are not accused of harbouring and assisting her.'

'She is not a witch and she is at present in Newgate, as I am sure you are aware.'

'I am relieved to hear it. Justice will be done.'

'Justice will only be done, Mr Pyke, when Joan Willys is released. Did you give the Scrope wench the money to pay for an action against her?'

Pyke rose to his feet and his face turned the colour of a rich claret. 'That is a disgraceful allegation against an officer of the law. How dare you suggest such a thing?'

'Did you?'

'I have told you that I do not know this woman. What mischief are you about, Dr Radcliff?'

'You have been seen entering Alice Scrope's house.'

'Seen by whom? A lie. A fabrication for which you are no doubt responsible. Leave this house immediately or a constable will be summoned.'

Christopher did not move but stared hard at the ugly face. 'You are a craven liar, Pyke. Because of you an innocent woman is in Newgate gaol and when I discover why, it is you who will face justice.'

Pyke began to splutter something but it was too late. Christopher slammed the door behind him. Outside he stood rubbing his hand and trying to breathe evenly. The disgusting little man should be thrown back into the swamp from which he had emerged. But at least there was a glimmer of hope for Joan.

CHAPTER 24

Shiva was over. Christopher walked briskly down Cheapside and Cornhill to Leadenhall, sensing that the mood Ell had noticed on the streets was still there — quiet markets, quiet voices, a sense of foreboding. He cursed himself for the fanciful notion. Places could not have moods. It was all in his head.

Nevertheless he found himself quickening his pace and keeping a wary eye on those he passed. A dagger hidden in a sleeve might deliver a fatal wound before the victim saw it coming. He kept well clear even of a one-legged beggar on Cornhill and clearer still of a pure collector gathering dog shit for the tanners who worked along the Fleet river. All in his head, perhaps, but a man's head directed his actions.

The door was opened by a servant — a young, dark-skinned girl in a black cowl, who showed him into the parlour where Sarah Cardoza sat alone, embroidering the hem of a white napkin with red and yellow roses. 'Isaac loved roses,' she said, looking up, 'and often bought them for me despite the expense. A clever man of business but he could be sentimental.'

'How do you fare, Sarah?' he asked.

'I am well, thank you, doctor. I miss Isaac beyond words but take comfort from knowing that he is with God. He was a good man.'

'He was, and a loyal one. I too miss him. What of the children?'

'Daniel and David have started work with Aaron Lopes. He has been generous to us and they will learn a good trade. Ruth is too young to work but helps care for her mother.' A tiny smile played around her eyes. 'I am blessed.'

'And the shop?'

'The landlord has taken back the lease.'

Christopher nodded. 'That is good. Some would insist on the terms being met.'

'Isaac had arranged for the landlord to do so in the event of his death. I have wondered if he foresaw it.'

'Surely not. He simply put his family first.'

'Always.'

'Sarah, I have news of the coiners. Would you like to hear it?'

She put aside the napkin. 'I would.'

He told her of the Pryses and his discovery at Guildford, keeping it as brief as he could. At the end, he said, 'The son, Hugh Pryse, is in Newgate and I am confident that he will tell us what we need to know.'

'He will not be tortured, I hope,' said Sarah. 'Our families left Portugal to escape the brutality of the inquisition. I would not wish to think that such an ungodly practice had come to England.'

Torture of prisoners was rare and required the consent of the Privy Council, but it did sometimes happen in cases of treason. Sarah did not seem to know this. 'He will be rigorously questioned, Sarah, but he will not suffer torture. You have my word.'

'That is sufficient. God will punish him for what he has done. Now, will you take refreshment?'

'Thank you, no. I must be on my way. I will call again when there is more to tell you.'

'Come again whenever you wish, Christopher. And take more care of yourself. You are too thin.'

'I will go to the market on my way home. *Shalom*, Sarah.'

'Be sure that you do. *Shalom*, Christopher.'

It was the first time that she had ever used his Christian name.

Last time, a penny-halfpenny for a plucked chicken. This time, two pence. Last time, two and a half pence for a small loaf. This time two pence and three farthings. He did not even bother asking why. The answers would be the same. And he could hardly tell the traders that the coiner of the false testons was in Newgate and there was nothing for them to worry about. They would not believe it.

No angry apprentices, at least. They would be thinking twice before attacking the traders again. Just unsmiling faces resigned to hardship and toil.

Christopher gathered his purchases into a bag and left Cheapside for Ludgate Hill. It was as he entered St Paul's churchyard that he saw a figure disappearing down the alley that Wetherby had been attacked in. He saw only the man's back but that was enough. The shadow had returned.

'You chased after him, of course,' said Wetherby, slouched on a chair, 'and demanded to know why the coward had attacked me from behind.'

'I did not. I would not have caught him in those alleys even without carrying my victuals.'

Wetherby had arrived unannounced and had settled himself comfortably into the study. He had lit the fire and poured himself a glass of wine. 'You disappoint me, Christopher. I would have thought you would abandon the victuals and run like a stag after him. Just as I would have.'

'I'll bear it in mind for the next time. Have you come just to drink my wine or do you bring intelligence from the palace?'

'Neither. I bring thoughts.'

'Your own, I trust, not those of a dead Frenchman.'

'If you mean the excellent Monsieur Rabelais, Christopher, they are not. Now calm yourself and let us consider what we know, although it is not much. We have found the mint operated by the Pryses and we have Hugh Pryse safely in gaol. But we do not yet understand what the false testons are about other than to cause trouble. Taken together with the slogans and plague crosses and of course the attack on Isaac Cardoza, there must be more to them.'

'On that we are already agreed, but what more? And why am I being watched?'

'That I do not know, but Pryse is a frightened man. Even in Newgate with the threat of the Tower and a traitor's death hanging over him, he has not spoken. Nor will he unless his fear of Scylla is greater than his fear of Charybdis.'

'Scylla being us and Charybdis the bringers of chaos and confusion?'

'Exactly. Let us go and see how Master Pryse is enjoying Newgate.'

'You will have my support in any action you take,' Leicester had said. God willing, he had meant it. They spoke first to the warden who took some persuasion and an assurance that he would not be held responsible for any mishap but finally agreed to Christopher's unusual request and ordered Pryse brought up from the cells. Christopher had searched his conscience and decided that Sarah Cardoza would not object.

A few days in Newgate and Pryse was a much diminished figure. He stood before them in what remained of his shirt and breeches, with his hands and ankles shackled and his head lolling on his chest as if it were too heavy for his neck to support. Even when Christopher spoke, he did not look up.

'Are you ready to speak to us, Pryse? Have you thought carefully about what awaits you if you insist upon this foolish silence?'

'Who is it that you are so afraid of that you would suffer at our hands rather than face them?' asked Wetherby.

'You have denied knowing Gerard Fossett yet we know that this man delivered silver and copper to you to be melted down and turned into false testons and later collected the testons from you for delivery to his masters.'

'And now Gerard Fossett is dead,' added Wetherby. 'His throat was cut and his face marked with a cross. Why would that be, Pryse?'

Still the prisoner did not look up or speak. Wetherby tried again. 'Why would that be?' he shouted. There was no reaction.

Christopher shook his head. Without food Pryse would not last much longer and he would be no use to them dead. Two years ago he could not have done it — the sound of a sheep's limbs popping from their sockets as the dead animal lay on the rack in the Tower still haunted him — but the prisoner must be made to speak. Wetherby had been attacked and Isaac was dead. If Pryse would not speak, Christopher would have to put aside his scruples and force him to do so. 'You will be tried for counterfeiting, and if found guilty, you will be hanged. Now we are going to show you what you will suffer if you continue to refuse to speak. Bring him to the pressing room, gaoler.'

The pressing room was a simple square chamber, empty but for four iron rings set into the stone floor and three stacks of weights along one wall. Christopher ordered the gaoler to unchain the prisoner and lie him on his back with his hands and ankles secured to the rings. 'Now, Pryse,' he said, 'I am not permitted to use pressing to cause you permanent harm, although I certainly would if the law allowed it, but I can demonstrate to you what awaits a prisoner who will not plead in court.' He signalled to the gaoler who took a small weight from the top of a stack and placed it carefully on Pryse's stomach. Pryse tried in vain to tip the weight off by wriggling and squirming. He moaned in agony and his face looked as if it might burst like an ugly pustule, but still he did not speak.

Christopher nodded to the gaoler who took a second weight, placed it on top of the first and held them steady. This time Pryse's eyes closed and his mouth opened in a silent scream.

Christopher sighed and bent to speak quietly to him. 'I had hoped to spare you this, Pryse. I do not enjoy inflicting pain, and if you tell me what I need to know, you will suffer no more.' From Pryse there was no sign that he had heard. Christopher straightened up and nodded again to the gaoler.

A third weight was added. Vomit trickled from Pryse's mouth and his eyes bulged, ready to pop from their sockets. 'Will you speak?' shouted Christopher, to be sure that he heard. There was a tiny nod of Pryse's head before it lolled to one side. 'Will you speak?' This time there could be no mistake. Pryse lifted his head a fraction and grunted.

Christopher signalled to the gaoler who removed the weights one by one. For a moment he feared that Pryse was dead. He did not move or make a sound, but lay still and silent, until the gaoler nudged him with a booted foot, and he groaned. Much relieved, Christopher ordered the gaoler to untie him. It had been as close to the illegal use of torture as he dared go.

The gaoler helped Pryse to sit up. 'That was but a taste of what you may expect if you will not speak in court,' Christopher told him. 'Tell us what we wish to know and you will suffer no more pain.'

'Water, for pity's sake.' The words came out in a painful croak.

'Bring ale, gaoler, and find food.'

They waited while the gaoler fetched ale and a chunk of bread and watched Pryse swallow a sip. A bite of bread, however, was too much and was out of his mouth almost as soon as it had gone in. Pryse retched and clutched his stomach in pain.

When he thought the creature was up to it, Christopher put aside a twinge of sympathy for him and began again. 'Did you meet the man named Fossett?'

'He came to the farm.' Now Pryse held his head in his hands and kept his eyes on the floor.

'To bring silver and collect the testons?'

'Yes.' The word was barely audible.

'Was there anyone else?'

A shake of the head.

'No one?'

'My father spoke of a Gabriel.'

'Gabriel. But you did not see him?'

'Never.' Pryse took a mouthful of beer and grimaced.

'What did your father say about this Gabriel?'

'He had set up the mint and paid us to operate it.'

'Nothing else?'

'No.'

'How were you paid?'

'We kept some of the silver brought by Fossett.'

Pryse was flagging. His voice was getting weaker and his chin was on his chest. 'I suggest we save him for another day, Christopher,' whispered Wetherby. 'In this state he will say anything to be rid of us.'

'One more question, Pryse. Why did you hate your father?'

Pryse's head jerked up. 'He was as tight as a nun's cunny. Always saying prayers and fingering his beads, but wouldn't give me a few shillings for ale.'

'Did you kill him for the money?'

'That's two questions. Fuck off.'

'It matters little. You'll hang anyway.'

Pryse glared at him, his eyes blazing with anger and hatred, and for a moment Christopher thought he was going to try to struggle to his feet. But the effort was too much. He slumped to the floor and lay there.

They would get nothing more from him. 'Back to the cell with him, gaoler,' ordered Christopher, 'and take care with your words, Pryse, if you don't want to starve to death.'

'Is the prisoner unharmed?' asked the warden on their way out of the prison. 'I could not be party to illegal torture.'

'Worry not,' replied Wetherby. 'We were quite gentle and he is recovered from a slight shock.'

'I am much relieved to hear it. It was unwise of me to agree to his being pressed, even lightly, and I feared that he might die. I will not permit it again.'

'There will be no need,' replied Christopher, 'although he has not yet told us everything.' He handed a coin to the warden. 'Keep him alive until we return.'

CHAPTER 25

I n his study, Christopher sat with an untouched beaker of ale, his eyes closed. He had hated witnessing the traitor Patrick Wolf suffer in the Tower at the hands of the queen's interrogator, Fulke Griffyn, and he had thanked God that he did not have to watch the man being racked.

And the images of the violence he had seen in Paris — men, women and children hacked to pieces and burned by rampaging gangs — would haunt him for ever. Bloodshed, torture and cruelty of a kind he would not have believed possible had he not seen it with his own eyes and for which he could find not a scrap of justification. Still the terrible dreams came and went as they chose.

He had changed. Of course he had changed. Did all men not change as the years passed? But Christopher Radcliff, Doctor of Law, and chief London intelligencer for the Earl of Leicester, hated himself for it. Once he could never have countenanced the threat of violence to obtain information, let alone actually employ it, as he had employed it on Hugh Pryse. Now he could do so without hesitation if it was necessary. Pryse had to be made to speak so it had been necessary. Pressing was only used when an accused refused to enter a plea in court in order to avoid his property being forfeit and his widow and children left destitute, as a convicted felon's would otherwise be. Pryse, fortunately, had not known that.

He had stretched the truth a little, only a little, and with justification, but even so it did not sit comfortably with him. Pryse was a foul creature who had fed his own father to the pigs but dying on the end of a rope would be punishment enough.

Warwick the chess-player thought the coiners were playing a game, moving their pieces seemingly at random but with a hidden purpose and he had urged Christopher to make the connection. If he was right that the murdered man was Gerard Fossett who had delivered silver to Guildford, returning with false testons hidden in consignments of glass, Fossett was a connection.

If the crosses on the slogans and on healthy 'plague' houses and cut into Fossett's face were not crosses but the letter *chi*, signifying chaos and anarchy, his disappearance from the deadhouse might be another connection. Rising prices, fear of witches' work, mysterious slogans recalling days long past — all to cause confusion and insurrection?

Possibly. But they did not explain Fossett's murder or the Dudley emblem or the shadow. Where were the connections there?

He arrived at the prison at noon to find Wetherby waiting for him. Pryse was brought up by the same gaoler. He held his head up and looked stronger than the day before. 'Has the prisoner had meat and ale?' asked Christopher.

'He has, sir, as you instructed.'

'Well then, Pryse, are you ready to answer our questions or must we return to the pressing room?' Pryse shrugged. 'Why did you kill your father?'

'He was old. He died.'

Christopher stared at him, searching for signs of a lie. There were none. 'Why did you feed him to the pigs?'

'Why not? Pigs have to eat, same as us.'

'What did you do with what was left of him after the pigs had finished with him?'

'Went in the midden. There wasn't much.'

It was Wetherby's turn. 'Gerard Fossett. He was the man who took away the counterfeit coins, was he not? Did you never see him?'

'Once only.'

'What more can you tell us about him?'

'He brought the silver and took away the coins. That's all.'

'How was it that you saw him only once?'

'My father sent me to town whenever he was due. I came back early that day.'

'How often did he come?'

'Every month.'

'How many coins did he take away each month?'

'A hundred. It's what he wanted.' A hundred coins every month for, say, twelve months. One thousand two hundred coins. Many more than had been recovered. Even allowing for those washing about in the markets, there must be a store somewhere. 'What else can you tell us about Fossett?'

'He came from London. That's all I know.'

'How did he know about you and your father?'

'Don't know. Might have had friends at the mint.'

'Did you wonder why Fossett wanted a hundred testons stamped with the Dudley bear and ragged staff each month?' asked Christopher.

'No. Didn't care as long as we were paid.'

'Why are you so frightened of Fossett if you never so much as met him?' Pryse closed his eyes and said nothing. 'What did he tell your father?'

'He told him what would happen to us if we were discovered or spoke of our work to anyone. He said we would not be able to hide.'

'And what was that?'

'Father said Fossett would cut off our balls and throw them to the pigs to give them a taste. Then he'd set them on us.'

'And you believed he would do this?'

'Father believed it.'

'Your father died six months ago. Why were you still there?'

'I liked it there.'

'What did Fossett look like?'

'Tall, black hair, black beard. Wore fine clothes.'

Christopher and Roland exchanged a glance. It was just as M. l'Église had said.

'We thought as much.' said Christopher. 'Take him down, gaoler. That is enough for today.'

'And if you have more to say,' added Wetherby, 'the warden will send for us.'

CHAPTER 26

Leicester sat with his elbows resting on his huge desk, listening quietly, not interrupting and showing no emotion. Only when Christopher had finished did he speak.

'You have not told me everything, of course, Dr Radcliff, and you are wise not to,' he said. 'You have found the source of the false testons and one of the coiners who has revealed a little of what we wish to know. I do not want to know how you persuaded him to do this.'

'The prisoner is unharmed, my lord.'

'Good. The Privy Council is sensitive about such matters, as, indeed, is Her Majesty. Worryingly, however, it seems that a large number of these coins have not yet appeared. How are you intending to find them?'

'I do not think the prisoner knows where they are. We must find them by some other means but as yet I do not know how.'

'My brother the Earl of Warwick believes that we are pieces in a game of chess, being moved by an unseen hand. Are you of the same opinion, doctor?'

Christopher hesitated. 'I think that the testons and the slogans and the plague crosses are all connected, my lord, but we have yet to discover their true purpose.'

'You have spoken of chaos.'

'Chaos, yes. But chaos with a purpose — and that the purpose of a man of considerable resources.'

'Mr Wetherby, I understand, believes that we are the objects of some sort of Rabelaisian jest and that if we wait long enough something unexpected will occur and order will emerge from the confusion.'

'A *coq-à-l'âne*, my lord, a sudden change of direction. He has spoken of it.'

'And your opinion, doctor?'

'Mr Wetherby's imagination is itself almost Rabelaisian, my lord.'

Leicester smiled. 'Quite so, doctor. Well put. And we will not be waiting at our opponent's pleasure. Even if the plague of testons is over, the culprits must be caught and punished. Take care with the prisoner but do not allow him to keep anything from you. A delicate touch, doctor, but a firm hand.'

'I understand, my lord.'

Christopher left the palace through the Holbein Gate and strode down the Strand. The bitter winter cold had abated and he felt the tiniest hint of warmth on his face. With a shock, he realized that it was the first day of March. The Easter assizes and the London sessions were fast approaching and Joan Willys was still in Newgate. The church clocks chimed four. There was time enough to call on Ell before returning to the prison, where with a firm hand and a delicate touch he might get something more from Hugh Pryse.

He had to wait in Grace's parlour while Ell finished entertaining but it did not take long and the stew owner gave him a glass of strong Rhenish to help pass the time. When Ell appeared she was fully dressed and looked as if she had just woken from a long sleep, refreshed and smiling. The lovely whore never failed to bring a grin to his face.

'Dr Rad,' she said, laughing, 'how did you guess? I was coming round later, as soon as Grace said I could. I've been watching that Alice Scrope's house.'

Christopher put a finger to his lips and spoke quietly, lest Grace could hear them. 'I hoped you would. Have you seen anything?'

'I have, doctor. Comings and goings from morning to evening and who do you think's been coming and going the most?'

'The coroner, Clennet Pyke?'

'Good guess but wrong. Ugly bugger, isn't he? He's been there, sure enough, but there's one I've seen more.'

'Who, Ell?'

'The magistrate, Gilbert Knoyll.'

'Knoyll? Are you sure?'

'Sure as I'm sitting here. No mistaking him, the fat-bellied pig.'

'Ha. Now there's a thing.' There were whores all over London. Why would both the coroner and the magistrate choose a raddled hag like Alice Scrope?

'I know what you're thinking, doctor,' said Ell, reaching out to touch his cheek. 'It's not just how a whore looks but what she does. I daresay Alice Scrope does things that even I've never been asked to do. If one of them told the other, she'd have two happy customers with the coins to pay for what they want. Good way to make money if you can bear it. I couldn't.'

Christopher took her hand. 'Pleased to hear it, Ell. Keep yourself clean and fresh and you'll always be beautiful.'

Ell's smile lit up her face. 'Thank you, Dr Rad. You've a way with words.'

'No, Ell, thank you. I think you might just have saved Joan Willys from gaol and me from having to find a new housekeeper.'

'Any time, doctor.' She held out her hand. 'Half a crown will do, as it's you.'

Christopher handed over the coin without protest. Like any whore, she had to make a living as best she could. 'I'll be paying Mr Knoyll a visit tomorrow.'

'Don't be gentle with him, doctor. Make sure he gets what he deserves for locking up Joan Willys and frightening her half to death, the poxed prick.'

'That I will, Ell. Be good.'

'Always.'

Outside the stew he huddled into his coat and looked up and down the alley. His being seen there would be as much a danger to Ell as to him. But apart from a single beggar, the alley was deserted. He set off for Ludgate Hill.

Pryse could wait until tomorrow, too. Ell's news had lifted his spirits and he did not want to dampen them with a visit to Newgate. What he did want was a beaker or two of ale and a good dinner. He would sleep well with Clennet Pyke and Gilbert Knoyll to look forward to in the morning.

The girl on Ludgate Hill selling beer from a jug for a penny was new. Christopher reckoned he would have noticed her if she had been there before. The usual vendor was a crabby old woman with a squint, whom he avoided. This girl was pretty and he was thirsty.

She took his penny, filled a wooden mug with beer and handed it to him with a smile. 'Drink it up, sir,' she said. 'It'll do you good.'

'It will.' He downed the beer in one and smacked his lips. 'Excellent.'

It was only a few paces up the hill to the house but by the time he got there and was trying to unlock his door, his legs were heavy and his eyes would not focus. He fumbled with the key and dropped it. He slumped down outside the house and shut his eyes. The beer had brought this on but it would pass. He would take a minute to settle and then go inside.

He heard a voice — a man's voice. 'Are you well, sir? Do you need help?'

He looked up and tried to see clearly. The voice jogged a memory. Had he heard it before? Must be a neighbour. His mind was fuddled. He laid his head on the cobbles and closed his eyes again. Within seconds he was asleep.

CHAPTER 27

Christopher awoke with no notion of where he was or how he had got there. His head throbbed and his mouth was as dry as dust. His first, muddled thought was that he was in the Tower. He fought back a moment of panic, lay still and listened. There was only silence. He turned on his side, stretched out his arms and felt cold stone. He was lying on a thin mattress, covered only by a woollen blanket. Probably not the Tower, but a prison of some sort.

He remembered buying beer from a girl, struggling up Ludgate Hill and lying down outside his door, unable to stay awake. He had been drugged. There must have been something in the beer — dwale probably, from the foxglove. A strong dose could knock a man out in minutes. Surgeons used it. Some said witches used it. The beer-seller had used it.

When he sat up his head swam and he had to lie down again. He put his hand to his belt. The poniard had gone but his purse was still there. Not a thief, then; not a cutpurse with an accomplice. The girl selling beer could hardly drug every one of her customers, so why him? And how had he come to this place, wherever it was?

Gradually, very gradually, his mind began to clear and he could make out the room he was in. He stood and felt his way around the walls. They too were of stone. The room was not large — four of his paces in one direction, six in the other.

There were no windows but he found a door. It was wooden, with iron fixings and a heavy round iron handle. He tried to turn it but it scarcely moved. Locked from the outside, he presumed. He tried to prise open what he thought was a spyhole but again to no avail. Apart from the mattress and bedding and a bucket in one corner, there was nothing in the room. He was in a cell.

What could he do but wait? His head ached and he was still drowsy. He lay on the mattress and dozed.

Sometime later, he was roused by the squeak of the panel over the spyhole being drawn back. He twisted to one side and pushed himself up. A dim light filtered through the hole and a voice spoke. It was a deep voice, the uncultured voice of a working man. 'My name is Gabriel. I have food and drink for you. Stay where you are and do not do anything foolish. I am armed and you are not. Is that understood?'

It might have been the voice of the shadow who had whispered in his ear but Christopher could not be sure. He managed a croak. 'It is.'

A key was turned in the lock and the door was pushed open. The man calling himself Gabriel took a step into the room. In one hand he held a candle. By its flickering light, Christopher could see that his hair and beard were unkempt. His nose was broad and his eyes deep-set. It was the face of a farm worker, perhaps, or an artisan. In the other hand the man held a pistol. 'It is primed and loaded,' he said, 'and not with hemp seed.' He put the candle on the floor and took a step backwards through the door, keeping his eyes on Christopher. Crouching down, he slid a wooden trencher into the cell. Christopher saw a jug, a beaker and a plate of food. 'I will leave you the candle. There is another by the plate,' said Gabriel, standing up.

'You are the one who has been following me. You attacked Roland Wetherby and me. Did you kill Fossett? Did you kill Isaac Cardoza? Where am I and why am I being held here?' demanded Christopher, his voice still hoarse. The question ended in a rasping cough from deep in his throat. From Gabriel there was no reply, just the sound of the spyhole being closed and the door locked.

Being careful not to allow the candle to flicker and die, he collected the food and took it to the bed. The beaker and the jug were full. He drained the beaker, refilled it and drained it again. The beer was strong and yeasty and it eased his throat. On the plate were bread with butter, a slab of cheese, four slices of beef and the other candle. He nibbled the bread and realized that he was starving. Like the beer, the food was good – the bread freshly baked and the beef lean and well seasoned. He did not allow himself to think but concentrated on eating and drinking. In Norwich gaol he had soon learned that it was a foolish prisoner who did not take the opportunity to keep up his strength when he could. He ate everything and emptied the jug.

Time passed but he could only estimate how much by the candle. It was a thick wax candle, such as a wealthy man might have in his library, and had been about six inches in height. When it began to gutter, he lit the second one from it. He reckoned that had been two hours, so he had two hours more of a little light.

The second candle was half done when the spyhole was opened and Gabriel spoke through it. 'Simon wishes to meet you and I am to take you to him. Remember that my pistol is primed.'

'Who is Simon?'

'That you will soon discover. Stand up and face the wall. I will tell you when to move.'

Christopher did as he was ordered. He heard Gabriel enter the cell and for a moment thought of hurling himself at the man. The thought quickly died.

'Turn around slowly, doctor,' said Gabriel, his voice even and calm. 'Pick up the candle and leave this room. I will be close behind you.'

Following Gabriel's instructions, he walked along a dark passage and up a short flight of steps. At the top, he turned right. A door barred his way. 'Open the door,' ordered Gabriel, 'and go through.'

Christopher turned the door handle and stepped into a great hall. There was more light here than in his cell but still it was gloomy. A feeble fire at the far end of the room gave off little light. He held up the candle. The hall was bare but for a table, a few plain chairs and a single high-backed chair set to one side of the fire and turned towards it. On it sat a hooded figure with his back to the room. He was playing a lute — a tune that Christopher did not recognize.

'Stand still and do not move. Simon will speak when he is ready,' said Gabriel in a hushed voice. Still holding the candle, Christopher stood and waited.

The music ended and the figure put down his lute. He did not turn around. 'An old piece, Dr Radcliff,' he said, 'but one of which I am fond. "La Vilanela". Do you know it?' The voice was that of a young man and, like the tune, light and musical, quite different to Gabriel's.

Christopher cleared his throat. 'I do not. Nor do I know you. Who are you and why am I held here?'

'All in good time, doctor. Do you play?'

'Who are you?'

'I am Simon. That is all you need to know at present.'

Christopher took a step towards him. 'No closer,' warned Gabriel. 'The pistol is pointing at your back.'

Simon spoke again. 'I regret having to put you in the cell. It is inhospitable, I know, but alas it is the only secure room in the house. It was once a food store. Are you comfortable enough there? Is Gabriel's fare to your taste?' Christopher did not reply. 'No matter. I quite understand your reluctance to speak. If we were to change places, I too would be cautious. Do be seated, doctor.' Christopher sat. Gabriel stood behind him.

'I regret also the need for a pistol. I dislike firearms but Gabriel persuaded me that it was necessary. I warn you not to cross him. He is a loyal friend but his temper can be fierce.'

'The pistol is pointing at my neck. What do you imagine I might try to do?'

Simon laughed. 'Who knows, doctor? Strangle me? Hurl me into the fire? I prefer not to find out.'

'Why do you not show your face? Are you a leper?'

'Simon of Bethany, Simon the leper? Very good, doctor, but I must disappoint you. I am not diseased. And I will show my face when I choose to.' The soft voice took on a harsher tone. 'Do not ask me that again.'

'How long am I to be held here?'

'That is in part up to you, doctor, although I do not anticipate that you will be here long. I merely wished to meet you to discuss with you an idea I have.'

'What idea?'

'That you will find out when we know each other a little better. Now I am tired and Gabriel will escort you back to your cell. We will speak again tomorrow.' Christopher rose. As he reached the door, Simon said, 'I regret also the death of Isaac Cardoza. It was unnecessary. His killer has paid the price for his stupidity.'

'Did Fossett kill Isaac?'

'He did.'

Christopher started back into the hall. He was stopped by the pistol at his cheek which turned his head. But not before he had seen Gabriel's face clearly. If there had been any doubt there was none now. Gabriel was his shadow. And had killed Fossett. And did the bidding of Simon. But who was Simon and why had Christopher been brought to this place?

CHAPTER 28

That night he dreamed not of burning women or slaughtered children but of Norwich gaol. He was locked in a windowless cell with headless creatures and limbless corpses. He cried out for water but there was none and he was forced to drink the blood of a dead man. When his own scream awoke him, sweat was dripping down his face and he was shaking. He dared not close his eyes for fear of the dream returning and lay wide-eyed until he heard the spyhole being opened.

Gabriel opened the door and put the trencher on the floor. 'Simon will see you when you have eaten. Make haste.'

'Where am I?'

Gabriel did not reply. The door was closed and Christopher fetched his breakfast – sweet ale, good mutton and fresh bread. It took his mind from Norwich.

This time Simon was playing Thomas Tallis's 'Like as the doleful dove', a tune that really needed a voice to lift it above its doleful melody. Christopher had never liked it. Thankfully, the hooded figure put the lute aside when he heard Christopher enter the hall.

Without being asked, Christopher sat on the chair that had not been moved since the day before. 'Fossett killed Isaac Cardoza, your servant Gabriel killed Fossett and it was Fossett who collected the testons from the Pryses, was it not?'

'Does it matter, doctor?' Simon did not move and spoke as gently as a man might to a lover.

'The testons matter. What is their purpose beyond embarrassing the Dudley family?' Simon's tone had angered him and his voice rose. It was as much as he could do not to hurl himself at the man, although to do so would certainly be futile. Behind him, Gabriel would be holding a loaded pistol.

'Must they have a purpose? Is there a purpose to our lives or are we merely at the mercy of capricious gods? What purpose is there in pain and suffering?'

'Did Fossett kill John Pryse?'

'He and the man's son killed him together. Fossett did not deserve to live. He was a preening fool of strong opinion and little intelligence. And he had disobeyed my orders. Isaac Cardoza should be alive.'

'Why was Fossett's body removed from the deadhouse?'

'Surprise, shock, fear. Confusion and paradox.' Perhaps Roland Wetherby had been right. Their enemy could indeed be François Rabelais or at least a disciple. 'There are few locks that Gabriel cannot pick and few street urchins who will turn down a penny in return for helping to move a body.'

'And many who believe in the power of witches. To change shape, to fly, to remove bodies.'

'Quite so.'

'The slogans. Were they your work also?'

'Not all. There are those who lead and others who follow. They served our purpose.'

'Plague crosses, a bag of testons outside the Cardozas' door, a cross on my door. Why?'

'You have answered your own question. They were there because you have to ask why.'

Riddles and puzzles. The stuff of fear. 'When will you tell me why I am here?'

'Soon, doctor. Meanwhile, Gabriel has visited your house.'

Christopher started. 'Why?'

'Do not be alarmed. Nothing has been damaged or removed. Except for one thing. It is beside you.'

Christopher looked down. Gabriel had made not a sound in placing his lute case by the chair. He reached down for it.

'Do open it,' said Simon. Christopher took out the lute and plucked the treble string with his thumb. The sound was true. 'I somehow knew that you would play and asked Gabriel to check. I do hope you are not offended. But really, doctor, to hide such a masterpiece under a pile of old clothes — it is almost an insult to the maker. Venetian, is it not? A magnificent instrument which I shall much enjoy hearing. I noticed the plate on the peg box. It was a gift from the Earl of Leicester. He must think very highly of you. Now what will you play for us?'

Not only had he been poisoned but his house had been entered and searched. Yet still he did not know what his captors wanted of him. Ignorant and powerless, he could only wait and try not to let fury and frustration cloud his mind. He tried a different tack. 'What is the meaning of the crosses? Or are they not crosses?'

Simon clapped his hands. 'Bravo, doctor. Now what might they be if they are not crosses?'

'The Greek letter *chi*, symbolizing chaos.'

'Exactly. Just as the music of the lute, when poorly played, may symbolize chaos. Or, when played well, harmony and order. Or love. The courtly noble or the jesting fool or the lovelorn youth. Have you ever wondered at the conversation a man may have with his lute? That is an extraordinary thing, is it not? A man and an object in conversation.'

'Why do you seek chaos?'

'Before the world began, there was chaos. Out of the chaos came order and it is order I seek. The order that comes with knowledge and truth.'

'And you are willing to kill to achieve this.'

For the first time, Simon's voice rose. 'Enough. I wish to hear you play, doctor. I wish to know if the music of your lute is as beautiful as it is. What will you play?'

'I will play nothing until you tell me why I am here and what you want with me.'

'That is a disappointment, doctor.' Now the voice had taken on its harsher tone. 'I trust you will not regret it. If you will not play, I have no further use for you today. Leave me.'

Christopher felt the pistol at his neck. He put the lute back in its case and stood up. As he did so, he turned suddenly and thrust the case into Gabriel's face. If he could overcome Gabriel, he could force Simon to speak. Before Gabriel could react, he picked up the chair and rammed its legs into his stomach. Gabriel yelped but did not drop the pistol. Christopher made a lunge for it. He was quick but Gabriel was quicker. He stepped aside and slashed the barrel across Christopher's face. Christopher stumbled and fell, blood running down his cheek.

Gabriel stood over him, the pistol pointing at his eyes. 'You were warned. A foolish attempt, doctor. Do not make another.'

'Gabriel is right,' said Simon. 'I did not see what you did, but whatever it was, it was foolish. Another attempt would be fatal.'

The weather must have turned colder and the candle had burned out. Christopher huddled under the blankets and touched the bloody bruise on his face.

'Out of the chaos came order,' Simon had said, 'and it is order I seek. The order that comes with knowledge and truth.' What did he mean by that? Knowledge of what? The truth of what?

Not diseased, yet unwilling to show his face. Why? A man who disliked firearms yet could not escape responsibility for at least two deaths. A man who played on human fears. In pursuit of ends he had not disclosed. Why not? More paradox, more enigma.

The food and drink came again. At least he was not going to starve to death and if Simon had wanted him dead, he would have ordered Gabriel to kill him by now. Nor was he being kept alive just to play the lute. What did Simon really want of him and how long was he to be held in this place? And what of Roland, what of Ell? Were they searching for him? Had Leicester sent for him only to find that he had disappeared? Would Christopher ever find out?

He guessed that it was mid-afternoon the next time Gabriel escorted him up the steps to the hall, but could not be sure. Heavy drapes covered whatever windows there were. It was a house that sunlight could not enter.

'Are you in better humour today, doctor?' asked Simon. 'I do hope you are ready to play.' There was an edge to his voice, as if he were nervous or excited.

'Why am I being held here?' asked Christopher, struggling to hold in check another urge to throw himself at the faceless figure.

'That you will discover soon.'

'Where am I? What is this place?'

'I am surprised you have not asked this before. Sit down and I will tell you my story of this house. It is my own story, one I made up while sitting here by the fire. Like all stories it may be true or it may not. I will tell it to you and afterwards you will play.'

Christopher sat and waited. After a few minutes, Simon began.

'Where this house stands there was once a small community eking an existence from the river and the land. The community was destroyed in a great flood nearly ninety years ago and now the land is almost deserted and such dwellings as remain are but mean hovels.

'A rutted highway, banked up with soil and stone to protect it from the river's incursions, still runs through the land and a hundred yards to the east of it, on a low plateau of higher, firmer ground, a single house remains, largely hidden from view by a copse of alder and birch, and protected by a maze of ditches that criss-crosses the treacherous land around it. Anyone unfamiliar with the marsh at this place risks his life if he tries to find a way through it.

'The house, two storeys high, with solid stone walls, a straw-thatched roof, shuttered windows and doors fashioned from thick oak panels, was built by a merchant who made his fortune in the trading of wool a hundred years ago. A man of social as well as financial aspiration, he brought the oak from the Essex forests and the stone from quarries in Kent and in doing so he risked much. The cost was enormous.

'When the house was completed he furnished it extravagantly, moved in with his servants and set himself to find a wife. Within a few months, however, his dream of a thriving community centred on his grand mansion had been swept away in the flood and he was forced to leave it to the mercy of the wind and the river. He never found a wife and died sick and broken.

'For decades the house remained deserted but it was well built with deep foundations. Its present owner paid little for it, the isolated location being a deterrent to other buyers. But not to him. His purpose it suited admirably. He did not do much to repair or refurbish it other than to replace the ancient, rotting thatch with grey slate tiles and to clear the chimney — a feature of which the merchant had been especially proud — of birds' nests and other debris. His furniture was plain and functional and his possessions few.

'The house had been designed around a great hall from which a grand stair curved up to bed chambers above and from which doors led to the kitchens, a cellar, storerooms and servants' quarters.

'Even in midsummer the shutters were never opened and the house was dark. Now, when winter has yet to give way to spring, it would take fifty wax candles to light the hall and fifty more the rest of the house. That had been one of its attractions. A shadowy house, black and silent, well hidden and unknown to all but a few. From here the owner wove his spider's web of shock and deceit and rejoiced in the chaos and confusion they sired. And he took pleasure in finding a certain symmetry in the house's history. One man's dream had become another's, entirely at odds though those dreams were.

'At one end of the hall the merchant had built a fireplace wide enough to accommodate six-foot lengths of timber but the owner allowed only small branches and brushwood to be burned on it and then only at night. He did not want unwelcome visitors calling to discover the source of the smoke. It was not that his presence was entirely unknown, merely that he wished to be solitary and to be asked no questions.' He came to an abrupt end. 'That is the story I have invented, doctor, and that is the house in which we sit. Now you will play for me.'

'I will not. I may be your prisoner but I am not your musician to perform at your request.'

'In that case you will not require your lute.'

As soon as the hooded figure began to play, he knew. In the right hands the ivory lute produced a sound unlike that of any other. Its notes held a particular clarity, a resonance that spruce could not offer. He longed to leap at Simon and take it back. The lute was his. It should not be played by another man, however skilled a musician.

He felt a hand on his shoulder and Gabriel spoke into his ear. 'It would be unwise to interrupt, doctor.' Christopher clenched his teeth and gripped the arms of the chair. Simon was an accomplished player − quicker and more fluent than he was − but hearing the music was like an arrow in the chest. Only with difficulty did he take Gabriel's advice.

Simon finished the piece and put down the lute. 'Venetian music for a Venetian lute, doctor. I do so enjoy music of that period, although it is sadly out of fashion now. Do you not agree?'

'That is my lute. You have stolen it from my house.'

'Borrowed, doctor, borrowed.'

'What is your purpose in holding me here?'

'Well now, doctor, it is almost time that I answered that question.' Simon stood up, his back to the room. He was not a tall man, slim and narrow in the shoulder, his head tilted a little to one side. He kept a hand on the arm of his chair and did not look round. 'For a man condemned to a life of solitude, music is magical in its beauty. The pleasure of discourse, the touch of a woman, even to walk down a street unmolested − all are barred to me. From an early age I read whatever I was given − the Bible, Plato, Machiavelli, Rabelais,

Chaucer — but the lute was my only real friend and the one thing that I looked forward to each day. I had no teacher but learned for myself. The lute asked me questions and I tried to reply. As I got older the questions became more difficult and I realized that there were no more answers. Our world is capricious and it is easier to accept that than to look for reason.'

Simon paused as if to gather his thoughts. 'Having spent most of my life in reading, playing and thinking, I have concluded that reality and illusion are not always easily distinguished. You will recall Plato's story of the prisoners in the cave. They see shadows moving on the wall but do not know what is causing them. For the prisoners, the shadows are reality.'

He paused again and took several deep breaths. The effort of standing and speaking was tiring him. 'I will not fulfil my three score years and ten, or anything like it, a fact to which I am entirely reconciled.' There was a short laugh before he continued. 'A brief fancy is often superior to a longer one, do you not agree? That is why I have also sought to amuse myself in other ways. The testons and the crosses and the slogans served that purpose well and brought you to me when the time was right. Bringing you here earlier would have been easy enough but unamusing.' He paused to take a few short breaths before continuing. 'Since the death of my mother, dear Gabriel, who has known me since the day I emerged from her womb, has been my only companion and my loyal servant. Although, sadly, he has no talent for music, I owe him a debt that I can never repay. And now I have need of your service, doctor.' He paused again. 'I wish to play for the queen.'

Christopher stared at Simon's back, wondering if he had heard correctly. 'And how in the name of God do you intend to do that? Is she to be invited here?'

Simon laughed. 'A delicious thought but alas, no. It is you who will make the necessary arrangements.'

'And how am I to do that? Even if I were not held in this hellish house of darkness, how would I persuade Her Majesty to allow you into her presence, let alone listen to you play?'

'I have given that much thought and believe I have a solution to the problem.'

'And what is your solution?'

'You will find that out later today. Meanwhile, Gabriel will escort you back to your room. Tell him if there is anything you need to make you more comfortable.'

'My freedom would help.'

'Oh, I almost forgot. I wish the Earl of Leicester to be present also. I believe that the queen would like him there and I am aware of his love of music.' He sat down. 'Gabriel will tell you when I am ready.'

CHAPTER 29

Gabriel had brought a new candle. Christopher sat in the cell that Simon had called his room and watched the flame flickering.

The man was clearly mad. A lunatic who should be in Bedlam. A madman who had been perfectly lucid but was capable of making such an outrageous and absurd demand. How in the name of the devil's whores did he imagine that Christopher was going to arrange for him to play for the queen and the Earl of Leicester? And how did Simon think he would escape capture? As the instigator of murder and coining he would certainly be hanged and probably drawn and quartered.

Then he realized. Simon was not so mad after all. It was perfectly simple. He was going to do exactly what the traitor John Berwick had tried to do. He was going to take a hostage and hold him — no, her — until he had played and been allowed to depart unharmed. While Christopher sat helpless in his cell, Gabriel would be paying a visit to Wood Street.

Yet there remained unanswered questions. What would Simon do to ensure that the whereabouts of this house were not revealed?

Where did he expect to play? And how would he leave after playing without being arrested or followed?

Nor would Leicester ever agree to a hooded stranger being permitted access to Whitehall, let alone into the queen's presence. The very idea was monstrous.

The candle was still burning when Gabriel returned. Christopher heard his footsteps and saw the spyhole cover being drawn back. He stood away from the door and watched while Gabriel opened it and motioned with the pistol for him to go up to the hall. He did not speak.

Simon was at his usual place by the fire, playing another old Venetian tune on the ivory lute. He was hooded. Opposite him, at the other end of the fire, sat another figure, also hooded and bound to the chair with rope. Although the figure was in shadow, Christopher knew at once that it was not Katherine.

Simon finished the piece and stood up. Keeping his face hidden, he took two steps, reached out and pulled the hood from the other figure. It was Roland Wetherby.

Christopher rose from his chair and was immediately pushed down by Gabriel behind him. 'Roland, are you injured?' he asked.

'My pride, only,' replied Wetherby. 'More importantly, are *you* injured?'

'No, I am uninjured, although if I am forced to remain in this place for much longer I shall certainly lose my wits.'

'Forgive me, Mr Wetherby,' said Simon. 'Despite my solitude, I have a taste for the dramatic. I once tried to write a play with a part for myself but, alas, I have not the playwright's skill and soon returned to my music. Perhaps someone more skilled will one day do it for me. Did you enjoy the tune?'

'I would have enjoyed it more without a hood over my head. Who are you and why are we here?'

Simon laughed. 'The very questions Dr Radcliff has been pestering me with. I am Simon and you are here because I wish to play the lute for the queen and the Earl of Leicester.'

'Although he has not disclosed how or why this is to be done,' said Christopher. 'Warwick's notion of a game appears to have been apt. This man, a coiner and a murderer, sees us as his pieces to be moved about the board as he chooses.'

'Dr Radcliff is ill humoured because I have borrowed his lute. However, Mr Wetherby, now that you are here, it is time that I explained what I have planned. Do, please, listen carefully.'

'Have we any choice but to listen? I am bound to this chair and Dr Radcliff has a pistol at his head. But kindly make your explanation brief. Already I tire of this game.'

Simon clapped his hands. 'If only things had been different, Mr Wetherby, I believe that we would all have been good friends. Your spirit does you credit. As does Dr Radcliff's. But I have long since given up wishing things were different.' While Christopher and Roland were seated, he remained standing. 'I am anxious to achieve my one ambition while I can. That ambition is to play the lute for the Queen of England and to do so in the Great Chamber of Whitehall Palace.'

Christopher scoffed. 'A noble ambition, but not one that is likely to be realized.'

'On the contrary, doctor, I have every expectation that it will indeed be realized because you will ensure that it is. Mr Wetherby will remain here while you return to Whitehall to persuade the noble earl to obtain Her Majesty's consent to my proposal. I feel sure that she will give it, especially when she is told that Mr Wetherby's head will be delivered to her, as John the Baptist's was to Herodias, if she does not.'

'The plan would have a better chance of success if I stayed here and Roland returned to Whitehall,' said Christopher.

Simon shook his head. 'Most gallant, doctor, but I think not. The silver-tongued lawyer should have no difficulty in winning his case. You will leave this house tonight, bound and your eyes covered. Gabriel will drive you to Aldgate where you will be left to find your own way to Whitehall. The guards at the gate will not detain you. Twelve hours later you will return to the gate where Gabriel will be waiting for you. You will inform him that the queen has given her consent and that you will meet me at the gate four hours later. From there you will escort me by coach to the palace. After I have played, you will return me to the gate where Gabriel will be waiting with Mr Wetherby, who will be released on my word.'

'And if I do not?'

'Then Mr Wetherby will die.'

Christopher looked at Wetherby. 'Then I had best persuade the earl.'

'Please do, Christopher,' said Wetherby. 'I do not wish to have my head removed for the sake of a galliard.'

'Again, Mr Wetherby, I am in awe of your courage,' said Simon. 'Dr Radcliff will now return to his room while I play for you. Would a piece by Francesco Spinacino be agreeable?' Without waiting for a reply he sat down, took up the lute and began to play.

Gabriel nudged Christopher with the barrel of the pistol and whispered, 'Time to go, doctor.'

'How long before dark?'

'Two hours. I will fetch you when it is time.'

It was a long two hours, spent largely in rehearsing what he was going to say to Leicester and what Leicester could possibly say to the queen, and trying to make sense of Simon's bizarre demand. Coining, crosses and slogans leading to this? Why had he not simply abducted Christopher and Roland and achieved the same result? Did he hope to become a royal lute or was he simply mad? Both, perhaps.

Over and over he turned the questions in his mind, but when Gabriel opened the spyhole he had found no answers. The door opened and Gabriel threw a hood into the cell. 'Put that on and face the wall,' he ordered. 'I am instructed to kill you if you offer the slightest resistance. Mr Wetherby, too.' Christopher slid the hood over his head and faced the wall. 'Your hands behind your back, if you please.'

Christopher almost cheered. There would be a moment when Gabriel needed both hands to tie him and would have to put away the pistol. He steadied himself and waited for the moment. When the rope tightened on his wrists he turned sharply, ready to smash a fist into Gabriel's face. Only his wrists were already bound and the pistol was pointed straight at him. Gabriel had prepared a knot that could be slipped into place with only one hand. 'I warned you, doctor,' Gabriel growled. 'No more chances.'

Another rope went around his neck and he was led up the steps. At the top they did not turn right towards the hall, but left. When Gabriel opened a door, cold air swept into the house. They were outside. 'Ten steps,' said Gabriel, 'and one step up into the coach. I will be sitting beside you.' So there was a coachman – no doubt some homeless felon scraped off a filthy alley and put to work for a shilling or two. He would be no help.

The coachman cracked the reins and they set off, slowly at first and then at a canter. The road beneath them was pitted and holed and Christopher found himself being shaken about like a sapling in a storm. The ropes remained well knotted and Gabriel did not speak.

If he had been brought to the house on this highway he must have swallowed a heavy dose of dwale. Then he had been conscious of nothing; now he was close to vomiting. He swallowed hard and tried to imagine he was at sea. He loved the sea as he loved the river and on a boat could happily put up with any amount of wind and rain.

He sniffed and detected a hint of salt in the air. So they were not far from the sea. And Simon had said Aldgate, which guarded the road from the east. He had been held to the east of the city. Among the salt marshes perhaps, where few ventured for fear of robbers and disease.

After a while the highway became smoother — a sure sign that they were nearing the city wall. The coachman urged the horses on and they increased their pace. Outside the walls there was always a danger of highway robbers. Simon might have gatekeepers and urchins in his purse but not highwaymen.

When they came to a halt Gabriel said, 'We are at the Aldgate. You will be admitted through the gate to the left of the portcullis by a guard who will untie your hands when he has closed it behind you. We will step out of the coach now.'

Christopher put a hand on the seat and felt for the door. It was open. He stepped out, the rope still around his neck. 'Twenty paces,' said Gabriel. Christopher counted them off. 'Enough.' He heard the gate being opened and a voice asking for a sign. 'The lute player,' replied Gabriel.

'Let me have him, sir. I'll take him inside.'

A church bell struck eight. 'Do not forget,' said Gabriel. 'It is now eight o'clock. I shall be here in exactly twelve hours. Do not be late.'

Christopher heard him climb into the coach before the rope was tugged and he was led through the gate. The gate was closed with a thump and his hands were untied. He pulled off the hood. The guard stood in front of him, sword drawn. 'On your way, sir. My job is done.'

'Am I at the Aldgate?'

'You are. Be gone and take care not to meet the watch.'

The watch would be about but they were seldom vigilant and would be content with a few coins if he ran into them. Without his blade he was more concerned about the creatures of the night who infested this ward and thought nothing of slitting a gentleman's throat for a purse.

He kept to the wider streets and away from the lanes and alleys into which even the watch seldom ventured. In Leadenhall Street he ducked into a doorway when he heard them coming and waited until they had passed. There were only two of them, chattering away as if at drink in a city tavern but he did not want to have to explain himself or to be delayed.

Without the hustle and bustle of the market, Cheapside was a ghostly place — silent and empty but for a single whore being humped against a wall. For a moment he wished that he could turn down the lane to Ell's stew where there would be a willing listener and a sympathetic voice. But he had not the time and in any case the chances were that Ell would be occupied. He hurried on to St Paul's and down to Fleet Street, where Isaac's shop showed no sign of a new occupant. The owner had better look sharp or it would not be long before packs of vagrants and vermin moved in.

The Strand was a favourite haunt of whores hoping for easy pickings from its grand houses. It was easy enough for a servant or a young man of the house to slip out of a side door for a quick dalliance and their whores expected to be paid well for their service. Taking care not to step in the heaps of horse shit waiting to be collected,

Christopher kept to the middle of the street, away from grasping hands and promises of untold pleasure.

A guard stood either side of the Holbein Gate, at that time of night closed to all but the queen's closest courtiers and members of her Privy Council. Many of the palace guards knew Christopher and would admit him without fuss. These two, however, did not. He explained who he was and that he must see the Earl of Leicester at once on a matter of great urgency, but without a letter of authority, they would not open the gate for him.

He told them that lives were at stake and that the earl would not be pleased to learn that his chief London intelligencer had been refused entry by them. He told them that the matter upon which he must see the earl concerned the queen herself. And, in desperation, he told them that it was in his power to have them dismissed from their posts.

The guards were unmoved. 'Our orders are to admit no one without authority,' said one of them, 'and you have none. Be off and come back in the morning.'

He gave up. There would be no getting past these guards. Best try something else.

Whitehall Palace had two landing piers — one for the queen's private use and a second, larger one for visitors arriving by wherry or barge. At night, the river was seldom used and the entrance which the pier served would be closed and guarded, but he had no better idea.

He made his way down the lane towards the river, passing the backs of the Great Chamber and the chapel, until he reached the riverbank. He climbed a short flight of steps on to the pier.

The pier was lit by torches. Three barges were tied up to it but there was no sign of bargemen. He walked up the wooden ramp to the iron gate that barred entry to the palace grounds. As he approached, a guard on the other side of it challenged him and asked his business. Christopher claimed to have arrived by the river and repeated everything he had told the guards at the Holbein Gate. The guard was unmoved. 'You have no authority to enter. Get back in your boat and return from where you came. No one enters the palace at night without authority.'

Christopher made one last attempt. 'Send messengers to the Earl of Leicester and the Earl of Warwick. Tell them that Dr Radcliff asks to see them at once.'

'No messages. Go, whoever you are.'

What now? Time was passing and he must be back at Aldgate by eight in the morning. He could not afford to wait until light.

From behind the gate came the clatter of boots on stone and three men appeared. Two were guards. The third Christopher recognized immediately. He had once sat in this man's library in his house on the Strand overlooking the river and been asked if he would consider leaving Leicester's staff to join his own. He had declined and later, after Berwick had been arrested and hanged, the opposite had happened and Roland Wetherby had left the man to join Leicester. Thomas Heneage and Leicester were rivals but Heneage, Treasurer of the Queen's Privy Chamber, had remained on friendly terms with him.

For Heneage and his guards the gate had to be opened. One of the barges moored at the pier would be his. It was but a short distance to his house but he was known to prefer the river to the streets. The three men waited while the guard fiddled with the gate. 'Make haste, man,' grumbled Heneage. 'It is time I was in my bed.'

'Mr Heneage,' said Christopher loudly, 'it is Christopher Radcliff. I must speak urgently with the Earl of Leicester but the guard will not admit me.'

Heneage peered through the iron bars. 'Dr Radcliff? What are you doing at this time of night? You should not be here.'

'Mr Wetherby is in grave danger. I must speak to the earl. Please have this gate opened.'

'Wetherby in danger? How so?'

'Mr Heneage, I have no time to explain. If you would have the gate opened, perhaps one of your guards would escort me to the earl.'

Heneage frowned and shook his head. 'The earl was not at the queen's masque this evening. He is unwell.'

'Mr Wetherby's life hangs on my speaking to him. Could he not be disturbed?'

Heneage hesitated. 'I am reluctant . . .'

'Wetherby will die if I do not speak to the earl at once.'

Christopher's tone must have persuaded him. 'Very well, Dr Radcliff. You may enter but I will escort you myself to the earl's apartments. I do hope that the inconvenience to both of us is justified.'

The guard opened the gate. Heneage's guards waited while he led Christopher into the palace. They walked down a long passage lit by torches, up a flight of stairs and into the gallery that overlooked the gardens. Leicester's apartments were at the end of the gallery. A guard stood outside his door. Heneage ordered him to step aside. The guard did not move. 'The Earl of Leicester is unwell,' he said, 'and will not receive visitors.'

'He will receive me,' replied Heneage. 'Tell the earl that Thomas Heneage asks to see him on a grave matter concerning Mr Wetherby.' The guard looked doubtful. 'Do it, man, or I'll have you on kitchen duty for a year.' From his initial hesitation, Heneage had become an ally. Did he see an opportunity to impress Leicester or to regain Wetherby's services? No matter if he did. Leicester must be woken.

'Remain here, sir,' said the guard. 'I will see if the earl is able to see you.' He opened the door and went in, leaving them outside in the gallery. Neither spoke while they waited.

In a few minutes the guard returned. 'Mr Heneage may enter,' he said, 'but the earl asks who is with him.'

'Dr Christopher Radcliff.'

The guard disappeared again. He was back immediately. 'You may enter, sirs. The earl is resting but will see you.'

They hurried through the antechamber and into the earl's apartments, from which a door led to his bed chamber. Christopher had never been through that door and he doubted Heneage had either. The guard knocked and they went in.

Leicester was propped up in his bed in a nightshirt, with the heavy bed drapes drawn back and candles in silver holders lighting the room. By the colour of his face, he had a fever. A book lay open beside him. In a voice thick with cold, he ordered the guard to leave them.

'What is this, Dr Radcliff? You disappear only to reappear having persuaded Mr Heneage to help you gain entrance to my bed chamber while I am suffering from a winter cold.' He coughed. 'You told me the coiner was safely in Newgate. And what is this about Wetherby being in danger?' Before Christopher could reply, he added, 'I thank you, Thomas. Do feel free to return home. I would not keep you from your bed.'

'I might be of some further assistance.'

'No, go home and let me deal with this. But please ask a guard to find my brother.'

'As you wish.' He sounded disappointed.

When Heneage had left, Christopher said, 'My lord, Mr Wetherby is a prisoner of the man responsible for the false testons, the slogans maligning Her Majesty and your family, plague crosses where there is no plague, my agent Isaac Cardoza's murder and the attack on Mr Wetherby at St Paul's. He also ordered the murder of Isaac's killer.'

Leicester sat up straighter. 'Where is he held and what is his captor's name? I will order the militia out immediately.'

'I do not know where he is held and only that his captor goes by the name of Simon. He has a servant named Gabriel who does his bidding.'

'This is making no sense, doctor. Is it my head or have you lost your wits? How can you not know where these traitors are? And why have they taken Wetherby?'

'I will make the story as brief as I can, my lord, because time is also our enemy.'

The chamber door opened and Ambrose Dudley, in a coat hastily thrown over his nightshirt, limped in. 'What is this, Robert? What new disaster has befallen us? I was about to retire.'

'Dr Radcliff is about to explain why we have both been disturbed.' He nodded to Christopher. 'Do proceed, doctor.'

While Christopher recounted the events since his own capture, Leicester sipped from a silver goblet and Warwick stood beside him. Their silence made his task all the harder. He felt their eyes upon him and sensed their disbelief. Even to his own ears the tale sounded ridiculous. He told it as quickly as he could and waited nervously for a response.

'Is that it?' scoffed Warwick, shaking his head.

Christopher ignored his tone. 'It is, my lord.'

'So if I understand you, doctor,' said Leicester, wiping his mouth with a napkin, 'if this Simon, who will not reveal his face to the world, is not permitted to play in front of our gracious queen and myself, Wetherby will die.'

'That is correct.'

'Why? What could this man possibly gain from it? And why would he put himself at risk? For all he knows, we might throw him into Newgate and drag the truth out of him, leaving Wetherby to take his chances.'

'I cannot answer that but we must assume that he does not believe we would do so.'

'Is there anything you can tell us about this Simon? Anything that might shed light on his purpose?' asked Warwick.

'I can only imagine that the wretched man is horribly disfigured. He claims that he is not diseased or scarred so he must have been born as he is and having lived a solitary life his mind will also be affected.'

'Good God. That a man so afflicted would want to play before Her gentle Majesty surpasses understanding,' said Warwick.

'As does the idea that I would cause Her Majesty to suffer such an experience,' added Leicester. 'The man is a lunatic.'

'And you really do not know where you were being held?'

'As I was left at the Aldgate, it will have been to the east of the city, but I could not say where. It might take weeks to find the house.'

Leicester wiped his brow with a white handkerchief. 'Damn this cold. My head is like a sack of wool.'

'Robert,' said Warwick, 'Dr Radcliff has had a day — several days, by the sound of it — that would have felled many a strong man and he must be hungry. Let us send for victuals for him. He can fortify himself while you and I discuss this problem.'

'The kitchens will find you something. There will be pies and pastries left over from the masque,' said Leicester, before sneezing.

It was an order. Christopher left the chamber, spoke to the guard and sat in the earl's apartment. The chair he chose was the one he had sat in when he had first played the ivory lute. A good omen or bad?

The food came with a bottle of Rhenish wine. He drained two goblets before setting about a chicken pie and a custard tart. He ate most of the pie as he waited for Warwick to emerge. When the earl did so, he was dressed. Christopher rose to his feet. The other man's expression was grave.

'My brother is dressing,' he said. 'We will go to the privy apartments and ask for an audience. The earl was most reluctant but eventually came to the conclusion that we should at least try. If Her Majesty will not see us or refuses your request, that will be an end to the matter.'

'Thank you, my lord. We can but hope that Her Majesty remembers the signal service Mr Wetherby once performed for her.'

Warwick nodded. 'You are to remain here. We will send for you if necessary.'

Leicester emerged from his bed chamber in a black doublet edged in gold over a white ruffed shirt and black hose. Sick or not he would never appear before his queen other than immaculately attired. He ignored Christopher, opened the door and left. Warwick followed him.

Christopher had nothing to do but twiddle his thumbs and imagine what the queen might say at being disturbed. He had once bowed to her but never exchanged words. He wondered if he should wait in the antechamber but decided to stay where he was. The antechamber was dominated by a portrait of the queen that he had always found unsettling. This was no time for yet more unsettlement.

As the minutes passed, he asked himself whether that was a hopeful sign or not. They would have returned by now if the queen had refused to see them but on the other hand she could not have been immediately swayed by Wetherby's past service and readily agreed to Simon's request.

He had been waiting for an hour when he heard the outer door open and footsteps on the wooden floor. He jumped up. Leicester's face was suffused by fever. He stumbled as he entered the room and had to steady himself with a hand on the chess table. 'I shall retire,' he said. 'My lord Warwick will give you your instructions.'

When Leicester had left them, Warwick reached for the wine bottle and took a gulp from it. 'Excuse my discourtesy, doctor. I too should be in my bed and my throat is dry.' Christopher waited. Warwick took another swig before continuing. 'Her Majesty was not best pleased to be disturbed in her private apartments and found your story hard to believe. She does not fear for herself but cannot understand, as we cannot, why this man wishes to put himself at risk by coming here.'

'I too have no answer to that, my lord.'

'However, she was eventually persuaded — largely by my brother, I should add — that if this man is responsible for coining and murder, we cannot allow him to remain at large and free to commit further crimes.' Warwick paused but Christopher's eyes did not leave his face. 'This is what has been agreed with Her Majesty. You will return to Aldgate by eight o'clock, where you will meet the coach. You will insist on returning to the house in which you were imprisoned — hooded no doubt — where you will inform the man Simon that Her Majesty has graciously consented to hear him play in return for the release of Mr Wetherby. On our part, there will be no subterfuge.'

Christopher tried to keep his face impassive until he knew what else had been agreed.

'You will tell the man Simon that he must return with you and that you will escort him here to the palace. Her Majesty has specified a time of three o'clock so that she can dine afterwards.'

Christopher nodded.

'You will also inform him that he will be permitted to play in the Great Chamber, as requested, in front of the queen, her ladies-in-waiting, the Earl of Leicester, you and me.'

'I am to be present?'

'It is Her Majesty's wish. There will be an armed guard in each corner of the room with orders to kill the man at the slightest hint of danger to her. It is up to you to persuade him to accept these terms. There will be no others.'

'Her Majesty is most gracious.'

'Indeed she is. I did not need to remind her of Mr Wetherby's past service and she appeared most concerned when she learned that he was in danger. I believe that is why she has agreed to this strange request.' He paused. 'That and curiosity. She wants to know why this man has made it.'

'And what will happen after the recital?'

'You will escort him back to Aldgate where Mr Wetherby will be waiting for you. If he is not, Simon will be arrested and taken to the Tower to be questioned.'

'By whom will he be arrested, my lord?'

'The guards will have been changed and will have been given their orders.'

'Simon is a traitor and a murderer. Are you willing to let him go?'

A tiny smile crossed Warwick's face. 'Fear not. We will keep our side of the bargain but afterwards he will be found and brought to trial.'

No wonder he had had to wait so long. The queen and the brothers Dudley had thought through the plan with great care. There were more than eight hours before the coach would be at the Aldgate and Christopher needed rest. 'If I may, my lord, I will return to my house to sleep. I will be ready in the morning.'

'Good. My coach will be outside your house at seven. That will allow plenty of time for delays.'

'Thank you, my lord.' Christopher rose to leave.

'Tomorrow, doctor. Be ready and whatever lies before us, pray for a successful outcome.'

CHAPTER 30

He was back in his own house and his own bed but there remained the lingering suspicion that, despite Warwick's assurance there would be no subterfuge, he had not been told everything. A known traitor and coiner would never be allowed to escape justice.

Sleep did not come easily. He dozed until St Martin's clock struck six to mark the end of the curfew. There was an hour until the coach clattered up the hill and came to a halt outside his door. He would hear it coming and he would be ready.

He dressed, combed his unruly hair and looked around for his poniard. 'You ape, Radcliff,' he said out loud. 'The thing has long gone.'

He found another knife in the kitchen and set about what remained of the pie. He found ale with which to wash it down and silently thanked the palace kitchens for providing his breakfast. A slice of squashed tart followed the pie. He was ready.

His hand ached. He rubbed the palm and stretched the fingers. The condition was getting worse. If it continued, the lute would lie unused. If he ever recovered it. Katherine came into his mind. If he didn't recover her, he would lie unused. He had been unable to help Joan Willys who languished in Newgate, put there by the slattern Alice Scrope with the help of the lying Gilbert Knoyll and Clennet Pyke. At least the murdering Pryse was locked up and would hang.

The coach drew up as the clock struck seven. The coachman wished him a cheerful good morning and set the horses off at a walk. He did not hurry and only occasionally had to yell at an urchin or a vendor to make way. The Dudley crest on the coach's doors were a deterrent to any man with mischief in mind.

At Aldgate, Christopher stepped down and sent the coachman on his way back to Whitehall. He preferred to wait alone for Gabriel, although if the shadow did not come he would face another long walk, followed by an unpleasant meeting with Leicester and Warwick. And Wetherby would be dead.

He did come. On the stroke of eight, Simon's coach arrived outside the gate and Gabriel jumped out. 'Well, doctor,' he asked, 'is Her Majesty looking forward to a performance on the lute?'

'She is. There are, however, conditions.'

Gabriel frowned. 'Conditions of what nature?'

'That I will tell Simon when you have taken me to the house. I am willing to be hooded.'

'Simon will not take kindly to conditions.'

'Then he will not meet the queen.'

'And Wetherby will die.'

'So be it.'

Gabriel shrugged. 'Very well. Board the coach, doctor, and I will secure the hood. Do not forget that I am armed.'

Christopher stepped into the coach. Gabriel produced the hood, slipped it over his head and tied it around his neck with a short length of rope. 'Your hands, please, doctor,' he said. Christopher held out his hands for Gabriel to bind his wrists. When it was done, Gabriel called to the coachman to be off.

It was not easy to measure time without being able to see but Christopher reckoned that the journey took about an hour. They did not speak.

When they came to a halt Christopher was led into the house, hands still bound. He sensed that they were in the Great Hall and that Simon was there. Gabriel untied the rope around his neck and removed the hood. He was standing in the middle of the room facing the fire, where Simon sat with the ivory lute on his lap and his back to him.

'Dr Radcliff,' he said, 'I was not expecting you but I am delighted to see you. I did not think you would leave Mr Wetherby to his fate, but, well, a man can be wrong. Happily, I was not. What have you to tell me?'

'We will travel in your coach to Aldgate. There we will be met by the Earl of Leicester's coach and taken to Whitehall.'

'Gabriel must accompany us.'

'To the gate, no further. Her Majesty will receive you at three o'clock this afternoon. She will be guarded and the Earls of Warwick and Leicester will be present, as will I.'

'No one else?'

'Only her ladies-in-waiting.'

Simon laughed. 'Of course, no queen could be seen without her ladies. It is part of being royal, is it not? Anything else?'

'Nothing.'

Simon shrugged. 'And after I have played?'

'When it is done, I will return with you to Aldgate in the earl's coach, where Gabriel will be waiting with Wetherby. If he is not there, you will not be allowed through the gate.'

For a minute or so, Simon did not speak and Christopher began to fear that he suspected a trap and would not accept the conditions. But Simon stood up and handed the lute and its case to Christopher. 'I have decided to play for Her Majesty on my own lute. Here is yours. It is a magnificent instrument. Take good care of it.' Under the hood his face was hidden by a linen mask.

'We should leave at one,' said Christopher. 'I trust Mr Wetherby is in good health.'

'As far as I know, he is. Gabriel will escort you to your room — you are sharing it now, I'm afraid — so that you can see for yourself. He will carry your lute for you. Until one, doctor.'

Wetherby sat on the mattress, back to the wall and knees drawn up to his chest. The cell was lit by three candles and the remains of a meal waited to be removed. 'I confess that I do not like cells,' he said as Christopher came in. 'This one reminds me of the Gate House where I was forced to spend several foul nights.'

'I remember. Free my wrists, Roland, and I will tell you the plan.'

Wetherby undid the rope. 'I am ready.'

Christopher told him what had been agreed. 'I am assured that there will be no subterfuge that might endanger you.'

'Most reassuring. But while you are backwards and forwards in coaches I must remain here until taken to the Aldgate and hope that the plan does not prove a miserable failure. Is that it?'

'I'm afraid it is. The alternative was to throw you to the hounds and be damned.'

'Hmm. Was it difficult to persuade Leicester to this?'

'It was not easy and I might not have succeeded without the help of his brother.'

'I much admire Warwick. Lacking his brother's looks but in every other way his equal. And the queen?'

'I did not speak to her but Warwick spoke of her curiosity.'

'Curiosity about his hidden face or the wish to play before her?'

'Both, I fancy.'

There was a pause before Wetherby spoke again. 'Christopher, while you were gone, I had the opportunity to observe our captors. I gained the impression that between them all is not quite as it seems.'

Christopher laughed shortly. 'I would be hard pressed even to explain how it seems. Being held prisoner and ordered to arrange an audience with the queen for a faceless man she does not know is strange enough. What did you observe?'

'That although Simon is the master, Gabriel is more than his servant. It is not so much what he says as how he says it. A certain lack of respect. Had you not noticed this?'

'No, but Gabriel has hardly spoken in my presence. What do you think is going on?'

'I do not know and I may be mistaken,' replied Wetherby with a shrug. 'Let us watch and listen and perhaps learn something to our advantage. And now, my friend, we can either pass the hours in discussion of important matters of politics and philosophy, or we can rest.'

'We shall do neither. Now that I have my lute back, I shall play a tune for us. What shall it be?'

'Hmm. I wonder what the sound will be like in this cell. Do you know "Qui Passa"?'

'I do. A simple tune with repeated melodies. A good choice. Make room and I will sit to play.' Christopher sat beside Wetherby with his back to the wall and his long legs stretched out. 'I have never before played while sitting on a mattress on a cold floor. Beware false notes.'

'Or in a cell, I expect. Or did you play in Norwich prison?'

'Be silent, Roland, and let me concentrate.'

He tested the treble string with his thumb and then the five pairs of strings below it. Simon had kept the lute in tune. He began to play and at once the cell filled with music. The notes seemed to bounce off the walls as if they were sitting in the middle of a family of lutes all playing the tune.

When he finished the piece, Wetherby clapped his hands. 'Are you sure Her Majesty would not prefer to hear our host play here?' he asked. 'It would be a new experience even for a queen.'

'I am pleased to have my lute back. I thought I had seen the last of it.'

'It sounds as if it is pleased to have you back and now we know how to occupy ourselves until the clock strikes one. I shall choose and you shall play.'

'I can but try.'

For over an hour Christopher played, until he could play no more. Wetherby chose galliards, a rather ponderous pavan, several fancies and finally 'My Lady Cary's Dompe', which Christopher knew well. His playing had been far from perfect but he had done his best. 'No more, Roland,' he pleaded. 'My fingers are sore.' He put aside the lute and rested his head against the wall. There would be no sleep but he could rest. Wetherby did not disturb him.

Gabriel came bearing meat and ale. He put the trencher down and told Christopher to prepare himself. Wetherby began to eat but Christopher could not. 'You must eat, Christopher,' Roland urged.

'Butterflies are cavorting in my stomach. I would not keep it down.' He tried a sip of ale but it tasted like river water. 'I shall just have to go to my work on an empty stomach.'

Gabriel was soon back, this time with his pistol. 'You will remain here, Mr Wetherby, while I escort Dr Radcliff and Simon to Whitehall. Pray that I return unharmed or you will languish here until you die.'

'And do please take care of my lute,' added Christopher, trying to sound cheerful.

Once again, the blindfold was secured over Christopher's eyes and his hands were bound. He did not resist. Gabriel led him outside and into the waiting coach. 'Good afternoon, Dr Radcliff,' said Simon, who must have been waiting for him. 'I hope you are looking forward to my recital. I see you have left your lovely instrument in the care of Mr Wetherby. I am sure he will guard it for you.' His voice was muffled a little by a mask.

Christopher heard Gabriel get in and sit beside Simon. He would have the pistol on his lap. Another journey to Aldgate and he was beginning to see the highway in his mind's eye. At first, a rough road which gradually became less rough and finally, as they neared the city wall, a paved highway on which the coachman would call for the horses to canter.

He imagined a flat landscape dotted with poplars and elms, a few hovels and the occasional farm. He sensed no villages or coaching inns, where there would be the sounds of men and animals. Even for a man who could see, it would be a journey of little interest. Twice Gabriel reached across to tug at Christopher's hood and hiss at him to sit still and not to speak. Otherwise they rode in silence.

When the coachman brought the horses to a halt, Gabriel reached over to remove the blindfold. 'We do not want the guards asking questions,' he said, undoing the rope around Christopher's wrists. 'Simon will go first, and you will follow.'

Christopher blinked in the afternoon light. Gabriel sat opposite him, Simon, his face invisible, was beside Gabriel with his lute case across his knees. He looked out of the window. Aldgate was a hundred yards ahead. Simon reached out to embrace Gabriel, who stared over his shoulder at Christopher. The menace in his eyes was clear — do as you are ordered or Wetherby will die. Christopher waited while they clung to each other. After some moments they pulled apart and clasped hands. Simon stepped out of the carriage. Gabriel waved his pistol at Christopher and ordered him to follow. 'Do not forget what I have said,' he growled. 'One mistake and your friend dies.'

At that time there were more leaving the city than entering. Through the gate came market vendors wheeling flat carts, milkmaids with empty churns and children playing, pleased to be going home. To the two men, one in a hood like a monk's cowl and carrying a lute case, the other fair and tall, they gave barely a glance.

But a guard stepped forward to bar their way and asked their business. Christopher's heart sank. Had the guards not yet been replaced? He would have to say something. 'My cousin and I are visiting my mother who lies sick in Leadenhall.'

The man scratched his groin and pointed at Simon. 'What is he carrying?'

'His lute. She loves the music of the lute.'

'Why does he hide his face? Not a leper, is he?'

'No, sir. He is disfigured by smallpox and is sensitive about his appearance.'

'He need not worry. There's whores aplenty who won't care what he looks like as long as he's got sixpence.' He reached out to lift Simon's hood. 'Let's have a look at him.'

His hand had not even reached the hood when he yelped in pain. Christopher had grabbed his arm and pulled it back. 'Better not, sir. He does not take kindly to being seen and he will haunt your dreams.'

The threat did not work. When Christopher let go of his arm the guard put a hand on the hilt of his sword and made to draw it. Christopher stepped in front of Simon and held out his arms. 'I meant you no harm, sir,' he said, 'but I urge you not to distress yourself further. My cousin's face is not easily forgotten.'

Christopher held the guard's gaze while he hesitated, clearly torn between duty and fear. Then he shrugged and pushed the sword back into its scabbard. 'One poxed scroyle more or less won't make no difference,' he growled. 'Move on, the two of you, and pray I don't see you when you return.'

'We shall, sir,' replied Christopher. 'Good day to you.' With an inward sigh of relief he led Simon quickly through the gate. Leicester's coach was waiting for them on the corner of an unnamed lane.

The coachman raised his hat to Christopher but did not speak or jump down to open the door. As soon as they had climbed in, Simon laughed and said, 'A fine show, doctor. What a player on the stage you would have been.'

'Invention bred of necessity. I would not care for a repeat performance.'

'Then we must hope there are no over-zealous guards at the Holbein Gate.'

They did not speak again until the coach rattled into Leadenhall Street when Simon said, 'I have much to thank you for, Dr Radcliff.'

'Thank me? I had little choice. You hold the winning card in Roland Wetherby.'

'I regret the inconvenience caused to the admirable Mr Wetherby, but that is not what I meant. Since my mother died two years ago, I have nursed a keen ambition to play before Her Majesty, but no means of achieving this until you presented me with one. Gabriel found you and through you I found a way to her. And, also, as it has turned out, to the good Earls of Leicester and Warwick. I invited Leicester but Warwick is a welcome addition to the audience.'

'And that is why Gabriel followed me.'

'It is. His task was to keep a watch on you and to keep you safe.'

'He assaulted Wetherby.'

'Regrettable, but Gabriel is skilled in such matters and does not kill unless it is necessary. Mr Wetherby was only slightly hurt.'

'And the testons and the slogans? What purpose did they serve?'

'In part they served for my own amusement — my life has not been one filled with entertainments — and in part they served to create chaos or at least the illusion of chaos.'

'Why?'

'From chaos and disorder come order and truth. From life comes death. From ignorance comes knowledge. The serpent in the Garden of Eden. It was ever thus.'

'Your meaning is lost on me.'

'Think on it, doctor. Nothing lasts forever.'

'You have had money at your disposal.'

'My mother died in Bedlam, but wealthy from her own inheritance. She had no other children.'

'They will find the house, of course.'

'I am aware of that. They will find the house but I doubt they will find anyone in it. I have tired of it and shall move on, although only God knows where I shall go. But no more talk, now, if you please. I must prepare myself for what lies ahead.'

What to make of such a man? For all that he had done, for all his crimes, Christopher could not help feeling some kinship with him and half wished that they had attempted a duet. There would not be another chance now.

Down Fleet Street and into the Strand. Simon raised his head and peeked out of the window. 'I see we are here. I find that I am calm, doctor. Are you?'

'I am not.'

At the Holbein Gate they were halted by the guards. The captain opened the coach door and beckoned for them to alight. 'My orders are to search the visitors. Dr Radcliff, you first.' Christopher stepped forward and allowed a guard to check that he carried no concealed weapon. 'Now the lute case, if you please.' Simon put the case carefully on the ground and stood back. The guard opened it and took out the lute. He shook it gently to make sure there was nothing inside the body, then ran his hands around the case. Satisfied, he closed the lid. 'And you, sir.'

'The gentleman's hood and face covering will remain in place,' ordered Christopher.

'Very well,' replied the captain. Simon held up his arms and stood still while he was patted down.

'Nothing,' said the guard.

'Very well, doctor, you may proceed. The coach will remain here with the driver.'

They were escorted to an entrance beside the Great Hall that led to the private apartments, where another guard awaited them. They followed him up a flight of stairs and through a door into the Great Chamber.

The chamber was a large, rectangular room, used both for official business and for the more intimate of the queen's entertainments. For the lavish masques and plays that she so enjoyed, the Great Hall was usually needed.

Tall latticed windows looked out over a cloistered yard, once used by the queen's brother Edward as a place for preachers to deliver their sermons, now simply a quiet retreat for courtiers and visitors to take the air. The queen disliked sermons and had been known to walk out if she felt a preacher was going on for too long.

The chamber walls were panelled. At one end a large high-backed chair, upholstered in fabrics of red and gold, had been placed on a raised dais. Smaller chairs, also upholstered, stood either side of it, with another, single chair to one side of the dais. The lutenist's seat, a plain oak stool, faced them from about ten paces. At each corner of the chamber stood a helmeted guard armed with a halberd and a sword at the waist. The guards did not move when they entered.

Without being instructed, Simon took his place on the stool and opened his lute case. He took out the lute, played a few notes, adjusted the treble string with a slight turn of the peg and laid it across his lap. At no time could any of the guards have caught sight of his face. Unsure of how long they would be waiting, Christopher took the single chair.

It was not long. A message would have been sent to Leicester as soon as the coach had arrived. With his brother beside him, he entered the chamber from a door that led to the privy apartments. Simon did not move but Christopher rose to his feet. Leicester barely glanced at him before taking his seat to what would be the queen's right. His face was flushed with fever and in his hand he held a large white handkerchief. Warwick acknowledged Christopher with a nod and took his seat to the queen's left. Christopher remained standing.

From somewhere in the palace a clock struck three and through the same door from which Leicester and Warwick had appeared, the queen, followed by two ladies-in-waiting, entered. She held her head high, her hands clasped at her waist, her face showing not a hint of what she was thinking.

Not a word was spoken, yet Christopher immediately sensed a change in the chamber. The guards squared their shoulders; Leicester and Warwick rose and bowed their heads. The queen did not acknowledge them but stood before her chair and allowed her eyes to traverse the chamber.

Christopher bowed. Simon, too, stood and bowed, face still hidden by the hood. The queen's eyes returned to him for a few seconds and then, assisted by her ladies, she took her seat. She wore a white lace ruff at her throat and a green velvet gown chosen to complement her auburn hair. Two strings of pearls hung around her neck. Christopher looked for a trace of disquiet or concern and saw none. The queen appeared entirely calm, as if, to the Queen of England, such an occasion was commonplace. Her ladies, demure in pale blue, arranged themselves behind her. The room was silent.

The queen sat perfectly still and upright, her pale blue eyes fixed on the hooded figure before her. Then she spoke, her voice clear and with no trace of emotion, as if she were addressing her privy council-lors on some dry legal matter. 'We are informed, sir,' she said, 'that our loyal servant Mr Wetherby is held at your pleasure and to secure his release we must hear you play. We are unaccustomed to receiving orders from musicians and murderers and are inclined to think that this is the request of a madman who would be better arrested and taken from here directly to the Tower. Can you say anything to persuade me otherwise?'

'A great prince knows when to employ a velvet glove and when a hand of iron. I throw myself on Your Majesty's mercy.'

'What is your name, sir, and why have you made this impertinent request?'

'I am Simon Lovelace, Your Majesty, and my purpose will become clear.'

'If your purpose is to do us harm, be assured, Master Lovelace, that my guards will kill you before you can lift a finger.'

'I am aware of that, Your Majesty, and I mean you no harm. I simply wish to play for you.'

'The royal lutes play when we ask them to. There are no finer musicians in England. Why must we hear you play — a man of whom we have never heard and about whom we know only that he holds prisoner a loyal servant of the Crown?'

'My request is humbly and loyally made, Your Majesty. My fate as well as that of Mr Wetherby is in your hands.'

The queen stared at him. 'You hide your face yet expect us to grant your wish.' There was a touch of anger in her voice.

'I will reveal myself when I have played, if that is your wish.'

The stare did not waver. 'We are tempted to have our guards save you the trouble. You must know that your crimes cannot go unpunished. The law will pursue you until justice is done.'

'I have no fear of justice.' Certainly, there was no hint of fear in his voice.

'Have we your word that after you have played, Mr Wetherby will be released exactly as has been agreed?'

'You do, madam.'

The queen glanced again at Leicester. 'As Your Majesty pleases,' he said quietly.

'Very well. With Mr Wetherby's safety in mind, we shall hear you play. But the merest sniff of deception and my guards will be upon you. What have you chosen for us?'

'It is an old tune entitled "The Maiden's Lamentation", and with Your Majesty's gracious permission I shall sing and play.'

That was a surprise. Christopher had never heard him sing and there had been no mention of it. From their expressions, neither Warwick nor Leicester seemed to care.

'As you wish, Master Lovelace. Proceed.'

Simon bowed his head and took his seat. He reached up to untie the cloth covering his face, leaving the hood in place, raised the lute, placed his fingers on the strings and began.

But late in place
A pretye lasse,
That was both fayre and yonge e,
Wyth wepying eie,
Right secretlye,
Untyll hersealfe she soonge e.
How showld I rock the cradle, serve the table,
blow the fyre, and spyn, a?

He sang in a clear tenor, finding an easy rhythm that suited the melody.

This lytle foote,
And ite toote,
With notes both sweet and cleere e.

She syght full ofte,
And soong alofte
In forms as shall here e.
How showld I rock the cradle, serve the table,
blow the fyre, and spyn, a?

Alas! she sayde,
I was a mayde,
As other maydens be e;
And thowgh I boste,
In all the coste
Ther was no more lyke me e.
How showld I rock the cradle, serve the table,
blow the fyre, and spyn, a?

Christopher did not know the song and wondered why Simon had chosen one written for a female voice. He glanced at Leicester, who had closed his eyes as if to concentrate better on the words, and at Warwick who sat tapping his fingers soundlessly on the arm of his chair.

For four more verses Simon continued, his voice steady and strong. He sang of the maiden's plight and of the child she must care for alone.

Clene out of syght
And all delyght,
Now heere in servitude e.
At the behest
Of most and least
That be, Got wot, full rude e.

How showld I rock the cradle, serve the table,
blow the fyre, and spyn, a?

I may not swerve
The boord to serve,
To blow the fyre and spin e.
My chyld to rock,
And plese this flock,
Where shall I first begin e.
How showld I rock the cradle, serve the table,
blow the fyre, and spyn, a?

Still the queen's face showed no emotion. And, beside her, Leicester and Warwick appeared uninterested in anything but having this over with.

Preserve, good God,
All maydynhode
That maydenlye entend e.
Let my defame
And endless shame
Kepe them from shamefull end e.
How showld I rock the cradle, serve the table,
blow the fyre, and spyn, a?

Beware, good maydes,
Of all such braydes,
Before all other thing e;
Or all in vayne,
As I complayne,

Thus wepyng shall ye synge.
How showld I rock the cradle, serve the table,
blow the fyre, and spyn, a?

Simon put down his lute. The maid had given her warning to others not to make the mistake she had and her lamentation was done. In the Great Chamber there was silence. The queen must speak first. Eventually, she did so.

'A strange choice, Master Lovelace, perhaps better sung by a maiden. I wonder why you chose it.' She held him in her gaze. 'Could it be a warning to your queen or is the song more personal?' She turned her head to Leicester. 'What do you think, Robert?'

Leicester wiped a drop of sweat from his lip. 'I think this man is a charlatan, your majesty, and should be arrested at once.'

'A charlatan? How so?'

'How do we know that he has not told us a pack of lies?'

Simon's voice was strong and firm. 'There have been no lies, my lord, and the song carries different meanings for different people.'

'An evasive answer, Master Lovelace,' said the queen, her face impassive, 'but you sing well and your playing is ravishing.'

Simon bowed his hooded head. 'I thank you, Your Majesty. To play for you has been my ambition. I am honoured to have been allowed to do so.'

Leicester coughed into his handkerchief. Warwick looked bored. The queen's expression did not change. 'Will you now show your queen the face of the man who is so accomplished and has risked all to fulfil his ambition?'

'I will.' And, slowly, he pulled back the hood. As he did so, there was a gasp around the room. From the corner of his eye, Christopher saw one of the ladies-in-waiting grip the queen's chair to steady herself, and the other put a hand to her mouth to stifle a scream. Leicester made to rise but was held back by the queen's hand on his arm. Warwick closed his eyes and mouthed a prayer.

Christopher stared at the face. It was the face of neither a leper nor a victim of the smallpox, nor was it a face scarred in battle. It was a face that could only have been fashioned in the depths of hell. The right side bulged as if pumped full of air by a bellows; the left was sunken as if all air had been expelled from it. A lump protruded from the forehead and hung over the eyes. The mouth and nose were twisted and the chin set to one side. Had he not heard Simon's voice he would not have believed that a creature so deformed would be able to speak. Yet his voice, except when he was angered, was almost lyrical. Christopher sat unmoving and unable to drag his eyes from this monstrous gargoyle who had held him captive. And who had now played for the queen.

Still the queen showed no emotion, as if she had known what to expect. 'Your life has been a hard one, Master Lovelace,' she said gently, 'although that does not excuse your crimes or explain why you are here. You must face justice, but before you do, we would hear your story.'

'And you shall, madam.' Without the hood, Simon spoke boldly, as if he was suddenly free of a great burden. He turned his head to look around the chamber as if wanting everyone present to see his face. Then he began. 'I was born in the year 1551 in the county of Essex. My grandfather, whom I never knew, had become wealthy from the trading of wool. He found it cheaper to ship his wool by sea from Lynn in Norfolk to London than to send it by road and thus increased his profits. My grandmother had died in childbirth and he doted on his daughter, my mother Caroline Lovelace, who was his only child.' The words flowed. They had been rehearsed.

'Where is this leading, man?' demanded Leicester. 'Her Majesty has no time for tales.'

The queen touched his arm. 'Hush, Robert, we will hear the story.'

Simon went on. 'We lived well and my grandfather often entertained friends at his house. Without a wife, he looked to my mother for support in matters of household management, although she was barely more than a child. This she was happy to give. In the year 1550, when she was sixteen years old, a young man of high birth came to stay. He was considering an investment in the wool trade and sought advice from my grandfather. While staying in his house, he seduced his host's daughter. An affair followed until my mother discovered that she was with child. The father could only have been the young visitor.'

Christopher stole a look at the dais. The queen's face was set, still expressionless.

'In her innocence,' carried on Simon, 'my mother expected the young man to marry her. He had declared undying love and she had no reason to doubt him. But on learning that she was with child, he rejected her utterly and refused ever to see her again. She was desolated.'

And afraid, too, thought Christopher, just as the maiden in the song had been.

'So great was the shock that she fell ill and could scarcely leave her bed for the duration of her time. She suffered great pain in her stomach and in her back. She could not tell the physician why she suffered so but he feared that the child she carried was not normal and its birth would not be easy. Then, as if she was not suffering enough, in the sixth month, my grandfather died, leaving her his estate but with the grim prospect of bringing up a bastard child alone.

'Imagine her grief when that child was born. Not only a bastard but an unspeakable monster.' Simon's voice rose. 'A creature from hell, deformed in the womb by the shock and grief she had suffered and who could never take a proper place in the world. She must have cursed the child's father with every waking breath. Yet she had given birth to him and would not allow the midwife to put him out of his misery. She fed him from her breast and, as he grew older, taught him to read and write and to play the lute. In this she was assisted by her servant, Gabriel Browne, who was devoted to her and became devoted to her son. It was thanks to them that the boy lived, albeit without the company of other children or the normal pleasures of childhood. The strain on her was great, her mind became fragile and at the age of thirty-eight, she died in Bedlam. She had given her own life for that of her monstrous son.'

When Simon paused to wipe a tear from his eye, the queen asked, 'And the son sought revenge on the world?'

'No, madam, not revenge but truth. Truth that should not be hidden.'

'Did she tell her son who his father was?'

'She did.'

'Your story has little meaning without his name. We would wish to know it.'

Simon stared at Leicester. 'His name was Robert Dudley.'

The earl was on his feet. 'This is outrageous. How dare you suggest such a foul thing?' He stepped down from the platform as if about to silence Simon himself. Christopher too was on his feet. Roland's life was at stake and Simon must not be harmed. If he had to, he would restrain the earl. Simon had not moved but sat calmly facing the man he claimed was his father.

'Hold, Robert,' ordered the queen. 'Leave us if you wish but we shall hear the end of Master Lovelace's story.'

Leicester stopped and turned to face her. 'Do not listen to this, madam,' he shouted. 'The man is deranged and should not be believed. Have the guards arrest him.'

Simon appeared unafraid. He spoke clearly but did not raise his voice. 'Why should I not be believed, sir? Is it for the shame of a man such as yourself siring a creature like me? Or is it for the shame of deserting my mother and causing her unborn child to be so affected?'

Leicester's handsome face was suffused with rage. 'Guards, arrest this man,' he spluttered.

'No, Robert,' ordered the queen, her tone allowing no further discussion. 'Allow Master Lovelace to finish his story.'

Simon took up his lute and fiddled absently with a peg. 'There is no more to tell,' he said. 'I have played before my queen and I have told my story. The truth is now known. That was my purpose and that is an end to it.'

The room was silent as if waiting for the queen to speak or to leave. She did neither, but sat looking at the creature before her. Simon watched her as he fiddled with the peg. Christopher thought he was going to spit in the hole to make it fit more closely. It was a common enough practice.

He was mistaken. Simon pulled the top from the peg, tipped something into his hand and swallowed it. Almost immediately, his body began to convulse and he fell from the stool. Neither Leicester nor the guards moved. Christopher rushed forward and knelt over the stricken man. Whatever Simon had taken was working fast. Blood seeped from his crooked mouth and one eye bulged in shock. The gargoyle was dying. Christopher lifted the grotesque head and turned it to one side. If Simon could be made to vomit, the poison might yet be expelled. He coughed and retched but spat out only blood. Christopher lifted him up and made to thump him on the back.

'Hold!' commanded the queen. 'Leave him. He must die as he wishes. We will not inflict more pain upon him.' Christopher looked up at her, and let the young man down slowly. Simon's body jerked once and then he lay still. 'For all his sins we shall be gentle with him in death, as God will be.'

Abruptly, she stood and left the chamber as regally as she had entered it. She was followed by her ladies. Neither brother moved or looked at the dead body. Unsure what to do, Christopher waited for instructions from Leicester. But Leicester seemed too shocked to speak. The instructions came from Warwick.

'Make haste, doctor,' he said. 'Mr Wetherby is in danger.'

Christopher carefully picked up the peg between finger and thumb and looked into it. It had been hollowed out. There were two small seeds in it. He sniffed. Hemlock. No more than four or five seeds could kill a man instantly. And they had been hidden so as to disguise Simon's true intention. A taste for the dramatic, even in death.

Deception and trickery. Disorder and chaos. And knowledge from ignorance.

CHAPTER 31

The coach was waiting at the gate. If the coachman had been expecting two passengers he gave no sign of it. Christopher ordered him to the Aldgate.

The coachman cracked his whip and the horses broke straight into a canter. In the Strand he bellowed at a rider blocking their way and in Fleet Street they sent a box of eggs flying into the road. Shrieks of outrage followed them down the street but did not detain them.

Christopher hung on to his seat and silently urged the coachman on. They had been tricked. Gabriel had known that Simon would not return from Whitehall so Wetherby was in danger. Gabriel had no reason to keep him alive.

They sped down Cornhill and Leadenhall and came to a halt at the Aldgate. Christopher jumped out and pushed his way through the last of the traders making their way home. He scanned the road. Of Simon's coach there was no sign. He ran back to the gate and asked a guard if he had seen a slightly built man with a lute case come through. The guard had not.

He hesitated.

'I am here, Christopher,' said Wetherby from behind him, 'and quite unharmed.' In his hand he held the lute case.

Christopher turned, laughed and gripped his shoulder. 'Trust you to have me worried, but I am truly relieved to find you well. How long have you been waiting and where is Gabriel? I imagined he would have killed you.'

'Happily not. Gabriel has gone. He left me here an hour ago. I thought it best to wait for you. He knew Simon would not be returning with you. Is he dead?'

Christopher nodded. 'He is. Hemlock seeds hidden in a hollow lute peg.'

'Did he play for the queen?'

'He did. "The Maiden's Lamentation".'

'Gabriel would have been happy to know it. He told me Simon's story and the unspeakable life the man had. Was his deformity appalling?'

'It was. I wonder that he could speak let alone sing.'

'And what now for us, my friend?'

'I shall return to Ludgate Hill. Leicester will be in his bed and best left alone.'

'And I shall request the coachman to take me on to Whitehall where I shall sleep the sleep of the just.'

Christopher left the coach on Ludgate Hill. He let himself in and put the lute in the study. There was neither food nor drink in the house. He considered the Brown Bear but could not persuade himself even to a quiet inn.

He went up to the bed chamber, thinking to rest, but found that sleep was impossible. That day he had seen one man die and another live. Simon Lovelace had chosen to die; Roland Wetherby had been allowed to live. How easily it might have been otherwise. And what of the faithful Gabriel Browne, a murderer who had devoted himself to caring for a child cursed as cruelly as any child could be? What did the fates have in mind for him?

Where would Simon's body be taken and where would he be buried? An unimaginable life, cursed from birth to death, yet blessed with a beautiful voice and a love of music. And he had been granted something denied to all but a very few — the manner and time of his death. Only then had he found the fulfilment his life had lacked.

He went down to the study where he sat idly leafing through sheets of music and wondering whether or not to play. He barely noticed the tunes he was looking at, until he came to a piece he had tried before but since forgotten. 'Awake ye woeful wights' had been inspired by the ancient story of Damon and Pythias whose friend-ship was so strong that Damon offered himself as a hostage to King Dionysius of Syracuse in place of the condemned Pythias. It seemed appropriate. He took up the lute and began.

It was a contemplative piece and he did not hurry it. He stopped once to adjust a fret in the hope of making the notes sweeter and missed a change of stops towards the end but otherwise felt that he had done the music justice.

He hid the lute under the pile of shirts and sat stretching his fingers. Abruptly, almost without conscious thought, he got up and put on his coat. The light had faded and the curfew had begun, but he could not sit still. Out of habit he glanced up and down the street before locking the door. No watcher, no shadow.

He stayed away from Newgate where the night creatures would be emerging from their secret places, and kept to the middle of the streets. The alley off Cheapside reeked of rotting food and human waste and he almost ran down it.

The stew owner opened the door. She took the clay pipe from her mouth and looked him up and down. 'Dr Rad, isn't it?' she asked in a voice raw with smoke and drink. 'Ell's busy but you can wait if you like.'

'Thank you, Grace. I'll wait.'

In the little parlour with a glass of Grace's thin Spanish wine he tried not to hear the humping and grinding above him. At least it was not Ell. Her room was along the passage. Or he hoped it wasn't her. He caught himself. Ell Cole was a whore. Why should he care?

Grace had lit a fire and the parlour was warm. He drank a second glass. His eyes closed and his head lolled on his chest.

He was woken suddenly. 'The devil's ball sack, Dr Rad. Don't tell me you've come here to sleep. Mistress Allington thrown you out of your own home, has she?' He opened his eyes. Ell stood over him, hands on hips and a wide grin on her face.

He shook the sleep from his head. 'No, not yet. I have not seen her for a while, though. I've been busy.'

'Wish I had. Quiet as the grave, it's been. Don't know why. Still, I've been getting more sleep. Does it show?'

Throw her into a dungeon with a pack of murdering felons and slavering hounds and Ell Cole would emerge unscathed and radiant. 'Lovely as ever, Ell.'

She poked out her tongue. 'Bit more enthusiasm, Dr Rad, wouldn't go amiss. What can I do for you?'

'Nothing really. My day has been one I hope not to see repeated. I just did not feel like being alone.'

Ell sat down in Grace's chair. 'Bad thing, being alone. When I'm in company I sometimes wish I was alone but when I am I don't like it. Difficult cow, aren't I? Sorry to see you low, Dr Rad. Would you like some food?'

Christopher realized that he was starving. 'I would, Ell. Have you got anything?'

Ell threw up her hands. 'Course we have. Grace keeps the cupboard full for our gentlemen. Some of them need a bit of meat first. Even I can't rouse one old fellow until he's had half a chicken. Poor sod. His wife treats him like a child. Made him queer in the head, she has.' She got up. 'I'll go and see what there is. Stay here and drink Grace's wine. Gets better with a few glasses, you'll see.'

It did, but not much. God knew what Grace had mixed in it. Gutter water, probably. Ell returned as he was draining his fourth glass. 'We've mutton and onions and fresh bread, doctor. Go up to my room and I'll bring it up. Be more private there and Grace wants her parlour.'

Ell had tidied the bed. Christopher sat down and waited for the food. Why had he come here? Why was he not asleep in his own bed?

Ell brought the food. She watched him eat and poured him another glass of wine. He felt better for eating but he could barely keep his eyes open. 'Lie down, Dr Rad,' she said. 'There's room for two.' He put his head on her pillow and knew no more.

Sometime in the night he woke. There was a figure sleeping beside him. He put his hand on a hip. 'Katherine, I . . .'

'Shush, Dr Rad,' whispered the figure. 'Go back to sleep.'

When dawn came, he woke again. He lay still with his eyes closed. The figure beside him had gone. Why had Katherine left the bed so early? With a start he sat up. This was not his chamber. It was Ell's. His shirt was loose and his legs were bare. Where was she? He lay down again and closed his eyes.

Voices outside woke him the second time. The lane was coming to life. He pushed himself up and swung his legs over the bed. Where was Ell? Had he spent the night with her?

The chamber door opened and Ell came in, carrying a bottle and a beaker. She was grinning. 'Good day, Dr Rad. Didn't know you talked in your sleep. Slept well, did you?'

'What am I doing here, Ell?' he croaked. 'Where are my trousers?'

Ell poured ale into the beaker. 'Drink that, Dr Rad. It'll make you feel better.'

He took the beaker and sipped the ale. It could have been rat's piss. He handed it back. 'Why am I here, Ell? Have I been here all night?'

'You have, doctor. Asleep in my bed. You were troubled so I let you stay. Chattering away, you were. Never heard anything like it.'

'What did I say?'

'Hard to tell. Jumble of words, it was. Simon, testons, Damon, Pith-something, lute, Joan.'

Oh God. Joan Willys. 'Did you undress me?'

'Might have. Fine legs you've got, doctor. Very shapely for a man. Do you dance with the queen?'

'Ell, did anything happen?'

'Like what? You falling asleep and chattering happened.'

'You know what I mean.'

'No, doctor, nothing happened. Could do now, though, if you feel strong enough.'

Temptation. Lie in Ell's bed with her beside him while the world outside went about its business. No sane man would refuse. 'I'd like that, Ell, but I've work to do.' Joan was still in Newgate.

'Work, work, always work, Dr Rad. It's no wonder you're so troubled.'

'Where are my trousers?'

Ell handed them to him. His shoes were on the floor by the bed. He put them on and stood up. 'Thank you for letting me sleep here, Ell.'

'You owe me two shillings.'

'Do I? Why's that?'

'To make up for the money I could have earned if my bed had been free.'

'Oh, very well. Where's my purse?'

Ell held it up. 'Any other whore and you'd have lost it. Shall I help myself?' Ell fished out two shillings. 'Take more care next time, doctor.'

Sarah Cardoza welcomed him in. She offered him wine and cake and asked after his health. 'I miss Isaac, of course,' she told him, 'but I speak to him every day. He will guide me until we meet again.'

'And the children, Sarah?' he asked. 'How do they fare?'

'They are a comfort to me as they were to him. I am blessed.'

'I envy you your family and your faith.'

The sharp eyes twinkled. 'Then you must find a wife and from her you might find faith. Life is so much harder for those with neither a family nor a god.'

Had Simon Lovelace had faith? he wondered. It would not have been surprising if he had believed in almost anything other than God, yet he was ready to die.

'Sarah, I have come to tell you that the man who murdered Isaac is dead.'

'He who lives by the sword, Christopher?'

'Yes. There were others involved in the counterfeiting, of course. Two are dead; one is in Newgate. Another has fled but he is no danger and I doubt he will ever be caught. Would you like to know about them?'

'No. It is over. I wish only to think of Isaac.'

Christopher rose. 'He was a good man and my friend. I too miss him. Good day, Sarah.'

'*Shalom*, Christopher. Call again. And remember what I have said. A man should not be alone in this world. Find a wife and have many children.'

A wife and many children. He would be happy enough just with Joan as his housekeeper. The cupboard was bare and must be replenished.

In Cheapside the prices had risen again. A penny and three farthings for six eggs and three pence a small loaf. Simon's testons were still doing their work. He bought cheese and apples and a piece of mutton and was wondering whether Ell could be persuaded to cook it for him when he saw her. At a confectioner's stall, Katherine was filling a bag with biscuits and cakes. She had not seen him.

To ignore her would be churlish. He swallowed his pride and walked over to the stall. 'Joy of the day, Katherine,' he said. 'Do I find you well?'

She looked up sharply. 'Christopher. I had not thought to see you here.'

'A man must take care of himself if no one else will.'

She took some coins from her purse and paid the confectioner. 'You know why that is so. Joan is in Newgate on a ridiculous charge and I will not keep house for you while you are seeing that whore. Or are you no longer seeing her?'

'She is my agent. That is all.'

'Then I suggest you ask her to cook and clean for you. I daresay she'll be delighted. Good day, Christopher.' She had gone before he could speak.

Infernal woman. Did she really not believe him or was it a pretence? Perhaps he should tell her that he had spent the night in Ell's bed. It would be the truth but also a pretence of sorts.

The slogan could not have been there long. It certainly was not there when he had left the house. He put a finger to the paint. It was wet. Three men and a woman stood looking at it. It was written on the wall of St Martin's church. *Chaos comes in many a guise, Death and fear and monstrous lies.* It was marked with a cross.

'What does it mean?' asked the woman.

'Nothing,' replied one of the men. 'Just like the others, it means nothing.'

'But it's painted on a church,' said another. 'It must mean something.'

'Or it's there to frighten us,' said the woman.

'Well, it doesn't frighten me,' said the third man. 'Not unless it was the devil himself who wrote it.'

Christopher walked on. Simon Lovelace had said that not all the slogans had been his work. There had been copiers. But this — mere chance or were the testons not the dead man's only legacy?

CHAPTER 32

Two days had passed since he had visited Sarah Cardoza. Two tedious days waiting for a summons from Leicester or a visit from Katherine. Two days of fiddling with his lute, tightening the strings, loosening them again, moving the frets up and down the neck and playing a few short pieces.

He had walked to Fetter Lane where Mr Brewster had sold him a ruled music book for his own compositions and he had ventured into Holborn Fields where the lawyers' horses were grazing and where he had watched a trained band drilling and he had visited Ironmonger Lane where he had bought a new blade.

He had received no callers and no messages from Whitehall. And he had not called upon Ell.

The summons came by messenger on the third morning. The Earl of Leicester wished to see him at once.

Leicester still looked a little fevered but he was out of bed and at his table. His brother sat beside him. Christopher doffed his cap, bowed low and waited. He had rehearsed this scene in his mind, practised answers to possible questions and tried to find some tactful middle ground upon which to pitch his tent. Now that the moment had come, however, and faced with both Leicester and Warwick, he could remember almost nothing of what he had planned to say.

Leicester began: 'Dr Radcliff, you will appreciate how difficult this is for my brother and for me.' He paused as if searching for a way forward.

'Our family name is at stake,' said Warwick, 'not to mention Her gracious Majesty's goodwill and the security of the realm.'

Leicester continued. 'What happened in the Great Chamber was a drama, a piece of theatre designed to cause trouble for the amusement of the dramatist.'

Taken aback, Christopher spoke without thinking. 'Drama, my lord? A man died. Was it not painfully real?'

Warwick leaned forward in his chair and rested his elbows on the table. 'Good dramas should wear the clothes of reality, Dr Radcliff, don't you think?'

Christopher did not know what to think. Were they suggesting that the whole thing had been a charade, a dream? Or that Simon had invented his story? 'I saw a new slogan painted on St Martin's church, my lords.'

'I am aware of it,' replied Leicester. 'Mischief-making, I fancy. Let us not concern ourselves with it.'

A brick wall against which Christopher knew he would only be banging his head. The brothers had made up their minds and would not be shifted. 'Should we have denied Simon Lovelace his wish and abandoned Mr Wetherby, my lords?'

'No, no, doctor,' replied Leicester hastily, 'Mr Wetherby's safety was of the greatest importance.' He glanced at Warwick. 'It is simply that Lovelace's story is best treated with a certain caution.'

Weasel words. Had Simon Lovelace told the truth or not? If not, why not bluntly deny his allegations? 'Caution, my lords?'

'Her Majesty is anxious that what occurred in the Great Chamber should not become known by her loyal subjects,' replied Warwick. 'It could do great harm to our country at a time of national danger and we all know the trouble that ill-informed gossip can cause.'

'Yet truth will out, my lord. The queen's ladies and her guards were present.'

Leicester tapped a finger on the table. 'Neither the four guards nor the queen's ladies will utter a word of what they heard and saw.'

'I am neither a guard nor a queen's lady. It was I who discovered the source of the false testons designed to blacken the Dudley name, my lords, and I, with Mr Wetherby, who was held captive by Simon Lovelace. I am in a trusted position on your lordship's staff. I will protect a confidence but may I not know the truth of the matter?'

Warwick shrugged. 'Truth, untruth, something between the two — what does it matter? What matters, Dr Radcliff, are the consequences. And you will serve our family and your queen best by a loyal silence.'

They were not going to say more. 'If that is what Her Majesty wishes.'

'It is.'

'And Mr Wetherby?'

'We assumed that Mr Wetherby would know what occurred and have secured his promise to say nothing of it.'

'And we thank you, doctor, for finding the coiners and for your loyalty. I am sure we have seen the last of them and their foul treason,' added Leicester. 'And Her Majesty has authorized a reward for your service.' He took a leather pouch from a drawer in the table and pushed it across to Christopher.

Christopher stared at it. 'There is really no need, my lords.'

'Take it, doctor,' said Warwick. 'It is just reward.'

Christopher reached out and took the pouch. It was heavy. 'Thank you, my lords. I am grateful.'

Warwick remained sitting but Leicester stood and extended his hand. 'I am fortunate to have you in my service, doctor.'

He sat in the Brown Bear with a tankard of beer. So much for rehearsing what he planned to say. The play had been written by the noble lords, not by him. Without denying the truth of Simon's story they had managed, without saying as much, to cast doubt upon it. And they had played on his loyalty. He should not be surprised.

He would tell no one what he knew. Of course he would tell no one. The Earl of Leicester was Master of the Queen's Horse and a member of her Privy Council. It would be treasonous to do so.

He grinned at the sudden thought that the pouch of coins hidden under his gown might be full of bear and staff testons. In an odd way, that would have endeared the brothers Dudley to him more than a pouch full of crowns.

For an hour he sat nursing his beer. Perception and reality. Order and disorder. Truth and untruth. As a lawyer it was the last that troubled him most.

A slight figure was standing outside his door. 'Have you no better occupation than to stand about and wait for me, Roland?' he called out as he approached. 'I have been at Whitehall.' He unlocked the door.

'I know,' said Wetherby. 'And no doubt you were treated to the same advice as I was. Did you come away with a purse of crowns for your trouble?'

'I did. Did you?'

'I did. For what I had suffered.'

'Come in and sit. We may tell no one of what we know but, as we both know, we will be telling no one. Does that make sense?'

'I believe it does. Lawyer's sense at least.'

Christopher poured two glasses of his best Rhenish, which they took to the study. He raised his glass. 'To Simon Lovelace. May he have found peace.'

'May we all, when the time comes,' replied Wetherby, raising his. 'Simon Lovelace.'

They sat in silence, each with his own thoughts, until Christopher asked, 'What do you think is the truth of the matter, Roland?'

'I did not hear Simon speak in the Great Chamber,' replied Wetherby, 'and know only what Gabriel Browne told me, so it is more difficult for me to form an opinion. However, I find it impossible to suppose that any man, even one as tormented as Simon, would fabricate such a story without good reason.'

'With that I agree. That which starts out as a story, however, can sometimes become truth in a man's mind.'

'You mean that we come to believe our own stories. That is true. Do you think that Simon had come to believe his own story?'

Christopher threw up his hands. 'I don't know. Perhaps — or perhaps it was the truth. Young, handsome Robert Dudley seduces beautiful Caroline Lovelace who becomes pregnant with his child. It is hardly a new tale.'

'Nor a particularly interesting one,' added Wetherby, 'until he deserts her and she suffers such grief that their unborn child is so affected that he comes into the world barely human.'

'She cannot have known when she first set eyes upon the child that, despite his deformity, his mind would be that of an intelligent and sensitive man. He would not have survived but for a mother's unconditional love.'

'And now the mother and her child are dead. We should let them rest in peace.'

'We should, yet, as you yourself suggested, there is more to Gabriel Browne than we know. I have a wish for the truth and we are forbidden only to speak of what we know, not to discover the truth of it.'

'How might we do that, Christopher?'

'The house. I believe I know where it is.'

Wetherby sat up. 'Where?'

'The journey to Aldgate took about an hour at a steady pace. The road was rough and there was salt in the air. I heard gulls and curlews — sea birds and marsh birds. Simon would have chosen a place where few live and to which travellers would have no reason to venture. My guess is that the house is in that place where the river turns south and then north again, creating the shape of a horseshoe. The Isle of Dogs.'

Wetherby considered. 'And if you are right, what do you suggest we do?'

'The house may hold secrets. I suggest we find it.'

'Gabriel may already have burned it down.'

'He may. In which case we will have had a wasted journey.'

'I am not sure, Christopher. What is to be gained?'

'The truth. No more.'

Wetherby sat with his hands steepled at his chin. He did not speak for several minutes. 'Very well, Christopher,' he said eventually, 'rather than suffer your jibes for the rest of my life I shall accompany you, but I hold out no great hopes of our discovering anything but a pile of ashes.'

'Good. Can you find us a coach?'

'I can find us a pair of decent mounts more easily.'

'More riding. How foul. Well, if it must be.'

'Be at the stables in Chancery Lane at eight tomorrow morning. I will make the arrangements.'

CHAPTER 33

Wetherby had found them a pair of tolerable palfreys and by nine they had left through the Aldgate and were on the road heading east. The days were getting longer and the worst of the winter was over.

'A joy to be out of the city,' said Wetherby, 'even if our journey proves wasted.'

'I doubt it will be,' replied Christopher, 'and I certainly hope not. This is a most uncomfortable beast.'

Wetherby laughed. 'You will soon get used to it. And you seem confident.'

'When you returned with Gabriel from the house to Aldgate you were hooded. He did not want you to know where you had been. Had there been nothing to hide, that would not have mattered.'

'We might be too late.'

'We might. It has been five days. If I were Gabriel I would have disappeared, leaving nothing for us to find but the satisfaction of knowing the place of our imprisonment.'

They left the river when it turned south and joined the causeway that ran through a forest of reeds and little else until they arrived at a crossroads. It was a bleak spot with neither building nor human in sight. A few sheep grazed what little grass there was while carrion crows squawked overhead, waiting for a lamb to be born or a rabbit to venture too far from its burrow. Here they took the road south.

'Do you not think this is it?' asked Christopher. 'Here there are the ruts and holes I am sure I felt in the coach.'

'Christopher, this far from the city wall any road is full of ruts and holes. But you may be right. Let us carry on.'

They passed deserted hovels and a mean cottage or two built in the lee of a thin copse or low mound until the road forked. They took the left fork, a rough path banked up against encroachment by the river. The trees here were taller and more numerous. In the distance they heard a dog bark.

Then they saw it. Through a screen of elms the roof of a large dwelling appeared. They dismounted and quietly led the horses closer until they had a clear view of it. It was an old, two-storey house, stone-built, with a grey slate roof and shuttered windows, just as in Simon's story. There was no sign of life. They looked at each other and nodded. Whoever had built this house a hundred years ago had sought to impress. And whoever had most recently lived in it had sought privacy.

They tethered the horses to a tree and approached the great oak door. For the journey Christopher had bought a new blade. He knocked on the door with its pommel. From within there came not a sound. He turned the handle and pushed the door. It creaked open and they entered. Christopher peered into the gloom. A chair had been set by a cold fireplace; two more stood opposite. There was no other furniture. They were standing in Simon Lovelace's hall.

The oak door closed behind them. They turned in surprise to see a figure holding in one hand a lantern in which burned a thick candle and in the other a cocked pistol. 'Welcome, gentlemen,' said the figure. 'I have been expecting you.'

Gabriel's beard had gone and his hair was neatly trimmed. He wore a high-necked doublet and long leather boots. The working man had become a gentleman. Even his voice sounded different, the vowels less flattened, the tone lighter.

Christopher was the first to recover his poise. 'Gabriel Browne. We imagined you long gone. Have you been watching for us?'

'I am not entirely alone in this miserable place, doctor. You were seen.' He gestured with the pistol. 'Sit down. I will take Simon's chair.' He waited for them to sit before he did. He put the lantern on the floor. 'Simon said you would come. I confess to having been less sure. But he was right. He was nearly always right, and here you are.'

'Unless that is a most unusual pistol,' said Wetherby, 'you have but a single bullet with which to shoot both of us.'

'Very good, Mr Wetherby. Simon approved of your spirit. However, one bullet is quite enough to kill Dr Radcliff, after which I will take my chances with you. Now, tell me why you are here.'

'We were curious,' replied Christopher. 'Curious to see the house in which we had been kept prisoners and curious to know whether Simon's story was as true as he made it seem.'

'And how did you expect to discover that? Simon is dead. Did you think to find a confession or a journal in his hand revealing all?'

'We expected nothing, Gabriel, least of all you. But our journey has proved worthwhile. Here we are and here you are.'

'Was Simon's story true?' asked Wetherby. 'The story which he told the queen and which you told me.'

'Why should I tell you? What is to be gained from it?'

'The truth,' replied Christopher. 'The very thing that Simon Lovelace claimed was his purpose. Reality from deception, and knowledge from ignorance.' He let that sink in. 'Was Robert Dudley Simon's father?'

They sat in silence. For some minutes Gabriel did not move or show any inclination to reply. Eventually, he spoke. 'Caroline Lovelace, Simon's mother, was a sweet child, beautiful and clever. My father was in the service of her father and I knew her from the day she was born. I watched her grow into a young lady who could have married any man she chose. She was talented and accomplished and, from an early age, young men doted on her. We all doted on her — her father, his servants, all of us. But she was no maiden pure. I do not doubt that Robert Dudley was her lover — he came to the house often enough — but he was not the only one.'

'Did her father not know of this?' asked Wetherby.

'He did not — or at least he chose not to. Are fathers not blind to the sins of their children?'

There was another long silence. 'So Caroline Lovelace did not know whether Robert Dudley was her son's father or not.'

'She chose to believe that he was. For her, that was the truth. He was young, handsome, of noble birth, destined to rise high. If he took her as his wife she would rise with him.'

'And she brought up her son to believe as she did.'

'Exactly. But do not judge her too harshly. How many women could survive the shock of rejection yet devote themselves to the care of a son like Simon? Caroline Lovelace was only seventeen when Simon was born, her life ahead of her, yet she did so and it hastened her death.'

'Why did she think that Simon's condition was caused by Dudley's rejection?'

'The doctors were agreed. So great was Simon's deformity that no one thought it could have been caused by anything other than a shock to his mother that played havoc with the balance of her humours and thus also those of her unborn child.'

'Did the doctors not ask the name of his father?'

'They did but she revealed it to no one until Simon was sixteen and then he was sworn to silence until she was dead. The doctors knew only that she had been left with a bastard child.'

'No one except you.'

'I too was sworn to silence and I gave my word that I would care for him until one of us died. He wanted to expose Dudley but I think he also dreaded being alone. He wanted to die before I did.'

'Why did you stay with him, Gabriel?' asked Wetherby.

'His mother asked it of me.'

'Simon was a clever man,' said Christopher. 'The testons, the slogans, the crosses, a disappearing body, even the hemlock hidden in the lute peg, and God knows he had good reason for wanting the truth to be known, but three men have died. He had blood on his hands and so do you.'

'Fossett killed Pryse and the goldsmith. Neither was necessary. And he could not keep his mouth shut. Simon wanted him out of harm's way.'

'Did you paint the slogan on St Martin's church?'

'I ordered it done.'

'Why?'

'To make you ask yourself why. Simon would have done the same.'

Christopher rubbed his hand. He had killed, accidentally, and been fortunate not to hang for it. Did this man who had killed on another's orders deserve to live or was he as much a murderer as a throat-cutting thief? Did it make a difference that his victim was also a murderer? Some might think so but the law said not.

He stretched his fingers. Jury? Law? Gabriel was armed, there was no rescuer outside and he would not want to leave them alive. He would put a ball between Christopher's eyes, take his blade and kill Roland.

'You seem deep in thought, doctor,' said Gabriel. 'Are you planning your escape?'

'I am,' replied Wetherby, 'but I cannot at present see one.'

'And you, doctor? Do you see one?'

'An escape, no, but a possible solution to our problem.'

'Our problem?'

'We do not wish to die and I do not think you wish to kill us. What you do wish to do is spend the rest of your years in peace and safety. You have the silver taken by Fossett from the Pryses — at least I imagine you do — why not take it and our horses and leave us here? It is a long walk back to Aldgate and by the time we reach it you will be long gone.'

'And pursued until I am found.'

'Not if we swear never to speak of this. Your face is known only to us. You will be safe.'

'Why should I believe you?'

'Because we came alone. We did not bring armed constables or the queen's guards. We were curious, that is all. We meant you no harm.'

'A lawyer's argument that does you credit, Dr Radcliff, although, like all lawyers' arguments, not to be believed.'

Christopher was watching him and trying to read his expression when, outside, something spooked the horses. A fox, perhaps or a dog. Instinctively, Gabriel turned his head and in that instant, without conscious thought, Christopher leapt at him. But he was not quite quick enough. Gabriel raised the pistol and fired. Christopher felt the bullet sear his cheek but his momentum carried him forward and he crashed into Gabriel, sending his chair and the pistol flying. He was probably as strong as Gabriel but the bullet had dazed him. Gabriel managed to reach the handle of Christopher's poniard and pull it out. He heaved Christopher off and raised the blade to strike. Christopher was on his back. Looking up, he was dimly aware of Wetherby standing behind Gabriel. With a crack, the butt of the pistol came down on Gabriel's head. The poniard fell from his hand and he collapsed on to the floor.

Wetherby helped Christopher to his feet and sat him down. 'You were lucky, my friend,' he said, peering at Christopher's cheek. 'A slight wound only and you will keep your looks. But why did you do it? He might have agreed.'

Christopher shook his head to clear his mind. 'I do not know. It was beyond my control. I did not think about it.'

'Well, it is done now. I will find something to bind his hands with.' He went outside and was soon back with a short length of rope with which he tied Gabriel's wrists behind his back.

There was a groan. Wetherby picked up the blade and put a foot on the back of Gabriel's neck. 'Stay still, Gabriel Browne, and you will live,' he growled. 'Move a finger and you will feel the point of this blade in your throat.'

Christopher had regained his senses. 'I offered you a solution, Gabriel, but you hesitated. That was a mistake. We should take you to Newgate and leave you there to face trial. But you can still save yourself from that fate. Do you understand?' Gabriel did not reply. Christopher nodded to Wetherby who pressed the blade into his neck. 'If we search the house, what will we find? Is there any evidence to support your story?'

'You will find nothing. The house is empty.'

'No papers, no letters?'

'Nothing.'

'Mr Wetherby will search while you and I remain here. Be quick, Roland. Now that we know the truth, I am anxious to be away from here.'

Wetherby took a candle and climbed the stairs. His footsteps echoed around the emptiness of the upper storey. It did not take long and he was soon down again. 'Nothing but a couple of mattresses,' he said, shaking his head. 'Not much comfort for the weary traveller in this inn. I will look below and in the kitchen.'

He was soon back. 'Empty but for the mattress in our cell. Not even a pot to piss in.'

'So, Gabriel,' said Christopher. 'We find you in the act of removing all trace of Simon's existence. But I doubt you've removed Simon's money. You would want to keep that close. Where is it?' Gabriel shrugged. 'Jog his memory, please, Roland. The earl would be pleased to receive an unexpected gift.'

'With pleasure,' replied Wetherby. He knelt beside their prisoner and ran the point of the blade down his cheek. Blood bubbled up and Gabriel squirmed. Wetherby applied the blade to the other cheek. This time Gabriel yelped in pain. 'There,' said Roland, 'now both sides match. A pity you have only one nose.'

'Where is Simon's money?' demanded Christopher.

'Take the knife away.' Wetherby did so. 'What remained of the false coins lies deep in the marsh.'

'Not those. His true money.'

'What money?' Another nudge with the blade, just under his left eye. 'His chair.'

Christopher stood up and felt under the chair. He had not before noticed it but the seat was unusually deep. He found a catch. The seat opened on a hinge. Inside were three bags. He took them out. 'Is this what remains of his inheritance?'

'Yes.'

'We will take it. Now listen carefully and be in no doubt. Roland and I will return to London and you will accompany us. Your hands will be bound and tied to the saddle of your horse. We know you have one. This house is a long way from anywhere on foot. The animal will be loosely hobbled to deter you from attempting to escape. If you try, I will kill you. Is that understood?'

'Entirely.' Blood was dripping down Gabriel's face. 'Undo my hands so I can wipe the blood away.'

'It will dry. Until then, put up with it.'

'Come, Christopher,' said Wetherby. 'It is a fine day and we have a most agreeable ride to look forward to.'

They rode in single file, Wetherby leading, Christopher at the rear. With Gabriel's horse hobbled, progress was slow. Wetherby looked back over his shoulder often to check that their prisoner was secure. Christopher kept his eyes fixed on the prisoner's back. They saw no one and, as far as they could tell, no one saw them.

They had almost left the marsh and turned left towards the city when a long-beaked curlew shot skywards out of the reeds, shrieking a warning to others. Half a dozen smaller birds rose from the marsh, all anxious to spread the word that there were strangers about. They swooped overhead directly in front of Wetherby's horse, spooking it.

The horse tried to bolt but stumbled in a rut and fell, throwing its rider off. Before Christopher could react, Gabriel had slipped out of the rope around his saddle, jumped down and run back down the causeway towards the house. He must have worked his binding loose. Roland or Gabriel? Christopher chose Roland.

He dismounted and led his horse around Gabriel's so that he could tie their reins together. Wetherby's horse lay on its side, a front leg twisted grotesquely backwards. If Christopher had had a pistol he would have shot it without hesitation. But he had no pistol, only a slim blade.

Roland sat up and rubbed his shoulder. 'God's bowels,' he grumbled. 'Fucking birds.'

'Are you wounded?' asked Christopher.

'A sore shoulder, nothing more. But the wretch has escaped. What shall we do?'

'There is no point in following him. Either he has disappeared down some secret pathway or he will be waiting for us, armed and keen to be rid of us once and for all.'

'So we travel on to London?'

'We do. Can you ride?'

'I think so. Unhobble the horse and I will take it.' He glanced at his own mount. 'This one is finished. Give me your blade.'

It had to be done. Christopher handed over the poniard and watched while Roland stroked the horse's head. When it was quiet, he held its mane with one hand and with the other drove the point of the blade into its throat. It eyes opened wide in shock and it struggled feebly to get to its feet. Wetherby pushed it down and when he removed the blade a fountain of blood gushed out, the animal twitched and soon lay still. 'Kinder than leaving it to die,' he said, wiping the blade on a tuft of grass before handing it back.

Christopher untied the hobbling ropes and held the horse while Roland mounted. He grunted in pain but managed to get on without mishap. Christopher untied the reins joining the two animals and clambered on to his. He patted the bags slung over the horse's back. 'At least the money is safe.'

'I would rather have had a prisoner to give to the earl,' replied Wetherby. 'Too late now. Let's be on our way.'

Two hours later they rode slowly down a busy Leadenhall Street. 'If all these good people had an inkling of what we are carrying, we would be food for the rats within minutes,' said Wetherby. 'What are we going to do with it?'

'We are going to take it straight to Whitehall, Roland. It will be safer there than at Ludgate Hill.'

'There is a great deal of it. Five hundred pounds at least and not a bear or staff to be seen.'

'Let us hope that their lordships are happy.'

They went first to the palace where they stored the bags in Wetherby's apartment and returned the horses to the Chancery Lane stables. 'Call tomorrow in the afternoon,' said Christopher. 'In the morning I shall be occupied.'

CHAPTER 34

His mother had loved the tune. He seldom played it now because it reminded him so sharply of her. She said that it had been composed by the queen's father at the time he was wooing her mother, Anne Boleyn, who was resisting his advances. It was a more difficult tune to play than it sounded and Christopher had taken time to master it. He had thought that one day he would like to write lyrics for it.

A repeating bass formed the ground over which were played four chords with variations as the lutenist wished. The more skilled the player, the more variations there tended to be. The tune was known as 'Greensleeves'.

He tuned the strings carefully, not wanting to break one and to have to replace it. He tried a few chords, adjusted two frets and started to play.

At first the fingers of his right hand were stiff and awkward and he had to stop and try again to find the divisions he wanted. Once started he was determined to play the tune as his mother had played it. For an hour he played it over and again until he was satisfied. If Leicester ever asked him to play again, this would be the tune.

He put the lute back in its case and hid it under the pile of shirts. Then he remembered that Gabriel Browne had had no difficulty in finding it there and took it up to his chamber. It fitted comfortably under his bed.

There was no food in the house but he had not the energy to go out. He went to sleep lulled by the melody of 'Greensleeves' repeating in his mind.

The storm began that night. Rain lashed the window and crashed like pebbles on to the roof. He lay awake and listened to it. Not a man or woman in London would be asleep. Water would be gushing down Ludgate Hill, sweeping away anything in its path and dumping it in heaps on corners and in doorways, where it would fester and rot until it ended up in the Fleet or the Thames.

When St Martin's clock struck six to signal the end of the curfew the wind had abated but it was still raining. There was no point in rising. He needed food but there would not be an inn open at that hour. He lay on his back, just as he had often done with Katherine beside him, and let his mind wander. Heavy bags of coins with Wetherby, on their way to Leicester and Warwick, the riddle of the false testons and the slogans solved and Pryse in Newgate. But dear Isaac was dead, Simon Lovelace was dead and Joan Willys was still awaiting trial. As to Gabriel Browne, who could say? Where would he go — the Low Countries, Denmark? Somewhere far away from the reach of the Dudley family, to be sure.

By eight the rain had ceased. He rose and dressed and went in search of sustenance. He avoided the worst of the torrent pouring down the hill by keeping to the middle of the street. Urchins splashed about in the puddles while their mothers collected what they could in pails and pots, for fresh rainwater was cleaner even than that drawn from Clerk's well.

He found what he needed in the Crossed Keys in the form of bread and beef washed down with a beaker of ale and steeled himself for Newgate. By the time he squelched his way through the great gates, his shoes were sodden.

The warden was in his room. 'Dr Radcliff, good day to you, although I see you have had a wet time of it. And not such a good day for the prisoners. The cells on the common side have flooded.'

'Can anything be done?'

'Nothing but wait for the water to drain away. It will eventually. If you have come to inquire after Pryse, I am afraid you are too late. He was buried two days ago.'

'How did he die?'

The warden coughed. 'I have recorded his death as being caused by gaol fever. There have been cases and the flooding will bring more.'

Christopher raised an eyebrow. 'Gaol fever. Not the result of his experience in the pressing room?'

'No, no, doctor. Gaol fever to be sure.'

The warden was lying but Christopher felt no remorse. Pryse would have hanged and deserved to die. He had other concerns. 'Is Joan Willys still here?' he asked.

'She is, on the master's side. Do you wish to see her?'

'If you please, warden. I shall not take long.'

The warden summoned a guard who escorted him to Joan's cell. She was wrapped in a thick shawl and perched on a stool, nibbling a piece of cheese. She jumped up when she saw Christopher, bobbed a curtsy and smiled her lop-sided smile.

'Dr Radcliff, are you well? How do you manage at home? Are you well fed?'

Christopher held up a hand. 'I am well, thank you, Joan, although I am in sore need of your honeyed porridge. Has Mistress Allington visited you?'

'Oh yes, doctor, almost every day. She brings victuals and clean clothes.'

'That she does,' said one of the women with whom Joan shared the cell, 'and we are grateful to her. A fine lady.'

'A fine lady,' echoed the other woman.

'She is indeed. Have you had other visitors, Joan?'

'No, doctor. My mother cannot come and who else would? Except you.'

'I would have come sooner but I have been away. Do you lack for anything?'

'Nothing. How many days more, doctor?'

A grand jury had yet to be summoned but he would not tell Joan that. 'Not many, Joan.'

Again the lop-sided smile. 'I have been saying my prayers as Mistress Allington told me. I knew you would come.'

'And I will come again soon, Joan, very soon.'

He walked back to the gate. Prayers. They would need more than prayers.

Gilbert Knoyll's servant answered the door, disappeared briefly and returned to say that the magistrate was not available. Christopher pushed past him and into Knoyll's study.

The magistrate was stuffing food into his mouth. When he spoke, he sent crumbs flying over his desk. 'Dr Radcliff, did my servant not make it clear that I am not available? Return tomorrow if you have business to discuss.'

Christopher ignored him. 'Why is Joan Willys still held in Newgate and why has a grand jury not yet considered her case?'

'That is not your concern.' More crumbs splattered the desk.

Christopher felt his temper rising. He stretched his fingers, breathed deeply and took his time before speaking. It was in just this mood that he had killed a man on the day of his mother's burial. 'Mr Knoyll, I know that both you and Mr Pyke have visited Alice Scrope at her house. I also know that the woman is a thief and a whore who holds a grudge against Joan Willys. And if Joan Willys appears at the sessions I shall not be the only one who knows it. A magistrate who supports the accusation of a woman with whom he consorts and lies about it will not be looked upon favourably by the judge.'

'Joan Willys has been tested. Justice must be done.'

Christopher snapped. 'Justice? You speak of justice, Knoyll? An innocent woman languishes in Newgate awaiting a trial that should never take place while you sit on your fat arse doing nothing. You are swiving a whore who has made a false accusation and if Joan Willys is not released today, you will be the one in Newgate, sitting in twelve inches of stinking water with an empty belly.' He glared at Knoyll, searching for a sign of fear. There was none.

He slammed the door on his way out.

Each time he saw Clennet Pyke, he thought the coroner looked more like a flounder. His face appeared flatter, his mouth smaller and his narrow eyes set closer together. Now the man sat by his fire, a beaker in his hand and reeking of drink.

Christopher recoiled at the smell of stale beer. He was in no mood for courtesy. 'My patience has run out, Pyke. You are swiving the woman Alice Scrope, despite the fact that she is a whore and a thief and has made a false accusation of witchcraft against my house-keeper. What have you to say about that?'

Pyke's eyebrows rose. 'And who is your housekeeper, Dr Radcliff?'

'You know perfectly well who she is. Joan Willys who now waits in Newgate for the Easter sessions. A monstrous injustice to which you are party.'

'How is that? Was she not properly tested in Mr Knoyll's presence and did she not appear in his court where witnesses spoke against her?'

'To hell with testing and witnesses. Which is where you and the fat magistrate will go if she is not released today. Today, Pyke, or you will join Knoyll in Newgate and it will not be on the master's side. Be sure of it.'

Pyke got to his feet. 'You do not frighten me, sir, with your threats. I am a coroner and will not be intimidated.'

More spirit from the revolting little man than he had expected. 'You are a thieving incompetent, Pyke. Persuade Knoyll to free Joan Willys or face the consequences of your crimes.'

As he had with Knoyll, Christopher glared at him before marching out. Had he seen a speck of fear in those mean eyes or was it his imagination?

He hardly noticed the prices in Cheapside. Two pennies, five pennies — he would probably have paid ten if he had been asked. His mind was on Joan and how to save her from the stocks and a prison term.

Wetherby had come bearing wine. 'I've counted it,' he said. 'Five hundred and fifty pounds in gold and silver coin.' He filled two of Christopher's glasses. 'When shall we hand it over to the earl?'

'The sooner the better. Today?'

'We shall have to explain where it has come from.'

'I fear so.'

Christopher's mind was not on the money and he was grateful that Wetherby did not push him. 'What of Mistress Allington? How does she fare?'

'Well enough, I suppose. I would know if it was not so.'

'Have you called on her since we returned?'

'I have been busy. Tomorrow perhaps.'

'Then all is not well between you. I am sorry for it. Is that what is troubling you?'

'In part. I am troubled also by my housekeeper, Joan Willys, having to face a judge and jury at the Easter assizes on a false charge of witchcraft. She is ill equipped to defend herself and is likely to spend a year in prison and four days in the stocks. I doubt she would survive.'

'Tell me how this has happened, Christopher.'

Christopher told him about Alice Scrope's accusation and Joan's searching and her examination in the magistrate's court. 'If it were any other magistrate than Gilbert Knoyll, it would not have happened,' he said. 'The man's a fat slop bucket and he's been swiving the woman Scrope. How can he be thought impartial?'

'Surely he cannot.'

'And his friend the coroner is swiving her too. Clennet Pyke is as bad as Knoyll.'

'Pyke? Clennet Pyke? A small man with narrow eyes?'

'That's him, the evil little toad.'

'Well, well. The Clennet Pyke I know is not a swiver of women, even whores. He is well known in certain establishments around Eastcheap, and much disliked for his meanness of purse and spirit.'

Wetherby frowned. 'Mind you, there are those who lie on both sides of the bed, if you understand me. He must be one of them.'

'And women who do too, so I've heard.'

'That I would not know. Clennet Pyke, however, I do know. He would do well in Newgate.'

When Wetherby left both bottles were empty. He staggered a little at the door, clapped Christopher on the shoulder and strode off down the hill. 'Call this afternoon, my friend. I will arrange an appointment for us with the earl.'

CHAPTER 35

In Cambridge he had often walked along the ancient path that ran alongside the river to the hamlet of Grantchester. It was a good way to clear the head after a morning's teaching and more often than not he had only cows in the meadows for company.

Holborn Fields were a poor substitute, with or without lawyers' horses — thick, clinging mud in winter and earth baked hard in summer. A day after the storm the fields would be like the marshes at Hackney. He would have to make do with the streets.

North from St Paul's, right into Gresham Street and then into Gutter Lane and Cheapside would take him about thirty minutes. Enough to restore his mind after the excess of the morning. It was Roland's fault for bringing two bottles and for entertaining him with his palace gossip.

Sir Christopher Hatton's laundress had found a ten-decade rosary among his undergarments. Thomas Heneage had upset the queen by calling the Earl of Warwick 'the limping sibling'. And a lady of the queen's bedchamber had taken too much strong wine, addressed her majesty as 'sir' and fallen over. Roland was never at a loss for a story. True or not — it mattered little.

Water still dripped off rooftops and lay about in puddles. It was worst in Gresham Street where the rain had settled on the paving rather than seep into the ground as it did more easily on cobbles.

He passed Wood Street, walked a few paces and stopped. A small boy shouted across the street. 'You lost, mister? A penny and I'll show you the way.' Christopher ignored him. He retraced his steps before turning up Wood Street.

'You are not at the mercy of some unseen force, Dr Radcliff,' he muttered to himself. 'You are a man of free will, doing as you please. Do not pretend otherwise.'

He rapped on Katherine's door. Nothing happened so he rapped again. The door opened and she stood, arms crossed, on the threshold. She did not smile. 'Christopher, you have saved me a walk to Ludgate Hill. I have news for you.'

'Good news, I hope. May I come in?'

'What needs to be said can as well be said here. My aunt is sick and will not live long. I have determined to return to Cambridge when she dies.'

'Has this something to do with Ell Cole?'

'No, Christopher, it is to do with you. Your work for the earl has changed you and you are not the man I followed to London. The whore is simply one way in which you have changed.'

'Katherine, that is nonsense. And I have told you endlessly that I have never touched Ell Cole.'

She glared at him. 'Can you tell me truthfully that you have never shared her bed?'

He sighed. 'No, Katherine, I cannot say that, but I have never—'

'Goodbye, Christopher. I shall pray for you.' She closed the door, leaving him standing in the street.

'Found 'er, did you?' said the boy as he brushed past. 'Penny to show you the way 'ome.' He scuttled off laughing.

Not the man she followed to London. No, indeed he was not. The dreams, of course, and a temper more likely to flare, as it had when she had last spoken of Ell. But what else? Had she not changed too? Who would not in London?

He walked slowly back to Ludgate Hill, his mind only half on what he was doing. Like rats sensing easy prey, chattering urchins skipped around his legs, grabbed his coat and barred his way until he tipped the contents of his purse on to the street and left them to fight over the coins.

He did not even notice the coach until he was almost at his door. It was a two-seater, painted a deep blue with gold trimmings, drawn by two black Neapolitan coursers and bearing the Dudley crest. The queen, he knew, had one much the same.

A messenger jumped out when he saw Christopher. 'Dr Radcliff, the earl requests you to come to the palace immediately. We are to convey you.'

Another reward? Another warning to keep the secret of Simon Lovelace? 'What does the earl want of me?'

'That I do not know, doctor, but he was most insistent that I escort you to Whitehall without delay.'

Troubles seldom travel alone, his father had been fond of saying. He climbed into the coach and sat opposite the messenger, with his back to the driver.

The Dudley crest ensured that they were not held up on the way or at the gate. He was escorted by a guard to the earl's apartments and shown straight through the antechamber. No waiting around today.

He had not seen the man standing beside the earl for more than four years, despite the fact that he spent as much time in London as he did in Cambridge — a matter that had long grieved the college fellows. John Young, Master of Pembroke Hall, was a slight man, neat in appearance and modest in his dress, as befitted a clergyman and scholar. He was the second John Young to be Master, his father having been one of those replaced by the queen for his Catholic sympathies. His son had sometimes hinted at the distress his father had suffered as a consequence of his dismissal and Christopher had wondered if he bore a grudge. It had been he who had ordered the removal of every trace of popery from the college chapel on the day news reached the town of the queen's wishes.

'I have invited Mr Young here, Dr Radcliff, because he has written to me on a sensitive matter concerning you. I felt he should speak to you in person,' said Leicester.

'Dr Radcliff,' said Young in his precise way, 'it is a pleasure to see you after so long. Five years, is it not, since you left Pembroke?'

'It is, master, and there are times when I still miss the college.'

Young pursed his lips. 'Indeed. And I for one was sorry to see you leave us. Alas, an unfortunate necessity. But you will be happy to know that little has changed since you were with us. Idle nobles, impoverished sizars, hard-working commoners, the town council arguing with the Caput Senatus about the watch and ward and the King's Ditch and our pupils at war with the apprentices.'

Christopher laughed. 'Then little indeed has changed.'

'I shall come to the point. The fellows of the college have given their consent to my inviting you to return. I am also advised that the Caput would not stand in your way. Five years have passed and the university has need of teachers of your skill. Naturally, I first advised his lordship of this and he graciously suggested this meeting.'

What was the expression? Struck dumb? 'Well, master,' he managed, 'I am at a loss. This is entirely unexpected.'

Leicester grinned. 'You lost for words, doctor? A thing I have never before encountered.'

'My apologies, my lord. It has been a day of surprises.' Christopher stopped stretching his fingers and made an effort to recover himself. 'Master, I am conscious of your generosity but I remain a convicted felon. If it were not for my lord Leicester, I would still be food for the rats in Norwich gaol or buried in the grave of a common criminal.'

'We are of course aware of that,' replied Leicester, 'but if you wish to accept Mr Young's offer, I believe that Her Majesty might be persuaded to grant you a royal pardon which would extinguish your conviction.'

'You are not married, doctor, am I right?' asked Young. 'I ask because Her Majesty's prohibition on married men taking up fellowships could not be circumvented.'

'I am unmarried, master, and likely to remain so.'

'Good. Then it is up to you to decide, doctor. Continue in the service of his lordship or return to Pembroke Hall with a fellowship awaiting you. Not immediately, of course, but in a year or two I would certainly support your election.'

'Do not make your decision hastily, doctor,' said Leicester. 'Give it careful thought. I should be sorry indeed to lose you but I would not stand in your way if a return to teaching is what you want. And to keep you here against your will would be foolish in the extreme.'

'I shall, my lord.'

'Meanwhile, I will speak to Her Majesty. It would be as well to be sure of her views. She takes a very close interest in the universities. "My Cambridge", she is pleased to call it. Good day, Dr Radcliff.'

'Good day, my lord, good day, master.' He bowed and turned to leave.

There was no coach to take him home. He found a wherry at the Whitehall steps. The river was calm. His mind was not. Whose idea had it really been? John Young's or Leicester's? Would he be welcome in Pembroke Hall or was it simply a means of removing him from the earl's service and sending him where there was less likelihood of his causing trouble?

And, most of all, what did he want to do? He would never now lack for money. A fellowship and the pleasures of Cambridge or discomfort and danger in the cause of the country? And Katherine? Would a fellowship change her mind or would it not? Not marriage, of course, but a reconciliation?

He alighted at Blackfriars steps. If Katherine had not that very day turned him away he would go to Wood Street. If Isaac were alive he would go to Fleet Street. He could do neither. And he had quite forgotten that Wetherby still had the money and was expecting him to call.

CHAPTER 36

It had rained again for most of the night and the dreams had come and gone. He dragged himself out of bed, pulled on a shirt and went down to the study without bothering to wash or dress properly.

He was trying without success to light a fire when he heard the door open. Surely Katherine had not changed her mind. He left the fire and went to greet her. 'Good morning, doctor,' said the little figure, smiling her lop-sided smile and putting the key back in her basket. 'I thought to come straight away. Have you taken breakfast?'

'Joan. You have been released. When was it?' He smiled in delight and only just stopped himself from embracing the girl.

'Yesterday evening, doctor. The warden came to the cell and told me to go, so I did. Luckily the key to your door was still at my mother's house.'

'Did the warden give any reason for your release?'

'No, sir. He just told me to leave. I've brought honey and oats for your porridge. How have you been managing?'

'Very poorly. It is a mighty relief to see you free, Joan, for both our sakes.'

'Mistress Allington will have taken care of you.'

'Mistress Allington has been much occupied. I have seen little of her.'

'Oh. I am sorry to hear that, doctor. Now, you go to your chamber and I will prepare your breakfast and set a fire. It's cold out after the rain.'

He could have cheered. Joan back and with a brisk confidence that he had not seen before. Where had it come from? Surely not Newgate. Perhaps she was a witch. He laughed. Knoyll and Pyke had been frightened off after all. For all their braggadocio, they had taken fright and run like the craven scroyles they were.

He was still grinning when he went down to the kitchen. 'I've made extra, doctor,' said Joan, spooning porridge into a bowl. 'You sit down and I will attend to the fire.'

He emptied the bowl and helped himself to another. He called out to her. 'You can move those shirts, now, Joan. I expect they could do with a wash.'

Joan poked her head around the door. 'They could, doctor, unless you are minded to buy new ones.'

'If you wash them, do you know anyone who would like them?'

'I do, doctor. There's many would be grateful.'

'In that case, take them and wash them and find them new homes. I shall visit the shirt-maker in Leadenhall.'

'As you wish, doctor. Be sure to buy good linen shirts, won't you? They do better than wool.'

He was in the study when Joan came to say goodbye. 'Do you need money for food?' he asked her.

'Two shillings will be sufficient.'

'Are you sure? The market prices have risen.'

'I know, doctor, but the traders will be pleased to see me. I can manage on two shillings.'

He handed her the coins. 'Tomorrow, Joan?' he asked.

'Tomorrow, doctor.' For the first time, Joan looked unsure of herself. 'And I thank you for what you and Mistress Allington have done for me.'

'You are well and free, Joan. That is thanks enough.'

Wetherby arrived at noon. He looked about the study and shook his head. 'You've found a new housekeeper, Christopher, unless I am mistaken. No dust, a good fire, and where are your old shirts?'

'Joan Willys has been released from Newgate. I shall never wear dirty shirts or go hungry again.'

Wetherby threw up his hands. 'That is excellent news. How did it happen?'

'It seems that the ungodly Clennet Pyke and Gilbert Knoyll took fright and saw the error of their ways.'

'Excellent. I wonder what caused them to change their minds?'

There was something in Wetherby's tone that made Christopher look up. A tiny smile played around his mouth and eyes. 'Roland, did you have anything to do with it?'

'I? Good God, no. It must have been your silver tongue and lawyer's demeanour. Now let us to the Brown Bear. I am hungry.'

The inn was quiet. They found a table in a corner and ordered food and ale. 'I tried to make an appointment for us with Leicester but could not. It seems he was much occupied with other matters. And I gather we had an unusual visitor at Whitehall,' said Wetherby while they waited. 'John Young, Master of your old college. Why would he come to the palace, do you suppose?'

'I really could not say. Perhaps Her Majesty had asked to see him.'

'I think not. He was seen entering the Earl of Leicester's apartments.'

'Was he?'

'He was, Christopher, and so were you.'

'In the name of God, is nothing secret in that place?'

'Very little. Are you going to tell me or not?'

'Tell you what?'

'Christopher, dissembling does you no credit and you are not good at it. Kindly tell me why the Master of Pembroke Hall and the noble Earl of Leicester summoned you to Whitehall.'

He knew Roland Wetherby. Like Katherine Allington, he would not let go of the bone until he had picked every last shred of meat from it. 'Oh, very well, Roland, but if you breathe a word I will do to you what Gerard Fossett did to John Pryse.'

'No you will not. Now tell me.' A girl brought their pie and two beakers of ale. Christopher waited until she had gone before he started.

'A difficult decision for you, my friend,' said Wetherby when he had finished. 'Disputation and dinner with the fellows or felons and traitors for the earl. I know which I would choose.'

'I know which you would choose, too. It is what I should choose that I do not know.'

'Have you told Katherine? What does she say?'

'I have not told her, nor intend to. Katherine has decided to return to Cambridge alone.'

'Ah. Then I shall inquire no more. Sit by your fire and think. I daresay the answer will come to you. Be sure to tell me, however, if you feel in need of wise counsel.'

They parted outside the inn. At Ludgate Hill, Christopher let himself in, took off his coat and went into the study. The fire was fading. He crouched down to put more wood on it. He did not see the blow that felled him from behind.

CHAPTER 37

He was on the floor, hands and feet tied, lying on his side facing the fire. His head throbbed and his mind was befuddled. He tried to focus his eyes but could not. It took a little while before he realized what had happened. He had returned to the house, come into the study and then nothing. He knew no more.

His attacker knew his business. The blow had been hard enough to knock him senseless but not hard enough to kill. Just like Wetherby at St Paul's. And at that moment he knew. Gabriel Browne had been waiting for him.

'Dr Radcliff,' said a distant voice, 'surely you did not think that I would disappear, that we would never meet again.' Christopher managed to roll over, unable to prevent vomit dribbling from his mouth. He looked up to see Gabriel Browne standing over him. 'Our business is not yet done,' said Gabriel. Christopher wriggled around and got his back against a leg of his writing table so that he could sit up. 'How wise of you to get rid of the shirts and put the lute under your bed. Much safer. Your blade is in the kitchen, should you need it.' He held up a wicked-looking long-bladed dagger. 'I have brought my own. I have never liked firearms, just as Simon did not. A good blade is so much more reliable, don't you agree?'

'The blade with which you cut Fossett's throat.'

'Fossett was a prick. He deserved it.'

'What do you want?'

Gabriel laughed. 'Not money, if that is what you think. You took but a fraction of what Simon had hidden in the house. Nor the lute, lovely though it is. No, I have come to reveal to you the truth.'

'The truth is known to me. You did Simon's bidding and helped him to end his own life.'

'The latter, doctor, I cannot deny. The former, however, I do.' In his manner of speech, it was as if he was transforming himself from servant to master.

Christopher stared at the face, now lightly scarred by a line on each cheek. 'How can you deny it?'

'Are you comfortable, doctor? I have a story to tell.'

'Another story? I rather tire of them.'

'This story is true and I shall tell it to you while I can.'

'While you can? Will you be taking hemlock or will you be using your blade on me?'

'That you must wait to find out.' Gabriel settled himself into the chair often occupied by Wetherby and began. He spoke without much emotion, without hurrying and in a low, clear voice. 'My story begins in the year 1530, when I was born. My mother died giving birth to me. My father was in the employ of Caroline Lovelace's father and I was brought up in their house, doing menial jobs in the kitchen and the garden. When he died, I was kept on. I gave little thought to it, just accepted life as it was and thanked God for a roof over my head and a full belly. There were many who had neither.

'Caroline was born four years after me, so I knew her for all of her short life. I seldom strayed far from the house and knew little of the outside world. When I was nineteen, however, word arrived of camps appearing around Norwich and Cambridge. That was the beginning of the popular uprisings led by the Kett brothers. They quickly spread throughout East Anglia and as far as the western counties. Without telling my father where I was going, I left the house and made my way to the nearest camp at Thetford. I wanted to find out for myself what the uprising was all about.

'I soon learned that it was about poverty and injustice. Wealthy landowners enclosing good grazing land, poor folk dying of starvation, no one listening to their complaints or offering help.

'One day, the camp was attacked by a force sent by the Lord Protector, Lord Somerset. It was led by the Earl of Warwick and two of his sons, Robert and Ambrose Dudley. When they left, the camp was a heap of ashes and bodies. I saw Robert Dudley pierce the throat of an old man with his sword and his father slice off the arm of a boy of no more than twelve. I was sickened.'

'Yet you escaped.'

'I did, and swore one day to take revenge.'

'For all his fine words, it was revenge that Simon Lovelace sought.' Christopher coughed and tried to wipe his mouth with his bound hands.

'Indeed, but revenge of a different sort. He was born two years after the uprisings were suppressed, leaving the people even worse off than they had been, in the year that the bear and staff testons appeared.'

'Was Leicester his father?'

'Ah, the sharp legal mind cuts to the chase. Of course, there is no way of being sure. Robert Dudley did visit the house often and he did have an affair with Caroline Lovelace. That I know. She was very beautiful, you know. But as to his being Simon's father, who knows? She had many admirers.'

'Were you one of them?'

Gabriel snorted. 'I was a servant. If I loved her, it was from afar. The point is not who was the child's father but that Caroline believed it to be Dudley. That, in her mind and Simon's, made it true.'

Christopher's head still throbbed. 'I tire of this story. If you are going to kill me, make haste and do so.'

'No, doctor, there will be no haste.' Gabriel moved a chair and sat facing him. The blade was still in his hand. 'You were foolish not to kill me when you had the chance. Are you capable of killing, I wonder?'

'I have killed before.'

'Have you now? I did not know that. Who was he?'

'I will not speak of it. I am defenceless. Why not use your blade and be done with it?'

'Patience, doctor. I have spent much of my life waiting for another man to die. I will not be rushed now.' Christopher moved a little to ease his back and saw the blade twitch in Gabriel's hand. Gabriel would not make the same mistake again. 'I was almost as much a prisoner as Simon. At Caroline's request I took care of Simon and kept him safe from prying eyes. I wanted the monstrous child to live, although at the time I could not have said why. Only later did it become clear to me that he might one day help me vent my festering anger at the Dudleys.' He paused. 'If you have killed before why did you not kill me?'

'I could ask the same of you.'

'*Touché*, doctor.'

'It was an accident.' Christopher regretted the words as soon as they were out of his mouth.

'Oh, not killing at all then. Merely a mistake. I did not think you would be able to look a man in the eye while you thrust your blade into his heart.'

'Why are you here?'

'I wanted to know more about the man who risked his own life by not taking another. Know thine enemy.'

'And know thyself: γνῶθι σεαυτόν. It was written on a wall in the temple at Delphi.'

'Alas, doctor, I did not have the benefit of schooling in the classics so I must take your word for it. I am merely a humble retainer.'

'You are a wealthy man. Find a wife. Take your money and go. The Low Countries, Denmark, even the New World. Why not?'

'I have of course asked myself that question.'

'And?'

'And I have no answer.'

'In London you are in danger. If Leicester or Warwick learns that you are here you will not be allowed to live.'

'Will you tell them?'

'Will I have the chance?'

'That I have not yet decided. I should kill you as you should have killed me, and I probably will. But first, allow me to finish my story. You will not learn your fate until I have done so. When his mother died — just another mad soul trapped in Bedlam — Simon began to speak of ending his own life. I did not discourage him and gradually an idea formed in my mind. It took a little while but I eventually persuaded him that his death could have purpose and that we could work together to achieve it. The plan — the testons, the slogans, the plague crosses, the capture of Wetherby, Simon's death — was mine. Simon merely agreed to it. Now he is dead and the Dudley name has been blackened in front of the queen. The plan worked.'

Gabriel stood up, threw some kindling on the fire, gave it a poke and moved his chair a little nearer its warmth. 'Now, doctor, we will sit quietly, each of us with our own thoughts, while I consider what to do for the best. Are you comfortable?'

'No.'

'That is unfortunate. Now let us be silent.'

What was this about? Was Gabriel really undecided about what to do? Surely the planner had not come here without a plan. Or was he simply prolonging the agony? That was more likely. Gabriel would leave Christopher to contemplate what was coming and then, when he was ready, he would cut his throat and go. He would do it when it was dark and he had a good chance of slipping away unseen. The silence was no more than another bluff, another deception. If he was to think of a way to escape, he had better do so while it was still light. Take his chances and hurl himself at Gabriel as he had before? No, he might as well cut his own throat. If Roland called, he would die too.

Isabel Tranter was dying. Soon Katherine would leave London and return to Cambridge where she would be able to choose from an army of young admirers. Unlike Penelope waiting for Odysseus to return from Troy, she would not spend her days at her loom, waiting for Christopher to join her. She would find a man with no interest in becoming a fellow and marry him. A young noble, perhaps, or a wealthy wool merchant.

John Young wanted him to return to Pembroke Hall. Leicester seemed ambivalent. Should he not go where he was wanted? If he ever had the chance, that was. More likely he would never leave the house again unless wrapped in a shroud.

There was a knock on the door. He opened his mouth but before he could utter a sound, the tip of Gabriel's knife was under his chin. Gabriel shook his head and put a finger to his lips. 'Not a squeak, doctor,' he whispered.

The visitor knocked again, this time with more force. Ell? Roland? A messenger from Whitehall? Whoever it was, he willed them to hammer on the door and keep on hammering until Gabriel lost patience.

But there was no more. His visitor had given up and gone. Slowly, Gabriel withdrew the knife and sat back on the chair. 'Very wise, doctor,' he said. 'If you had so much as coughed, you would now be dead.'

Christopher closed his eyes. There must be a way. 'In your position, Gabriel,' he asked, without opening them, 'what would Simon have done?'

'That is exactly what I have been asking myself. Simon knew that you would find the house but he did not tell me what to do with you when you did, so I planned to dispose of you and disappear. Unfortunately, you thwarted that plan.'

'Why not the same plan now?'

'The light is fading. I shall decide soon.'

'Why wait? I am ready.'

'But I am not. Be silent.'

In the distance, the clock at St Martin's struck six. The curfew had begun. Surely Gabriel would act soon. Christopher waited, trying in vain to work his bindings loose and wondering what was going through his captor's mind. The clock struck seven. The streets would be all but deserted. If Gabriel wanted to avoid the watch he should go now. At that time, the constables would believe a story of being detained or lost or drunk. Much later and they would be less accommodating.

He heard Gabriel stand up and opened his eyes. The knife was in his hand, its tip pointing at Christopher's eye. He rolled to one side to protect his face. Gabriel laughed. 'That will do you no good, doctor,' he said. 'A throat is more easily cut from behind.' Christopher clenched his teeth and readied himself for the touch of the blade. Let it be quick.

'However,' went on Gabriel, 'I have made my decision. Today is not the day upon which I shall kill you. Today I shall let you live. When I have gone, make as much noise as you like.' He paused. 'But, and it is a but you would be unwise to ignore, do not suppose that you are free of me. When you are summoned to Whitehall, I shall be watching. When you go to Smithfield or Cheapside, I shall be close by in the shadows. When you visit Mr Brewster's shop I shall see you walk down Fetter Lane and return here with your music.'

Christopher rolled back to face him. 'And how will you do that? Even you must sleep.'

'The eyes that watch you will not always be mine. You will never know which child, which beggar, which vagrant the eyes belong to but I will always know. Simon's money will be put to good use.'

'Why do this?'

'Deception, ignorance, fear. You will never know who is behind you or when they might strike. You bested me at the house. Think of it as my revenge.'

'You are mad.'

Gabriel's voice rose. 'Take care, doctor, lest you talk yourself into a swift grave. I can easily change my mind.'

'At least let me lie in my bed. I will freeze to death here.'

'If you can crawl up the stair, you may lie in your bed. I will not untie you.'

Christopher pushed himself on to his elbows and knees. With wrists and ankles tied, movement was slow and painful. He reached the bottom of the stair and crawled slowly up on his knees and elbows. Gabriel followed him. In his chamber he managed to scramble on to the bed and lie flat, trying to catch his breath. Gabriel produced two more lengths of rope with which he attached Christopher's bound hands and legs to the bed posts, leaving him almost no room for movement. Then he covered him with a blanket.

'There, doctor,' he said, as if speaking to a child. 'Warm enough, I hope? Such a pity if the cold takes you and my eyes have no one to watch.' Christopher did not answer. 'I shall leave you now. Be sure to look over your shoulder.'

Christopher heard the door close. He wriggled his hands in the hope of finding slack in the ropes. There was none. Nor was there in the ropes around his ankles. Gabriel knew what he was doing. And he had brought the ropes with him. He had known all along what he was going to do.

For most of the night he had been in that strange place between sleep and wakefulness. Dreams, if they were dreams, had come and gone; half-formed thoughts had slipped in and out of his mind. He had seen Simon Lovelace kissing Katherine Allington and heard Joan Willys cursing Roland Wetherby for calling her a witch. He had struggled against the ropes that bound him and tried, unsuccessfully, not to piss in the bed.

With the dawn came the early morning sounds of voices and beasts and carts. He tried shouting but after his voice became hoarse he realized that it was useless. He could not be heard.

He could not be sure if he was asleep or awake when he heard the voice. It seemed to come from within the house but it was an odd, quiet voice. He turned his head to the wall and ignored it. It would go away.

But the voice came again. What was it saying? It came once more, a little louder. 'Dr Radcliff, are you here?'

His throat was like tree bark. 'Here.' It was a croak. He tried again. 'I am here, Joan.' He heard footsteps on the stair and Joan's face appeared. Her hand flew to her mouth. 'I cannot move, Joan. Untie my hands.'

Joan was shaking as she fumbled with the knots, squealing when she broke a nail. At last she freed one hand and then the other. With a groan, Christopher sat up and reached down to his ankles. 'Dr Radcliff, who has done this?' she sobbed. 'Are you hurt?'

The ropes fell away. 'I am unhurt, thank you, Joan.' He rubbed each wrist where the rope had chafed the skin, grimacing at the pain, before gingerly feeling the back of his head. The lump where Gabriel had hit him was excruciatingly tender and about the size of a small plum. When he stood up, he stumbled. 'Give me your shoulder, please. I am a little unsteady.' With his hand on her shoulder, they went down to the kitchen.

Joan was still weeping. 'Sit down, doctor,' she said. 'You need food. I have brought honey and oatmeal.'

Christopher massaged his red, raw wrists again. 'There is ale in the jug,' he said. Joan filled a beaker and handed it to him. He took a gulp and the fire in his throat eased. 'I am sorry to shock you, Joan. I was attacked last night. He has long gone.'

'Who was he, doctor? Did you know him?'

'I do not think so. A thief, I daresay, who hit me from behind, tied me up and ran off. No doubt my purse has gone.'

Joan looked doubtful. 'How did he get in, doctor, and how did he get you up to your chamber?'

'He hit me hard. I remember little. Perhaps it will come to me.' He took another gulp of ale. If Joan knew that he was being watched, she would be afraid for him and for herself. 'Honey porridge should refresh my memory.'

'Yes, doctor. Drink your ale and I will make it.'

He sat while she mixed the oatmeal with water, heated it over the fire and added a good spoonful of honey while it was simmering. When it was ready she put a bowlful on the table. 'There, doctor. Try that. I will clean your chamber while you eat.'

While she was in the chamber he slipped into the study. His purse was on the table. He hid it under a stack of papers.

'Excellent, Joan,' he said when she came down. 'I will stay here while you clean the study and set the fire. Be careful with my papers, please. Best not to move them.'

'As you wish, doctor.' Poor child, he could tell she was confused. He waited until he heard the fire before leaving the kitchen. 'I was right. My purse has gone.'

'Should you not report it to the magistrate, doctor? Or shall I fetch a constable? A hue and cry could be raised.'

He put a hand on her arm. 'I would rather not, Joan. There was little in the purse and I shall recover from a sleepless night. Better to forget it.'

When Joan looked directly at him, the cast in her eye made it appear that she was looking over his shoulder. 'Seems wrong, doctor, me being in prison and a thief going free. Not right at all.'

'No, not right at all. But we cannot make everything right.'

'No, doctor. If we could, Alice Scrope would be the one in gaol.' Joan put on her coat. 'I will go to the market tomorrow and I will bring a salve for your wrists. Lock your door tonight and open it for no one. Thieves often return.'

'I will, Joan. Thank you.'

Lie upon lie. Should he have told her the truth? What truth and how much of it? No, the lies were necessary and served their purpose.

CHAPTER 38

'The Maiden's Lamentation'. A mournful song which could have been written for Caroline Lovelace. He wondered where Simon had found it. The words of the verses had gone but he remembered the refrain. *How showld I rock the cradle, serve the table, blow the fyre, and spyn, a?*

It was worth a try. He opened the lined music book bought from Mr Brewster, sharpened a pen, and played a few notes on the lute. The tune came slowly, very slowly, but when he thought he had a passage right, he wrote it in tablature form in the book, until he had the verse.

He put down the pen and played. And suddenly the words of the last verse came to him. He wrote it down quickly and played the tune again. He knew his voice was weak but, with no one listening, he sang as he played.

> *Beware, good maydes,*
> *Of all such braydes,*
> *Before all other thing e;*
> *Or all in vayne,*

As I complayne,
Thus wepyng shall ye syng e.
How showld I rock the cradle, serve the table,
blow the fyre, and spyn, a?

A sad song but a pretty enough tune and cleverly chosen. Had it been aimed at Leicester or was it a warning to the queen not to depend upon him? Both, perhaps. He would ask Mr Brewster if he knew where it might be found.

Two days since Gabriel and he had barely left the house. It was not fear that had kept him at home, more a childish wish not to be dictated to. If there were eyes on Ludgate Hill they could stay there until he was ready.

He heard a coach draw up. Just as Ell knew his knock, he knew Wetherby's. It was a rat-a-tat-tat knock used by no one else who came to the house. 'Come in, Roland,' he shouted. 'The door is unlocked.'

Wetherby let himself in. 'The earl is concerned for your health, Christopher,' he said, 'and has sent me to convey you to Whitehall.'

'Concerned for my health? Why?'

'I was in jest. The earl cares not a jot for your health but summons you to the palace. Your lute will not be required.'

'Then I shall put it away.'

'And brush yourself down while you are in your chamber. You are in a poor way today and you know how the earl dislikes unkempt intelligencers. Brush your hair, change your shirt and clean your shoes. I will wait for you.'

He must be in a poor way. It was unlike Roland to speak so bluntly. The lute went under the bed, he found a shirt newly washed by Joan, ran his fingers through his hair and went downstairs.

Wetherby inspected him. 'Shoes, Christopher.'

'For the love of God, Roland, I'm not going to meet the queen. Leicester is quite used to me by now.'

'Shoes.'

Christopher sighed, and went to the kitchen to find a cloth.

'Better,' said Wetherby when he came back. 'Not good, but better.'

They were in Fleet Street when Christopher said, 'I had a visit from Gabriel Browne.'

'What? When?' Wetherby looked as if he might fall out of the coach.

Christopher told him the story hurriedly. He finished as they arrived at the Holbein Gate.

'Why did you not tell me before?' asked Wetherby.

'Had you called, I would have. Have you delivered the money to the earl?'

'I have. He seemed surprised.'

'That you had not kept it or at its origin?'

'Both, I fancy. I told him about our visit to Simon's house, but did not mention Gabriel.'

'Wise of you. It would have done no good.'

The coach drew up. Wetherby escorted Christopher to the earl's apartments. Outside the door to the antechamber, they clasped hands before Christopher was admitted by the guard and Wetherby returned to his own apartment.

The portrait of the queen which dominated the chamber looked even larger than usual and Her Majesty looked even more regal. She seemed to be staring at him as if he were a naughty child caught in some forbidden act.

Leicester threw open the door. 'Dr Radcliff, Her Majesty wishes to speak to you and I am to escort you to her immediately.' He spoke gravely, the dark eyes holding Christopher's.

'May I know why Her Majesty wishes to speak to me, my lord?' asked Christopher, taken aback by the news.

Leicester's tone did not change. 'That she has not confided in me but doubtless you will find out soon enough. Follow me.'

Leicester led him along the gallery that overlooked the queen's garden and into the Great Chamber where Simon Lovelace had played for her. From there they passed through to the privy chamber. 'We will await the queen here,' said Leicester, and to a guard: 'Tell Her Majesty that Dr Radcliff is here.'

Christopher looked around. The walls were panelled, the floor tiled and painted and spread with rush mats. At one end of the room was a stone fireplace. On a raised platform at the other end stood a single tall chair with a cushioned seat and a matching crimson footstool. In one corner water tinkled in a small fountain. A huge painting adorned the wall opposite the window, and another, smaller one hung beside the fireplace. There was a second door beside the platform. It was a room designed to impress but not overpower.

When the guard had left them, Leicester said, 'Mr Wetherby told me about your visit to Master Lovelace's house and handed over the money you found. It is a great deal. I have given the matter thought and decided that it should be divided into three equal parts, one each for you and Wetherby and one for the queen's exchequer. Her Majesty has agreed to this.'

Suddenly, Christopher was wealthy. 'My lord, I am grateful, of course, but—'

Leicester held up a hand. 'It is decided. I will keep your share safe and you may call upon it at any time. I will not ask how you intend to use it.'

Christopher bowed. 'Thank you, my lord. The money will be put to good use.' Before he could continue, the door beside the platform opened and the queen entered, followed by the very same two ladies-in-waiting who had been with her in the Great Chamber. Again Christopher bowed. The queen stepped on to the platform and sat, her ladies standing either side of her. She wore a pale blue gown with a low ruff and the double string of pearls around her neck. To Christopher's eye, regal, but less formal than on the day Simon Lovelace played for her and died.

'Thank you, Robert,' she said. 'You may leave Dr Radcliff in my care now.' Leicester bowed and left Christopher standing alone in the middle of the chamber. The queen smiled and held out her hand. 'Dr Radcliff, we are happy to welcome you again to Whitehall.' The voice was calm and measured, just as it had been in the Great Chamber.

He hesitated before stepping forward and kissing the hand and was relieved when she smiled again. Being close to the queen, as he had been in the privy garden and in the Great Chamber, was one thing, being addressed directly by her was quite another. He made an effort not to rub his hand or stretch his fingers.

'You are wondering why I have asked to see you, Dr Radcliff.'

'I am, Your Majesty.'

'The Earl of Leicester has told me much about you. I know how you came to leave Cambridge and join the earl's staff and of course I know of the part you played in foiling the plot to burn down this palace and put a bullet through my heart. You have served us well.'

Should he speak? No, better to keep quiet until she asked him a question. She went on. 'And were it not for you, the criminals behind the recent outbreak of coining and the treasonous slogans that have impugned not only the Dudley family but also my own would not have been apprehended.' Christopher inclined his head. 'I have found that it is the decisions one makes that determine the course of one's life, rather than one's virtue or competence or, indeed, the vagaries of fortune. A wise man may make a bad decision and live to regret it while a foolish man may make a good one and thereby profit from it. Master Lovelace, may he rest in peace, made his decision and who is to say that he was wrong? Poor man, an unimaginable life, mercifully short. I thought his choice of song interesting and have wondered to whom he was really addressing it. One might only guess.'

The queen rose from her chair and stepped down from the platform. 'The painting behind you', she said, 'is by the younger Holbein, a great favourite of my father. It depicts my grandfather and father, his queen Jane Seymour and Elizabeth of York. It is almost life-size. What do you think of it, doctor?'

'It is very fine, Your Majesty, formidable and imposing. A worthy painting for a family such as yours.'

The queen clapped her hands together. 'My lord Leicester said that you have a way with words, doctor. But then you are trained in the law, are you not?'

'I am.'

'Half my advisers are lawyers. If ever I am in need of an advocate, I shall be well served.'

The queen walked over to the smaller painting by the fireplace. 'But it is this painting, also by Holbein, that I wished you to see. The two men in the painting are Jean de Dinteville, who commissioned it, and Georges de Selve, French visitors to my father's court. It was a preliminary study for a larger painting which now hangs in de Dinteville's chateau at Polisy. Holbein gave it to my mother when she became queen in 1533 and it subsequently passed to me. Holbein called it *The Ambassadors*. Look hard, doctor, and tell me what you see.'

Christopher stood a yard or so in front of the painting and studied it as best he could with the queen hovering nearby. The taller man wore a fur-trimmed coat over a shirt of pink satin or silk, the other a sombre clerical robe. They stood either side of a low table underneath a draped shelf, on which stood a celestial globe, a sundial and various instruments whose purpose he did not know. On the table were another globe, this one terrestrial, a flute box, an open book and a lute. In the foreground was a strange object he could not identify. Both men looked straight at the artist.

'Your Majesty, I see two men of wealth and influence — ambassadors, no doubt — surrounded by evidence of their learning and erudition. I see globes, books, scientific instruments and a lute. These are cultured men with a love of knowledge and science.'

'Very good, doctor. And what do you make of the object in the foreground?'

'I cannot make it out at all.'

'Move to your left, doctor, and look again.'

Christopher took a pace to his left and looked again. The object became clear. It was a human skull.

'Why did the artist show the skull as he has, do you think?' she asked.

'Could he be reminding us of our mortality?'

'Perhaps, doctor, but I think he is reminding us of something else. That life, like people and objects, can be viewed from more than one perspective. And the lute, what do you make of that?'

Christopher looked closer. 'The lute has a broken string.'

'It does. I am told by wiser judges than I that the broken string represents the religious conflict of forty years ago when Holbein painted the picture. The split with Rome leading to the intolerance and disharmony that blights us now. But I wonder, also, if Holbein is telling us that nothing in life is certain or simple. A storm may blow down a house; a lute string may break. The painting is full of symbols and contrasts. A globe showing us God's earth and another his heavens. One man is sumptuously attired; the other is in a simple robe. Like Holbein's painting, our lives are full of contrast and paradox. And we must make decisions that are not always easy.' She turned to face him. 'Decisions of the head, doctor, not the heart.'

The queen returned to her chair. 'If you are minded to return to Pembroke Hall, Dr Radcliff, you will do so with my blessing. I will grant you a royal pardon for the crime of which you were convicted and you will be able to teach again. I cannot rescind the prohibition against fellows marrying but the pardon I can grant.'

Was she pushing him towards Cambridge? 'I am grateful, Your Majesty.'

'Think carefully, though, before you make your decision. Where does your true loyalty lie? To your college or to your country? Where would you best serve your queen — by teaching young minds or by seeking out those who would do us harm, as you have so bravely in the past? Ask yourself these questions and you will arrive at the right decision.' The queen's smile lit up her face. 'I am sure of it. May God bless you.'

He barely had time to bow again before the queen and her ladies had swept out of the chamber, leaving him to be escorted back to the Holbein Gate where Wetherby was waiting for him. 'I do not want to know what advice the queen gave you, Christopher,' he said, 'I just want to offer a little of my own.'

'As long as it is only a little. My head is rather full of advice.'

'I think you should ask Leicester for protection from Gabriel.'

'Or I could return to Cambridge. I doubt Gabriel would bother me there.'

'Are you going to return?'

'Her Majesty would be disappointed if I did but I need time to decide.'

'Well, tell me when you do. Whatever you decide, you will of course have my blessing, although I should miss you greatly if you were to leave London.'

Christopher took Wetherby's hand. 'I will let you know.'

Wetherby nodded. 'Good. You know where to find me.'

CHAPTER 39

Christopher rose early to play. He ran his right hand over the ivory of the body and the fingers of his left hand over the frets. He settled himself and began.

'Greensleeves' followed 'My Lady Cary's Dompe'. But if the broken string on Holbein's lute signified discord, his playing signified confusion. He missed changes of stops, left out notes and played too far from the rose, making notes grate. With a grunt of dissatisfaction, he put the lute back in its case.

With Roland he had been less than courteous and regretted it. With the queen he supposed that he had been courteous enough but not perhaps at his brightest. He was trained in argument and disputation not respectful silence. But she had spoken frankly and kindly to him and for that he was grateful.

Joan let herself in and found him in the study, a big grin on her plain face. 'Dr Radcliff,' she almost shouted, 'Alice Scrope is in the Clink. She was caught thieving in Eastcheap.'

'No more than she deserves, Joan, but what about her child?'

'In there with her, doctor.'

Christopher nodded. The child would save her from the gallows but what to do with the child of a convicted felon was a problem to which the courts had no good answer. Most likely it would be put in some place of safety until it was old enough to join the ranks of homeless urchins on the streets. The child of a criminal parent invariably became a criminal himself. He had sometimes thought of it like an inheritance — passed down from one generation to the next.

Joan took a sealed letter from her basket. 'Mistress Allington asked me to give you this, doctor.'

'Thank you, Joan. I'll read it while you stir plenty of honey into my porridge.'

'That I will, doctor.' She took out a small bottle. 'And I have mixed this salve for your hand. Rub it in every morning and evening.'

He took the bottle from her. 'Thank you, Joan. I shall do as you say.'

He broke the seal and spread out the letter. It was not long.

My dear Christopher,

Isabel Tranter died peacefully yesterday and will be buried in the graveyard of St Michael's church on Friday. Kindly respect my wishes and do not attend.

I shall return to Cambridge within the month.

May God bless you.

Katherine Allington

He crumpled it up and threw it into the grate. Damn the woman. Her blessing, the queen's blessing, Roland's advice. But only he could make the decision.

Joan poked her head around the door. 'Your porridge is ready, doctor. I hope Mistress Allington is quite well.'

'She is, Joan. Quite well. Have you mixed enough honey in?'

'Plenty, doctor.'

'Good. My humour needs sweetening.'

It was a contrary thought but entirely deliberate. To get to Cheapside he went past Newgate, where two cheerful beggars were roasting a pair of fat rats on a fire in the street, and down Dog's Head Lane. He stopped once to look back but saw nothing. If Gabriel's eyes were on him they were well hidden.

Ell's alley was, as usual, running with muck. He stepped carefully around it and knocked on the stew door. 'Early for you, Dr Rad,' said Grace. 'Ell got you excited, has she? Does that for a man, Ell. Go on up,' she cackled, 'she'll be pleased to see you.'

Ell was sitting on her bed, examining her face in a hand mirror. As he came in, she put it away. 'Lines and wrinkles, Dr Rad,' she said. 'A few more every month. Be on the streets soon at this rate.'

'You, Ell? Never.' A line or two perhaps but the blue eyes would always sparkle and the lips would always smile. Hers was a beauty that might fade but would never entirely leave her.

'Never is a long time, doctor. What can I do for you?'

Christopher sat on the bed. 'I was hoping I could do something for you, Ell.'

'Good God, and what might that be?'

'You told me once that if you had the money you would buy a house in Southwark and let the world go to hell. Or something like that.'

'I did, doctor, and meant it. All I need is the money. A sack full of naughty testons might do it. Have you got one?' The throaty laugh made her shoulders shake.

Her eyes opened wide in surprise when he reached out to take her hand. 'Now, Ell, I am serious and I do not want you to tell me to fuck off.'

'Never, Dr Rad, not you.'

'Good. Find a house you like and I will give you the money for it. Not naughty money, real, honest silver.'

Ell's eyes opened wide and then narrowed in suspicion. 'Why?'

'Because I want to. Isn't that enough?'

'Has the queen given you a cart full of silver, doctor?'

'Not the queen, but someone else. What about it?'

The brown eyes twinkled. 'Will you be moving in with me?'

Christopher laughed. 'No, Ell, I do not much care for Southwark. I might buy a house for myself though. A small house in Westminster village would suit me well.'

'Lord, doctor, two houses. It must have been a big cart.'

'Big enough.'

Ell picked up the mirror and took another look. 'Can't keep the wrinkles away forever. Be an old hag soon, grateful for a few pennies from a blind beggar in a dark doorway.'

'Never, Ell, not you. Well?'

'Are you really in earnest?'

'Never more so.'

Ell leaned over and kissed his cheek. 'Then be sure to visit, doctor. Southwark's not so bad.'

Author's Notes

Ambrose Dudley, known to posterity as 'the good Earl', was the fourth surviving child of John Dudley, Earl of Warwick and Duke of Northumberland, and older than his brother Robert by two years. He married three times (Christopher could not recall whether it was two or three), but left no heirs.

He was made Earl of Warwick in 1561 at which time Warwick Castle was restored to him, having been confiscated by Queen Mary from his father who had been executed for supporting Lady Jane Grey, his daughter-in-law, in her claim to the throne. Robert's Kenilworth Castle was nearby. Like Robert, Ambrose was imprisoned in the Tower and only narrowly escaped execution.

The queen was known to be fond of Ambrose (although he lacked the looks and charm of his brother) and appointed him to the important post of Master of the Ordnance. He was also close to Robert, who said 'Him I love as myself'.

In 1549, Warwick, Ambrose and Robert were active in putting down the popular uprisings, later known as Kett's Rebellion, in East Anglia, and in 1562–3 Ambrose commanded an army sent by the queen to support the Huguenots in France, where he was severely wounded in the leg. In 1590 he was forced to have the leg amputated and died soon afterwards.

Had they been born 450 years later one feels that Robert would have been an enthusiastic user of social media to promote his cause, but Ambrose would not.

During the reigns of Henry VIII and Edward VI, there were sporadic outbreaks of **slogans** written on walls in public places. The *Hempe* prophecy was one such. *Mouldwarp* also appeared, although not in the form in which Christopher sees it. The other slogans in the story were invented by Simon and Gabriel.

Counterfeiting, or 'coining', was a serious problem during Henry VIII's reign because his debasements of the coinage, especially the 'Great Debasement' of 1542, not only caused widespread mistrust of the value of coins but also made coining easier. Silver was extracted from legal coins by 'clipping' bits off, 'sweating' them by shaking them up in a bag and collecting the resulting silver dust, and 'culling' better coins to melt them down and remix them with copper. Counterfeiters were often mint-workers or goldsmiths.

One of the slogans Christopher mentions is *Beware the coin of reddish face, not silver pure but metal base.* The slogan is fictional but its warning was not. The redness came from copper mixed with silver — the more copper, the redder the face. Queen Elizabeth did much to restore confidence in the coinage but the problems of counterfeiting persisted. In 1562 the coinage, by that time hopelessly unreliable as a result of debasement and counterfeiting, was revalued. As part of this process, the coins known as testons were divided into two groups. The value of a 'better' teston was set at 4¼d., and of a 'worse' teston at 2¼d.

The first stories of a teston with the Dudley marks of a **bear and a ragged staff** appeared in 1551, during the reign of the young Edward VI, for whom the Earl of Warwick, father of Ambrose and Robert, was regent. There was a rumour — never proved — that the testons had been produced in a secret mint at Warwick Castle. Using the iron dies known as 'trussels' and 'piles' it would not have been difficult to produce large quantities of 'naughty' coins. The difficulty would have been in keeping the activity secret.

Simon Lovelace and Gabriel Browne employed the Pryses to make the dies and to produce the 'Dudley testons', although their purpose was rather different to that of the coiners of twenty years earlier. They chose Guildford because it was safer than London and because of the glass-blowing which existed there at that time and which gave them a means of smuggling the coins into London hidden in consignments of glass.

The **lute** was an instrument which educated young people of the early modern period were expected to learn. At court, lutenists were commonly known as 'royal lutes'. By the end of the sixteenth century it had evolved from the lutes of two thousand years earlier into a six-course instrument, five of the courses consisting of pairs of strings. Christopher did not sing but the lute was often played as an accompaniment to the human voice, as it was by Simon in the Great Chamber.

The body and neck of a lute were commonly made from a hardwood, often edged with ebony, the strings from animal gut and the bridge from a softer fruitwood. The lute given to Christopher by the Earl of Leicester was very unusual in that the body was made of ivory. It was made in Venice and would have been very expensive.

By 1574 the earl had built up a considerable collection of musical instruments.

The jolly galliard and the more restrained pavan will be familiar to many readers, at least in name. Less so, perhaps, the dompe and the almain, the latter being somewhat more sombre than the former. 'My Lady Cary's Dompe' was a particularly popular tune in the late sixteenth century (and one of Christopher's favourites).

The composer of 'The Maiden's Lamentation', Simon's choice of music to play before the queen, is unknown but the lyrics have survived. The queen describes his playing as 'ravishing'. To us this may sound odd but it was an adjective used at the time to compliment a player.

The Ambassadors, painted by Hans Holbein the Younger in 1533, now hangs in the National Gallery. It is a double portrait full of symbolism over which experts have argued for nearly five hundred years. The skull in the foreground actually reveals itself from either the left or the right but not from directly in front. I know of no evidence for a preliminary painting but it is not impossible that one existed.

Following the horrors of the St Bartholomew's Day Massacre, in *Chaos* Christopher is suffering from what we would call **post-traumatic stress disorder (PTSD)**. For those wondering about his hand, he also suffers from **Dupuytren's Contracture**, a condition found among people of Nordic and Northern European descent, in which the fingers are pulled progressively down towards the palm. His height and fair hair suggest Scandinavian ancestry.

It is a condition which neither Joan's salves nor anyone else's would have helped; today it is treated surgically.

ACKNOWLEDGEMENTS

One of the joys of being a historical novelist is the wonderful, interesting people one meets, either in person or through the ether. Without exception, the experts I have consulted on *Chaos* have gone out of their way to be helpful and constructive and I thank all of them. Of all the benefits the World Wide Web brings, making it easier to find an expert on almost anything is, for me, the most valuable.

In particular, I offer grateful thanks to Professor James Sharpe of York University who advised on the discovery, examination and prosecution of those accused of witchcraft and to Dr Katherine Butler, senior lecturer at Northumbria University, Newcastle upon Tyne, and an expert on Tudor musical culture.

Chris Goodwin, Secretary of the English Lute Society, kindly allowed me to visit him at his house and answered with practised ease all the questions thrown at him by a most unmusical author. He also made suggestions, checked the passages in the story in which the lute plays a part and corrected my mistakes.

Without their expert and generous help, and that of others who prefer to remain unnamed, Christopher Radcliff could not have played the lute, Joan Willys could not have been accused of witch-craft and the bear and staff testons could not have reappeared.

The libraries at the Goldsmiths' Hall and Royal Holloway, University of London, yielded much invaluable information and I thank the librarians at both for their help, as I do the librarians at the National Gallery.

Finally, to my brilliant agent David Headley of DHH Literary Agency and to Simon Taylor, my patient editor at Transworld Publishers, my gratitude for putting up with me and for nursing me through the writing process all the way from idea to finished book.

Any errors of fact in the story are of course my own.

Andrew Swanston's
THE THOMAS HILL TRILOGY

'Wonderful – rich, deep, intelligent and thoughtful with clearly drawn characters and exactly the right amount of suspense'
MANDA SCOTT

THE KING'S SPY

Summer, 1643. England is at war with itself, but for bookseller and cryptographer Thomas Hill the conflict feels far away. Until, that is, a stranger knocks on his door and summons him to the king's court at Oxford where his singular ability with codes and puzzles is required to help unmask a traitor . . .

THE KING'S EXILE

Spring, 1648. Thomas Hill has been condemned to life (and most likely death) as a slave on Barbados. As news of the king's execution reaches the island, chaos ensues. A fleet sailing in Cromwell's name arrives to take control, but the violence increases and Thomas' long-planned bid for freedom seems ever more unlikely . . .

THE KING'S RETURN

Spring, 1661. Cromwell is dead and England awaits its new monarch and the stability his coronation will bring. But a murderous plot that threatens king and country is uncovered. Called upon to decode the conspirators' correspondence, Thomas Hill suddenly finds himself more deeply embroiled and in danger than he had ever imagined . . .

Available in paperback and ebook editions.

THE INCENDIUM PLOT
A. D. Swanston

Gripped by fear . . .
It is 1572 and in Elizabeth I's England fear of heresy
and insurrection, and of plague and invasion, is constant.

Surrounded by enemies . . .
Lawyer Christopher Radcliff is the Earl of Leicester's chief
intelligencer. His task is to seek out treachery at home and the
ever-present papist threat from abroad — and he is under
pressure to get results.

With a fanatic on the loose . . .
Then two brutal, seemingly motiveless killings alert Radcliff
to a new plot against the queen. All he has to go on is a single word:
Incendium. Whatever it means and whoever is behind it, it has the
power to tear the nation apart.

The fuse has been lit and time is running out . . .

Available in paperback and ebook editions.